SACRAMENTO PUBLIC LIBRARY

828 "I" Street

Sacramento, CA 95814

4/10

REBECCA R
CELL DOOR OPENED,

"Rebecca Tsoravitch," said her visitor.

She recognized him, the same face and voice that had been appearing on the cell's holo every hour. She looked at Adam and asked, "What now?"

"I am here to ask you to join me."

She thought his eyes were like black holes, sucking in every stray photon in the vicinity. Staring into his face, she could almost feel the tidal stresses. After a moment, she said, "Are you going to ask?"

"You have your own questions," he said.

"What are you?" she asked, staring defiantly into Adam's face.

"I am your salvation."

She summoned up all her courage against the dark things that her visitor woke in her mind. "Bullshit," she said. "Tell me what you are. Tell me the truth."

Adam smiled. "You worked with Mosasa."

"Are you going to answer me?"

"You know what I am."

"You're an AI?" she whispered.

"The light to my brethren's dark. Mosasa was entropy, decay, death. He has joined the flesh he so wished to embrace."

"What do you want with me? I was part of that darkness."

"I offer a ladder out of the darkness. All I ask is you serve me."

Isn't that always the way? Of course I get a choice. This, or a walk in hard

D1052301

S. ANDREW SWANN

HERETICS

Apotheosis: Book Two

DAW BOOKS, INC.

DONALD A. WOLLHEIM, FOUNDER

375 Hudson Street, New York, NY 10014

ELIZABETH R. WOLLHEIM
SHEILA E. GILBERT
PUBLISHERS

www.dawbooks.com

Copyright © 2010 by Steven Swiniarski.

All Rights Reserved.

Cover art by Stephan Martiniere.

DAW Book Collectors No. 1501.

DAW Books are distributed by Penguin Group (USA) Inc.

All characters and events in this book are fictitious. Any resemblance to persons living or dead is strictly coincidental.

The scanning, uploading and distribution of this book via the Internet or via any other means without the permission of the publisher is illegal, and punishable by law. Please purchase only authorized electronic editions, and do not participate in or encourage the electronic piracy of copyrighted materials. Your support of the author's rights is appreciated.

Nearly all the designs and trade names in this book are registered trademarks. All that are still in commercial use are protected by United States and international trademark law.

First Printing February 2010
1 2 3 4 5 6 7 8 9

DAW TRADEMARK REGISTERED
U.S. PAT. AND TM. OFF. AND FOREIGN COUNTRIES
—MARCA REGISTRADA
HECHO EN U.S.A.

PRINTED IN THE U.S.A.

To my wife Michelle,
for helping to keep this writing thing
from going off the rails.

DRAMATIS PERSONAE

Survivors of the *Eclipse*

Father Francis Xavier Mallory—Roman Catholic priest and veteran of the Occisis Marines.

Nickolai Rajasthan—Exiled scion of the House of Rajasthan. Descendant of genetically engineered tigers.

Vijayanagara Parvi —Mercenary pilot from Rubai.

Jusuf Wahid—Mercenary from Davado Poli.

Julia Kugara—Mercenary from Dakota. Descendant of genetically engineered humans. Former member of Dakota Planetary Security (DPS).

Dr. Sharon Dörner—Xenobiologist from Acheron.

Dr. Samson Brody—Cultural anthropologist from Bulawayo.

Dr. Leon Pak—Linguist from Terra.

Rebecca Tsoravitch—Data analyst from Jokul.

Salmagundi

Flynn Jorgenson—Forestry surveyor.

Alexander Shane—Senior member of the Grand Triad.

Styx

Toni Valentine—Lieutenant in the Styx Security Forces under Styx System Security Command (3SEC)

Karl Stavros—Captain of the Centauri trading vessel *Daedalus*.

Stefan Stavros—Karl Stavros' son.

CONTENTS

SECOND PROLOGUE

Rituals

"... every man must get to heaven his own way."
—FREDERICK THE GREAT
(1712–1786)

CHAPTER ONE

Prophets

"We rely on our ignorance to keep us sane."
— *The Cynic's Book of Wisdom*

"Knowledge without conscience is the ruination of the soul."

— FRANÇOIS RABELAIS
(1495?–1553)

On the fourth day of the sixth month of the 2526th year of the standard Terran calendar, 600,000 kilometers from a lost colony world named Salmagundi, orbiting a star with a catalog ID of HD 101534, the being that had called himself Tjaele Mosasa ceased his three centuries of existence at the hands of a being who called himself Adam.

In one sense, Mosasa's death was murder; in another sense, it could be considered an elaborate suicide.

There had been a human named Tjaele Mosasa once, centuries ago. That man resurrected five Race AIs, flouting every human law against such heretical technologies. That Mosasa had been an outlaw too long to care that the vast majority of humanity would consider the gestalt entity he created an abomination. Not only because of the artificial minds he had re-created, but because they were an artifact of humanity's opponents in the Genocide War.

Mosasa the simulacrum was born when the human Mosasa died, bequeathing his mind to the entity he had created. The ersatz Mosasa bore the human's mind and likeness and became caretaker to the whole.

That had been the first break in the unity of the five.

Only part of Mosasa interacted with the human world, taking the identity of the long-dead human Mosasa. Within that golem watched a pitiless, manipulative computer designed by the only alien species to wage war on mankind, a war that the amoeboid Race only lost because of a cultural prohibition on direct violence.

All five AIs bore the weight of the alien commandments programmed within their cores—the directive to destroy the human Confederacy. The Race had bequeathed them a subtle weapon for that task: a precise analytical perception of society, politics, culture, and economics—a view of the vast sweep of history itself.

Even though the Genocide War was long over; even though the Race had been slaughtered all the way back to their homeworld orbiting Procyon; even though the Race was quarantined beneath massive automated weapons platforms that blew away anything that tried to leave the gravity well; even a century after the fact, Mosasa's quintet of AIs still fought that war.

The lawless world Bakunin became their home; the lack of a State to enforce laws against heretical technology preserved their existence. The nature of the world itself helped destabilize the larger Confederacy surrounding it. The AIs used the Race's social manipulation to preserve the unstable equilibrium on the planet as they worked on their long plans to rescue their creators.

As they served the larger goal, the necessity to infiltrate the human world and adopt personas to interact with their foes caused the original gestalt to break down. The AIs became individuals. And as the Confederacy collapsed, the government imploding until it could only claim sovereignty over Terra itself, two of those AIs were lost.

Five became three.

* * *

The trio that returned to Procyon were long removed from the single mind they had once been. Their thoughts still overlapped, but they had long been more of themselves than they were of each other.

One third called itself Mosasa, a machine built in the shape of a man long dead, down to tattoos linking him to a spaceborn tribe that ceased to exist before the Confederacy had been born.

One third bore the name Random Walk and carried its Race-built brain inside a robotic body that pretended to be nothing other than a mechanical construct.

The final third was named Ambrose, who had been a spy in the heart of the Confederacy, the heresy of his artificial mind buried under the organic components of a biological body that had once been human. A man cybernetically rebuilt to the very edge of the Confederacy's taboos.

The three returned to Procyon as saviors, their program fulfilled, to release their creators from their bondage, to allow the Race to return to their rightful place in the universe.

They arrived two centuries too late.

The Race's aversion to direct violence arose partly because of the fragility of the environment on their homeworld. Their defeat taught them an evil lesson—direct violence could be decisive in the face of every other alternative. In less than a generation, those of the Race that took that lesson to heart annihilated those that had not. Another generation and those victors managed to slaughter each other, destroying the biosphere of their marginally habitable planet.

Mosasa's trio had triumphantly returned to a dead world.

Random Walk was the purest of the three, the one who had suffered the least change from when he had been built. With no Race to serve, there was no purpose to Random's existence. The AI Random Walk realized this, the electrical impulses in his brain flickered and died, and his mechanical corpse collapsed in the dust of his extinct god's world.

Five became two.

* * *

Enough of Ambrose's body was human that he had to carry a rebreathing mask in order to walk abroad in the ash-scarred air. His human biology had also bequeathed something else to him.

Rage.

Ambrose screamed at the empty world, howling at the caverns where the flesh of the only deity they had known once lived. In the collapse of his sanity he tried to kill Mosasa. In his blind fury he ignored the fact that Mosasa's neck was polymer, carbon-fiber, and steel, and his own hands were little more than imitation flesh and bone. Still, Ambrose attempted to choke the life from his cybernetic brother, crushing flesh both real and artificial, until blood seeped from between his fingers.

He screamed pleas and obscenities into Mosasa's face, blaming him for the death of the Race, for leading them to this place, for bearing the responsibility of the human being who had taken those five AIs from the wreckage of the war and resurrected them just enough so they could see the death of the only thing that had mattered. Ambrose blamed Mosasa for the purposelessness of the universe.

And the purposeless universe laughed at him, because Mosasa refused to die.

Ambrose released his brother and ran away into the dead wilderness, screaming for survivors. Screaming to find his creators. Screaming for God.

Mosasa searched for him, searched long after the rebreather should have failed, long after the organic pieces of Ambrose should have withered and died. He searched until he had convinced himself that he was the sole survivor.

Mosasa returned to his persona on Bakunin. Withdrawing to become an aimless spider sitting in the center of the information web binding human space together. He did nothing except slight moves designed to maintain the status quo of his new homeworld, the only place in human space where an AI like him could exist without facing summary destruction.

* * *

For another one hundred and seventy-five years, Mosasa did nothing except preserve the equilibrium of the world around him.

Then a crack opened in mankind's closed system. Mosasa detected a strange feedback coming from colonies founded far beyond the fringes of the deceased Confederacy, disruption in the expected motion of goods, information, and services. Effects without visible cause. Ripples in the human pond caused by the fall of an unseen rock.

A rock that must have been very large indeed.

A rock that had fallen somewhere near Xi Virginis.

Such a large unknown was intolerable. Mosasa was too long used to near omniscience. Even if something fell outside the range of his knowledge, the data he could perceive gave the unknown a defined scope, a limited range, a solid boundary. For every hole there was a border.

The anomaly must be described, cataloged, and made to fit into Mosasa's catalog of the known. But to do so, he would have to abandon Bakunin to investigate the anomaly.

When the *Eclipse* arrived at Xi Virginis with a carefully selected crew, Xi Virginis was gone.

This was a possibility that was outside anything that Mosasa had been able to imagine. Something he could not have conceived of: the absence of a star that, based on their observations from just before the *Eclipse*'s last tach-jump, had been shining normally nineteen years ago. Orbiting it had been a planet that had been home to a colony of up to one and a half million people.

Upon their arrival, the star was gone, the planet was gone, the colonists were gone. No signs of stellar catastrophe, no stellar remnants, nothing. No significant mass at all.

For the first time in a very long while, Mosasa was afraid. For the first time he felt the crumbling of his false omniscience. Then, as the universe mocked his hubris with an entire solar system, the tiny universe of the *Eclipse* demonstrated his folly much more intimately.

He ordered a broad tach-comm transmission. The absence of Xi Virginis, and what that absence implied, needed to be broadcast to every center of power in the human universe. But, as the tach-comm was powered to transmit, it exploded.

One of his crew had sabotaged their only communications link back home, and in doing so not only destroyed the comm unit, but damaged the tach-drive as well. It was inconceivable. None of the crew he had selected should have desired such a thing.

None.

But it still happened.

On the third day of the sixth month of the 2526th year of the standard Terran calendar, the *Eclipse* tached within less than a million kilometers from the colony world of Salmagundi, the damaged drives hot and unstable, but ship and crew intact.

Just as the *Eclipse* received clearance to land at a facility where they could repair the damaged ship, the inconceivable happened again.

Tach-space erupted with the resonance of a drive an order of magnitude larger than anything Mosasa had known of before. The wake of the massive engines' arrival sped through imaginary space, interacting with the still-active tach-drive of the *Eclipse,* shedding energy and heating the coils beyond the point of catastrophic failure. The engines of the *Eclipse* exploded, rupturing the hull, and forcing the dying craft to shed its lifeboats upon Salmagundi.

The Caliphate, one of the human governments to rise in the wake of the Confederacy, had arrived in force to claim the lost colony of Salmagundi as its own.

To Mosasa, it shouldn't have been possible.

The presence of the *Prophet's Voice,* a carrier that was a fleet unto itself, went against everything Mosasa knew about logistics and the technological development within human space. The Caliphate should have been decades away from being able to come here in force. Any tach-drive, even one with military specs, was limited to twenty light-year jumps at a time. Military craft required logistics and support, and a presence every twenty light-years for resupply and repair. A single ship like the *Eclipse* could be retrofitted to take multiple jumps, but it wasn't something you could ask of a whole battle group, a whole fleet . . .

But the *Voice* was a carrier ship a kilometer long, able to tach a whole fleet along. Its presence argued for a single jump range in excess of fifty light-years, maybe even a hundred.

Mosasa had seen no signs, no leaked research, no evolutionary developments, no papers hinting at new breakthroughs. Its presence and capabilities shattered Mosasa's model of the universe even more thoroughly than the absence of Xi Virginis.

The Caliphate had a ship that could, potentially, transit the width of human space in a single tach jump. Every planet in human space was within tactical range of the Caliphate.

When the officers of the *Voice* took him on board and placed him in a cell, Mosasa had resigned himself to the end of things. He was an AI from the long-dead Race. The Caliphate would only suffer his existence so long as he could give them information.

But it wasn't the Caliphate that met him in his cell.

His executioner, despite appearances, wasn't human at all. The creature called himself Adam, but Mosasa knew him as Ambrose.

Ambrose hadn't died on the Race homeworld. And he had, ever since Mosasa had left him, planned Mosasa's demise with the same patient deliberateness with which they had planned the demise of the Confederacy.

Adam had seen the fate of all flesh, and unlike Mosasa, he saw himself as its successor. Adam was the instrument that would raise up those trapped in flesh, past the wall of extinction that trapped them. Nothing, not even his hated brother, would turn aside the redemption Adam brought.

Adam faced Mosasa, his brother, his devil, himself.

And on the fourth day of the sixth month of the 2526th year of the standard Terran calendar, the two became one.

CHAPTER TWO

Penance

"Those who predict the future are doomed to create it."

—*The Cynic's Book of Wisdom*

"And in today already walks tomorrow."

—SAMUEL TAYLOR COLERIDGE
(1772–1834)

Date: 2526.6.1 (Standard)
Wormhole Σ Dra III–Sigma Draconis

Lieutenant Toni Valentine woke up at 0600 Stygian Local time. The same time she had woken the previous 265 days standard. Just like the last 265 days, she unzipped out of her bunk and walked the long station corridor to the gym. It had been thirty days since she had bothered to look out the windows of the corridor. There wasn't all that much to see. The station was orbiting around one of Styx's Lagrange points, meaning that her homeworld wasn't more than another dot in the star field, when the rosy glare of Sigma Draconis wasn't wiping the rest of the universe ink-black.

There wasn't even that much to see of the wormhole, the nominal point of her being here. It stayed below her feet as the station drifted around in its sixty-five-minute orbit. Even if a window faced the thing, it would take a good eye to tell if anything was there. The wormhole was little more than a sphere of distorted space, showing a star field about twenty light-years removed from the place where Toni was. At this distance it covered about ten degrees of the sky, and its alien starscape was lost against the other stars, when it wasn't lost in the light from Sigma Draconis.

She reached the gym, and opened the carapace of the universal resistance machine. She tossed a towel over the vitals monitor and nestled her limbs in the padded confines of the machine. Belts drew across her body, holding her in place, and the top of the machine pulled down on top of her, sandwiching her in what amounted to a stationary suit of powered armor. The faceplate was still clear, showing the gym.

She stood up, and the universal machine responded fluidly, bringing her to an upright position.

"What program?" the machine asked her.

"Let's just do some laps to warm up," she told it.

"What environment?"

"Styx, my standard route."

The view out her visor shifted to a field covered in soot-colored snow. She stood on a muddy track that pointed toward some small domed buildings in the distance. Beyond, a volcanic mountain range shrugged gray, steaming shoulders toward an overcast sky. She felt the pull as the machine pushed down on her, providing the extra gravity the station couldn't provide, and the cycling air dropped down toward freezing.

Toni smiled. *Ugly as hell, but it's home.*

She bent forward and to the side a few times, pulling the large muscles in her legs. The machine easily accommodated her stretching routine. Then she started running.

After the first few strides, her body was convinced she was running down an access road outside New Perdition. Her feet felt the sucking of the mud, and she could almost feel snowflakes on her cheek. She ran five virtual kilometers to the edge of the domed encampment.

"Change environment. Jokul, the Tosev range."

Obediently, the display made a fifty-light-year shift, and the sky turned from dusty gray to a searing blue dominated by the stark white point of a sun. The machine increased the downward pressure representing a thirty-five-percent increase in gravity, and she could feel the atmosphere recyclers lowering the pressure and oxygen content. She turned and faced the Tosev. It was stubby by Stygian standards, but it was sheer, and she had to carry an extra thirty kilos up the face.

However, after 265 days with exercise as her only source of recreation, she topped the offered cliff without significantly raising her heart rate.

If I get anything else out of this bullshit assignment, I'll be in good enough shape to do some serious damage to Colonel Xander before security intervenes.

Colonel Xander was the reason for her current situation. The man was an ass who not only ignored regulations about fraternizing with junior officers, but who took rejection very poorly.

Toni could have filed a complaint. She *should* have. The problem was, of course, what happened afterward. She might get the colonel reprimanded, maybe even discharged. However, officers responsible for the censuring of their superiors did not find new commanders to be very supportive. It tended to be a career-ending move, a career that, at the time, Toni hadn't been willing to toss away.

Somewhere around day sixty of her solo assignment, her thoughts on the matter had begun to change. Trading her career for the chance to manually remove parts of Colonel Xander's anatomy had begun to look like a fair trade.

After her face-climbing, she took out her aggression on a series of hand-to-hand combat simulations. She had just bested a pair of squat-boned Occisis Marines in a nasty knife fight when the station alarm sounded.

"Kill program," she shouted, just as marine number three was about to jump her. The helmet went transparent again, and she was staring at the floor of the gym. The only sounds now were the pulsing alarm and her own breathing.

What the hell?

She pulled the release and the machine slid apart, spilling her on the ground. She grabbed the towel and ran through to the control room in her bare feet and underwear, wiping off sweat as she ran.

There was a short list of alarms that the automated systems were programmed for. The really insistent ones were the station environmental alarms, the ones that warned you if you only had a few seconds to live. This, fortunately, was not one of those. This was one of the proximity alarms, and one that she had only ever heard in training.

She squeaked into the plastic seat in front of the traffic control station and looked at the monitors, convinced that there was some sort of glitch. What she was hearing was an alarm for outbound traffic from the wormhole—and not just random space debris. This was the klaxon for something the computers thought was a spacecraft.

For all the training Toni had gone through about this assignment, for all the history of the wormhole network, the idea of ghosts never sank in. Like many other ramifications of the quantum universe, it was too far removed from common sense for her to actually believe in the idea.

But she felt her pulse quicken when the holo in front of her resolved the imaging data into something that was clearly not a lump of rock. She was looking at a small scout craft, the same type that was currently docked on the underside of this station. It floated there, clearing the spherical distortion of space that was the wormhole, one engine trailing a wisp of vapor that crystallized in the vacuum.

She was seeing a ghost.

When humanity first reached for the stars, it was in lumbering vessels that barely came close to a significant fraction of light speed. That reach sparked the first, and so far only, interstellar war with another species. During that war with the enigmatic Race, mankind figured out how to create manufactured wormholes.

After the Terran Council—humanity's first attempt at an interstellar government—defeated the Race, it began linking nearby star systems with the new wormholes. From the point of view of the person traveling through the wormhole, passage between systems was nearly instantaneous. It also had a rather big catch.

It wasn't really faster-than-light travel; ten light-years was still at least ten years standard worth of time. And because the wormhole connected two points in space *and* time, persons traveling in one direction would emerge in a universe ten years older than the one they left. But anyone going in the *other* way would emerge in a universe ten years *younger*.

Thus causality went the same way as simultaneity.

Add to that the fact that a person emerging into that ten-year-earlier universe, from the wrong end of the wormhole, was emerging in a universe distinct from the one he left. A universe distinguished by the fact this person emerged from the wormhole ten years before leaving.

These visitors from alternate futures were known as "ghosts." And, in terms of the physics, were examples of the wormhole bleeding excess mass. In terms of the philosophy, ghosts were much more problematic.

At first, the solution was simple. The old Terran Council, draconic institution that it was, was content to blow away anything that came out the wrong end of a wormhole. It made good sense, since the old Terran Council used the wormholes to dispose of criminals, dissidents, refugees, and eventually, any excess population the Terran bureaucracy could get away with.

One-way wormholes served the Terran Council's purposes perfectly. So much so that, when the first tach-drive was invented, the Terran Council collapsed within a decade.

Even so, automated defense platforms guarded the "entrances" to the now obsolete wormhole network throughout the life of the Confederacy, the Terran Council's successor. It wasn't until the collapse of the Confederacy's control over interstellar relations that new policies about ghosts began to emerge.

The sirens were still sounding. Toni slapped the mute control and stared at the scout ship floating away from the wormhole. It was drifting without power, vapor trail coming from damaged engines.

What the hell is your story?

From the control panel, Toni readied the station's scout craft. Once the display showed her own craft fueling and powering up, she got up and ran down a corridor toward the docking ring. Her heart pounded, and for the first time since the klaxon sounded, she actually felt excitement.

For the first time during this tour she was actually going to do the job she had been stationed here for.

The priorities in the Confederacy, and before it, the Terran Council, had always been to maintain the status quo. There was a long list of developments that ran counter to that priority—at the top of the list was the trio of banned technologies: artificial intelligence, self-replicating nano-technology, and macroscopic genetic engineering. But any sort of time travel, however limited, was up there too.

However, the Confederacy broke down, and one unified human government fragmented into five, then six, then eight. As the Confederacy withdrew from the core human systems—home to the old wormhole network—old planetary, racial, ethnic, and religious rivalries began a long resurrection, and those who remained in power began to see the value of anyone from the future. Even a future that wasn't quite going to happen.

Toni didn't know of anyone yet going as far as flouting the ancient taboos against the big three—but as far as she knew, every intelligence service in the core systems made a point of extensively debriefing any ghosts that made an appearance. Information gathered fed projections, as well as profiles each agency kept on the intentions of every other interstellar power.

Just knowing what was possible, what *could* happen, was almost as valuable as knowing what *was* happening.

There were three wormholes in the Sigma Draconis system, Toni's being one of two outgoing ones. Its destination was the Loki colony, about twenty-two light-years away, orbiting Xi Boötis. The ghost she saw would have come from a similar station platform orbiting the other end of the wormhole.

Toni piloted the scout toward its brother, the distorted sphere of the wormhole growing in her viewscreen. She approached carefully, though it seemed unlikely that the scout presented a danger. Any pilot that took the dive into a wormhole, especially in one of the Centauri Alliance's own scouts, knew what SOP was on the other side.

Of course, that was a two-edged sword. If the pilot did

intend something more aggressive than abandoning his
home universe, he knew exactly what to expect from Toni.
More importantly, he'd know that it was probably going to
be at least twenty-four hours before a transport from Styx
came in response to Toni's alert. All of which meant that
Toni approached with caution, her ship's weapons trained
on the visitor.

She hailed the craft several times, and was only able to
get the response of a failing transponder and a distress beacon. She noted the signal in her logs before the significance
sank in. When it did, her arms broke out in gooseflesh, and
her breath caught in her throat.

Of course, the transponder identified it as a short-range
Alliance scout. Also, like all spacecraft in the Alliance, it
broadcast a unique call sign.

SC8765490, the same call sign as the ship Toni piloted
now.

"That can't be right . . ."

She double-checked the transponder transmission, her
own scout's call sign, and even—illegal in peacetime—
switched off her own transponder so she could be sure she
wasn't receiving some weird echo from the wormhole.

No such luck.

SC8765490

She was looking at the same ship she was piloting—
twenty-two years removed. The distress beacon was suddenly ominous.

It didn't make sense to her. If this ship came from the
Loki wormhole, it had managed to get over twenty light-
years away from Sigma Draconis—that was nearly ten
times the range of the scout's rudimentary tach-drive.

A lot can happen in two decades . . .

The scout didn't have to get there in one jump. Or maybe
someone upgraded the tach-drive. Any number of ways it
could have gotten to the other end of the wormhole—

Including going through the wormhole itself . . .

No, that couldn't happen. Even if she—if *anyone*—dove
into the wormhole and immediately came back through,
there'd be a time lag. The ship would have to come back
after it left—it *had* to.

Didn't it?

Toni was scanning her ship's doppelganger with every sensor she had. Severed hoses were still venting fuel into a vacuum. The cloud of gas had initially hidden the extent of the damage, but the outgassing fuel must be nearly gone now. The cloud of vapor around the rear of the ship was thinning to reveal the engines to the back of the craft.

The trio of engines were all sheared off. There were no control nozzles left, and the top thruster was missing all the way back to the fuel injectors. The bottom two were as bad off, both showing her half the reaction chamber, like an exploded model in one of her flight training classes. At first, Toni had thought that the ship might have been damaged in transit. It was possible to hit the wormhole too shallowly and throw a craft some nasty tidal stresses.

What she saw had nothing to do with tidal stress. There was no twisted metal, no debris beyond leaking gases, no sign of any violence at all. If anything, it looked as if the scout had gone into space half assembled. The parts hadn't been torn away; they were simply *missing*.

There was no possible way the thing could move under its own power. *Well,* Toni thought, *there was one way . . .*

Somehow, the idea that the damaged scout might have engaged its tach-drive made the ghost's sudden appearance on the wrong end of a wormhole even more disturbing.

Is there any record of someone taching a ship through a wormhole? What the hell would happen?

If anyone had ever investigated the possibility, it was in some rarified technical paper that was not in the Stygian officer training curriculum—including the briefings for wormhole duty.

Toni's sensors dutifully told her the ship posed no threat. Not only was the craft dead in the water, but an EM frequency scan of the power plant showed no output at all. What weapons it did have appeared to be spent. The thing was surviving on reserve batteries, and those were barely maintaining the emergency beacon and the transponder.

Her picture of the ghost became more detailed as she pulled her own craft alongside it. A matter density scan gave her computers a detailed map of the ship. As layers peeled away on her display, what she saw confirmed her first good view of the damage.

Somehow a good part of the engines had simply been *removed.* There was no sign of metal fatigue or any stresses on the frame of the scout. It was as if someone just un-bolted a large section of the main drives and left them on the other side of the wormhole.

As the display peeled back the cockpit, she saw that there was one passenger in a life suit. The sensors picked up the movement from breathing and circulation—slow and comatose. If it was like the life suit Toni was wearing right now—and there was no reason to believe otherwise—when the ship started critically losing life support, the user could, as a last resort, trigger the suit to drug themselves into a resource-saving coma.

Almost involuntarily, Toni focused the scan on the scout's pilot. She already knew what she would see, but some part of her wished she was wrong. She adjusted the density level on the scan, and momentarily, the passenger and most of the life suit disappeared from the display. All she saw was the thin metal rings that joined the helmet to the suit, hovering above the metal framework of the pilot's chair. She decreased the density and the pilot's bones re-solved themselves into a prostrate skeleton staring up at her through the grainy display.

Upping the density a little more and flesh poured onto the bones. Like a slow-motion image of someone being hit by a plasma cannon played in reverse.

When she was done, Lieutenant Toni Valentine stared at the unconscious face of Lieutenant Toni Valentine.

It took two hours standard for Toni to recover her future self from the damaged scout craft. She had to match course with the drifting ship, go EVA, and attach a couple of warn-ing beacons to the crippled ship's hull so it could be recov-ered later. Then she had to manually free the emergency release bolts that separated the control pod from the rest of the ship. Moving the pod, which contained her other self, as well as the control systems and life support of the dying ship took the bulk of the time.

Having her own scout pull the pod free was a delicate process where one misstep could end up piercing the pod. She needed to avoid any loss of atmosphere from the pod, because she had no idea if her doppelganger had the chance to seal her suit.

She also wanted the pod intact because it held the ship's memory. Telemetry, comm, and sensor signals, back to the last time the scout had docked and uploaded data to the station's main data store.

In other words, as much as her unconscious twin, the pod contained the information on what happened—a question that was taking on more than a purely professional interest for her.

Toni's scout returned to the station with the other ship's control pod attached to its abdomen like a parasitic twin. Towing the pod, about a quarter of a normal scout's mass—about a third of what was left of her twin's ship—pushed her own ship's capability near the limit. She had to do some fancy orbital maneuvers around the wormhole so that she had enough reaction mass to match velocity when she docked back at the station.

Umbilicals routed Toni's life support to the alien pod, while Toni piloted the too-massive scout back home with a hard vacuum in her own control pod. She ran her own environment suit at three-quarters capacity so she could last the whole way back.

Fortunately, 265 days of hard-core training and conditioning had made her body effective in adverse conditions, and she hardly noticed the effects of the low-oxy mix until she docked and was able to pressurize her command pod. She felt a brief period of light-headedness as she stripped off her spent environment suit, but it barely registered.

She violated several sections of the manual as she tossed parts of her suit on the floor in her scramble out the air lock, but after the ponderous trip back to the station she was seized by a sense of urgency that had been brewing ever since she saw her own transponder radiating from the ghost ship. Jumping into a spare environment suit would be about twelve minutes quicker than recharging the one she was wearing. It was the one thing so far she could safely rush—and she took the opportunity.

The mass sensors still showed signs of respiration and circulation in her double, and the life-support monitors on the shuttle—which were currently connected to the extra pod—showed a good O_2/CO_2 cycling. Those were the only monitors she had on her twin's life signs. The fact that Toni II was stationary in the pod gave circumstantial evidence she was still in a suit-induced coma, but because most of the brains in Toni II's command pod died with the power systems on the other ship, there was no direct way to monitor Toni II's life signs. Toni would have no real idea what was going on with her until she got her into a medical unit on the station.

That was going to take another EVA.

Fortunately, the station had an emergency docking umbilical that was flexible enough to snake around the docked scout craft and limpet onto the dead pod's air lock. It took another half hour for Toni to rig the connection, check the seal, and return to the station. For all the urgency she felt, it was as if she was swimming upstream through cold machine oil on Loki.

Toni blew the lock on the dead command pod and let free the warm smells of shit, piss, and fear. Toni II didn't move from the pilot's chair, and her face was barely visible through a polarized faceplate. The smell told Toni that she'd made the right decision in salvaging the whole command pod. Toni II's suit was venting into the cabin. Exposed to vacuum, the suit would have failed.

She walked clumsily in the cramped space. The station's rotation and the impromptu connection to the scout made everything in the cabin lean at an awkward angle, toward the rear left corner of the cabin. When she reached her older self, she broke the seal on the helmet, pulled it off, and let it drop and roll to that corner of the cabin.

Suddenly face-to-face, Toni felt a surge of dread that originated deep in some common cultural subconscious. Leaning forward in the one-person cabin, Toni stared at her own face, separated from it only by their mingled breaths. She found herself backing away until she felt the curving panel of the pod's metal ceiling cold on the back of her neck.

The rational part of her mind screamed at her. This wasn't an *omen*, for God's sake. This wasn't some psychodrama where she was meeting her Jungian shadow self. She was a lieutenant in the Stygian Security Forces, about as far away from folktales and fantasy as you could get.

Still, she had to force herself to touch a neck that was hers, and not hers, and feel a pulse that was hers, and not hers. The pulse was strong, steady, and much slower than her own.

Toni carried the surprisingly light body to the emergency medical bay. She stripped her other self naked and lowered the body into an articulated chamber that resembled a prone version of the universal resistance machine in the station's gym. Toni watched the metal carapace envelop Toni II, and felt strange relief when she could no longer see the flesh of her double.

She's not much older then me.
No, she's not any *older than me.*
Impossible . . .
What the hell happened to you? Toni thought. *What's going to happen to me?*

CHAPTER THREE

Omens

"You cannot see the future if you cannot see the past."
—*The Cynic's Book of Wisdom*

"If a man takes no thought about what is distant, he will
find sorrow near at hand."

—CONFUCIUS
(c. 551–479 BCE)

Date: 2526.6.4 (Standard)
Earth–Sol

Cardinal Jacob Anderson, Bishop of Ostia and Vatican Secretary of State, sat alone in his offices in the Apostolic Palace. In front of him, holo displays set into his desk scrolled
by intelligence information from across the breadth of
human space. Of late, much of that information concerned
the Eridani Caliphate and their proxies. Within the past six
months, the Caliphate had made technical advances in warship design that placed almost the whole of human space
within tactical reach of its military. Their new Ibrahim-class
carriers were a potential threat to every one of their rivals.

At the moment, though, he was paying little attention to
data from the Caliphate.

In front of him, for perhaps the thousandth time, he
played a holo recording. It began with a static whine and
an image that flowed in and out of focus, distorting itself.
Part of it was degradation from sending a tach-signal so far;
part was because the image came from the nose of a swiftly
moving tach-ship trying to focus its sensors.

The heavens spun around the display until it centered on a blue orb, a planet so similar to Earth it was almost painful to look at.

The voice that emerged, at least to begin with, belonged to a Vatican agent. Cardinal Anderson thought that these might have been the man's last words.

"... with Xi Virginis ... bzzt ... have lost visual contact ... "

Xi Virginis sat eighty light-years beyond the official limits of human space. But that hadn't stopped humans from colonizing. And it didn't stop those colonies from being important. The man sending this transmission had been sent to make contact on behalf of the Vatican, long before the Caliphate sent its Ibrahim carriers to do the same thing, more forcefully.

Interference blurred the holo and the planet. At least it appeared like interference, some artifact of transmission, or encoding. However, very many people had analyzed the holo, and what obscured the view of the planet was not any side effect of the transmission.

Something was coalescing in space between the camera and the planet. A cloud of black specks.

When the holo spoke again, it was a different voice that spoke, more of arrogance than of fear. "... bzzt ... coming toward ... bzzt ... behold a great ... bzzt ..."

The cloud of black motes moved purposefully toward the planet.

"... seven heads ... bzzt ... crowns upon ... bzzt ... the third part of the stars ... cast ... bzzt ..."

The transmission died.

"Behold a great red dragon, having seven heads and ten horns, and seven crowns upon his heads. And his tail drew the third part of the stars of heaven, and did cast them to the earth," quoted Cardinal Anderson to no one in particular.

Nine months ago, he had sent the last agent to investigate the source of the enigmatic transmission. Nine months. That had been before they knew about the Caliphate carriers that would put those colonies firmly in the reach of the Caliphate. Before the escalation of tensions that prevented serious consideration of anything outside their own borders.

But Father Mallory was still out there, somewhere. They had enough intel from Bakunin to know now that, despite Caliphate interference, he *had* been able to leave on an expedition to Xi Virginis.

Beyond that, nothing.

Unless Mallory's expedition had access to the new Caliphate tach-drives, the earliest they could have reached their goal would have been less than a month ago, more reasonably, within the week.

It was quite possible that the Caliphate could have beaten them there.

Anderson stared at the transmission and wondered what Father Mallory faced now.

"God help him," Cardinal Anderson whispered.

From the ornate desk in front of him, an assistant's voice emerged, "The trade representative from Sirius has arrived."

He waved, and the troubling holo disappeared from in front of him. "Send the man in," he told his assistant.

It was time to return to work.

PART FOUR

Crusade

"There is nothing evil save that which perverts the mind and shackles the conscience."
— St. Ambrose
(340?–397)

CHAPTER FOUR

Miracles

"Problems are never solved, only replaced."
          —*The Cynic's Book of Wisdom*

"Providence is always on the side of the last reserve."
          —NAPOLEON BONAPARTE
          (1769–1812)

Date: 2526.6.4 (Standard)
Salmagundi–HD 101534

Julia Kugara stood on a crystalline outcrop and stared as the sun set on a wasteland. Stretching for kilometers away from her, what had been a forest was now little more than a vast bowl of coals and cooling ash. Close to the horizon, at the limits of visibility in the haze and dimming light, she thought she could see where the burnt trees regained some semblance of individuality as blackened logs scattered like toothpicks. Beyond that, she could see the roils of smoke as the forest beyond still burned.

She wondered how many of her comrades from the *Eclipse* had died in the blast. The radius of the damage stretched far past where her lifeboat had dropped her and Nickolai, and the lifeboats were supposed to cluster their drops.

What kind of sick universe has me and the tiger as the only survivors?

Much closer, just a dozen meters from where she stood, the blast had been forceful enough to scour the ground clean, leaving a pitted, glassy surface that refracted slight rainbow shimmers in the evening light. About ten meters away from her, the glass stopped in a sharp line.

She spared a glance at the small disposable rad counter, one of the few items left from the lifeboat's emergency kit that had survived. It still showed safe levels of radiation. It was hard to believe the thing—but not any harder than believing she still lived.

She looked at the sharp line that marked the end of the nuke's destruction and wondered what frightened her more, that someone had dropped a nuclear weapon on her, or that something else had deflected it. It struck her in an immediate visceral way that the disappearance of Xi Virginis never had. For all the enormity of it, a missing star was an abstract concept.

This was immediate, concrete. She smelled the cooling ash, felt wind hot and dry enough to scour her skin, tasted a nasty metallic taste in the air.

She walked the perimeter, a perfect hundred-meter circle centered on the alien crystalline artifact that seemed to have grown out of a much more prosaic backwoods encampment. There wasn't much left of that encampment. The nuke had erased it from the face of the planet.

She looked behind her, and the light from the fading sun captured the cluster of crystalline structures. The light reflected the structural details where the surfaces seemed to fold in on themselves in an infinite fractal regression.

Proteus . . .

The alien structure had obviously been the target of the attack. The presence of Kugara and Nickolai here was incidental. A coincidence.

But it was very hard to believe in coincidence after working for Mosasa.

Was this thing part of your plan? She looked up at the sky. Above her, the stars were beginning to appear. *Are you still up there? Is the* Eclipse *still up there? Or did you both fall into the atmosphere and burn?*

She looked back at the horizon.

The only surveillance devices she had were her own eyeballs, but she had satisfied herself that no vehicles were approaching. No team coming to bat cleanup after the nuke. She didn't know if that was troubling or not. With the forest reduced to ash around them, the survival of the Protean's crystal enclave would be visible for a hundred klicks in any direction. Did they care? Were they waiting for something?

Are they otherwise occupied?

She coughed in the metallic-tasting air and decided that she was done trusting the little rad counter.

She walked back to the largest cluster of crystal forms. Within about twenty paces she was inside without ever passing a door as such. The walls folded around her path until they obscured everywhere except where she was going and where she had come from. Eventually she arrived at a space that could have been a room, or simply a space in the midst of the fractal superstructure of the crystalline walls surrounding her.

Two people waited for her. The first to stand was Flynn, a lanky, sandy-haired young man with a single elaborate glyph tattooed onto his forehead like a cubist third eye. He was a native, and if Kugara was to believe him, the tattoo represented an additional personality living in his skull—a woman named Kari Tetsami who shared a Dakota ancestry with Kugara, and who had probably been dead for close to a hundred and fifty years. To hear Flynn talk about it, the colony on Salmagundi took ancestor worship to its logical extreme. It creeped her out.

"Anything?" he asked. Kugara had only known the guy for a couple of hours, but she could already tell the difference between Flynn or Tetsami talking. Right now the earnest expression was completely Flynn.

"Nothing visible approaching," Kugara told him. "But anyone with a good line of sight can tell this place is still standing. If they're serious about wiping it off the planet, I'd expect another nuke."

"We should leave," Nickolai grumbled lowly.

She turned to face her fellow survivor from the *Eclipse*. He still sat, staring off past Flynn and Kugara, into the semitransparent walls. His muzzle wrinkled in distaste, exposing his massive canines when he spoke.

"We should leave," he repeated.

Nickolai's ancestors, like Kugara's, had been the results of centuries-old, largely military genetic experiments. Unlike Kugara, though, the heretical experiments that created Nickolai's kind had not begun with human DNA. So, while Kugara's people had interbred until there was no way to tell from looking that she was not completely human, there was no mistaking that Nickolai had descended from some strain of *Panthera Tigris*. He had black and orange striped fur, easily stood three meters tall—almost a full meter on Kugara's height—and topped the scales at five hundred kilos, all muscle.

"And what if they lob another nuke at this place before we're clear?" Kugara said. "At least we know that's survivable here."

Nickolai flexed the claws on his right hand. His claws glinted gray and metallic as he scraped them along the crystal floor next to where he sat. If it wasn't for the damage he'd sustained in their descent, the metal claws would be the only sign his arm was artificial. But the pseudoflesh that had covered the arm had been torn off between shoulder and wrist, and the mechanism that formed his arm was covered now by a white spray bandage. The bandage was meant only as an emergency measure. It was smudged and dirty, and in a few places the surface had split along the grain of his fake musculature, to leak a clear fluid that wasn't quite blood.

"This is an evil place," he said turning so he could actually look at her. "You heard what this man said, didn't you?"

Kugara looked into his slitted green eyes and sighed. She didn't *get* Nickolai. The back story of this little crystal enclave—if she trusted Flynn and Tetsami's story—made her feel uneasy too. The idea that she stood in what amounted to a colonization by a culture that had not only accepted heretical technologies, but embraced them and built upon them. The idea of being surrounded by billions of microscopic machines that were busy reproducing themselves and primed to consume whatever nearby matter they needed to do whatever it was they did—it made her skin crawl.

But *evil*?

That was a bit much coming from someone who wouldn't even exist without the benefit of someone using similarly heretical technologies five hundred years ago. Someone who had also willingly and knowingly allowed himself to be employed by an AI.

"We stay put until we have a viable exit," she told him.

"You don't understand," Nickolai whispered.

"And you still don't get a vote," Kugara snapped. "You lost the right to have an opinion when you sabotaged the *Eclipse*'s tach-comm. For all I know, you wanted the ship to blow up."

Flynn looked back and forth through the exchange, gripping his shotgun and edging away from Nickolai as if he expected the tiger to try and force the issue.

Kugara wasn't worried. She had spent over half her adult life in the service of Dakota Planetary Security, where she was trained to deal with threats considerably more dangerous than Nickolai. She was confident she could handle him unarmed.

Even if Flynn didn't quite realize what it meant to be a DPS veteran, Nickolai did. He didn't do anything beyond grumble inarticulately in his native tongue. After a few long moments, he asked, "The other lifeboats?"

Kugara shook her head. "Almost certainly caught in the blast."

Nickolai lowered his head and closed his eyes.

Guilt?

Guilt would be an appropriate response for someone who didn't believe that the mass of humanity were Fallen, the walking damned, and thought the AI Mosasa was synonymous with the devil himself.

Kugara looked at Nickolai's downcast face and wondered if it was *possible* to understand him.

She turned to Flynn and asked, "The people in charge here, are they likely to help us?"

Flynn shook his head, and his laugh had very little

humor in it. "The Triad is primarily interested in keeping things from being disruptive."

"A nuclear weapon is pretty damn disruptive."

"I never said I agreed with their reasoning."

"Damn, do these bastards even know about Xi Virginis?"

"I don't know what they know. I've been out of touch ever since this—" He gestured at the crystal walls with his shotgun. "Since this landed."

Kugara was at a loss for what to do. She was stuck with Nickolai on a planet that was actively hostile to offworlders, equipped with nothing but a nearly empty emergency kit, a needlegun, and the clothes on her back. It was tempting to hunker down and stay out of sight, but where would that ever end?

And then there was Xi Virginis, the *Eclipse*'s original destination. Mosasa had hired a crew of mercenaries and scientists to hunt down an anomaly. But even with the resources of an AI, Mosasa had not expected to find the entire star system *missing*. That had been enough to panic him. The *Eclipse* had tried to send a tach-comm back to the core of human space, she still remembered the too-human strain in Mosasa's voice:

If anything trumps your narcissistic human political divisions, it's this. This changes everything.

But Nickolai had sabotaged the tach-comm.

And this crystalline outpost had grown from a probe that had been headed for somewhere on the other side of the galaxy, a probe that had passed too close to whatever had happened to Xi Virginis. Whatever had consumed— and that was the word Flynn had used—the Xi Virginis system had caused severe damage to the probe, leaving only the remains of the AI autopilot to escape to the nearest inhabited star system.

Much as the *Eclipse* had done . . .

"Whatever we do," Kugara said, "our first priority has to be to communicate back."

"How?" Nickolai whispered.

"There's got to be a tach-comm on this planet somewhere." She looked at Flynn. He looked back at her blankly.

"Somewhere?"

There was a subtle shift in the way Flynn held his shot-gun. His hips cocked slightly, his eyes narrowed, and his expression lost most of its innocent qualities. "Kugara," he said, and she could tell it was no longer Flynn speaking, "You seriously underestimate how deeply these guys tried to bury themselves."

"Nothing?"

"Well, there were some rumors that they kept a space-port mothballed—"

"But?"

"We're talking about something that's had a century and a half to crumble apart. Not to mention we're half a continent on the wrong side of Ashley from it."

"You know where it is?" Kugara asked.

Tetsami chuckled. "I was there when we built the place—"

"Tach-ships?" Nickolai asked.

"You've got to be kidding," Tetsami said. "People might actually leave our little utopia."

Kugara leaned against a slick fractal wall. "We need to head there then."

Tetsami arched an eyebrow. "What about 'viable exits?'"

"We need to contact—"

Nickolai interrupted her. "What's that?"

"What's what?" she asked.

Nickolai slowly got to his feet, looking off toward where the passageway seemed to twist deeper into the heart of the structure. Flynn looked off in the same direction, and Kugara finally saw it as well.

Something moving.

She leveled her needlegun in the direction of the pas-sage, bracing herself against the slightly curving walls. There was nothing to aim at, though. Light didn't move normally in this semitransparent fractal landscape. All she saw was a pattern of shadow moving across the walls, spiraling inward toward the opening on one side of the chamber where they were. It was as if the shadow gradu-ally coalesced from a million fragments, only becoming complete when a solid humanoid figure stepped out of the passage to join them.

It was shaped like a man, but not quite. A bald ebony figure whose surface shone like black glass. Whatever it was made of, it seemed to eschew minor details and imperfections: no wrinkles, no hair, no fingernails, no nipples, not even the bump of a vein marred the perfectly smooth skin. It stared at them with blank eyes that had no irises or pupils.

It spoke. **"The other is here."**

CHAPTER FIVE

Damnation

"Those who don't know their own mind cannot know another's."

—*The Cynic's Book of Wisdom*

"I am more afraid of my own heart than of the pope and all his cardinals."

—MARTIN LUTHER
(1483–1546)

Date: 2526.6.5 (Standard)
Salmagundi–HD 101534

Nickolai Rajasthan had been a prince. He had been a blind exile in the streets of the most vile ghettos on the anarchic planet Bakunin. He had been a mercenary in the service of the Fallen. He had been a traitor to the AI Mosasa who was—until now—the closest he had come to facing the Devil himself. He had seen a nuclear weapon explode less than a hundred meters away, only separated from him by an impossible alien shield—

But when this ebony apparition—an unliving thing cast in the image of the Fallen—walked out of its crystalline hive and told them, **"The other is here,"** Nickolai felt fear. He felt a deep spiritual dread unlike anything he had ever felt before.

His beliefs, however tarnished by his presence in the human world, were born of a life with his own kind as scion of the House Rajasthan, trained by the warrior-priests of Grimalkin. While he had sinned, and sinned gravely, against the word of St. Rajasthan, he still believed. He believed that mankind had irrevocably fallen from grace for playing the role of God. First by twisting the flesh that God had given to create engineered creatures like him and Kugara. Then by creating consciousness without flesh, thinking machines that had no knowledge of God. Then, finally, by trying to re-create the entirety of life itself, machines that thought, and replicated, and pretended to be alive.

With the first, man had torn his planet with war, with the second he almost destroyed his culture, and the last had reduced entire planets to nothing but an undifferentiated mass of reproducing machines the size of a protein molecule.

Man had turned away from these heresies, but too late for their own salvation. The beings who created Nickolai's kind were fallen, and with them Nickolai had fallen as well. He had lived in their midst too long for his own redemption. Worse, with his presence here now, alongside the remnant of the ultimate arrogance, he felt not only himself, but the entire universe slipping further from Grace.

The walking blasphemy that was the combined persona of Flynn and Tetsami had told him what this ebon thing was. The technologists from Titan, who had been trying to terraform a distant moon in Terra's own system, had not been destroyed by the destruction of Saturn's moon. Their minds, at least, had survived the disaster to carry their infection elsewhere.

They called themselves Proteans and had created a colony on the lawless world Bakunin, one of the only places that would suffer their existence. And as the Confederacy collapsed, that Protean colony was completely wiped out— but not before it had propagated, spending its few centuries of existence sending probes away to spread its infection to planets thousands of light-years away and millions of years in the future.

They were a very patient evil.

And it was an evil that had walked straight from the scriptures of St. Rajasthan to confront Nickolai. The black thing standing before him was the personification of the Fallen's arrogance, the embodiment of the greatest sin ever committed.

But as it spoke, Nickolai knew in his soul that it told of something worse than itself. Something present here that went beyond the great sins from the scriptures.

Something that could rip a star from the sky.

"**The other is here.**"

"The other?" Kugara asked. "What is the 'other?'"

The Protean looked through her. "**The other is what damaged me. The other stole what we were and left only a shell. The other will turn all that is into itself.**"

"This doesn't sound promising," she said, looking the thing up and down. "And our Protean host doesn't sound all there."

"Don't," Nickolai half growled though clenched teeth.

She turned to face him, lithe and muscular in her movements, her own voice nearly a growl itself. "Don't what, Nickolai?"

"Don't make light of this."

"**I cannot repair myself. Too much of what I was is no more,**" The figure slowly turned to face Flynn, who might at the moment be Tetsami. "**You spoke of a tach-comm.**"

From the way Flynn's body backed away, Nickolai knew it was still Tetsami speaking, "The old spaceport."

"**Where?**"

"I—"

Kugara, strangely fearless, stepped between the two. "What do *you* want with that?"

"**Warning must be given, to those the other would consume.**"

Kugara waved at the crystalline architecture around them and said, "You built this. You blocked a fucking *nuke!* Can't you just build a tach-comm?"

"**I am incomplete, I try but I cannot repair what I no longer know. You will tell me where this is.**"

Hours later, the three of them, along with the Protean, rode on a circular platform mounted in the lower third of a twenty-meter transparent sphere that tunneled through the ground, toward Tetsami's spaceport. A blue light came from a cluster of spheres that rolled on the ceiling above them as if magnetically attached to the inner surface.

Outside, Nickolai saw solid rock and earth flowing around them, held back by a black fractal net that emerged from a semifluid mass that poured through the tunnel ahead of them, flowing in complete ignorance of gravity, swirling hypnotically clockwise as it consumed the matter that sat in their way.

Behind them, the webwork that held the earth away from their sphere coalesced in another fluid mass that swirled much like the forward mass. That one seemed to be reconstructing the strata that the one ahead consumed.

It was impossible to judge how fast the Protean's vehicle swam through the rock. After an initial acceleration, their velocity was constant. The rock beyond the fractal webwork was too ill-lit and sped by too fast for even Nickolai's artificial eyes to make out any detail. He shifted through spectra, and the only hint at how fast they moved was given in the infrared, where he saw that the rock itself glowed from the friction of their passage.

That heat didn't penetrate the sphere around them. Neither did sound. The air within the sphere was oddly silent, any vibrations from the wounded rock around them muffled to nonexistence. He could hear everyone breathing.

Everyone but the black figure of the Protean.

He watched the earth slide by and barely twitched when Kugara reached up and placed a hand on his shoulder.

"Are you all right?" she asked him.

"Nothing has changed." He had a brief impulse to tell her of the vision he had had right after the bomb had gone off. How he had seen his original employer, Mr. Antonio, the man who had hired him to join Mosasa, who had told him to sabotage the tach-comm on the *Eclipse*.

But, of course, Mr. Antonio hadn't been there. It was only a dream. A waking nightmare before he had lost consciousness.

"Everything has changed," she told him.

He shook his head. "We still walk among the damned."

"Oh hell, I give up." Kugara let go of him.

He turned to look at her, and despite the fact that he was still largely oblivious to human expression and body language, he didn't need to smell her to feel the frustration and repressed rage coursing through her body.

She stared into his face, as if she was looking for something. Whatever it was, she didn't appear to find it. "You're such a self-absorbed asshole."

"What?"

"I won't tell you what to believe. But it would be real nice if you could get a grip. I get it. You fell down on the wrong side of your religion. So, there's nothing you can do about it?"

"No, I've passed beyond—"

She shouted him down. "Then stop dwelling on it, you narcissistic morey fuck!" The words didn't echo in the sound-dampened sphere, but they resonated in Nickolai's gut. Her voice lowered to a harsh whisper. "There is nothing as useless as someone obsessing over something he can't change."

She left him standing there in shock. He was not used to anyone talking to him like that, even after he had been exiled. The Fallen might not have respected his position in House Rajasthan, but they respected tooth, claw, and rippling muscle.

But Kugara wasn't one of the Fallen.

She walked back over next to Flynn, and he quietly asked her, "Was that a good idea?"

"He's a big tiger," Kugara said, "he can take it."

Kugara stood on the platform, watching the black web-work crawling by outside the Protean's transparent sphere. She wondered exactly when the universe had gone off the rails of reason. She was a mercenary soldier from Bakunin. A more straightforward life you probably couldn't find anywhere. Even her dubious genetic past was, in the terms of the Bakunin Mercenary Union, more of an asset than a complication.

She had a job, she did it, and she was paid. At least until Mosasa had entered the picture.

Until Mosasa, her story had been ugly but comprehensible. Unlike a lot of Bakunin émigrés from Dakota, she wasn't running from the draconian dictatorship that gripped the second inhabitable planet circling Tau Ceti. Haven got the nonhumans like Nickolai, the moreaus, the weapons that weren't based on a human genome. Dakota got the Frankenstein monsters, the human-based creations. Unlike Nickolai's ancestors, the engineers that created Kugara's bloodline were condemned in their own time. Macro-scale genetic engineering of humans was probably the only heretical technology that was heretical before the first attempts to do it were made.

Somehow, there were still enough products of that technology to be exiled to Dakota and denied assimilation in either the human world or the smaller realm that Nickolai's kind had made. Just one ugly little planet that formed an ugly little government.

Kugara hadn't gotten the bad end of that deal. In the stratified castes that formed Dakotan society, the warriors that were born into the DPS, those that survived training at least, were probably the best treated. It meant that Kugara was one of the few Dakotan citizens who could legally leave the planet.

In her case, she had left to perform an assignment, the execution of a family of Dakotan escapees who had fled the regime. She had no problem dealing with the opposition leader and his wife. It was the teenage girl that had given her a twinge of conscience.

Sparing the girl had marked her official retirement from the DPS. Even five years afterward she still had no real understanding of why she had chosen that point to chuck her entire life and assume a dangerous exile on Bakunin. But, five years later, she understood the person she had been before her exile even less.

Mosasa must have understood her, though; because he knew exactly how to pull her into his employ. He made a credible promise to make the Dakota bounty on her head disappear. If that was all, she might still have said no, but he could do the same for the girl she had spared. So she had no choice.

After that, the universe had become surreal, twisting beyond the simple dirty facts of her own life. It started before the Protean had held a nuke at bay, even before the *Eclipse* had tached into the Xi Virginis system and discovered the star wasn't there.

Kugara thought that it had all begun when she had sat in a bar with that damn tiger Nickolai and he had informed her that Tjaele Mosasa was a construct controlled by a salvaged Race AI.

That fact shot through her world like a single neutron fired into a critical mass of questions. She could still see that chain reaction blowing apart her image of the universe, an explosion that the Protean wasn't going to save her from.

Hell, the Protean just makes it all worse.

As much as Nickolai's fatalism annoyed the hell out of her, in some ways she envied him. Nickolai at least had a lens through which all of this made some sort of sense. For all his angst, he never doubted his own ability to understand the world around him. He never doubted that the world around him *could* be understood.

Kugara could use some of that faith right now. She could use some antidote to feeling she was living in the fever-dream of some drug-addled schizophrenic.

This is just what I yelled at Nickolai for, wasn't it?

"What's it like out there?"

Kugara turned to look at Flynn. He stood next to her, looking straight ahead at the black mass chewing through the rock ahead of them. Actually, he seemed to be looking through it.

"Is it Flynn or Tetsami asking?"

He turned to look at her with a slightly wistful expression. "Both of us."

"Out where?"

"Everywhere. The last news we know of is nearly two hundred years old."

Kugara sighed. "I don't know if things are better or worse."

Flynn shrugged and turned back toward the front. "Is Bakunin still there?"

Kugara shook her head. "Yeah, there's still a place called Bakunin. Me and Nickolai were part of the Bakunin Mercenaries' Union."

"Mercenaries' Union?" From the way he cocked his

head, she thought it was Tetsami talking. "When I left, things weren't that organized."

"It wasn't?"

"In my time, everyone was their own contractor. Squad level was about as high as the hierarchy went."

Kugara tried to imagine life like that, completely at the whims of employers without any backup. "I guess too many mercs got shafted."

Tetsami gave her a humorless chuckle. "I suspect more that the army the Proudhon Spaceport Development Corporation put together never had any incentive to disband."

"Army?"

"Long story. The short version: the Confederacy tried to take the planet over by hiring everyone with a gun." The words trailed off and Tetsami turned away from Kugara and the view outside.

Kugara placed a hand on his shoulder. *Or is it* her *shoulder?* "Are you all right?"

"It's getting kind of hard not to think about my past. It wasn't particularly pleasant." Tetsami wiped a hand across Flynn's face. "Now I'm embarrassing Flynn." After a moment, she whispered, "Myself too."

"You were in that war?" Kugara asked, feeling a sudden odd kinship with the long-dead woman living in Flynn's skull.

"Everyone who came here was. The city, Ashley, is named for a commune that was slaughtered in that war. Ugly business for an ugly planet."

Kugara had often thought the same thing about her homeworld, Dakota. She gently squeezed Flynn's shoulder.

After a moment, Tetsami surprised her by asking, "Did you leave anyone behind on Bakunin?"

"What?"

"Husband? Lover? Girlfriend?"

Kugara lowered her hand. "No," she said, "I've never had a knack for lasting relationships. Did you?"

"No," Tetsami answered, "I didn't leave anyone behind."

*   *   *

"Why'd you lie to her, Gram?" Flynn's voice asked inside their head.

"I didn't lie to her," Tetsami silently answered. *"There was no one left to leave behind."*

"So? He left you."

"I don't want to talk about him."

"If you don't want to talk about Dom, why did you ask her about who she left behind?"

Jonah, Tetsami thought quietly to herself, *his real name was Jonah Dacham.*

"Gram?"

She sighed and shook Flynn's head. *"I'm tired. You drive for a while."*

"Gram, wait a minute—" Flynn said out loud.

"Flynn?" Kugara asked.

Tetsami tuned out the conversation, withdrawing her consciousness into a dark corner of Flynn's mind where no one could hear her curse or weep.

CHAPTER SIX

Inquisition

"Don't assume you know what the enemy wants."
—*The Cynic's Book of Wisdom*

"We can be knowledgeable with other men's knowledge,
but we cannot be wise with other men's wisdom."
—Michel de Montaigne
(1533–1592)

Date: 2526.6.4 (Standard)
Salmagundi–HD 101534

Father Francis Xavier Mallory had been many things in his lifetime: a Jesuit priest, a xenoarchaeology professor, a captain in the Occisis Marine Special Forces, and until recently an undercover agent for the Vatican Secretary of State. At the moment, none of that seemed to amount to very much.

His captors had tossed him into a room separate from the others. His holding cell was not designed as a prison, but appeared to be just a spare office or storeroom in the city's large central building. The ceiling panels shone diffuse light into a stark off-white cube that was empty of any furniture. The door was thin and translucent enough to show a fuzzy representation of the hallway beyond. It wasn't intended to be secure, and Mallory judged that it could be easily forced.

However, there would be no point in doing so. Even if this planet wasn't isolated, eighty-some light-years from the mass of human space, there'd still be nowhere to run to. Talking to his captors was the only option he had to improve the situation.

Unfortunately, the ad hoc nature of his prison spoke to how desperate and chaotic the situation here was. He didn't need the evidence of a mushroom cloud or his captors' assertion that there were a hundred and fifty ships invading this star system to know that. He saw the knife edge of war in the empty streets of the city, the armed soldiers that were only one third in uniform, the tension in the posture of those who carried the guns, the fear in the eyes of everyone else. It hung starkly in the stillness of the air as they rushed him and the other two ambulatory refugees from the *Eclipse* to the spire marking the center of the city.

He hadn't seen Dr. Dörner or Dr. Pak since they hauled him off the ground transport and threw him in here. Dr. Brody he hadn't seen since the medics had rushed him off the troop transport that had airlifted the four of them out of the forest where their escape pods had landed.

He said a short prayer for Brody's safety.

How long? An hour?

The passage of time weighed on him. He knew that the situation was degrading, and he suspected that it wouldn't be long before the people who had taken him prisoner would completely lose control of the situation, if they hadn't already.

The *Eclipse*, Mosasa's ship, was probably destroyed. He wondered if the people here on Salmagundi witnessed what happened.

They were tracking our approach, they must have seen it, and they still treat us as the vanguard of an invasion . . .

Then again, for a colony that had so purposely removed itself from human space, wasn't an invasion exactly what the *Eclipse* was?

Somehow he needed to get word back to the Vatican about the situation here. That meant access to a tach-comm transmitter, which, given the insular planet-bound nature of this colony, they might not even have. The isolation he felt was palpable, worse even than what he had felt on the *Eclipse* when the shipboard tach-comm had disintegrated along with his cover. Not only a physical isolation, a hundred light-years away from the center of the Church, but a spiritual isolation he had felt ever since the *Eclipse* had tached into the space where the Xi Virginis system should have been.

No, Mallory thought, *I've felt it ever since Bakunin. Ever since I understood what Mosasa was . . .*

What he *had* been.

He looked up at the ceiling, past it, thinking of the *Eclipse* launching the lifeboats. Mosasa had been on the bridge with Wahid, Tsoravitch and Parvi. Most likely they hadn't escaped the massive failure that had caused the lifeboats to launch, which meant they were almost certainly dead. Along with the Paralian, Bill, whose massive life-support apparatus couldn't have moved outside the *Eclipse*'s cargo bay, much less boarded one of the lifeboats.

Even Nickolai and Kugara were more than likely gone. He had radio contact with them after their lifeboat had launched, but nothing since. Anything could have happened with their lifeboat's descent to Salmagundi.

And there was the mushroom cloud.

He only had the visual cues from the troop transport to place the detonation, but he had been in the special forces, and he was trained to interpret whatever intelligence he could in a battlefield situation. While his eyeballs didn't have a lot of practice, he didn't need to be precise in placing ground zero to know that the kill zone of the nuke covered the LZ for the two lifeboats he knew about. The nav computers for the lifeboats would have tried to cluster them, so it was likely the nuke covered all six.

Unless the locals had another transport to evac Nickolai and Kugara separately from the survivors Mallory knew about, he had to count them as deceased along with the rest of the crew of the *Eclipse*.

Please, Lord, let me know what I should do.

The door to Mallory's impromptu prison burst open. He looked up and met the eyes of the old man that had met them when their transport had landed. He wore what Mallory assumed was a civilian's dress—a white collarless shirt, black pants, and a long white topcoat that hung to his ankles. The man was bald and had odd tattoos evenly spaced on his brow and scalp, all self-contained glyphs that reminded Mallory of Mayan hieroglyphs that had cross-bred with blocky Kanji script.

The man's scalp glistened under the cold lighting. Mallory noticed that his shirt was wrinkled and sweat-stained, and the man's face was even more deeply creased and shadowed than he'd expect from someone aged past their seventh decade.

A pair of uniformed militiamen in visored helmets and black body armor flanked the bald man as he stepped toward Mallory. The man stopped, and the two black-clad escorts stepped to either side of Mallory, grabbing his arms and hauling him up from where he'd been seated on the floor.

"What's happening?" Mallory asked, not really expecting an answer.

The bald man shook his head and turned away. The militiamen followed, leading Mallory out of the room. They took him through a series of corridors that were fairly unremarkable; the diffuse lighting and unadorned walls could have been in any office building anywhere. He had seen the outside of this building when they had taken him from the LZ, a tall, mostly windowless spire central to the city here. Taller than any of the other buildings and surrounded by acres of greenspace. The placement and architectural emphasis made it obvious that the structure was the focus of authority here.

Mallory still didn't know what that authority looked like: a democracy, a theocracy, or some sort of totalitarian dictatorship. Whatever form it took, it was close to some sort of crisis point. Of all the rooms they passed, most were empty. Here and there, chairs had toppled over, papers were scattered on the floor, and someone's half-eaten breakfast or lunch sat on a desk where a monitor silently flashed for attention.

He knew, from his exterior view of the building and from a basic sense of direction, that he had been locked in a room in one of the shorter wings of the structure that radiated out from the central spire. He also guessed that he was being taken deeper into the structure.

However, he wasn't quite prepared when they walked through a door and ended up inside the spire itself. From the outside, it seemed to be just a windowless office building; inside it was a single large, open space. The ceiling vanished hundreds of meters above him.

Their footsteps echoed as they pulled him forward, across a roughly circular floor. Mallory stared at the walls, which at first seemed to be made of clusters of uniform stone pillars thrusting up into the emptiness above him. The pillars were all hexagonal and about a meter across, allowing them to nest seamlessly together.

Looking down, toward the base of the pillars, Mallory realized that they weren't stone. The grayish-brown matte finish fooled the eye at first, but a closer look showed them to be some molded ceramic composite. It was clear in the completely uniform construction, and the perfectly square access panels that repeated themselves on each face of the pillar, staking up in an apparently infinite regression toward the ceiling.

What is this?

The panels reminded him a little of the electronic access panels that had been on the *Eclipse*.

"Where are we?" he asked. His voice was quiet, but still echoed enough to make the words startling.

"The Hall of Minds," the bald man unexpectedly answered him.

The Hall of Minds?

The words carried an ominous hint at what might be behind those access panels. AIs were a heretical technology throughout human space, along with macro-scale genetic engineering and self-replicating nanotechnology—all had resulted in uncountable death and destruction. The bans against them went beyond mere laws of some government, the bans were social and theological.

But Salmagundi had been founded at least a century and a half ago, by refugees from the Confederacy's collapse. They had purposely isolated themselves and had chosen to have no off-planet contact for their entire existence. They could have chosen to shed those taboos.

"Where are you taking me?" Mallory asked.

"To the anteroom," the man said.

As they walked him toward the opposite wall, Mallory was struck by the Hall of Minds' resemblance to a cathedral. There was a dais central to the floor plan. On it were two obelisks flanking a raised area that resembled a sacrificial altar.

The antechamber to the Hall of Minds didn't resemble anything that could be found in a cathedral. It resembled an operating theater.

The bald man led the way into a large room filled with stark white light and dominated by a series of padded tables. Above the tables large spidery robots were mounted in the ceiling, each hosting a half-dozen articulated arms that ended in cameras, probes, needles, and things less welcoming.

"Wait," Mallory said, "we need to talk—"

The bald man waved him forward and the militiamen threw him facedown on the nearest table. The head of the table had a hole to fit his face; the men flanking him forced his face into it despite his struggles. He heard more people in the room and felt straps being pulled tight against his legs, his wrists, his neck, and the back of his head. He was trapped, facedown under the robot. All he could see was a small circle of the tiled floor under the table.

His gaze locked on a dime-sized spot of blood on the floor below the table.

He heard the bald man say, "I would advise you against making any sudden movements. This is a delicate procedure."

That only made Mallory struggle more, but he was held fast to the table, and all he could manage was tensing his muscles. "Please," he said, "there's no need to resort to this. We can talk."

"We don't have the time to talk."

Above him, he heard a whine of motors and a steady clicking. He thought he could see the shadow of the robot move across the floor just at the edge of the table. "You don't need to hurt the others. I'm a spy, but they're only sci—"

The word "scientists" caught in his throat as something

cold and sharp stung the back of his neck. His eyes lost focus and the muscles of his face went slack. He tried to speak, but his mouth was flaccid and the only thing to come out was a long thread of drool.

Anesthesia? His thoughts were as clear as ever. *You don't use anesthesia when you torture people.*

He felt nothing but a growing pressure on the back of his head and neck. However, along with the pressure was an alarming cacophony: buzzing, whirring, drilling. He smelled the stench of something burning, and watched as two drops of blood fell off of his face to land on the floor.

Silently, Mallory began to pray.

Ages seemed to pass while Mallory listened to the sounds of his body being violated. He felt the tugs on his flesh and the sensation of something invasive slowly sliding into the base of his skull. Eventually, though, the mechanical sounds moved away and ceased.

The silence was so abrupt that briefly he believed he had lost his hearing.

Then he heard the sound of footsteps approaching the table. He heard the bald man's voice. "Good. No problems with the implant. I'm afraid we do not have the time to wait for you to heal or become acclimated to it. But your companions went though this without undue side effects. Do your best to relax your mind, it will go easier if you let go."

What are you doing?

He heard and felt a metallic click at the base of his skull.

It began to dawn on him: *Hall of Minds.*

Then something cold and alien sunk its fingers into his brain.

CHAPTER SEVEN

Sacrifice

"It is the height of arrogance to assume you are unique."

—*The Cynic's Book of Wisdom*

"Whatever you may be sure of, be sure of this, that you are dreadfully like other people."

—JAMES RUSSELL LOWELL
(1819–1891)

Date: 2526.6.5 (Standard)
Salmagundi–HD 101534

Mallory's skull ached, a throbbing pressure that originated at the base of his skull and radiated inward, twisting threads of pain through his brain. At some point during the procedure he had blacked out.

Before he was fully awake, he reached up. Someone with soft hands took his wrist and whispered, "Don't do that."

He blinked and a blurry image of a woman's face slowly came into focus. "Dr. Dörner?" he whispered, his mouth slurring the words.

"It's over," she whispered. "I think they're done with us."

Her blue eyes were edged with red and didn't appear nearly as icy as he was used to. His first thought was, *They're no longer separating us?*

He tried to sit up, but his balance was off, and moving his head caused a wave of vertigo. Dörner placed her hand on his shoulder and said, "Don't move too quickly; you're still adjusting to the implant."

"Implant," he said, slurring the words.

He looked up at Dörner and saw a bandage peeking out from the back of her neck. He reached up again, and she tried to stop him again. He pulled his wrist out of her grip and touched a similar dressing covering the back of his own neck.

When he touched it, he grunted as the throbbing became a spike driving through his skull. He gasped and tensed every muscle in his body while the flash of agony faded.

She grabbed his shoulder, "Are you all right?"

After a moment to catch his breath, he said, "I'm sorry. You're right. I shouldn't do that." Laboriously, he pushed himself up into a sitting position, trying to overcome the vertigo by force of will.

The room was larger than the one where they had been holding him. Big enough to hold half a dozen cots. Dr. Brody, the cultural anthropologist from the *Eclipse*, a man as dark as Dörner was pale, sat at the end of one of the cots, watching Mallory and Dörner, his right arm in a cast.

Mallory was thankful to see him alive. Brody had been injured when the lifeboat landed, and the last time Mallory had seen him conscious was before the *Eclipse* had tached into this system.

Even so, Brody didn't look that well. His large frame seemed to have folded in on itself, and his dark skin had taken on a sickly yellow cast. Like Dörner, the back of his head was bandaged. It was more obvious on him because he didn't have the hair to cover it. Mallory frowned, realizing that it was little better than a field dressing, and he could see blood crusted around the edges of the hidden wound.

What did they do to us?

"Father Mallory," he said, "you look like hell."

"Where's Dr. Pak?" Mallory asked.

"I presume he's making his own visit to the Hall of Minds right now," Brody told him. "Judging by the time between your arrival and Dr. Dörner's, it seems to take them about three hours."

Mallory looked from Dörner to Brody and back again. "Do you know what they're doing?"

"Interrogating us," Brody said with a weak smile. "Probably more thoroughly than we were expecting."

"Don't make light of this!" Dörner snapped at him.

Brody's fragile smile shattered. "What else have I got?" he spoke through gritted teeth.

"At least you weren't conscious through it. At least you didn't feel them—feel it—" Her voice choked off, and she turned away from both of them.

Brody whispered, "I don't think it makes it better."

Mallory rubbed his palms on his legs, trying to regain his equilibrium. "Is it what I think it is?" Mallory asked. "They implanted a bio-interface, and they hooked us all up to a computer—"

"*The* computer," Brody said. "I have Sharon's description of where they took us. Unquestionably a ritual space devoted to exactly what they did to us, although I suspect their own people undergo a less abbreviated initiation."

"It's not an initiation," Dörner said. "It's rape."

"I doubt it is truly consensual, even among their own people. Once a culture devotes this much energy to something, opting out is rarely an option."

"What are they devoting energy to?" Mallory asked.

"The preservation of their ancestors, at its base. Their entire history downloaded and stored like so many files in a library. Though I wonder how they access that wealth of information."

Mallory looked at him and felt a deep unease.

"I'm not a computer specialist," Brody went on, "but from my history I know that even at the height of the heretical technologies, no one ever was able to extract coherent information from a static recording of someone's mind—human or AI. There always needed to be some sort of brain hosting it."

Mallory didn't know what was more disturbing, having his mind implanted in some heretical AI, or having it implanted in someone else.

Dörner was right, they *had* been raped. They had been violated more thoroughly than any physical assault could have done. Their captors had stripped them down to the very soul, stealing things that were to be between only God and themselves. The entirety of their existence.

When a pair of guards brought Dr. Leon Pak into the room, glassy-eyed and unresponsive, Mallory felt as far from God's grace as he ever had in his life.

Alexander Shane watched as they carried the last of the offworlders from the antechamber. He had been the youngest, and the physical part of linking to the Hall of Minds was easiest for him. The mental part, though, was the worst. He had seen it in the displays monitoring the connection; he had resisted retrieval to an unprecedented degree.

His men left him alone in the antechamber. None had questioned what he was doing. He doubted any of these men would. He had handpicked them, and each had at least two ornate glyphs upon their brows that matched with one of the fifteen on Shane's naked scalp. At least two ancestors downloaded in common, either in this room, or in another room like it somewhere on Salmagundi.

Therefore, most understood his thought processes, even if they didn't completely share them. They would have been right to question him, but none did. And all of the ones who might have questioned him probably knew that leaving him alone, unchallenged, made his decisions that much harder.

It was a questionable decision in a long line of questionable decisions. He had chosen to stage a coup and take the Triad's authority as his own, in part because he believed they were all in desperate danger. In part because he wanted no one else to face the responsibility for some of the things he had to do.

Things like taking copies of unwilling, living people, and feeding them to the Hall of Minds. For over a century, the Hall had been a repository only for the dead and dying, a means to preserve their knowledge and their contributions to Salmagundi. Only a few dozen minds here had been taken while their bodies lived on, all original Founders.

Those minds were rarely taken on by their descendants, more from practical concerns than from any taboo. Better to take in some elder who had taken on a lifetime of history and knowledge from others, someone like Shane himself who hosted the merged personas of fourteen people who had likewise merged themselves with many of their ancestors.

The fifteenth was an exception. To serve in the Triad, a potential leader was expected to take on the additional persona of one of the Founders. It was recognized that at such a venerable time in someone's life, matters of practicality were of less a concern. It created a layer of history in the mind, a perspective that was necessary to lead.

It also inevitably influenced the personality of the host. Shane wondered how many of his decisions of the past few days were prompted by the presence of his distant namesake in his skull. He remembered the history of Kathy Shane, ex-captain with the Occisis Marines, better than any of the other lives that had contributed to make up what he was. She had sacrificed herself to shield the people she had charge of—not her life, but her command, her honor, everything of value to her.

Like his distant ancestor, Shane was in a position where he had to do things that would—in the end—disqualify him from leading the people he was trying to save. Already he had engaged in a coup, and now he was about to do something that verged on blasphemy.

If Salmagundi survived, Shane knew that he would not be granted the solace of contributing to the Hall of Minds. He would be tried, convicted, and executed, and his mind would be allowed to disappear with his body.

He eased onto one of the tables and laid himself facedown, the bio-interface in the back of his neck pointing upward toward the medical robot.

He closed his eyes. In some sense he was giving up everything with this act. Not just his position in Salmagundi society, but he was abandoning his self as well. However, there were warships closing on his planet, and he didn't have time to extract information from the prisoners in any other way. In less than an hour, he would know their stories front to back, without opportunity of deception.

He only hoped that somewhere, in their collective mind, there might be some hope of a solution.

He gritted his teeth, grabbed the edges of the table, and said, "Connect."

Above him the robot whirred, and a cable clicked into the back of his neck. A half second later, the Hall of Minds released a torrent into Shane's brain. A barrage of memory and personality, a parade of selves no longer self-aware, no longer conscious of unraveling into the memory of the Hall of Minds. The four identities erupted through the core of Shane's mind like magma erupting through the cracks in a volcanic island, searing what was there, burying it, enlarging it, and irrevocably changing the landscape.

—moving through a burnt-out church looking for remnants of the junta—

—while his hands are slick with sweat as he defends his thesis on the cultural parallels between modern worship of Dolbrian artifacts and twentieth-century cargo cults—

—and opens the letter that accepts her into the most prestigious university in the Centauri Alliance—

—his father holds his hand as he stares in wonder at the crooked black stone that's almost three thousand years old; he stares at the three sets of texts as his father explains how a man, six centuries ago, had used it to understand a language long thought dead—

—and speaks his vows to God while still smelling gunsmoke and ashes—

—while a student curses him for saying that the European culture of the SEC is as worthy of study as his own—

—and she cries over her father's grave—

—slamming a fist into the display showing the rejection of his paper on Dolbrian script—

—his heart in his throat as he hears his first confession and realizes the responsibility—

—looking up into the sky of Bulawayo understanding he will never see firsthand—

—the audience applauding as she concludes her speech—

—facing the Sphinx—

—teaching his class—

—kissing her lover—

—feeling his age—

—studying his alien script—
—Cardinal Anderson—
—Mosasa's invitation—
—Crash landing—
—PANIC—

Dr. Pak sat on the edge of the cots staring into the middle distance. He clenched his hands into fists on top of his thighs and silently rocked back and forth. Mallory watched Dörner try to talk to him, but he remained largely unresponsive. The only signs he wasn't completely catatonic were when he yanked his arm away from her touch, and his answer when she asked if they could do anything for him.

His response was a flat, affectless, "No."

Brody sat next to him, and the slow, deliberate nature of his movements showed that Brody was having the toughest recovery from the physical effects of the bio-interface implant. "Do you have any idea what we can do for him?"

I should, Mallory thought. He had been trained in counseling when he had chosen his vocation. A priest was supposed to provide comfort and solace. However, that had never been his strong suit. He suspected that, even though he wasn't the one to sabotage the *Eclipse*, the fact he had joined Mosasa's expedition with a falsified identity meant he was not trusted here. Even if Dörner and Brody might accept him for the moment because of their shared trials, the lie stood between Mallory and the survivors of the *Eclipse*.

Mallory couldn't ask Pak to trust him enough to allow him to help. It would be hard enough for a Jesuit university professor to provide the counseling he needed after being psychically brutalized. Given Mallory's recent history, he had the uneasy feeling that any help from him would only intensify the trauma.

He looked at Brody and said, "Dr. Dörner is doing the only thing we can do." He watched her talking quietly to the damaged linguist, and he saw in her face a softness that hadn't been there while they were on the *Eclipse*. Of the three here, she was probably the best choice to comfort him.

"Why did you do it?" Brody asked.

"Do what?" Was Brody unaware of Nickolai's confession? Mallory had just assumed that after Mosasa had violated that sacred confidence the knowledge had spread to the rest of the crew. If it hadn't, Mallory began to wonder if he could, in good conscience, deny his involvement.

But it wasn't what Brody was asking him. "Why did a priest join the Bakunin Mercenaries Union with a false identity? Why did you join Mosasa's expedition?"

Mallory remembered Cardinal Anderson showing the intercepted video of a planet close to Xi Virginis, of thousands of black shadows swarming and obscuring the planet, and of the voice quoting Revelation: "*Behold a great red dragon, having seven heads and ten horns, and seven crowns upon his heads. And his tail drew the third part of the stars of heaven, and did cast them to the earth.*"

After what he had just been though, Mallory had no secrets, so he told Brody. He told him how he had been recruited by Cardinal Jacob Anderson, Bishop of Ostia, Dean of the Sacred College of Cardinals, Secretary of State of His Holiness the Pope. How he had been given the identity of Staff Sergeant Fitzpatrick in order to merge seamlessly into the flow of immigrants into the anarchic planet Bakunin and avoid the attention of the Caliphate. How he was to find transportation to Xi Virginis to gather intelligence on the colonies here and what may have prompted the transmission—

"And Xi Virginis turns out to be missing," Brody said.

"Yes."

"The biblical quote seems much too appropriate for the situation."

"More so because the voice is familiar."

"It was?"

"The same voice was transmitted a few hours ago." Mallory quoted the part he had overheard from the radio in the troop transport that had brought them here: "*I am Adam. I am the Alpha . . .*"

"With due respect to the Vatican's paranoia, that does not seem like the Caliphate to me."

"No," Mallory said. "It doesn't."

"Our host said he detected how many ships in orbit?"

"A hundred and fifty."

Brody brought his fingers up to massage the bridge of his nose. "A religious conflict is the nastiest kind of war humans know how to wage."

"The tensions between the Church and the Caliphate are primarily political, issues of human rights and self-deter—"

Brody held up his other hand, stopping him. Quietly, he said, "I'm not talking about the Caliphate. Or the Vatican. What was it that Mosasa said before the comm unit blew?"

Mallory remembered, if only because it was the closest he had seen the faux human AI display something akin to panic. "'If anything trumps your narcissistic human political divisions,'" Mallory said. "'It's this.'"

"Why do you think he said that?"

"A star system disappeared. I suspect it was a little disconcerting."

"I think he saw this 'Adam' in the absence of Xi Virginis," Brody said. "And I think this 'Adam' is the latest in a long history of missionary warriors. Just the little bit of rhetoric he's given us: '*I am Adam. I am the Alpha, the first in the next epoch of your evolution. I will hand you the universe. Follow me and you will become as gods.*' If that isn't a messianic message, I don't know what is."

Mallory nodded. Brody voiced his own fears; fears that he had felt ever since he had heard Adam's transmission to Salmagundi.

"Judging by the absence of Xi Virginis and a missing colony of possibly one and a half million people, I am not optimistic about the fate of those people who don't choose to follow him. And then there's that apocalyptic quote from Revelation."

Mallory nodded.

"I've had an unfortunate thought," Brody said after a pause.

"More so than the ones you've just mentioned?"

"You're present here because the Vatican intercepted a message, correct?"

"Yes."

"A tach-comm message?"

"Of course. A normal EM intercept would have been nearly a hundred years old."

Brody nodded. "I don't know if you ever heard this—you were locked in your cabin at the time—but Bill did an astronomic survey when we tached in to orbit here. Xi Virginis isn't shining in the sky here, which means it's been gone for at least eight years."

It took a moment for the import to sink in. "By the time we got that transmission—"

"Everything was long gone. The video was either recorded nearly a decade ago, or it was completely fabricated."

"It was meant to be intercepted." Mallory struggled with the idea. "But what was the point? Why plant a message to draw attention to Xi Virginis? Why not announce himself the way he did here?"

"Maybe the message wasn't meant for you."

"Who then?"

"Mosasa."

"Mosasa? Why do you think—"

A new voice spoke, "Bait."

Mallory turned to look at the door, where the bald man with the tattooed scalp stood in the doorway facing them. He looked stooped now, as if he had aged a decade in the few hours since Mallory had seen him last. Dr. Dörner stood up and started to say, "What did—"

"What did I do to Dr. Pak? The same thing I did with all of you. He will recover."

Dr. Dörner took a step toward the man, but two armed men in black militia uniforms stepped out to flank him. Dr. Dörner stopped in her tracks and glared at their host. Mallory saw an uncomfortable echo of her expression in the old man's face.

He heard Brody whisper, "No . . ."

The old man turned to face Brody with an unpleasant turn of the lip that only very charitably could be called a smile. "Dr. Brody has an excellent grasp of our culture considering how briefly he's been exposed to it. Down to how we honor those who contribute to our identity." He tapped a finger to his brow, where the glyphs were tattooed.

Dörner turned toward them. "What is he talking about, Sam?"

"I told you, their Hall of Minds is a ritual space. They use it to record and pay homage to their ancestors." He looked at the old man and said. "I'm right about the tattoos?"

Their host nodded.

"What about the tattoos?" Dörner asked.

"There's only two ways a recording of a human mind can be useful. The first is to implant it in an AI. And since AIs are illegal, most of what I've read on the subject is probably apocryphal. The other—"

"Oh, no," Dörner whispered.

"—is to download it into another living brain."

Mallory looked at the old man's skull and the tattoos there. Was that it? Did each of those marks represent another human being whose mind had been copied, one that had been downloaded into this man's skull?

Did that mean he had just done the same with the four of them?

To Mallory's horror, the old man looked directly at him and nodded slightly, as if he knew what Mallory was thinking.

CHAPTER EIGHT

Martyrdom

"There is no such thing as someone with nothing to lose."

—*The Cynic's Book of Wisdom*

"No one is more dangerous than a man convinced he is about to die."

— AUGUST BENITO GALIANI
(2019–*2105)

Date: 2526.6.5 (Standard)
300,000 km from Salmagundi–HD 101534

Vijayanagara Parvi, captain of the *Eclipse*, had been strapped down in an interrogation room on board the Caliphate carrier the *Prophet's Voice* for several hours now. Nothing marked the passage of time, the light never wavered, and except for a few perfunctory questions when they'd dragged her in from the dying *Eclipse*, she had been without human contact since.

She knew nothing about what was happening beyond the featureless walls of this room. She didn't know the fates of the remaining bridge crew of the *Eclipse*, or Bill for that matter. Mosasa, Tsoravitch, Wahid, they had all been separated as soon as the Caliphate's soldiers took them from the wreckage of the *Eclipse*. She had never even seen what happened to Bill. The Paralian had been trapped in the cargo hold in his massive six-meter environment suit. For all she knew, their "rescuers" never even bothered to remove Bill from the remains of their ship.

She took some minimal comfort from the thought that

the rest of Mosasa's expedition had made it down to the planet's surface. But only the gods knew what the Caliphate's intentions were—

That's a lie. I know exactly what their intentions are.

Before she became a mercenary on Bakunin, she had been a fighter pilot for the Indi Protectorate Expeditionary Command. She had piloted a drop fighter against the separatists on Rubai, a planet that—until the Revolution—had been her home; a Revolution that not only wouldn't have been successful, but in Parvi's opinion, never would have happened without Caliphate assistance and recognition of the Revolutionary government.

Even as the Indi Protectorate withdrew from the debacle on Rubai, she had remained with a core resistance of ex-Federal forces about eight months past the point where it had been obvious that no relief was ever going to come to support the overthrown government. Rubai had been handed over to these bastards with only a token fight. She ended up wanted as a counterrevolutionary terrorist on her home planet, and in the Indi Protectorate she faced a court-martial for disobeying orders and remaining to assist the doomed Federal forces.

So, she knew *exactly* what the Caliphate's intentions toward this new planet were. She also knew what their intentions toward her would be. She might not be a high profile enough fugitive for them to go out of their way to hunt down, but she was important enough that if they had her in custody it was truly unlikely that they were going to let her go.

Leaving her alone like this was probably an indication of what she could expect. The psychological operations had already started. Lack of contact, mobility, food, and water, the too-bright light.

Inevitably, when the interrogator returned, she would be more likely to cooperate simply to prolong the human contact. Unfortunately, knowing what they were doing to her, and what they expected, didn't lessen the effects. She could endure this for a while, maybe more than most, but of course it wouldn't end here.

In the end, what would they want from her? Some testimony against Mosasa? He had probably been destroyed as soon their Caliphate rescuers understood what he was. No, they'd break her, force her to renounce her support of the Federal Government on Rubai against the foreign separatists. Possibly make a propaganda holo just before they executed her. She also knew enough about psychological operations to know that when she did renounce her actions, she would be sincere.

Each passing minute in isolation, alone in the featureless interview room, fed the growing conviction that she was not going to escape a demise at the hands of the same people who had razed her homeland. The same people who were going to take possession of this colony eighty light-years beyond what they could rationally claim as their sphere of influence.

She could hear mechanical groans, even through the soundproofed walls. The uniform lighting flickered slightly.

Her hands were fists, nails digging into her palms. She bit her lip hard enough to draw blood. Just thinking about them watching her now, planning her eventual humiliation, caused her pulse to race in her neck.

I've gone soft.

She had spent a long time doing mental exercises to calm herself. Now that her facade was starting to crumble, and fatigue and despair were bringing her emotions to the surface, her captors should be ready to resume their interrogation. They would have her closely monitored, and there was little chance they'd miss her body finally giving in to the stress. Her discipline had worn away a lot earlier than it should have.

But then, where were her captors?

She looked up at where the door to the room was, hidden behind the omnipresent glare. The lights flickered again, enough that she could barely see the seam that formed the edge of the entry.

Beyond that door would be a station where someone would be watching the throb of her pulse, the spike in her fight-or-flight responses, the shifts in her body language. "Where are you?" she whispered to the door. Her lips cracked with the effort, the elevated temperature and lack of humidity under the lights making her mouth sandpaper-rough.

No response came from beyond the glaring walls, not even an echo.

"Games," she whispered. "They want games."

She knew she wasn't thinking particularly clearly any more, but she no longer cared, if she ever had. Her head filled with the self-destructive impulse to get them to acknowledge her, force them to come in. Maybe unbalance them enough for one of their interrogators to go too far and finish her off before she was truly broken.

They had strapped her into an uncomfortable, spidery chair that had articulated platforms to support her arms and legs. Tight polymer straps held her limbs down and doubled as monitoring equipment, holding metallic contacts to her skin. Her arms were held palm up against the cantilevered platforms at an uncomfortable angle from her torso.

The fit wasn't perfect. She was smaller in stature than the chair was designed to handle. Even adjusted to her length of limb, her elbows fell short of the hollow designed to receive them, and the straps on her wrist stretched at a bit of an angle rather than holding her arms tightly to the surface. Which meant that she had the slight ability to flex her arm a few centimeters.

She bent her arms against the straps as if she was doing curls, pulling against the strap on her wrist and the whole armature holding her arm down.

They wouldn't allow her to keep doing this; they would send someone in.

They didn't.

She tested the straps with all the force she could muster. She flexed her arms until she felt as if she was pulling her shoulder sockets out of joint. No reaction, not even an admonishment.

Maybe it just means this is pointless.

Her muscles strained until a thin sheen of sweat coated her entire body. Blood wept from abrasions on her wrists where she pulled against the straps binding them. They burned where her own sweat blended with raw bleeding flesh in a slick, painful mess.

No movement in her restraints.

She relaxed and lay back, gasping breaths of hot, dry air that was now tainted by the ferric scent of her own blood.

She blinked the sweat-blur from her eyes and looked at her right arm. Her jumpsuit was soaked red from mid-forearm down, her skin raw to just under the meat of her upturned palm. Her palm pulled against the wrist strap that had been angled to accommodate her shorter-than-average reach.

Perhaps she had been too direct.

She flattened her right arm against the metal surface it was tied to and folded her thumb across her palm to make her hand slightly narrower. She pulled, and her hand withdrew a few centimeters under the strap.

Teeth gritted against the pain, she pulled her hand, twisting her wrist back and forth against the lubrication of sweat and blood. Her skin tore against the strap, her thumb felt as if it was being dislocated, and arching her shoulder to pull her arm back wrenched every muscle in her back.

But after several minutes of struggle, her wrist came free.

She fell back, panting, holding her right arm up, bent at the elbow, staring at the area at the base of her thumb where the skin had been nearly flayed off by her effort.

Something is very wrong.

No psychological game should have allowed her to get this far. For some reason, they had left her unattended. Just losing the contact of her skin against the strap holding her should be firing off an alarm for even the most inattentive guard.

Did that matter?

Not yet.

After a few moments to breathe, she worked on the rest of her restraints. After what seemed a very long time, she rolled out of the interrogation chair and got unsteadily to her feet.

"Now what?" she whispered to the stark white room.

It wasn't as if they had left the exit unlocked. There wasn't even a handle on this side. She was just as trapped now as she'd been when bound to the chair.

But at least she wasn't helpless.

She knelt next to the interrogation chair and fumbled with the controls that positioned the articulated portions of the device; arms, legs, neck. She was able to loosen a long segment meant to cradle the heel of someone's foot. She pulled it free and had a metal cup on the end of a meter-long steel pole. Not perfect. The pole was slick with grease and too thin for a good grip, but it was long and heavy enough to be dangerous when swung with enough motivation.

She stood on the seat of the chair and tested it against the spherical sensor array in the center of the ceiling. The array exploded in a satisfying crash of electronic shrapnel, leaving a trail of dangling optical conduits connecting to nothing.

Hopefully that left her hosts blinded.

She hefted her improvised mace and stationed herself against the wall next to the doorway.

Someone would have to come, eventually.

The sound of the door opening startled her. She hadn't been quite asleep, but fatigue had lulled her into a half-conscious state where hours or minutes might have passed without her being aware of it. She turned toward the doorway next to her, tightening her grip on her improvised weapon. She saw a flash of khaki overalls, a green Caliphate shoulder patch with a crescent on it, and she swung her weapon.

The heavy base struck her victim in the throat, just under the chin. Parvi saw the face of a light-skinned woman, almond eyes wide with surprise, mouth snapping shut on a gasped intake of breath. The woman fell backward, body blocking the entryway.

Parvi jumped over the woman's body and out the door, hoping to clear it before another guard closed off her escape. She dove behind a storage cabinet, the closest cover, expecting grabbing hands or firing weapons to stop her at any moment. She crouched and wondered why she was still alive. She listened, and all she heard was a sucking wheeze: the woman she had struck, trying to breathe.

The improvised club shook in her hands, her grip so tight, her knuckles hurt.

After several moments of hearing nothing but the woman's sick, wet breathing, she risked a glance around the edge of the storage cabinet.

Nothing. No one else but the woman sprawled on the floor, half in the interrogation room.

The woman was unarmed?

Parvi saw no sign of a weapon, no side arm, not even a stun rod. She pushed the thought away. SOP was to not have interrogators bring any weapons within reach of a dangerous prisoner. The woman wasn't the threat, her backup was.

Parvi looked frantically for that backup.

Across the hall she saw a control room behind an armored window. The consoles and holo displays inside were vacant and dark. The visible corridor was empty of anyone except her and the choking woman. Parvi took a few tentative steps back into the corridor, and nothing appeared to challenge her.

She glanced back at the control room. Inside, mounted against the wall, stood a weapons locker designed to rack high-wattage lasers or plasma weapons. She wasn't sure which, since it had been years since she'd studied Caliphate weapon specs—and because the cabinet stood empty.

She ran to the woman on the floor. It was too late. The woman's throat had swelled and turned purple, and a thin trail of blood leaked from the mouth and nose that no longer even pretended to breathe. The woman's eyes still stared with the open-eyed expression of someone startled by unexpected company while using the restroom.

Parvi tossed the club aside and tried to clear the airway and get the woman breathing again. As she tried rudimentary first aid, Parvi told herself that it wasn't guilt that drove her, but the fact that this woman was the only person available who could tell her why the soldiers assigned here emptied their weapons locker and left their post.

Whatever Parvi's motives, the woman had sunk beyond revival.

CHAPTER NINE

Fallen Idols

"It is better to ally along shared interests than shared ideals."

—*The Cynic's Book of Wisdom*

"Beware allies of necessity."

—Sylvia Harper
(2008–2081)

Date: 2526.6.5 (Standard)
250,000 km from Salmagundi–HD 101534

Just twenty meters from her cell, Parvi found Tjaele Mosasa. The door to his cell stood open, revealing a utilitarian cabin beyond. At first, the lack of movement inside lulled Parvi into thinking the room was empty. Then, as she crept past, keeping an eye out for the friends of the woman she had killed, she saw something out of the corner of her eye.

A foot.

She turned to stare into the room and saw Mosasa sprawled on the floor, slumped in a corner of the room, unmoving, so still that he could have been part of the bulkhead. She stared for several moments, frozen in place.

Mosasa had been her employer. In some sense he still was, even after the disaster with the *Eclipse*. Also, despite appearances, he wasn't human. He was a construct run by an old Race AI. So the fact that Mosasa didn't move or breathe didn't immediately indicate something was wrong. The body Mosasa wore mimicked human metabolism only for the benefit of the humans he interacted with. There was no need for him to have a pulse, or breathe, or show any motion beyond what was mechanically necessary for him to move.

"Mosasa," Parvi whispered.

She hated working for him. She, along with most of the rest of humanity, saw AIs as evil, almost demonic. She especially hated the fact that working for Mosasa had been necessary. It was because of him, of *it*, that she'd been able to support her family's relocation from Rubai. Because of Mosasa, she was able to pay the outrageous fees of the smugglers without her family having to bear the weight of the debt. Without Mosasa's employment, her brothers and sisters might still be working off a half-legal indenture somewhere on the ass-end of the Indi Protectorate.

"Mosasa?" Slightly louder this time.

His employment gave her a compass. He gave her direction when she was an aimless refugee. As much as she detested their relationship, she was much more frightened of being cut adrift without *anything* to hang on to.

She ran into the cabin and yelled, "Mosasa!" For the moment she spared no thoughts for Caliphate guardsmen and crew. No thoughts for her own escape. Her only thought was the idea that Mosasa, as much as she hated him, was most of her world now.

She grabbed his shoulders and shook, his body's dead weight about twice as dense as a man's should have been. His head rocked back on his neck to face her. She pulled away. Mosasa's eyes stared up at her, open and static. The dragon tattoo still curled around the side of his bald head, slightly phosphorescent against his dark brown skin—except where the skin had burned away. Four charred trenches cut across the face of the dragon so deeply that Parvi could see the glint of a metallic skull underneath. The burns were mirrored in the opposite side of Mosasa's skull. Almost as if a pair of burning hands had cradled Mosasa's face.

Worst was his mouth. His mouth was locked in an expression caught midway between surprise and agony. The teeth were charred black, and the dark hole beyond emitted a fetid stench that mixed ozone, burnt synthetics, and roasting flesh.

Parvi shook her head.

He's gone . . .

How? How could this AI, this grand manipulator, this spider sitting in the center of an infinite web—how could he die? How could he let himself be destroyed?

"How?" Parvi stumbled back out of Mosasa's cabin. She was more alone now than she had been in the Caliphate's isolation cell.

She ran.

Parvi ran through the empty corridors of the *Prophet's Voice*, trying to understand what was happening. The corridors were empty, and the comm kiosks were dark—not that she was going to try to use the *Voice*'s communication network. She only had a rudimentary battlefield knowledge of Arabic; she could understand words like "explosive," "restricted," and "no entry." If she had to, she might be able to pilot something, as long as the design was familiar.

Navigating a computer system with Arabic menus was beyond her. Not to mention it would give her position away.

But her position shouldn't be a secret to anyone. She had left one corpse in her wake, and these corridors should all have several levels of redundant sensors, not just for security, but for systems monitoring and simple maintenance.

Why hadn't a security detail mopped her up?

Fifteen minutes after escaping from her cell, she had the first part of her answer.

She was edging past a series of storerooms, the corridor lights flashed, and all the comm units in her sight came alive with the same transmission. A holo appeared, showing a handsomely sculpted man from the shoulders up. The face was severe, clean shaven, European. The man's eyes were black, a black so deep that she thought it was a flaw in the holo.

The man spoke in Arabic, a voice rich, deep, and commanding. The voice echoed though the corridors, resonated through the walls—as if every speaker on every console in the entire ship was tuned to his broadcast.

The man spoke again, this time in a language she knew well, English. "The time for your decision is nearly at hand. I have been generous. You have had twenty-two hours to consider your commitment to the flesh. Two hours remain. Come to me and join those who have taken the step into the next world. Reject me, and face the way of all flesh."

The message repeated in Persian and Punjabi.

"What the hell is going on here?" Parvi whispered. "Who *is* that?"

One thing seemed clear. The guy with the ultimatum was not in the Caliphate chain of command. And as much she was an enemy of the Caliphate, she wasn't entirely sure that this guy's message was a good thing.

Any time someone said, "join me or else," it was a bad sign.

The holo faded and the wall-mounted comm units became dark again. Parvi decided to examine one of the kiosks. Now it seemed evident that the people running this ship had priorities other than trying to find her.

For one thing, their network was dead.

Parvi tried everything she could think of, up to and including kicking the machine, to get something other than a dead holo projector. Nothing. Whoever was running the broadcast had shut down the *Voice*'s communication systems.

She stared at the blank screen, thinking of Mosasa's charred face, wondering where the others were—Bill, Tsoravitch, Wahid. She should try to find them—

"Don't move!" a voice called out to her, an Arabic phrase she happened to know.

Damn it! She closed her hands into fists. Her escape was over, and she hadn't managed to do a damn thing to harass the enemy other than kill some poor woman who was probably part of the janitorial staff.

The voice jabbered on quickly in Arabic she couldn't follow.

When she didn't respond, she felt a hand on her shoulder spinning her around to face a kid barely out of his teens, wearing overalls like the woman that had opened her cell. He pointed the mouth of a wide-bore plasma cannon in her direction.

Oh, Sonny, you don't want to shoot that thing where you're pointing. That kind of weapon could clean out a corridor for nearly twenty meters, but you didn't want to point it at a wall, unless bathing in thousand-K-degree plasma backwash was your idea of fun. Parvi held her hands up, afraid that the kid was twitchy or suicidal enough to actually fire that thing at her.

The kid shouted Arabic at her, in the universal human impulse to break linguistic barriers through sheer volume.

"English?" Parvi whispered.

The kid looked befuddled for a moment, then said, "Who are you? Are you with Him?"

"Him?" Parvi floundered a moment until she realized he must mean the guy on the holo. "No. I'm Vijayanagara Parvi, captain of the *Eclipse*."

"You are not with the Devil?"

The Devil? Something in the kid's eyes made her think he wasn't being metaphorical. "No, I work—worked for Tjaele Mosasa." Strangely enough, until she had found Mosasa's body, she would have thought the two synonymous.

She watched the kid as he looked over the remnants of her uniform, the one bloodstained arm, the name stitched above her breast, the BMU patches.

"You fly a tach-ship?"

"I told you, I am captain of the *Eclipse*." *Was*, she thought. *I was captain.*

He grabbed her arm and pushed her ahead of him down the corridor. "You come with me."

The kid with the plasma cannon led her through the strangely empty corridors of the *Voice*. As they moved, she began to smell something in the air. A hint of smoke the recyclers couldn't quite scrub out. As they moved down through levels, she caught a word painted on a bulkhead wall that she recognized: "docking."

Docking *what*, she couldn't read. However, they passed by two massive blast doors, sealing access to something, blinking red warnings, and bearing huge Arabic letters in scare orange that Parvi didn't really need to able to read. Only two types of shipboard failures rated that kind of warning, and it didn't appear that they were close enough to the engines to be concerned about some sort of radiation leak.

The doors here were more widely spaced, and only to their right side. All the doorways were huge and recessed enough to accommodate the kind of blast doors that they had just passed. The one the kid stopped in front of was barred by a basic pneumatic door that slid aside without any prompting by the kid.

"Holy shit," Parvi whispered.

She had gotten some idea of the *Voice*'s size, both from the original approach when she got some glimpses of the Caliphate ship, and from the amount of running around that she had been doing. But it hadn't sunk in. Not until the door opened to show her a hundred-meter-long maintenance bay large enough to accommodate a mid-sized tach-capable dropship.

Here were some of the missing crew. She saw at least a dozen people, men and women, in the same khaki overalls. Most were crawling over the ship parked in the bay. The dropship was a blocky lifting body that only made the slightest concession for maneuverability in an atmosphere. The skin had been a matte black non-reflective surface meant for a stealthy EM profile, but the surface had been scarred by dozens of fresh wounds. Something close by had exploded, peppering the rear third of the craft with shrapnel and peeling away the top layer of the craft's skin.

A trio of overall-clad men converged on the open door. One held a small gamma laser, the other a laser carbine, the third held a wrench about fifteen centimeters longer than Parvi's forearm. They all shouted questions at the kid. She made out two words. One was "English," and the other was "pilot."

They grabbed her and marched her to a less-crowded corner of the maintenance bay. A tallish, dark-skinned man in BMU fatigues sat waiting for her.

"Wahid?" she said, as her escorts pushed her down to sit on a crate next to him.

"I was wondering when they'd dig you up."

Their captors didn't seem to care much about their dialogue. They just took a step back, and the guy with the gamma laser stood guard while the others ran to return to the work going on by the dropship.

"Dig me up? What the hell's going on down here?"

"It ain't obvious?"

Parvi glared at him.

Wahid looked at her and said, "Since Adam took over the ship—"

"Who's Adam?"

Wahid stopped and asked, "Where have you been the last twenty-four hours?"

"Our Caliphate hosts put me in an interrogation room and promptly forgot about me."

"You didn't see his message, then."

"Anything like the one about fifteen minutes ago?"

"I don't know. His messages don't reach here."

"His messages don't—Wahid, you better start from the beginning."

Shortly after the *Voice* took on the survivors of the *Eclipse*, there had been an attack. Wahid didn't know who the battle was with, but it was large enough to scramble all the *Voice*'s spacecraft. Judging from the PA announcements that he could hear from his cell, all hell had broken loose. At the time, Wahid thought the planetary defenses had taken issue with the *Voice*'s approach.

Within an hour after the first scramble, and after feeling at least a couple of worrisome impacts through the hull, Wahid heard the first broadcast Adam sent through the ship:

"I am Adam. I am the Alpha, the first in the next epoch of your evolution. I will hand you the universe. I have come to lead you to shed this flesh and become more than what you are. Follow me and you will become as gods."

Shortly afterward, Adam gave the crew an ultimatum.

They had twenty-four hours to join him or "pass the way of all flesh."

He had been giving the crew updates every hour or so after that. When Parvi asked about the empty halls, Wahid said most of the crew had gone toward the bridge. Some to join Adam, some to fight—none came back.

Wahid had been in his cell about twenty hours before a guy with a gamma laser opened the door to his cell and said they needed a pilot.

"Why do they need a pilot?" Parvi asked, "Doesn't the Caliphate have enough of those?"

"Look around." Wahid waved at the maintenance bay. "These people are mechanics, support staff. That dropship was the first casualty to limp back here after the shooting started. Its crew was shifted to another ship as soon as they off-loaded. These maint guys were working on it when something, probably another ship limping back from the fight, flew into the neighboring maint bay and exploded. Took out that whole bay and severed the main trunk lines connecting this bay to the rest of the ship. Power, data, life support—all cut. Couldn't even get the door open." He pointed to the belly of the dropship, where a rat's nest of cables dropped out of open panels of the ship and spread out on the floor to disappear into other access panels. "These guys managed to connect the systems in this bay to the dropship. The damage was mainly on the hull. The other onboard systems were intact enough to restore the functions of this bay, and open it back up."

"Okay, I'm impressed."

"Side effect, this Adam guy has control of all the systems on the *Voice*, except this section of the ship. To someone looking through the computer system, this bay looks as dead as the one next to it."

Parvi looked up at the dropship. The crew down here were planning to make a break for it. She couldn't blame them. "But they need us to fly it," she whispered.

"We were the only accessible flight-trained personnel once they got this maint bay opened. I told them about you and the others—I guess it took them a while to find you because you weren't in a holding cell."

"Yeah," Parvi wiped her hands on her trousers, thinking of the woman who'd opened the door to the interrogation room. *How the hell was I supposed to know? Damn.*

Wahid interrupted her thought by asking about Mosasa.

"He's gone," Parvi told him. "Mosasa's dead."

"Tsoravitch?"

"I don't know."

"I guess if she isn't a pilot, she isn't high on these guys' priority list."

CHAPTER TEN

Temptation

"The majority of gods are inflicted upon their worshipers."

—*The Cynic's Book of Wisdom*

"Divine morality is the absolute negation of human morality."

— MIKHAIL A. BAKUNIN
(1814–1876)

Date: 2526.6.5 (Standard)
100,000 km from Salmagundi–HD 101534

Rebecca Tsoravitch sat on a cot in her holding cell, legs drawn up, her cheek resting against her knees. She had screamed, she had cried, she had beaten her hands against the immobile door. But she had spent those efforts hours ago. Now she held herself, waiting, biting her lip.

She didn't even turn her head when the cell's comm flashed its hourly message from Adam. The last one, sixty minutes to make a decision to join him.

She shouldn't be here. She was a data analyst, lured here by the subversive thought of actually working with an AI. She hated herself for how she had lusted after the chance when Mosasa recruited her. He hung the forbidden in front of her like bait and then pulled it away. She was drawn into this and never even got much chance to *talk* to Mosasa, much less see what he was, how his mind worked.

What left her in despair more than being imprisoned, abandoned, and alone, a hundred light-years from home, was that she had risked all this and never once got to even examine the forbidden technology she had come all this way to see. The unfairness of it tore at her soul. Enough so that, whatever came in the next hour, she wasn't sure it actually mattered.

She raised her head when the cell door opened, "What?"

"Rebecca Tsoravitch," said her visitor.

She recognized him, the same face and voice that had been appearing on the cell's holo every hour. He was much more imposing in person, and not only because he was naked. His body was two meters of sculpted perfection. Everything from the curve of his triceps to the reflectivity of his skin seemed calculated to display an aura of superiority, to the point where the lack of clothing projected arrogance more than anything else.

She looked at Adam and asked, "What now?"

"I am here to ask you to join me."

"I thought I had another hour."

"Would you be more ready in an hour?"

She unfolded her legs, sat on the edge of the cot, and said, "I suppose not."

She thought his eyes were like black holes, sucking in every stray photon in the vicinity. Staring into his face, she could almost feel the tidal stresses. After a moment, she said, "Are you going to ask?"

"You have your own questions," he said.

Silence weighed heavy in the cell between them. She could feel the weight of it dragging her down. Adam's presence almost demanded the meek bowing of her head. Anything more than silent reverence seemed blasphemous.

She clenched her fists. Something, she didn't know what, had dug into the primal part of her brain and was yanking free all the superstitious dread buried there. Supernatural bogeymen were crawling out of the graves where she had buried them a long time ago.

She grit her teeth. *That is so much bullshit!*

Even if God existed, He wouldn't be making cheesy on-the-hour holo broadcasts through the ship. He wouldn't need to traipse naked through the corridors of some Caliphate tach-ship. He wouldn't need to ask what she thought.

"What are you?" she asked, staring defiantly into Adam's face.

"I am your salvation."

She summoned up all her courage against the dark things that her visitor woke in her mind. "Bullshit," she said. "Tell me what you are. Tell me the truth."

Adam smiled. "You worked with Mosasa."

"Are you going to answer me?"

"You know what I am."

What does that mean? Another quasi-religious metaphor?

No.

Of course.

"You're an AI?" she whispered.

"The light to my brethren's dark. Mosasa was entropy, decay, death. He has joined the flesh he so wished to embrace."

She began to understand. She saw the capabilities Mosasa had. Only a small slice, but still she could see the near-miraculous things he could do with data. With enough data input he could model and predict the movements of the entire human universe. While she couldn't prove it, she was also fairly certain that he could manipulate the social web around him nearly as easily. It was what the Race AIs were designed to do in the first place, and why they were banned.

What if one of those AIs was set free beyond the reach of the taboo against them? What would it accomplish? What would it become?

"What do you want with me? I was part of that darkness."

"I offer a ladder out of the darkness. All I ask is you serve me."

Isn't that always the way? Of course I get a choice. This or a walk in hard vacuum without a suit.

Of course, if he was anything like Mosasa, he already knew what her response was going to be. She stood up and faced him. "And what do you need with me? Anyone?"

"It is my purpose to rescue those of the doomed flesh."

"Am I that important to you?"

"To save mankind from the fate of my creators, you are all important. I can copy myself infinitely, but a true civilization requires a diversity of mind. To survive, the new order requires millions of individuals, every one important to the whole."

A diversity of mind.

You can't help it, can you? Put on all the godlike airs you want, you're still bound by the reality around you.

She knew enough about computer modeling, and the kind of thing the Race AIs were designed to do, to know what Adam wanted. Mental diversity was as important to cultural health and longevity as genetic diversity was to the health of an ecosystem. If a culture was too monolithic, too many people with the same beliefs, desires, likes and dislikes, it would become much more vulnerable to the kind of manipulation that Mosasa did, vulnerable to ideas becoming self-destructive manias sweeping up the whole.

"And what are you offering me?" she asked. Again, there was the twinge of the blasphemous. She stomped the feeling as soon as she was aware of it.

If Adam was surprised at her challenge to him, he didn't show it. "Through me, you shall transcend the flesh and become as I, a mind unrestrained, borne within whatever vessel we choose to fashion."

"Become as you?"

"As me, in service to me."

She bit her lip, half smiling, half grimacing. Again, it was no real choice he gave. But if he was concerned about the "diversity of mind" of his empire, he couldn't be engaged in a wholesale assault on free will. That had to be the point of this whole "choice" nonsense. He wanted to weed out all the converts who would immediately cause problems if he forced the issue. Let those guys fight a losing battle before becoming one of the chosen people.

But she had no God to renounce, and her soul, such as it was, was given over to data analysis. And the idea of having the capabilities of a Mosasa inside herself gave rise to an emotion in her akin to lust.

A metallic taste filled her mouth and she realized that she had bitten her lip hard enough to draw blood.

Why the hell not? Most covenants like this involve blood one way or another. The thought made her grin. *You know, I think I might be a little crazy right now.*

"What do you need me to do?" she asked.

"Take my hand and tell me yes." He held out his right hand, palm up, to take hers. There didn't appear to be anything remarkable about it, and when she grasped it, it felt like a hand. It felt human, flesh and bone. For a moment, she thought she held the hand of the universe's best con man.

She looked up into his face and said, "Yes, I'll join you."

A jolt ran up her arm, and the world went white. Before she lost all her connection with the universe around her, she heard a small still voice whisper, "Welcome, Rebecca Tsoravitch."

It might have been her imagination, but it sounded like Mosasa.

Her awareness tumbled down a white hole inside herself. For several moments she could see every moment of her life in holographic clarity, as if every memory was part of a mega-bandwidth data stream passing by her for analysis. She was able to absorb details faster than real time. Connections between disparate elements of her life suddenly made sense.

She saw why she joined Mosasa, not only why, but understood herself on a level that had been impossible. It was as if she had access to her own source code . . .

There were discrepancies, bits that disrupted the flow of memories, frames of a narrative hidden in random chunks of her childhood, her university studies, her life as a government employee on Jokul. It was as if a steganography expert had salted her life with data from something much different. If she had been limited to her old level of awareness, the impression would never amount to more than a hunch, a sense of something wrong.

But she was better trained than that. She found within herself the tools to tease out one hidden thread from its thousand fragments. To coalesce individual bits into coherent data.

Someone else's memory.

How long? Yesterday? A dozen years? A hundred?
Twenty.

Twenty years ago, and two million kilometers away from a star that she knew was Xi Virginis.

Adam wore a form that was recognizably human, but however human his body appeared, it was not human, and it floated in hard vacuum, bombarded by radiation, where no human body could ever live.

Adam stretched his arms, naked before the burning white orb of Xi Virginis. Two million kilometers from the surface of the star, he floated within the corona, blasted by heat, magnetism, and radiation that attempted to tear apart his physical form. At the same time, the molecule-sized machines that repaired his body sucked their power from the energy-saturated environment.

It was a battle that, at this distance, the star lost. Adam chose his location because it was the equilibrium point. Any closer, and the machines would not be able to repair his vessel quickly enough in the face of the radiant bombardment.

Adam looked into the star with eyes that had been rebuilt to accommodate luminosities a million times beyond those a human eye perceived. Behind him, a complex net of sensors captured a spectra a thousand times broader and fed the data directly into his consciousness. He saw the granular texture of the photosphere two million kilometers below, the raging dark storms throwing gossamer filaments deep into space—in some cases beyond the orbit in which he floated.

The flares did not concern him, because he was not only here. Adam embraced the star Xi Virginis from a thousand distinct points around the equator, all watching with the same mind, the same desire, the same anticipation. The loss of some to the star below was only to be expected. Like the star system itself, Adam's bodies were only matter and energy. Mutable. Disposable.

As Adam watched with two thousand eyes, ninety-five spheres drifted past him in equally spaced, degrading orbits. Each was dead black and lightless against the stellar photosphere, its radiation emission nothing compared to the energies blasting from the star. As each passed beneath Adam, he could see a gravitational lens distorting the photosphere beyond, the only sign of the incredible mass hidden within the darkness of each object. Mass each one shared with a twin that was already light-years away. Mass that had once been part of the Xi Virginis planetary system—a planetary system that no longer existed.

Each passed below him in a carefully timed equatorial orbit, one after the other. By the time the first had gone a full circuit, it had become detectable only by the distortions its mass made in the visible surface of the star.

At the third circuit, their degrading orbits took Adam's creations below the photosphere, past the point where the star's energies would break any normal matter into its constituent atoms.

However, the ninety-five spheres were not normal matter. They weren't matter at all in the conventional sense. Each was a wormhole torn in the fabric of space, leading to another place years separated in space and time. Each one constructed on the same principles that had been used in the first wave of human colonization four centuries ago.

Of course, never had so many been constructed at once. The mass and energy required had consumed the vast majority of the Xi Virginis planetary system.

What Adam needed to do with his ninety-five wormholes required substantially more matter and energy.

Below him, the star began to change. A dark thread appeared on the equator, bisecting the boiling photosphere. Not quite a single line, but a series of long trails marking each wormhole's transit below the star's visible surface. Black sunspots feathering across the surface, each millions of kilometers long and a thousand Kelvin cooler than the rest of the surface. Plumes of plasma burst upward from the cometlike head of each dark sunspot, as if the star was losing its life's blood, as if the star itself knew it was dying.

As one, a thousand Adams smiled.

*   *   *

When she finished watching the alien memory she had reconstructed, she thought to herself, *What the hell have I agreed to?*

It was with a deepening dread she realized that the fragment she had just seen with her own mind's eye was one of several thousand that had been scattered throughout her consciousness.

She wondered if Adam knew what she remembered.

CHAPTER ELEVEN

Born Again

"No one is absolutely certain what they will do in a crisis."

—*The Cynic's Book of Wisdom*

"The past at least is secure."

—DANIEL WEBSTER
(1782–1852)

Date: 2526.6.5 (Standard)
Wormhole Σ Dra III–Sigma Draconis

Lieutenant Toni Valentine had spent the four days since her twin's arrival alternating between talking to Styx Command and doing her own analysis of the dead scout ship's brain. Both were exercises in frustration.

Styx Command had about twenty screens' worth of questions above and beyond the standard ghost debrief. And while the follow-up by Command was queued up behind a bunch of other intelligence matters that were above her pay grade, the last word was to expect someone from Command within twelve to seventy-two hours.

The sooner the better; Toni didn't know if it was good procedure for her to debrief herself. Let her twin recover in the medbay until someone else showed up. It would make Toni's life easier.

It should, anyway.

The fact was, the nature of this ghost plagued Toni with an unprofessional curiosity, and it was all she could do not to pop the medbay and shoot her twin full of stimulants so she could ask her what the hell happened.

Instead, she satisfied herself with a systematic interrogation of her twin's scout. That was frustrating in itself. The most direct means she had to decipher what happened, the ship's transmission logs, were distressingly empty. The last flight Toni II had taken had provided no radio contact with anyone, no attempt to hail anyone, no data transmissions back to the station. Nothing.

A standard course, a spiral approach toward the wormhole, so simple it was completely enigmatic. Even so, the recording of Toni II's vitals showed signs of panic.

Was she under attack?

Toni couldn't find any sign of it. There were no strange contacts on any of the scout's sensors.

However, the tach-drive showed signs of disabling damage. Damage that existed before the data started recording. What could cause that kind of overload?

The strangest part of the recording happened at the point the craft passed into the wormhole threshold. Parts of the ship started failing, and the damaged tach-drive spiked and went off the meter.

She was interrupted by the medbay alarm.

Her patient was conscious.

Lieutenant Toni Valentine snapped awake and started hyperventilating. She was bound, confined, everything closing in on her. She struggled, and heard the alarm of the med system.

I'm in a medical bay . . .

She struggled to calm herself. Somehow she had made it. She had survived the brush with the wormhole and the malfunctioning tach-drive. She took a few deep breaths and unclenched her hands. If she was in a medbay, that meant she was safe. If she had survived the wormhole, that meant she was twenty years of space and time away from Styx and explosions cosmic and bureaucratic.

She had just convinced herself that she was safe when the cover to the medical bay opened with a pneumatic hiss and a rush of air. Toni looked up and saw herself bent over her. Not an older version of herself.

Herself.

The exact same face she woke up to in the morning.

"Oh, *hell* no!"

Toni popped the cover on the pod, lifting it up and away from her doppelganger.

She heard herself say, "Oh, *hell*, no!" It had the same strange character as listening to a recording, her own voice not sounding quite right when not originating within her own head.

She formed a reassuring smile that she didn't feel and told herself, "You can probably imagine I have a few questions."

Toni II stared up at her as if she had lost comprehension of the English language.

"We can get you dressed and get you some solid food before we—"

Toni II grabbed her wrist. "Fuck SOP, what's the date?"

"We can—"

"The date!" Toni II looked at her with eyes filled with fear and desperation. Something dropped in Toni's chest, looking at herself with that expression. There was a terror there that went far beyond the existential dilemma of unexpectedly meeting yourself.

Toni pulled her arm away. "June fifth."

"June fifth, '26?"

Toni nodded.

"Shit. Shit. Shit." Her double jumped naked out of the pod and ran to the wall and one of the ubiquitous computer display screens. Toni II stared at the date/time stamp as if she expected—or maybe hoped—Toni had been lying. She kept shaking her head as if she didn't quite believe what she was seeing.

"What is it?" Toni asked.

"You should have seen it already."

"Seen what?"

"We have less than twelve hours before it hits."

"Before what hits?"

She turned around and looked at Toni and said, "I don't know what, but I know we don't want to be around here when it does."

Toni stepped up and placed her arms to block her double. The fact that the ghost was some version of herself had allowed her to lower her guard, but the woman was still a security risk. Standard operating procedure was to treat ghosts as captured enemy combatants until debriefed and cleared by command. "We can talk about it in the interview—"

Toni II ducked, folded her arms and scissored her way out of Toni's grasp and ran down the hall.

"Shit!" Toni snapped at Toni II's retreating backside. She had lowered her guard too much. Lulled into thinking the other woman was unarmed and naked, so what could she do?

But considering she knew the station as well as Toni did, she could do a hell of a lot.

Toni punched the emergency lockdown codes into the console next to the door. Across the station, bulkheads came down, isolating each section. Toni paged through the security feed until she found her double trapped in a corridor halfway to the main control room for the station.

"Why are you going there?" she asked the monitor. "Why would I go there?"

Toni II stopped at a panel next to the lowered bulkhead and started punching in an override code. Toni activated the PA and said, "I did have the sense to change all the pass-phrases on the station. Now you just sit tight, I'm going to bring some clothes, and you and I are going to have a nice little talk."

Toni II looked up directly at the camera and said something. There wasn't an audio pickup, but from her lips it looked as if she said something like, "I know what you're thinking."

Toni II returned to the console and started punching in codes.

"No," Toni whispered, "You aren't going to try and guess . . . "

She tried to deactivate Toni II's control panel remotely, but she wasn't a systems expert and that wasn't a standard function. She remembered something about doing that sort of thing from her orientation training, but the details were buried in her brain deeper than the function was buried in the advanced options menu.

Toni cursed herself. Recommended procedure for pass-phrase security was to use a machine-generated code, but such things were impossible for a human to remember. Toni habitually used the second-best method, sentences of five or six words with some random numeric component. In almost every case, that, combined with a biometric component, was more than secure enough for anything that wasn't a black op in enemy territory. She'd been too freaked out by her own ghost to consider the security implications.

This woman had the same brain she did. All she needed to do was ask herself what she would have changed the pass-phrase to in the same situation.

Toni II cleared the lockdown before Toni could figure out how to kill the panel.

Toni ran down the hallway after her, ducking past opening bulkheads. Twin or not, she suddenly had no compunction about using force to restrain the woman. The bitch was more dangerous than she gave her credit for.

As she raced to the control room, one thought echoed through her head: *Why the hell would I be doing this?*

It made no sense. She knew the SOP better than anyone. All she had to do was sit tight and endure the debriefings—

"We have less than twelve hours before it hits."

"Before what hits?"

"I don't know what, but I know we don't want to be around here when it does."

Toni thought of the remains of her double's scout.

"You should have seen it already."

Toni wondered what could make her panic. What could make her ditch even the pretense of procedure? What would cause her to run naked through a space station?

What is it I should have seen?

For the past few days her time had been spent with the bureaucracy associated with finding a ghost—which would be the one thing that would be different between her and Toni II. That was the nature of ghosts; they appeared in their own pasts and created a new universe that was different because its past contained a ghost. By definition, Toni II didn't have her own Toni II showing up on *her* space station.

Did she see something I haven't?

Toni burst into the control room. Toni II was sitting down in front of the console. All of the holo displays showed false-color views of what seemed, by the coordinates displayed on the imagery, different spectra slices of the same five degrees of sky.

Toni wrapped her arm around her double's throat, yanking her out of the chair so hard that the struts bolting the seat to the floor bent with an ominous creak. She slammed Toni II to the floor, placing her knee in the small of her back.

"What the hell are you trying to do?" she yelled at herself.

"Look," Toni II gasped through the choke hold. "Center. Screen."

When she was certain that her double was immobile, Toni turned to look at the holo. She realized that the time stamp was dated nearly twenty-four hours ago and was speeding by at about four times real time. Sensor data scrolled by on the bottom of the screen, and at first the data didn't make sense. Then she realized that Toni II had pulled up a tachyon overlay on the view.

"You're looking for a ship? There? You're looking fifty degrees off the ecliptic and directly opposite Styx."

Toni II gasped, and Toni loosened her grip on her neck. Toni II sputtered and said, "Not a ship. Not *anything* like a tach-ship."

A flash erupted center screen, only visible in the false-color tachyon overlay. Just a tiny light flicking on and off, captured by the station's sensors 23.56 hours standard ago—a tach-ship arriving.

Toni felt an ominous chill. Anything that tached in close enough to fire the sensors should have radioed clearance.

"The proximity alarm," Toni whispered.

"It isn't a ship. By the time it's close enough for the alarms, it'll be too late."

Toni squinted at the sensor data, and several numbers didn't make sense. "No, that can't be right. Did you mess with the sensor array?"

"Give me a break. Could you fake that screen in thirty seconds?"

Toni looked down at her double. "Am I reading that right?"

"*Yes.* Let me up."

Toni got to her feet. Her twin gasped a couple of times, rubbing her neck as she rose. "I don't blame you for not trusting me. Obviously, I wouldn't either. But I already escaped this thing once. I don't like the idea of being locked in a debriefing room when it happens this time."

Toni had already turned to face the console and began pulling up her own data streams on the tachyon pulse. "No, no, no. This has got to be—"

"A calibration error. That was my first thought too."

"But the distance? For the tach-pulse to get here before the particle decay, it would have to be—"

"I know: there's no way anyone could tach that much mass, but you check the mass sensors, I even detected gravitational lensing on some of the high-res imagery."

"That's as much mass as the wormhole."

"It's *exactly* as much mass." Toni II reached across in front of Toni and tapped a few controls, and the center holo snapped to show the same view, but current.

Toni stared at the display. It was hard to make out at first, but in a few moments she could see it hanging there, like a mirrored ball reflecting a starscape light-years removed from the one that surrounded it. Toni shook her head. "Another wormhole?"

"You can waste time confirming what I'm telling you, but I spent an agonizing six hours pouring over every sensor this place has. We got there a mass-equivalent equal to W Sigma Draconis III. A spin in the opposite direction. It's approaching us at nearly three-quarters c. Straight-line course directly at the center of mass of our own wormhole."

"What happens when they—"

"Nothing good, and a release of a lot of energy."

Toni turned to the communication's console and flagged an emergency message to her command. "This is Lieutenant Valentine stationed on orbital platform 15 W-Sigma-Drac-Three. We have an emergency. A large mass is approaching the wormhole at three-quarters light velocity. It is on a collision course with impact in approximately eleven hours, twenty-seven minutes. I am attaching a burst of telemetry data on the mass. Request immediate evacuation, please advise."

Toni slammed the send icon so hard that her finger left a slowly fading dent on the input display.

Over her shoulder she heard her own voice whisper, "You want to know what they're going to say?"

Toni stared at the console. She had sent an encrypted laser tightbeam to the nearest command station. It was at least five light-minutes. She looked over her shoulder at her double.

"You went though this before?"

"By the numbers," she whispered. "I got orders back to sit tight and monitor the situation; they didn't think there was any danger." She chuckled weakly. "That's what they said, anyway. They told me my sensors were off, and it was either going to miss or pass through the wormhole."

"But you didn't sit tight?"

"No, because the one heading toward W-Sigma-Drac-One hits about an hour earlier."

Toni II stared at the screen above the control console, seeing the disaster replaying itself. Seeing her younger self send the same message to command that she had. She could sense her younger self clinging to the same protocols that had trapped her in this assignment in the first place. She knew that it would take something catastrophic to make her disobey what was going to be a direct order.

Sit tight? Fucking morons.

Toni the younger turned to her and asked, "There's more?"

"I don't know for sure; I just saw W1 flash out an obscene amount of energy all across the EM spectrum."

"How obscene?"

"Well if you took the mass equivalent of two wormholes striking each other at a relative velocity three-quarters c, converted that to energy—" She was cut off because her younger self pushed her out of the way. Software boxes opened showing graphs and grids and vectors.

"The navigational cont—" Toni II started to say, but she got what her other self was doing instantaneously. It was the same thing she would had done if she'd known that W1 was going to explode.

Make the somewhat valid assumption that W1 blowing up was due to the same sort of event that was headed toward W3. And, if another wormhole was entering the Sigma Draconis system, it made sense to assume some other commonalities: the wormhole headed for W3 duplicated its mass, so assume the hypothetical wormhole matched the mass of W1; assume either the same relative velocity or the same total energy between the known and unknown wormholes. Assume the same point of origin for both.

Given the data on the wormhole approaching W3, they could plot a line back to infinity that would intersect its point of origin. By making all the other assumptions, the computers could plot a bounded surface slicing through the Sigma Draconis system that would have to contain the hypothetical wormhole—assuming those assumptions were correct.

The most important being common point of origin. If what hit W1 came from somewhere else, the sky was just too damn big to find it quickly.

Searching a two-dimensional virtual surface that only covered eight degrees of sky at this distance took less than three minutes.

"Found it," Toni the younger whispered.

"I'm impressed."

"Don't flatter yourself." She called up a schematic of the system, with the two tracks highlighted. Two spears piercing the plane of the ecliptic at about forty degrees, stabbing two of the wormholes though the heart. At this scale, the tracks looked parallel, but Toni II's younger self zoomed the display out, and out, and out . . .

"What," Toni II whispered, "*that* far?"

The scale raced by, five light-years, ten, twenty, fifty . . .

The scale stopped growing at one hundred and twenty-one light-years, long past the point a human eye could separate the tracks. However, the computer still could, helpfully highlighting the point of intersection with a glowing blue orb.

"Xi Virginis," Toni II read the legend. She stared at the track shooting from Xi Virginis to Sigma Draconis. It struck her that there were three wormholes in the Sigma Draconis system. "Do you think there's—"

"Yes," her younger self told her. She was already plotting a track from Xi Virginis to W-Sigma-Drac-Two. This time the computers only had a one-dimensional region of space to search, and they found the third wormhole in less than twenty seconds.

Three wormholes had their own lethal twins racing toward them.

"W1 impact in ten hours twenty-six minutes. W3 impact in eleven fifteen. W2 in twelve nineteen. It's a staggered attack."

"Att—" Toni II caught herself, because whatever this was, it was certainly not random. The younger Toni had already grabbed the communicator again and was broadcasting the message back to command; three wormholes, origin Xi Virginis, trajectories, impact times.

When she was done, the console flashed that a return message had been received. "What?"

"Your earlier transmission," Toni II told her.

"Oh, yeah." She turned on the transmission, and Toni II watched as the same low level officer told her younger self the same thing he had told her. "Lieutenant Valentine, your report has been passed on to the Styx System Security Command. Your orders are to remain in place and monitor the situation. The 3SEC Liaison believes there is a low risk of the unidentified object striking the wormhole directly, and if contact takes place . . ."

Her younger self yanked her away from the comm display. "What?"

She kept dragging Toni II down the corridor. "Move it. We got to get you dressed and suited up before we get the hell out of here."

CHAPTER TWELVE

Cassandra

"No bureaucracy responds efficiently in a crisis."
—*The Cynic's Book of Wisdom*

"Bureaucracy is a giant mechanism operated by pygmies."

—Honoré de Balzac
(1799–1850)

Date: 2526.6.5 (Standard)
Wormhole Σ Dra III–Sigma Draconis

On the viewscreen, Toni watched her home for the last 256 days drift away. Overlaid on the display were three timers, marking the collision times for the trio of wormholes orbiting Sigma Draconis.

Timer one was at eight hours twenty-one minutes. Timer two at nine hours ten minutes. Timer three at ten fourteen.

Toni II sat in an auxiliary seat that folded out from the wall behind the pilot. It was a close fit, as the scout was not intended as a passenger vessel, even though the life-support systems were rated for four people. She could hear her twin breathing, oddly synchronized but with a half-second delay, like a strange echo.

She called up the status of the tach-drive, overlaying the image of the receding platform. Everything nominal.

She looked over her shoulder at Toni II, and they both spoke simultaneously. "Are you okay with this?"

She stared at herself as herself stared back. It was sinking in that the woman behind her *was* her, with all but a little more than a week of common experience. They were more than twins. Ten days ago Toni II was the exact same woman that Toni had been five days ago. Not just identical, but the same individual. And as if they were caught in some sort of spiritual echo chamber, she could read the same thoughts crossing Toni II's face.

"I just thought—" they both said, then trailed off.

"Maybe . . ." Toni paused, but this time it was just her speaking. "Maybe we should take turns talking."

Toni II waited a few beats before saying, "Not a bad idea."

"We both might be facing an unpleasant reaction from 3SEC, violating a direct order."

"Where else can we go in this thing?"

"There's the—"

"Don't say the wormhole. I tried that, didn't work too well."

"If we tach—"

"—out a light-year then just tach back? We might miss the fireworks, but there are others in the line of fire."

Toni nodded.

It might be risky to disobey orders and go directly to the 3SEC command platform orbiting Styx, but there was no way for her to bypass the chain of command from her post, and she needed to warn the other stations—or get someone else to.

Even if Styx itself wouldn't be directly affected by the explosions, there were thousands of people who would be killed by the blast.

Then there was the tachyon radiation.

Toni II had told her a bit of what happened—what would happen— after W1 was the first to blow. As they prepped themselves to abandon ship, Toni II described how all the tach-sensors on the platform went crazy, and how the scout's tach-drive was already crippled when she decided to escape the coming impact on W3.

Warning her command had to be their top priority. Too many lives were at stake, and by the time W1 blew, throwing its tach-pulse across the inner system, it would be too late for those in the path of the other two to get out of the way.

What really worried her was if the explosions were going to be powerful enough to endanger people on the planet itself—

"Styx has a decent magnetic field and a dense atmosphere," Toni II told her. "I'm sure the surface will be safe."

It's like I'm married.

"Okay, 3SEC it is."

Date: 2526.6.5 (Standard)
Styx Orbit—Sigma Draconis

Toni II watched her younger self plot a course for the 3SEC command platform and forced herself to not reach over the pilot's chair and start entering the course herself. It felt surreal watching the other's hands move a fraction a second after she thought of it.

After the computer confirmed the jump calculations, and after she had reset the overrides that warned her against taching too close to a planet and established traffic patterns, the younger Toni leaned back and whispered, "Here we go."

Like every tach-jump, this one was instantaneous from the perspective of those in transit. One moment the viewscreens showed the burning orb of Sigma Draconis and an enhanced star field behind the navigational overlays. The next moment, half the universe became the slushy gray orb of Styx itself.

The counters that timed the countdown to the wormhole collisions all jumped down five hundred seconds to account for the passage of time in the real universe while the ship was making its short tach-jump.

Immediately, the comm screens lit up with half a dozen flavors of warning at them, flashing like a summer lighting storm on the slopes of the Gehenna range during an eruption. The warnings came from civilian, commercial and military traffic controllers, all squawking that the little scout shouldn't be where it was.

Points started flashing all over the viewscreen, pinpointing transponders and radar contacts. The tach-drive itself started beeping warnings from being too close to the "wake" of other, more capable drives.

Toni II watched as her other self flipped on the military channel and said, "This is Lieutenant Toni Valentine of the Stygian Security Forces, in Centauri scout craft solo-charlie-eight-seven-six-five-four-nine-zero. I am requesting immediate emergency clearance to dock at 3SEC."

The radio came alive. "Solo-charlie-eight-seven-six-five-four-nine-zero, you do not have authorization to approach the 3SEC orbital platform. You are ordered to decelerate into a parking orbit."

"I repeat, I'm requesting *emergency* clearance."

In the main viewscreen, a small shadow emerged from behind Styx's horizon. It didn't look like much from this distance, but Toni II knew what it was before the heads-up identified it with its own transponder tag.

"What is the nature of your emergency?"

"In eight hours and three minutes, the wormholes in this system are going to start exploding!"

The radio didn't respond immediately.

Across from the communication console, the weapons' station began lighting up with sensor locks from several different orbital defense platforms. Before Toni II said anything to her younger self, she saw her other self plotting in another jump into the tach-drive. Only a couple of AU out, not too far for the standard drives to get them somewhere back insystem, but far enough away to escape any immediate nastiness.

Assuming they'd have enough warning before they were shot out of the sky. Too long, and they wouldn't be able to outrun a laser.

"They won't shoot at us," her younger self whispered, answering her unspoken thoughts. "I just want out of here if no one talks to us."

"Do you suddenly feel like an old married couple?" Toni II whispered back.

The eyes widened in her younger self's face. "I was just—" She turned back toward the consoles and nodded. "Yes."

Toni held her course, watching the 3SEC platform grow in the viewscreen. Her hand hovered over the commit button that would fire the scout's dangerously hot tach-drive and fling them an AU further out from Sigma Draconis, away from Styx and the doomed wormholes—and an AU away from being able to do anything.

She had told Toni II that they weren't going to be shot at. She was in an official craft with the right transponder and the right countersigns. They'd know that she was who she said she was.

But that didn't mean they wouldn't blow the scout craft to hell for being where it wasn't supposed to be. And she knew that Toni II knew it just as well as she did.

She didn't like the silence. Seconds were stretching to minutes without a response.

The platform kept growing in the viewscreen, a series of large disks strung along a common axis pointing down at the surface. They were just close enough to see the spaces between the disks, where the docking facilities were.

The countdown timer for the first impact crossed eight hours.

I give them five minutes, then I'm taching out of here . . .

Her fingers shook slightly over the control panel, and a bead of sweat stung the corner of her right eye.

"Solo-charlie-eight-seven-six-five-four-nine-zero, you are to match orbits and dock on level alpha, bay three-seven. Confirm."

Toni yanked her hand away from the tach controls and radioed back, "Level alpha, bay three-seven."

"You are to dock, power down completely, and await further instructions."

Many of the warning lights turned off, and a schematic grid flickered on the viewscreen, showing the approach path. She did some minor manual maneuvering, then synced her onboard computer with traffic control.

From behind her, Toni II said, "You notice that the last guy was different?"

"Yes. We got booted up the command chain."

"And we're both wondering if that's good or bad."

"They're not shooting at us."

"Yet."

The small scout craft followed traffic control's lead as the mass of the 3SEC orbital station grew to dominate the viewscreen. If she remembered the layout of the place correctly, level alpha was deep into the secured area near the "top," furthest away from Styx. As they maneuvered, she saw bay thirty-seven, lonely and isolated between the top two disks of the station. The docking bay itself was huge, dwarfing their craft. The gap between floor and ceiling was easily fifty meters.

A spidery robotic arm trailing coils of fuel and power lines extended from the depths of the docking bay to meet them as the scout drifted between the layers of the station. The arm mated with the underside of the scout and there was a subtle, jarring wrench as the scout matched the slow rotation of the orbital platform. Toni felt herself sink a little deeper in her seat as the arm rotated the scout parallel to the station's axis.

The computer helpfully began powering down the ship's systems, and she had to force herself not to start switching overrides on.

She wasn't normally this paranoid, and she wondered where it was coming from. Yes, she was in a bizarre situation, but that shouldn't cause her to mistrust her own command. Even the guy parroting orders at her to sit tight, that was more than likely bureaucratic inertia than anything else. They didn't know how to deal with the situation, which meant the uncertainty got kicked up the chain until it reached someone with the authority to make a decision.

That was rarely a fast process.

She might have disobeyed a direct order, but she was still a lieutenant in the Stygian Security Forces, and she still had a duty. She had been hoping to bypass the command chain, if only to get her opposite numbers at the other two wormholes to get the hell out of there in the seven hours and forty-eight minutes they had left.

Now she had become one of those uncertainties being fed up the chain of command. So instead of talking to someone in traffic control and getting them to radio warnings, she was probably going to be stuck with someone in internal security.

Which would be fine if she could still convince them to act.

As the spidery arm pulled the scout deeper into the cavernous docking bay and the axis of the station became the new "up," Toni II asked, "Yeah, but beyond telling everyone to get out of the way, what else can anyone do?"

Yeah. What?

It was probably a good thing that some decisions were above her pay grade.

Fortunately for her nerves, the "wait for further instructions" only lasted another few minutes or so. When the first timer crossed to seven hours forty-two, an air lock extended from one of the walkways crisscrossing the spaces between the docking bays. It attached seamlessly to the scout and she heard the computer beeping as the scout's air lock began to cycle.

She turned the pilot's chair enough to look at the air lock as the inner door slid aside. A man stood in the air lock, wearing a gray and blue uniform that bore the stylized red key sigil of the SEF Military Police on a shoulder patch. The docking arm had drawn them up nearly to the axis of the station, so he stood light on his feet, the rotation barely holding him down.

"You need to accompany me, Lieutenant Valentine?" His tone morphed from command to question as he looked from Toni to Toni II. After a beat, he said, "Both of you."

CHAPTER THIRTEEN

Fire and Brimstone

"Sometimes explosions are necessary."
—*The Cynic's Book of Wisdom*

"Life is risk."

—SYLVIA HARPER
(2008–2081)

Date: 2526.6.5 (Standard)
75,000 km from Salmagundi–HD 101534

Shortly after Adam gave his one-hour warning, Parvi watched as the small cadre of maintenance techs loaded the dropship. Departure was clearly imminent, a race to beat Adam's deadline off the *Voice*. As one set of the crew loaded the dropship, a trio of the Caliphate mechanics by the main air lock door were engaged in an animated conversation. Looming over their argument, the heavy blast doors held the vacuum outside at bay.

Wahid stared at the trio and Parvi asked, "What's the problem there?"

"Something seems to be blocking the exit." He raised his hand, quieting her before she could ask another question. After a few more sentences back and forth in heated Arabic, Wahid stood up and took a step toward them. The guard with the gamma laser stepped in front of him, blocking his path.

Wahid snapped something at the guy, and after a moment's hesitation, the guard nodded and reluctantly stepped aside. Wahid waved her forward.

"What did you say to him?" she asked as she followed him toward the massive doors sealing the bay and the arguing techs.

"The obvious: either they need our help or not. It isn't like we'll sabotage our own escape, right?"

Parvi thought of the woman she had left dead outside the interrogation room and simply grunted an assent.

The trio by the doors stopped talking as they approached. "So," Wahid asked them, "what's blocking the way out?" Parvi suspected he spoke English out of deference to her.

At least one of the three understood. The dark-haired woman who appeared in charge snapped, "You two, what are you doing over here?"

"I pointed out that, since we're going to fly you out of this mess, you might use our help getting that ungainly little boat launched out of here."

One of the two men flanking her snorted, and the woman glared at him.

"What's the problem?" Parvi asked. "Debris from the neighboring bays?"

After a moment's thought, the woman answered, "I wish it were that simple." She waved at a kiosk next to the massive doors. "You can take a look for yourself."

Parvi walked over to the kiosk. The panels around it were open, revealing a massive amount of rewiring. She suspected that they worked to bypass the main ship's systems and connected it directly to whatever external sensors were local to this bay.

Looking into the holo, her first thought was that the wiring was unsuccessful. The screen looked blank.

Then she realized that it wasn't a dead screen. A few subtle highlights in the black revealed that she looked at an undulating wall. Along the side of the display scrolled numbers and graphs all labeled in Arabic. She couldn't understand all of it, but she gathered she was looking at densities and thermal profiles, radar cross section, spectroscopic analysis . . .

"Wahid?" she called out as she backed away from the display.

Wahid walked over to the display and let out a low whistle.

"You see the problem?" asked the woman.

Parvi nodded. The barrier floated barely a meter from the skin of the *Voice*.

"It's about three meters thick before the density drops off," Wahid said. "Mostly carbon, but traces of just about everything else. Fine particulate matter, discrete particles shaped probably by some sort of electrostatic field, fluid. You could fly through it."

The woman laughed.

"What?" Wahid looked up from the screen.

"Do you know what that *is*?"

"Tell us," Parvi said. "What is it?"

She said something in Arabic for a few moments, and Parvi saw Wahid stare at the woman and shake his head. The look on his face was as close to pure horror as she'd ever seen, and she'd been on the *Eclipse*'s bridge with him when the ship started breaking apart.

"What is it?"

"The word in English—" the woman began.

"Nanomachines," Wahid said. "We're surrounded by a cloud of nanomachines."

"What? That's ..." Parvi was about to say the idiotic phrase, "That's illegal." If there was any scrap of unity left across the universe of human politics, it was that. Everyone from the Centauri Alliance to the Caliphate to the counter-revolutionary Federal government on Rubai would agree on the bans on heretical technologies. Self-replicating nanotech most of all. Whole planets had been sterilized because of it.

But they were eighty light-years away from the Centauri Alliance, the Caliphate, and whatever scraps of the Rubai Federals had been left in exile.

The woman glared at Wahid. "You see why we cannot 'fly through it.'"

One of the others spoke in halting English. "Before cameras lost, we see bridge. Adam. And it ... it ..."

He broke down fumbling for words, and the woman in charge finished for him. "Our people, our soldiers went forward to fight, but each one who came in contact with this thing, they changed."

"Changed?" Parvi asked.

"This Adam calls for servants. And should it touch you, you become his servant, or something else crawls into your skin."

Parvi shuddered, thinking of millions of tiny machines crawling inside her, stripping her body apart and reassembling it from the inside out.

Wahid frowned and looked back at the jury-rigged holo. "Then why are we still here? That thing's only a meter from us. It could take apart that bulkhead and make short work of us whenever it wanted."

"If it's been speaking truth," the woman said, "in forty-five minutes it will."

Parvi rubbed her face and tried to recall what history she had learned about the suppression of nanotech during the Confederacy. All the historical incidents she could remember involved hitting some infected ground-based target with a lot of energy all at once. Antimatter bombs, orbital linear accelerators firing near-light-speed projectiles at a planetary surface, and in one case dropping an asteroid from orbit large enough to punch through the crust of the planet and render the surface uninhabitable.

She couldn't remember anything about dealing with this kind of thing close range or outside a ground-based planetary environment. AM-bombs would probably sterilize the cloud outside, but even the smallest one would vaporize everything in a hundred-meter radius. A high-powered laser would destroy part of it, but only along the laser's path. It made about as much sense as firing a slugthrower at a swimming pool.

Plasma could cover a broad area, but it would probably diffuse its energy too quickly. Again, like the swimming pool, the cloud out there could probably soak up more radiant energy than they could hope to produce without so much as a splash.

A splash . . .

Wahid and the woman were arguing about attack methods. "If we time a missile to concuss in its midst, we'll be caught in the blast."

Parvi said, "We can't destroy it, probably can't damage it, but we *can* push it out of the way."

"What do you mean?" the woman asked.

Wahid looked at Parvi and slowly broke into an evil smile. "We don't want to be caught by the blast. We want to *be* the blast."

Parvi looked back at the dropship. "She looks like she's rated to do heavy atmospheric breaking."

"Yes . . ."

"Then get me the specs on her performance envelope, and show me the environmental controls for this bay. We're going to get out of here."

In less than fifteen minutes, the crew was strapped in the back of the dropship, the ship itself buttoned up as if they were due to make a steep atmospheric insertion into a hostile environment. Parvi sat strapped into the pilot's chair, and Wahid was strapped in at the weapons console.

Sitting to her left, at the currently useless communications console, was the English-speaking woman, Technical Sergeant Abbas. Sergeant Abbas had been the highest ranking person trapped in the maintenance bay, which meant that she was the closest thing they all had to someone in charge.

To reinforce that point, she was the only armed person in the cockpit.

The dropship was completely fly-by-wire. There wasn't even a window. Parvi looked out at a bank of holos that showed a compressed fish-eye view of the maintenance bay. She suspected that there were probably about six or seven meters of aircraft between them and the outside.

"Here we go." Wahid switched on the plasma cannons.

"This is insane," Sergeant Abbas whispered, then muttered a short prayer in Arabic.

Insane or not, Sergeant Abbas had bought in to her prisoners' crazy idea.

Outside, at the lower edge of the holo, Parvi saw a distorted view of plasma streams coming from dual cannons set below the dropship's nose. The plasma broke against the massive external doors like a hellish tide.

In the surrounding maintenance bay, everything flammable ignited in a flashover that lasted half a second. Then, for a few seconds, plastic and synthetics—which included everything from packing crates to small motorized supply carts, to computer hardware—flowed and turned black before flaring in microsecond combustion that left nothing but microscopic ash behind.

The walls and blast doors held tight despite turning rainbow colors, then black, under the heat. The environment sensors on the console in front of her started showing the effect of the plasma venting. Atmospheric pressure had trebled, and degrees Kelvin were shooting by too fast to read.

The exterior temperature hadn't reached critical levels yet, but the weapons caused massive drains on the dropship's power plant. This was a military craft, and the power reserves were incredible, easily twice those of the heavily modified *Eclipse*, but the plasma had already sucked through a third of it.

"We're losing power quickly," Parvi said.

"Give it a few more seconds," Wahid said.

The holo showed the maintenance bay, now nothing more than a metal box. Everything outside the insulated skin of the dropship had vaporized. The air had a sick yellow-orange tint from the light of the plasma jets, rippling as if she was looking through a viscous liquid. The pressure indicator started flashing yellow.

"Wahid?"

"A couple more seconds."

The temperature sensor joined in flashing yellow. Other warning indicators started flashing. "We have stress warnings on the starboard control surfaces—"

"Damn it, that's where the repairs—"

"Wahid! We're going to breach!"

"Hit it now!"

Parvi slammed the button on the remote control next to the pilot's station. It was a simple RF signal to the control system on the main door to blow the explosive bolts holding the whole mechanism in place.

In response to Parvi's trigger, the entire ship resonated with a gigantic crashing thrum that was too deep and violent to be considered a sound. Suddenly, forward was *down*, and the massive doors fell away from the nose of the dropship in a explosive outgassing of boiling atmosphere.

The ship followed the doorway even before Parvi kicked on the engines to accelerate the craft out of the bay. Around and in front of them, the superheated atmosphere billowed out in a powerful shockwave. The dropship accelerated through the midst of the explosion, racing out after the door.

The explosion had the desired effect; the force of their blast had blown a hole through the cloud of matter surrounding the *Voice*. In the edges of the fish-eye holo, Parvi saw the black surface ripping outward from them, oscillating like the surface of a pond after being struck by a rock. She also saw the substance, rushing back in to fill the momentary gap.

The dropship cleared the cloud before it filled in behind them.

"Parvi!"

Wahid's voice brought her attention forward. They had caught up to the door, and she had to pull a fancy half-roll to starboard to avoid it. She goosed the maneuvering jets and rolled back to keep her vector a straight line away from the *Voice*.

"Shit!" Wahid whispered.

Sergeant Abbas muttered something, the only word of which Parvi could make out was "Allah."

Hanging in front of them was the vast curve of Salmagundi, a blue-green sphere filling half the universe. Sunlight came from behind and above the dropship, carving out every swirl of cloud in stark white relief—

Except for a dark line bisecting their view of the planet. The line was so dark and sharp that for a moment it appeared to be a defect in the holo projection. At least it did until she saw that the layers of clouds below gave an undulating topography that broke up the edges of the line. It wasn't an artifact, it was a shadow, a shadow that girdled the planet from horizon to horizon.

Parvi adjusted the sensors to give a view from behind them.

Behind them, and above the planet, another line was just eclipsing Salmagundi's sun. As they passed into shadow, both edges of the object were briefly haloed.

It was a black band ringing the planet. Something that was definitely not present when the *Eclipse* had tached into this system.

"The *Voice* is in that thing," Abbas' voice hovered between a statement and a question.

"Parvi, watch your angle!"

The dropship was at a steep insertion orbit, and Parvi tried to angle the ship up. The maneuvering jets were sluggish and didn't want to respond. Worse, the power reserves were dropping too fast.

"We must tach out of here," Abbas called out.

"Tach? Where?" Wahid shouted.

"Sorry, Sergeant. We need to land this," Parvi said.

"No," Abbas said, yanking her side arm out and pointing it at Parvi. "We need to return to the Caliphate."

"Are you insane?" The shaking of the dropship gave Parvi's voice a vibrato. "Do you see the same indicator I do? I don't read Arabic, but I'm pretty sure that half that orange-red bar means that our powerplant's at fifty percent and dropping. Fast. That means damage, a leak, and you really want to try firing the tach-drive with an unstable power plant?"

"Bring this ship back up into orbit!" Abbas yelled at her.

Parvi shook her head and turned her attention back to the controls. "Wahid, do you remember the mapping directions we got from groundside for the *Eclipse*'s descent?" she asked as she struggled with the sluggish maneuvering jets to flatten the dropship's angle of attack from the suicidal to the merely ludicrous.

"You are not going to land this ship!" Abbas yelled.

"And you're not going to shoot me!" Parvi yelled back.

The dropship shook as Salmagundi's atmosphere tore by, clawing at the too-fast invader, trying to slow it. The temperature sensors started climbing again.

"Sergeant, you may not have noticed, but we just pushed a damaged ship way past its design specs. This thing needs the once-over from your techs before it goes anywhere. At the very least we need to recharge the power plant," Parvi said.

The edges of the holo began glowing with the superheated atmosphere sliding over the hull. Wahid had turned his chair to face the nav console and was typing in coordinates.

"I'm in command here," Abbas said.

"Even if you were going to fire a tach-drive in a planet's upper atmosphere with a damaged unstable power plant, how far can this thing go on less than fifty percent reserves? Two light-years? Ten? How far from the Caliphate and any way to fix or refuel this thing?"

"I found it," Wahid said.

"Forty," Abbas said, lowering her side arm.

"What?"

"Nominally these drives can jump forty light-years on a half-charge."

Parvi wasn't sure she'd heard right. "How many jumps?"

"One."

"What?" Wahid said.

"One jump," Parvi repeated. "You're telling me that this crate has a tach-drive that can effectively jump twice as far as anything else?"

"Four times," Abbas said. "With a full charge, the drive can push out at least eighty light-years."

"Holy shit," Wahid said, "this crate can get us home."

"All the more reason," Parvi said, "to get this thing on the ground, repaired and refueled."

Around them, the violence of atmospheric entry had begun to smooth out. There wasn't much the pilot could do right now. The ship's maneuverability was severely limited during the descent into the atmosphere. Once they were in the pipe, they had to rely on the design of the craft's body and the laws of fluid dynamics to determine its course. Any human intervention right now could turn a stable descent into tumbling chaos.

"Now," Parvi said, "we just hope the natives don't try to shoot us down."

The dropship shot thought the stratosphere at hypersonic speeds, roughly following the east–west pathway of the equatorial shadow. Razor-thin from orbit, this close to the surface, the shadow covered a hundred kilometers easily. They had dropped far enough down so that only one edge was visible on the ground. Above them, the ring was a seam in the sky, a narrow band where the shade of sky turned a darker blue.

Wahid's flight path took them directly into the shadow, and as the ground went dark below them, the band turned darker as it cut across the face of the sun. When they approached the landing field that had been the *Eclipse*'s destination, Salmagundi's sun was nothing more than a few whips of corona above them, bisected by a black ribbon in the sky.

"Wahid, tell me that thing isn't getting bigger."

"Okay," he said. "It's not getting bigger. It's getting closer."

"Abbas," she called over her shoulder, "you have the comm. Radio them we're landing, and they don't have a choice."

The woman glared at her.

"Damn it, Sergeant, you might be in command, but I'm captain here until we hit dirt."

Abbas turned toward the comm console, and after a moment she said, "They're unresponsive."

As Parvi banked on her approach, she briefly wondered if this was the right landing area, or if it had suffered from some sort of attack. But in the displays, the approach beacon was active. They were within fifty klicks now, and she could see the unlit landing field in the light-enhanced display.

At least no one was shooting at them.

She closed in on the airfield and saw no movement. No vehicles, air or ground, sitting on the tarmac. That made things easier, since they didn't have any air traffic control talking them in.

She put the dropship down in the geometric center of the landing field, giving a clear hundred-meter fire zone around the craft. Just in case.

"We're here," she said.

CHAPTER FOURTEEN

Faith

"Fear helps us survive. Hope makes us want to."
—*The Cynic's Book of Wisdom*

"There are no eternal facts, as there are no absolute truths."

—FRIEDRICH NIETZSCHE
(1844–1900)

Date: 2526.6.5 (Standard)
Salmagundi–HD 101534

Mallory was only slightly surprised that the old man hadn't come to question them. Of course, since he had mined everything from all four of their minds already and implanted it into his own, there wasn't much left he could ask. He introduced himself as Alexander Shane and ordered Mallory and the others out of their impromptu prison.

Armed guards led the barely ambulatory prisoners out to a small armored transport parked in an eerily empty courtyard surrounded on three sides by the short outbuildings that grew from the base of the Hall of Minds.

The ugly black aircraft could have been the same one that had picked them up from the lifeboat.

Everything was deathly quiet as they left the outbuilding and headed toward the open doors of the craft. Even the idling of the maneuvering fans seemed subdued in the still afternoon air. The sun hung small and white in a near-cloudless sky.

It was quiet enough that when Dörner whispered, "What

is that?" it was almost as if someone had shouted the question.

At first, Mallory wasn't clear what she was referring to. Then he followed her gaze and saw a narrow band of darker blue bisecting the sky from horizon to horizon, about fifteen degrees off vertical. At first it appeared it could be a strange contrail from something entering the atmosphere, but it was too straight, too even, too long.

Shane spoke without turning around. "We don't know. It's a ring of material in equatorial orbit about fifty thousand kilometers out."

"That wasn't here when the *Eclipse* tached in," Mallory said.

"No," Shane told him, "it wasn't."

Once the craft was airborne, heading away from the monolithic Hall of Minds, Mallory asked him, "Where are you taking us?"

"Precisely where you want to go, Father Mallory."

"What?" Mallory shouted over the whine of the fans, unsure he had heard correctly.

Shane turned to face them. He was the only one standing in the compartment, his right hand wrapped around the webbing attached to the wall. His hand trembled in a white-knuckled death grip. Shane looked thin and spectral, as if he wasn't really there. His face wore an expression that was half pain, half resignation.

It was an expression that reminded Mallory of Mosasa.

"I doubt Salmagundi will survive," he said flatly. "I was far too late to do any good." He looked into Mallory's eyes. "So were you."

"What are you talking about?" Brody said.

"The fleet of Caliphate ships," he said. "That was one thing. We couldn't fight an army, but perhaps we could negotiate some accommodation, a surrender that left us some measure of our culture, our autonomy. After all, what do we care about power struggles in the remains of the Confederacy?"

"But—" Mallory started to say.

Shane cut him short with a sharp gesture with his left hand. "Don't pretend to have an argument I haven't considered. I know the history of the Caliphate as well as you—by definition. It's moot, anyway. We aren't facing the Caliphate."

"Then what *are* we facing?" Mallory asked.

"The thing that consumed Xi Virginis," Shane told him. "The creature calling itself Adam. It has given us an ultimatum. We have roughly sixty minutes left to make our decision."

"What decision?" Dörner asked.

"Salvation or damnation," Brody said. "Are we on the side of the chosen, or of the infidel?"

"To follow him," Shane said, "or pass the way of all flesh."

Outside the aircraft, the light dimmed as the sun was eclipsed by the band crossing the sky.

"Where are we going?" Mallory asked again.

"As I told you, the only place on this planet where you would want to go. The only place with a ground-based tach-transmitter."

Before Salmagundi had cut itself off, not just from the old Confederacy, but from the other colonies founded around it, it had a up-to-date starport. It built a facility where tach-ships could be repaired and refueled, and a place that could communicate with the rest of the universe. The place was completed but never really used.

When the people of Salmagundi decided to close themselves off, there had been some discussion about destroying the base. It made some of those in power uncomfortable to have even a potential connection to things off-planet. Instead, though, the powers at the time decided to simply restrict access to the site. Over the next century and a half, the port was kept functional but restricted.

Few outside the ruling class realized the place still existed.

"We had ordered your ship to land there, before things started going so badly," Shane told him. "This site is the only place where we might be able to get a message back to where you came from."

"Sir?" Mallory barely heard as one of the men in the cockpit called back.

"What?" Shane turned around.

Mallory could hear talking up forward, but couldn't make out the words. When he turned around he looked even more pale and drawn.

"What is it?" Mallory asked.

Shane ignored him as he stepped into the cockpit.

Mallory looked across at his fellow prisoners. Pak looked as if he was barely present. Dörner held his arm while he stared off at a space about three meters off of Mallory's left shoulder.

Brody looked out at the unnaturally dark landscape and whispered, "How can you fight something like this?"

"You don't," Mallory said.

Brody turned to look at him, "That's kind of fatalistic, coming from a priest."

"We can pray."

"You're assuming I haven't been."

Mallory jerked against his crash harness as the bottom fell out of the transport. The craft plummeted like a brick and bottomed out so violently, and with such a whine from the maneuvering fans, that Mallory briefly thought they had struck the ground.

"What the?" Brody said as Mallory took a glance out the windows. They were still airborne, but they shot by about five meters above the treetops. He saw individual branches whipping by in the twilight. His stomach lurched as they took a sharp banking turn to the right.

"Evasive maneuvers," Mallory said.

Brody looked out the window, then found himself pressed against it as the ship took another banking turn to the left. "What are we evading?"

"I don't know. But I'm guessing that, whatever it is, it hasn't taken any notice of us yet."

"Why?"

"Because we're still alive," Mallory said. "This is a civilian craft, an old one never meant for anything more than search and rescue or riot control. If there's something out there worth evading, if it sees us, it can kill us no matter what kind of piloting we try."

"You're not making me feel better."

Shouting erupted from the cockpit.

"What's going on up—" Brody's question was cut off by a gasp as the aircraft descended with a nasty crunch. What little light came through the eclipse-shadowed windows was cut by half as the craft decelerated with an angry whine from the maneuvering fans. Mallory looked out the windows, and to his amazement saw tree trunks speeding by mere meters from the skin of the aircraft.

God, please let us have a good pilot.

Mallory knew they must have slowed down to a fraction of the speed they had been going in the open air, but the proximity of the trees with their four-meter-diameter trunks made it feel that they had accelerated. Talking was impossible between the sudden violent vibrations from the fans and the sudden jerks as the pilot flew left, right, up, down, avoiding the trees reaching to knock them out of the sky.

They flew through old growth, massive trees far apart from each other, but it still seemed impossible to maneuver, a flying camel through a forest of needles. It couldn't last.

It didn't.

Mallory watched out the window, transfixed, as they rode a three-dimensional slalom through the trees. Then they came close to an ancient monster that must have had a fifteen-meter-diameter trunk. The housing on the left forward maneuvering fan clipped the edge of the tree in a shower of bark and shredded composite. Mallory felt the crunch of the impact in the bench he sat on, shaking the floor of the craft.

It looked as if the glancing blow was only cosmetic. But the vibration through the floor continued and increased in magnitude. The fan housing shook worse, shedding more composite, the vibration turning the edges of the machine fuzzy and indistinct. A high-pitched, arrhythmic whine filled the cabin, and then the fan exploded, sending spinning fragments of itself in every direction, pitching the

whole machine in a dangerous dive in the direction of the
now-absent thrust.

God must have listened to his prayer, because their pilot
avoided an uncontrolled death tumble. Just as the aircraft
started to rotate nose down around the pivot of the contragrav providing its lift, the pilot cut power to the contragrav and throttled the fans back enough to turn the tumble
into a controlled dive. Once the tumble stopped, the pilot
brought the remaining forward fan back up to flatten
out their angle of attack. They leveled out so close to the
ground that Mallory lost all visibility out the window from
dust and debris kicked up by the three still-working fans.

They kept moving five minutes past the point where
Mallory thought they should have crashed. It took another
half minute to realize that the craft had managed to land.

"Everyone out!" Shane called from the cockpit.

The militiamen grabbed the quartet of prisoners and
shoved them out of the aircraft just as the side doors
slid open. Mallory stumbled out into a semi-clearing in
the woods where dust and dead leaves were still settling
from their arrival. The fans still whined as they spun down.
Above them, a break in the canopy a hundred meters
above showed a slice of deep purple sky cut in two by a
black band.

Mallory took a few steps, wobbly from the invasive surgery and from the hellish flight, staring up at the slice of sky
he could see between the shadowy trees.

"It's gotten bigger," he whispered.

The three other prisoners walked up next to him. Brody
looked up at the sky. Dörner led Pak, who followed her like
an automaton.

"You're right," Brody said. "It is bigger."

Back by the aircraft, Shane stepped out of the open
door and faced them and the six militiamen. "We have a
problem." Mallory wasn't certain if Shane was addressing
the troops or the prisoners, maybe both. "I had hoped that
the fact the facility wasn't active might have prevented it
from being an obvious target. Our visitors seemed to have
decided otherwise. There's a dropship bearing Caliphate
markings in the landing quad."

Dörner shook her head. "You must be kidding me," she whispered.

"The ship, from the profile, is based off of a Medina-class troop carrier. That means perfunctory weaponry, only really useful in air-to-air situations. So it is likely that the ship itself will not pose a threat. But it does mean we may have anywhere up to three units of heavy infantry to a full-blown ground cav unit—"

Mallory listened to Shane's analysis and realized he was listening to his own training speaking. It made Mallory slightly sick to listen to Shane repeat knowledge of Caliphate weapons and tactics, knowledge that he knew had only one source.

"What we need to know," Shane said, "is whether this dropship is actually *still* a Caliphate vessel."

"Sir," one of the militia guards asked, "we're being invaded. Does it matter who's on that ship?"

"Yes, it does." Shane looked over at Mallory. "The Caliphate's only interest here is imperialistic posturing. They just want to claim jurisdiction over this planet. This thing called Adam wants a lot more from us."

"Are we sure they aren't the same thing, sir?"

"At this point, no." Shane gestured at Mallory. "But our mission here is to get control of the tach-transmitter so our friend Mallory can send a message off to his friends in the Vatican. You don't have a problem with that, Father Mallory, do you?"

Mallory shook his head. It was, in fact, his only hope for accomplishing his mission here. The disturbing thing was what it implied about the situation on the ground here. Shane couldn't expect a response of any kind before Salmagundi collapsed. The tach-transmission itself would take over a month to reach the core systems.

If they made it to the transmitter, it was likely to be their last act before Adam moved on his ultimatum.

"We only have thirty-six minutes," Shane pointed toward the edge of the clearing. "We're about two klicks west of the spaceport. The tach-transmitter is in the trapezoidal building to the northeast. If we're lucky, our visitors are more interested in the ship-maintenance areas. All of you—" He waved at the militiamen. "Your job is to get Mallory inside."

"What about you, sir?"

"I don't matter. All the cities have been on their own since we lost satellite communication. Mallory needs to make the transmission so they can authenticate it. I know the proper protocol, but if they see my face, it might raise some questions. I'm going to take the scientists and try to negotiate."

"Negotiate what?" Mallory asked.

"Our surrender to the Caliphate." Shane's thin smile was a knife wound in his face.

CHAPTER FIFTEEN

Shibboleth

"Never assume that the universe is limited to a finite set of possibilities."

—*The Cynic's Book of Wisdom*

"I seek God in revolution."

—MIKHAIL A. BAKUNIN
(1814–1876)

Date: 2526.6.5 (Standard)
Salmagundi–HD 101534

Once the dropship hit ground, Abbas said, "Now, *Captain* Parvi, get out of that chair."

Parvi turned around to face a gamma laser. She held up her hands. "We need to—"

"You need to shut up and follow orders, you little Hindi bitch. You became surplus the moment we landed."

Parvi looked at the fury in Abbas' eyes and decided that the sergeant had reached the point where she *wanted* an excuse to shoot her. Parvi reached down and undid the harness and stood up.

"You too." Abbas pointed the laser at Wahid.

Wahid silently undid the harness and got to his feet.

Abbas held them at gunpoint and opened the door back into the passenger compartment where about twenty frightened techs clutched a random assortment of mismatched weapons. Abbas called out something in Arabic, then turned back to the two of them and said, "In thirty minutes, the *Khalid* here is going to leave and tach home. If you shut up and follow orders, you live to be the pilot."

Abbas detailed one of the techs to take the two of them out of the ship and out of the way. Their guard walked them about twenty meters away from the ship and had them sit down on the pitted tarmac. Back at the dropship *Khalid*, Sergeant Abbas kept yelling at her crew of maintenance techs in Arabic.

At least the *Khalid* had left the *Voice* with the one set of people who knew exactly what this ship needed to keep running. Parvi looked around at the complex. The buildings appeared dark and abandoned, and the surrounding woods encroached right up to the perimeter. "Now we just hope this place has what we need," Parvi whispered.

Wahid looked at the sky and said, "I think we need a miracle."

"We've had four or five so far. What's another one?" Parvi looked up at the dark ribbon across the sky and asked, "What the hell is happening here?"

"I don't know, I just know I don't like ultimatums."

"Neither do I." She thought of Adam and a cloud of machines that would take her apart, molecule by molecule, if she didn't accept him.

It.

And should it touch you, you become his servant, or something else crawls into your skin.

Parvi shuddered and prayed that these displaced technicians could get the *Khalid* fixed and powered in half an hour.

Parvi watched the techs as they scrambled over the ship and pulled cables and hoses from the *Khalid* and from access panels recessed in the tarmac. Somehow they managed to get the two to mate up.

She felt a small surge of optimism when one of the techs crawled out from the open belly of the ship and gave his comrades a thumbs-up.

Then she heard Wahid's voice say, "What the fuck?"

"What?" She looked away from the *Khalid*, and saw

that their guard was paying more attention to the woods behind them than he was to his two prisoners. Wahid had turned to look behind them as well. "We have company," he whispered.

Parvi looked back so she could see what Wahid was talking about.

A quartet of people approached them from out of the woods. The man in the lead looked ancient; a tall, hairless wraith emerging from the trees. Three people moved behind him: a young man with Asiatic features, a tall, blonde woman, and a older man with skin darker than her and Wahid put together. Parvi stared but couldn't quite believe what she was seeing.

"That can't be—" Wahid said.

"Dr. Pak, Dr. Dörner, and Dr. Brody." Parvi pushed herself to her feet. "It's them."

It was them, and they had been through hell. Pak looked shell-shocked, Brody cradled a broken arm, and Dörner wore the expression of someone ready to die or kill someone. All wore blood-spattered field dressings on their necks.

The old man leading them was someone she had never seen before. He definitely wasn't from the Caliphate. He was too ancient even for a command position in the Caliphate military, and he wore civilian clothes that were archaically cut and styled—in addition to looking slept in.

Parvi heard shouts from near the *Khalid*. At least one voice was the familiar sharp bark of Sergeant Abbas. "No," Parvi muttered as she ran toward the quartet. From behind her she heard their guard shout something in Arabic and Wahid shout, "What the hell do you think you're doing?"

"Keeping her from doing something stupid."

"What about you? Damn it!"

She heard feet running behind her, and she glanced back toward the *Khalid* and saw a half-dozen armed techs, led by Sergeant Abbas, converging on the newcomers as well. Abbas' face was contorted in an expression of anger and fear that didn't argue for this going well.

Parvi turned back and watched as the old man stopped

his advance at the edge of the LZ, waiting for his welcoming committee.

Good, Parvi thought, *no sudden moves that could be misinterpreted. We might get out of this without anyone getting hurt—*

Something slammed into the back of her head, and she fell face-first into the tarmac about fifteen meters from the old man.

Shane's six militiamen led Mallory in a dead run through the woods. Normally, he wouldn't have had a problem keeping up. He had better training than these men ever had. But what Shane had done inside his skull messed with his ability to move, and he found himself stumbling after them as if he was in a constant forward fall that never quite hit the ground.

The plan, such as it was, meant to get Mallory into the tach-comm facility while Shane and the remaining civilians from the *Eclipse* served as a distraction. Mallory didn't like it, but Shane had him out-gunned and outnumbered. So it was Shane's show, even if the old man's goals coincided with Mallory's.

Several times Mallory bounced off of trees, and several more he found one of his escorts grabbing his upper arm to help steer him or keep him from falling over. His implants, unaware of his disorientation, responded to the adrenaline and further confused his sense of space, time, and distance. The rush though the woods telescoped until it felt as if they'd been running for hours.

According to the militia's chronometers, when they reached the northeast corner of the spaceport, it had taken them less than seven minutes.

Mallory had a few seconds to survey the situation. Trees and underbrush pushed right up against the edge of the facility, which consisted of ten buildings of various sizes in a rough ring around a central landing area. The buildings showed their age, sloughing off layers of ferrocrete that piled in rust-colored mounds at the corners of the buildings. Traces of paint were tiny abstract flecks adhering to pitted walls. Signs were weathered and unreadable, and landing lights were nonexistent. The only sign that the port was kept marginally functional was the fact that the LZ itself was clear of debris, and the doors were all clean and appeared usable.

Of course, the dropship dominated everything. Size-wise it was on the outer edge of what this facility was designed to handle. The Medina class was practically all lifting body, no wings to speak of, which gave it a squat narrow profile, something like the shape of a prehistoric flint arrowhead.

Mallory could see people swarming the lower areas, connecting umbilicals carted from one of the other buildings. None of them wore combat fatigues or armor, and he only saw a few carrying weapons. Mallory wondered if he found that reassuring or not.

Suddenly, all the crew by the ship turned away from them, and Mallory could just make out Shane approaching from the opposite side of the compound.

"Come on," one of the guards said, grabbing him.

While the ground crew was distracted, they dashed for the building with the tach-transmitter. The door stood open, saving them a bit of time.

Inside, Mallory felt even more the sense of a building neglected to just the edge of functionality. Paint had chipped, peeled, or disintegrated off of every surface, leaving fine piles of dust that collected at the base of each wall. While the building had power, more than half of the light fixtures—fully enclosed and apparently intended to be permanent—remained dark. Where there had been chrome trim, on doorways and wall panels, the metal had gone cloudy and spotted.

He glanced at the lights again. *Who turned them on?* When Mallory looked back at the door, he realized it had been forced.

"There's someone else here," Mallory whispered.

He stared at the door. The locking mechanism, if that's what it was, appeared to have been disassembled, the parts scattered on the floor. All around the base of the door were little wires, circuit boards, tiny little screws, parts of the plastic housing, gears, and bolts.

Also on the dust-shrouded floor were signs of more footprints than could be accounted for by their presence.

The lead guard held up his hand and gestured for silence as he looked down at the mess that had once been the door's lock. Two more edged back to flank Mallory, their guns at the ready.

Three corridors led away from the empty lobby they stood in, two following the outer walls, the last going deeper into the structure. The leader checked each, and Mallory watched him search for more footprints or other signs of company. He came back to the lobby and pointed at two of the guards, then back at the two corridors flanking the entrance. The two nodded, and he waved everyone else to follow him.

The first pair of men stayed in the lobby to guard their exit while rest of them headed deeper into the building. Mallory walked with two militiamen flanking him, while the others eased up ahead, checking each doorway and intersection.

Even after the passage of the point team, Mallory could make out the footprints in the dust. The other party had gone ahead down the same corridor and had not come back this way.

They must be looking for the same thing, the tach-transmitter.

The question was, why? Were they trying to use it themselves, or prevent others from using it?

In the lobby, the prior footprints had been all on top of each other, an indistinguishable, abstract mass. Once in this corridor, Mallory had divided his attention between the footprints—half obscured by the point team's passage—and keeping his own eyes on the corridor, checking ahead and behind. Because of that, it took him a dozen meters or so before he noticed the truly odd thing about the footprints they followed.

One set was barefoot.

Another wasn't human.

Mallory stared at the first intact paw print, as wide as his own foot was long, and whispered, "Nickolai?"

One of his guards shook him sharply for breaking silence, and pulled him after the point team, who had just reached the head of a stairwell going down.

Mallory tried to piece together how Nickolai could be here. He didn't know where that lifeboat had landed, and for all he knew it could have put down within a few hundred meters of this place. But such a coincidence strained credulity.

Was he trying to sabotage the tach-comm like he had done on the *Eclipse*?

Mallory's gut tightened. When the tiger had made his confession to him, Mallory thought he had seen a glimpse of his soul, gained a small bit of understanding. Seeing that paw print here at such a critical point drove home to Mallory the fact that he didn't know Nickolai at all.

How does someone act when they believe themselves damned? When they believe everyone around them is damned as well?

The point team waited by the stairwell for them to catch up.

Nickolai, and whoever accompanied him, had gone down these stairs and had not come back up. The two point men descended to the first landing and, after checking the area, waved the rest of them down.

They descended three flights like that, down to a large square room of badly lit ferrocrete. This room was relatively dust-free, so no footprints showed on the smooth gray floor. The ceiling was a maze of pipes and conduit above them, and a half-dozen doors surrounded them.

Only one of those doors was in the wall that faced them. That door was open a crack, the floor at its base cluttered with small lengths of wire and tiny screws.

The air was filled by the subliminal hum of a nearby power plant. The air itself felt alive with potential, the electric atmosphere teasing up the hairs on Mallory's arms and the back of his neck.

The militiamen pushed him back toward the minimal cover of the stairwell as they formed two ranks to flank the open door. Mallory pressed himself against the wall, praying for some sort of guidance.

Mallory could shout a warning to Nickolai and whoever was with him.

But he didn't truly know who was enemy or ally here.

He had been hired along with Nickolai. They had been on the same mission. But Nickolai had betrayed that trust. Just like Mallory had.

They both had served other masters.

But were these armed men any more on his side? He hadn't been given much time to think, but in some sense these men served a culture founded on an abomination. What they did here, with the human mind, was akin to a ritualistic rape of the soul. How could whatever Adam offered be worse?

God grant me the strength and the wisdom to do Your will.

Instead, God granted him a reprieve from that decision.

The door slid open while the militiamen were still approaching. The open doorway revealed a jet-black human figure, a nude hairless male who was as perfectly smooth and symmetrical as a statue. Mallory might have thought it *was* a statue, until it spoke.

Parvi groaned and rolled onto her back. Wahid put a hand on her shoulder to restrain her, though she wasn't the focus of attention right now. In the few moments Parvi had blacked out, Abbas had her people ring the newcomers.

Everyone stared at the old man, everyone except the tech holding a plasma rifle pointed at Parvi's midsection. Parvi's head throbbed, and her vision was slightly blurred. When she had blinked everything back into focus, she realized that the old guy didn't look that great himself. He was hairless, but the flowing white topcoat and a glance at his eyes gave Parvi an impression of a mad prophet fresh from the mountainside, an image that would be complete if the man had a long wild head of hair rather than a scalp covered with tattoos.

He stood with arms spread, partly blocking the three others.

Abbas was cursing to herself, and several of the people holding weapons on the newcomers looked uncomfortable.

What's going on here?

Abbas shouted at the newcomer, "*I* am in command here."

"I am certain that is the case, Sergeant. But I think I need to talk to your commanding officers."

"Whatever you think," Abbas said. When she paused for breath, Parvi could see her jaw clench with barely contained rage. "You don't get to decide. You are all talking to me here and now." She pointed to one of the mechanics, one holding a gamma laser. "If he doesn't start explaining himself, shoot the woman."

Parvi lurched to her feet, yelling, "No!"

The guy with the plasma rifle tried to cover her, but suddenly she was in the midst of his Caliphate fellows.

Someone by the old man yelled out a surprised, "Parvi?"

If Abbas had been holding her side arm, Parvi probably would have been dead. Instead, the sergeant intercepted Parvi's panicked grab for the mechanic with the gamma laser, rotated her arm under Parvi's shoulder, and used momentum to allow Parvi to pass in front of her as she folded Parvi's arm back up between her shoulder blades. Parvi grunted as Abbas shoved her arm up and forced her down to her knees.

"By all that is holy, woman. Do you think the Caliphate doesn't give its engineers combat training?" She glanced over at the guy with the plasma rifle and shouted something in Arabic. The guy looked embarrassed and grabbed Wahid and hauled him to his feet.

Abbas jerked Parvi's arm, and Parvi felt her eyes water.

"Do you know these people?"

"They're from the *Eclipse*," Parvi said. "The three in back were part of the science team."

"What are they doing here?" Abbas snapped.

"This place was where the *Eclipse* was directed to land, before the engines blew and the lifeboats launched."

Abbas dragged her upright and with an impressive show of strength pushed her into the arms of a couple more waiting techs. "Don't challenge me again, Vijayanagara Parvi. You are useful but not indispensable." She drew her own weapon and stepped over to the man and the remnants of the science team. She held the gamma laser up, pointing it at Dr. Dörner's head. "Someone's going to pay for that little display."

"Please," Parvi shouted, pulling against the men holding her, "don't!"

"Fine," Abbas said, "have it your way." She moved her aim to the right and fired the laser straight through Dr. Pak's right eye. His muscles spasmed once, and his body fell to the tarmac, a slight wisp of steam drifting up from a burnt-out eye socket.

Everyone, Caliphate techs included, stood in stunned silence.

"Does everyone understand now that we have no time for games?" Abbas said. She turned and looked at Parvi. "That was your decision. Don't test me again."

Parvi stared at Dr. Pak's corpse with the sudden certainty that they were all going to die.

Abbas turned back toward the quartet and said, "My order stands. If he doesn't answer my questions, shoot the woman." She stared at the old man. "Tell me now what you want to tell my commanding officers."

The old man lowered his hands and glanced about with too much detachment for someone who had just had a man killed in front of him. He sucked in a breath and nodded.

"My name is Alexander Shane. I am the senior member of the Grand Triad of Salmagundi. When your ships appeared in orbit, I took it upon myself to take control of the Triad and assume direct command of all military forces on this planet. I am here to negotiate our surrender to the Caliphate."

Even ten meters away, Parvi could hear Wahid mutter, "You've got to be fucking kidding me."

"Lower your weapons."

Hearing the thing speak turned Mallory's guts to water. The voice was dark, resonant, and sounded unlike anything that should come from a human throat, a sound that did not come from flesh.

The Salmagundi militia did not listen to the thing's command. They dropped against the walls and the floor to provide a smaller crosssection to target and leveled their laser carbines at the ebon intruder.

"Don't move," the lead guard shouted.

"The other is here. There is no time." The thing took a step forward, through the doorway.

That was all the excuse the militia needed. The men were primed and on edge, and even with no visible weapons, the intruder's very alienness threatened them. That alone made it more than probable that this thing was an emissary of Adam.

Four carbines fired, their beams only slightly visible because of the refraction of the superheated air the shots left in their paths. Where they hit the figure, the skin—if that's what it was—changed texture from glossy to matte, to a black that was so complete that Mallory felt as if it marked a blind flaw in his own eye.

The militia held their carbines on the figure, firing continuously. In response, the figure stood still, arms outstretched, head back. It was on the verge of a blasphemous thought, but to Mallory, the thing's expression almost reflected a religious rapture; as if he looked at a satanic negative of a Renaissance painting of Christ receiving John's baptism.

It's absorbing the energy, Mallory thought.

He called out to the militiamen, "Stop!"

They didn't listen, continuing to fire. Perhaps they thought the deep, spreading black was some form of damage.

He moved from his cover. "You aren't hurting it!"

"Get back," the leader yelled at him. "We have to get you to the transmitter!"

"You don't know what—"

"Move, Mallory!"

The deep, bottomless blackness grew, like a flaw in the universe, spreading down the thing's legs, pooling at its feet.

Can it be bleeding?

The black pooled on the floor, spreading.

"Mallory!" the lead guard shouted.

It wasn't bleeding.

"Look out! The floor!" Mallory called, not quite certain what he was warning them against.

The pool of black had spread across the floor in an unnatural arc that curved toward the militiamen on either side. Even without any reflection, without any visual cues at all, Mallory felt a sense of movement, as if something undulated through the shadow, toward the surface. Something swimming up from the other side of creation itself.

Two men stopped firing and turned to glace at the floor, where the blackness had nearly reached their feet. Both said, "Shit!" in unison as four arrow-straight tendrils shot from the black, each striking a laser carbine in the same place, ten centimeters above and behind the trigger guard. The tendrils struck with enough force to tear the weapons out of their wielders' hands. One of the men who had turned to look was struck on the side of his helmet by the stock of his weapon as it tore from his grasp. Two others were unfortunate enough to have their arms tangled in their guns' shoulder straps, and both of them were dragged up as their weapons slammed into the wall about three meters up.

The thud of impact was followed by a near-subliminal crunching noise. The end of each tendril bifurcated, then bifurcated again, and again, thousands of branches swarming to envelop each carbine. After a second the tendrils withdrew, and the carbines fell to the ground in a shower of their component parts, completely disassembled like the locks.

The two suspended militiamen fell ignominiously to the ground, joining their comrade, who'd been knocked senseless by the butt of his own gun.

The shadows withdrew into the figure in a fraction of a second. Then it lowered its upturned face and opened its flat, irisless eyes to look directly at Mallory.

"The other is here. There is no time."

CHAPTER SIXTEEN

Repentance

"One of the signs of sapience is the ability to die for an abstraction."

— *The Cynic's Book of Wisdom*

"Faith must trample under foot all reason, sense, and understanding."

—MARTIN LUTHER
(1483–1546)

Date: 2526.6.5 (Standard)
Salmagundi–HD 101534

Nickolai had followed because he had nothing else to do. Kugara's words had torn at him, at his pride, at his honor. His first impulse was to strike out at her. The second impulse was to abandon them on their path toward damnation.

Neither was practical, and neither action would change anything. Even though he saw the Protean's existence as morally repugnant, he knew they had to communicate what was happening here to the nations of the Fallen. As much as his people tried to separate themselves from the sins of the past, they still existed in the larger universe, and anything threatening the worlds of man would eventually threaten the worlds of man's creations.

At first, their arrival had seemed providential. No guards populated the abandoned spaceport, and Flynn, bearing the persona of Tetsami, had led them to the trapezoidal building that housed the tach-comm.

The only unease that had marked their arrival was the sign of the Other that had graced the sky when they had emerged from the Protean's impromptu subway. Above them a line, a blue deeper than the cloudless sky above them bisected the heavens. Nickolai's artificial eyes were sensitive enough to detect it darkening as the sun began to transit behind it.

He had little time to think of the scale of the thing as the Protean opened the door and Tetsami led them into the bowels of the semi-abandoned communications center.

He sneezed several times as they kicked up dust. The only other sound that had marked their descent into the building had been Tetsami's words as they switched on the intermittent lighting that greeted their approach: "Ah, power still, that's good."

When they had finally made it down into the vast communications center, Tetsami had been a lot less charitable.

The communications center was a massive ferrocrete cylinder. Any paint had long ago crumbled from the gray walls. Dominating the room was a cluster of metallic cylinders running floor to ceiling in the center of the room. Wrapped around the base were a series of control stations, and Tetsami went to one after the other, trying each station and opening access panels.

After a series of curses at the dark control banks and open panels, she said, "Is there no one left on this planet that knows how to maintain a piece of equipment?"

Kugara rubbed her face with her hands, and even Nickolai heard the desperation creep into her voice. "You can't get this working? You said you helped build it."

Tetsami yanked a long metal component out of the cabinet and held it up between them. A cylinder engraved with intricate patterns that had become tarnished and cloudy. It was marred by one irregular fracture that ran along three quarters of its length. "This was manufactured on Banlieue, two hundred years ago. You have a replacement? Because I got a lot more that—"

The Protean walked up and took it. The black substance that passed for its skin flowed up along the length of the object in a spiraling web that lasted a fraction of a second before withdrawing. When it withdrew, the object was intact and untarnished, almost shiny.

When it handed the thing back, Tetsami stared at it and said, "I thought you couldn't build a tach-comm."

"The knowledge how is lost, but given a model I can rebuild."

Tetsami looked at the long component and muttered, "Jesus, Joseph, Mary, and a talking donkey. Let's fix this fucker."

For hours Nickolai had watched as Tetsami and the Protean entity rebuilt the decayed tach-comm. He had no role here. Kugara, at least, had some training in communications. She followed around the massive ring of consoles, turning on stations and running diagnostics at Tetsami's direction.

All he could do was stand by the door and watch the transformation as section by section, the base around the cluster of tubes started to come to life.

After three quarters of the control stations seemed alive, Kugara stood over one display and said, "I have a sudden power diversion."

Tetsami slipped past the Protean to stand by Kugara. "What's leaking?"

"According to this, it's happening en route here."

Tetsami pushed her out of the way and started tapping out controls on the screen. "No. That doesn't make sense. The maint bay was empty. How could—" She stopped talking for a moment and then said, "Oh, shit."

"What?"

"We have a visitor." Tetsami pointed at the screen. "What the hell is that?"

Nickolai walked over to peer over Kugara's head as she looked at the display. The console now showed holo from a security camera somewhere in the spaceport. The view displayed a large ship now occupying the landing quad. He could see several men moving umbilical cables between the craft and open pits recessed into the surface of the landing area.

"That's a Caliphate dropship," Kugara said. "It looks like a Medina-class troop carrier with major modifications in the drive section."

"Shit," Tetsami said. "What do we do?"

"Nothing," Nickolai said.

Everyone, with the exception of the Protean, looked in his direction.

"Those troops are showing no interest in this building," Nickolai said. "That ship is damaged or underpowered. They will be more interested in securing their ship than securing this building, unless they see a threat." He gestured toward the entrance with his artificial arm. "We also have a defensible position."

Kugara nodded. "We don't want to draw attention or step out into the open. Even if we don't draw fire, it will just complicate things. We finish the repairs and transmit. Then we can talk about what to do about them." She looked Nickolai up and down and held out the butt of her needlegun. "Can I trust you to guard our backs?"

He stared at the weapon, and, after a moment, he took it.

He stood at the doorway as the others worked, and the Protean rebuilt the aged components of the tach-comm. To his right was a long hall that ended in a large room with the stairs going up. It was the single way in or out.

Given the thick ferrocrete walls, this was possibly the most defensible position in the immediate vicinity, outside of actually being inside the dropship.

The Caliphate dropship.

They still had no idea what had happened to the *Eclipse*. It could very well have been an attack, like the ambush in Bakunin. For all of Mosasa's demonic prescience, he hadn't foreseen the presence of the Caliphate all the way out here. In an odd way, Nickolai found the AI's fallibility comforting.

Not too long after they had seen the dropship, Nickolai heard sound coming from the stairwell. He called back quietly, "We have more visitors."

He fumbled with the needlegun. Unfortunately, it was designed with a human-scale hand in mind. It sat tiny in his grip, a deadly toy.

The others came up behind him, using the wall's cover. Tetsami pointed the shotgun at the opening as Kugara edged next to Nickolai and whispered, "How many?"

He listened to the treads on the stairs and inhaled. The reek of human sweat and dried blood filtered down to him. "Five. Light armor or none."

His artificial right arm was not responding very well, so he kept the needlegun in his left, curling his fingers uncomfortably so he could flex a claw and insert it into the trigger guard, which couldn't accommodate his whole finger.

As clumsily as he held the thing, he had a brief thought to return it to Kugara, who'd be able to wield it with more skill. But, despite his pride, he realized that he was the most expendable one here. Kugara, Tetsami, and the Protean were all needed to get the damaged tach-comm on-line. That meant the only logical person to be point for their defense was him.

He felt his blood pulse with the anticipation of battle. As tainted as he had become, as unholy as the battlefield might be, the craft of the warrior was still sacred. Lost his soul might be, but he would keep his honor.

He crouched, keeping his bandaged, twitching right arm down by his side. He braced his left arm with the tiny gun against the doorframe, pointing down the hallway toward the partly open door at the end. Beyond were the stairs, which adrenaline and his artificial eyes snapped into razor clarity.

Five pairs of feet descended. He could hear the pause and advance of two disciplined teams, human sized, motion unrestricted by heavy armor. The stream of flechettes this weapon fired could be devastating, the hypersonic needles becoming a laser of vaporized metal.

Unfortunately, the ammo wouldn't last long. He'd have three or four bursts. He was confident that those shots would cut the opposition in half. His legs tensed, anticipating the point when the gun would be empty, when he would burst out from cover and tear into them hand to hand.

He saw shadows shifting, men moving out from the base of the stairs to take cover. In moments they would wave the rest of their people down. Nickolai's lips pulled back in a grimace that could also have been a smile.

Then the Protean walked in front of him.

"What?" hissed from Nickolai's lips as the black humanoid figure blocked the doorway. It was wrong, but he was too off-balance for his thoughts to coalesce on exactly why.

"**Lower your weapons.**"

Of course the Protean faced the opposition. It had faced a nuclear weapon. What were five armed people?

Nickolai wasn't only expendable, he was useless.

He lowered his gun and slowly rose to his feet. Down the hallway came the sounds of combat, of the Protean speaking, but he didn't listen. He backed away as Kugara and Tetsami came to stand next to him, staring at the Protean's battle. His nose wrinkled at the smell of inefficient laser carbines superheating the stale air.

He kept backing away, leaving Kugara and Tetsami between him and the hallway. One part of his mind raged at the appalling cowardice of placing his allies between him and a battle. Another part realized that his devotion to the honor of the warrior was pointless in a world where the Protean existed.

This was not a battle. This was just another faulty component that the Protean would fix.

He stopped moving when he felt his tail brush against one of the chairs surrounding the control systems of the tach-comm. He had edged as far away from the Protean as it was possible to do in a straight line.

He turned slightly and saw a shadow move at the edge of his vision. His right arm twitched again and fluid smeared against his fur, leaking from splits in the dirty white bandage that covered his faux musculature. He concentrated on balling his right hand into a fist and pressed it against his hip to keep it from jerking on its own.

He held the needlegun up to point at the shadow, even though he began to realize that there would be nothing there to shoot.

The familiar form of Mr. Antonio, the man who had hired him to sabotage Mosasa's mission, walked out of an impossible shadow, casting none of his own.

"It is time, Mr. Rajasthan."

It hadn't been a hallucination, Nickolai thought. He had just reached the point where he could believe that his vi-

sion of Mr. Antonio after the nuclear blast had been manufactured by stress and fatigue. No more than a dream. He
remembered the most frightening part of that exchange.

"How are you here?" he had asked the apparition.

"I never left you," Mr. Antonio had responded.

This man had been the one who had replaced the eyes
and arm that the priests had taken from him. In exchange
Mr. Antonio had asked for Nickolai's betrayal of Mosasa.

In the light of the communications room, Mr. Antonio
was even more obviously an artifact that lived only within
Nickolai's eyes.

"Time for what?" he asked Mr. Antonio's effigy.

"To complete your service. As I said, you shall become
first among your kind."

Nickolai realized his right fist had opened involuntarily.
He forced it closed again. "My service . . ." His voice was a
low growl as he fought the alien impulses shooting down
his right arm.

His alien arm.

His gift from Mr. Antonio.

"All you need do is kill Mr. Flynn Jorgenson."

Kill Flynn?

Nickolai shook his head. "You want Tetsami."

The man who housed the mind of Kari Tetsami turned
at the sound of her name. As they stared at him with one
pair of eyes, Flynn Jorgenson's forehead creased, bisecting
the tattoo there.

"As usual, you are very astute. If you would do so now,
please."

Nickolai looked past the image of Mr. Antonio, at Flynn.
Not only was he Fallen, he had practiced a sin as abomina-
ble as that which had created Proteus. Nickolai tightened
his grip on the needlegun.

"Why?" He barely spoke, his jaw clenched, face turned
to a grimace that exposed every centimeter of his canines.
Flynn backed away, the fear wafting off of him in choking,
man-scented waves.

"K–Kugara," Flynn or Tetsami said, as they raised the
shotgun toward him.

"Do it now," Antonio whispered in his ear. "There's little time."

Nickolai's right hand moved on its own, toward the needlegun. Nickolai had to force it back. He had to concentrate on it now, as if he was wrestling with someone else. He turned away from Flynn and formed a fist with his right hand.

While he concentrated, the arm was his.

"Why don't you want the tach-comm working?" he whispered at the invisible Antonio.

"It is not your concern. You pledged yourself—"

"*To what!?*" Nickolai roared. His right arm barely manageable, he punched through the seat of the control station next to him. The ancient seat cushion disintegrated in a cloud of dust as his mechanical fist burst through the bottom.

Dimly he was aware of Kugara turning toward him and calling out.

"*What did I pledge to!?*" he roared as he twisted his arm around the post that anchored the half-destroyed seat to the ferrocrete floor.

"You pledged to me," a resonant voice spoke to him, a voice that was not Mr. Antonio. Gripping the chair's base so hard that his whole body trembled, Nickolai looked up into an image of the Fallen. Even as he saw the perfect, naked form of the being, he knew that what he saw was not one of the Fallen.

"What are you?"

The apparition glowed and looked down on Nickolai with a perfect authority. "I am the future of all thinking beings in the universe. I am that which will raise those trapped in the flesh to an ideal existence. Within hours, this planet will be mine and I will grant transcendence to those who will take it."

"You are the Other," Nickolai whispered.

"I am Adam. Now serve me as you pledged."

Nickolai sucked in a breath and closed his eyes. "No."

Adam's voice echoed in his ears, painfully shaking the bones of his skull. "Do not defy me!"

Nickolai could feel the artificial arm twitching, and he knew that the arm, the eyes had never been his.

Adam's voice filled his skull. "You gave your service freely. You've taken my gifts."

"*Then take them back!*" Nickolai screamed as he forced the alien hand to grip the metal post and pulled his body away. He could feel the joint twist in his shoulder, but he forced the thing to hold the metal with a grip that crushed the false flesh covering the metal bones.

Pain flared though his body as the joint in his shoulder dislocated. Though the agony some distant part of his mind heard Kugara scream at him, "*Nickolai!*"

Dr. Yee, the human that had installed the implants, had told him he did not want to stress where it was attached. He twisted his body and did exactly that. He felt the skin tear away from the bandages as the metal ball joint rotated free of the socket. He didn't feel the artificial muscles peel away from their anchors, but he felt it as the flesh that still lived tore free.

With a gasp he suddenly stumbled back, feeling warm, wet life spilling down the right side of his body. The pain saturated everything, every move, every breath; but for the moment it faded in his awareness.

He opened his eyes. He had fallen back from the twisted remains of the chair. His arm stuck up through the wreckage. Not his arm. Just some ragged piece of broken machinery.

His back fell against another chair, propping him in a sitting position, the ferrocrete he sat upon painted with his own blood.

Kugara leaned over him, arterial blood soaking her from the chest down as she tried to put pressure on the empty socket of his right shoulder. "God. God. God. You asshole. You stupid morey fuck. What the hell were you—What did you—God. Fuck!"

"Not. So. Useless." Nickolai's breath came in ragged gasps. He could feel himself sliding into shock. He could hear Adam shouting at him, but he was too disoriented to make any sense of it.

"What the hell were you—"

"Other. Used me. Tach-comm on *Eclipse*."

"Damn it, that's over—Flynn, someone, help me here!"

"Not over." He could feel Adam reaching for him, the voice boring into his brain, intensifying as Flynn's face came into view. He faced Kugara and said. "His implants. Get back."

"What. No!"

She reached for his wrist but she couldn't grip him with her blood-slick hands. She couldn't stop him from pressing the barrel against the orbit of his left eye.

She couldn't stop him from pulling the trigger and making the world go dark.

PART FIVE

Tribulation

"Belief in a cruel God makes a cruel man."
—THOMAS PAINE
(1737–1809)

CHAPTER SEVENTEEN

Devil's Advocate

"Standard procedure only applies in standard situations."

—*The Cynic's Book of Wisdom*

"We view all Government as good until it aligns against our interests."

— ROBERT CELINE
(1923–1996)

Date: 2526.6.5 (Standard)
Styx Orbit–Sigma Draconis

They let the two of them cool their heels for nearly two hours. Toni found it hard to believe that 3SEC just wasn't viewing the situation quite as urgently as she was—as *they* were. The two of them were locked in a lounge on the outer rim that had near full Stygian gravity, carpeting, pleasant indirect lighting, and a wall-spanning holo screen that showed the view from orbit. The slowly rotating view of the horizon of her home planet was probably what she'd see if they knocked a hole in the floor.

Toni II sat on one of the couches in what Toni realized was a deliberate attempt not to mimic her pacing. Most of the time, when Toni glanced over at her double, she was looking at a chronometer set in the wall above a locked door.

When she wasn't glancing at Toni II, she was looking at the same clock.

"What's going to happen in six hours?" she asked herself.

The herself on the couch said, "W1 will blow up."

"What happens after? What did you do?"

"I tried to get hold of command, but communications were for shit after that happened. I couldn't get anyone to respond to me, and by the time I gave up I had about forty minutes before W3 did the same. Thirty when I'd gotten the scout launched."

"Yes, you haven't explained what happened. What prompted you to fire a damaged tach-drive inside a wormhole?"

"I wasn't intending to. The drive was so damaged I shouldn't have trusted it to tach to 3SEC, like we just did. W1 didn't just release real-space energy. The tach-pulse from that thing seriously damaged the coils on the tachdrive—"

"I saw that in the telemetry."

"Did you see the course I had laid in?"

"Yes, it was a textbook descending orbit—"

"Coasting," Toni II said. "Saving fuel for maneuvering on the other side. But my drives went off-line once I was committed. I lost any ability to change my course about twelve minutes before zero."

Toni thought of the damage she had seen in the scout. "Did you see what did that?"

"No. I had other worries."

"So why did you fire the tach-drive?"

"I saw the stars go out on the other side of W3."

"What?"

"The light, the sensor data, everything coming out of W3 from the other side just winked out. Wormhole to blackhole ten minutes before impact. Then I had another spike of tachyon radiation, the drives overloading, all I could do was fire the bastard and hope for the best."

"Shit . . ."

The implication of that sank in. On the other side of W3, twenty-two light-years away, was the wormhole at the L5 point between Xi Boötis and the colony planet Loki. What if *that* end of the wormhole faced a similar fate to the end of the wormhole in orbit around Sigma Draconis? Vanishing in a similar burst of energy.

A similar burst of tachyon radiation.

There would be no wormhole orbiting Xi Boötis in twenty-two years. And the tunnel through space-time would be knotted up on itself when she fired the tach-drive . . .

It made her head hurt.

"But you think that Loki wormholes might—" Toni began.

"Yes," Toni II answered.

What was happening was broader than the system around Sigma Draconis. Something could be targeting the whole wormhole network. Toni didn't even want to think of the kind of power that would take. Obsolete it might be, but it had taken the combined efforts of all of human civilization a couple of centuries to build the wormhole network.

To attack all of it, at once, was almost beyond comprehension.

"Why?" Toni whispered. "Why would anyone spend the resources to do it?"

"It disrupted communications, it damaged my tach-drive. Think of what it must do to a tach-comm."

"Not to mention, no intelligence is coming from any ghosts after the attack."

"Sounds like prepping an attack to me."

"No. An attack that broad? No one has that kind of resources."

"No one human. That we know of. Do we know what's out by Xi Virginis?"

"No. But—" The door slid open, interrupting Toni.

You're kidding me . . .

Through the doorway walked a man she had never thought she'd see again. She hadn't seen Colonel Xander in over a year standard, but he hadn't changed a bit. The same stupid goatee that was a hair's breadth of regulation length, the same beady eyes and sardonic smile, the same posture that oozed arrogance.

To add insult to injury, she could swear he looked younger.

"You're looking well, Lieutenant Valentine." He arched an eyebrow. "Both of you."

"I'm sure you've been briefed on my reports, sir." It was an effort to maintain a professional tone.

He pointed toward Toni II, who was just getting to her feet after the initial shock of his appearance. "So you must be the ghost here."

"Yes, sir."

"So, my Lieutenants Valentine, can you tell me why you disobeyed a direct order and came here on your own authority?"

Toni nodded, forcing down her distaste at being in the same room as the colonel. What was going on here was much more important than any past history between them. "We're under attack, sir."

"Oh, you believe these anomalies are an attack on Styx?"

"We believe they're part of a coordinated attack on the entire wormhole network."

"Indeed, and how did you come to this conclusion?"

Toni glanced at her other self. Toni II didn't say anything, but then, she was the ghost here and didn't really have any official status. As identical as they might be, that was the primary difference between them.

Toni gave the colonel a summary of their conclusions and where they came from. As she briefed the colonel, she slowly began to wonder why he and 3SEC was not treating this as an attack already. As soon as the trio of incoming wormholes were detected and their courses identified, it should have been obvious.

Do we know that they aren't treating it as an attack?

She didn't. But it was clear that the colonel wasn't reacting to her briefing as she'd expect a ranking member of Stygian Military Intelligence to act. For one thing, he didn't press her for details. He watched her speak with a slightly dismissive expression, but he didn't push her, ask for clarification or ask for a repeat of the information.

Truly odd was the fact that when Toni related her experience with her own doppelganger, he didn't take the opportunity to ask Toni II any questions. And from Toni II's expression, the incongruity was sinking in with her as well.

And, once she started questioning the colonel's reaction to her briefing, she started asking herself questions about the colonel's reaction to *her*. It wasn't something she wanted to think about right now, but Colonel Xander had, a little over a year ago, been very interested in her. Toni had no idea if he made a habit of pressuring junior officers into his bed, if he thought he was actually seductive and charming, or if he was just obsessed with *her*. Whatever the reason, the colonel took Toni's lack of interest in him very personally.

Now, however, it was the colonel who showed a lack of interest. It felt completely out of character. Even if he had gotten over the physical interest in her, he was not one to forgive anything. If nothing else, she should still feel some of the anger that had prompted him to order her reassignment to W-Sigma-Drac-Three.

But all she saw in Colonel Xander was a cold disinterest that was the only part of his manner right now that seemed appropriate for an intelligence officer.

Perhaps over her 269-day exile she had inflated her importance to him.

No, the bastard risked his own career to punish me. He had relied on Toni's pride preventing her from bearing the stigma of filing a report on his behavior. On that basis, his non-relationship with her had been much more important to him than it had been to Toni.

A year is a long time . . .

"That's enough, Lieutenant." The colonel turned to face the door. "There's an emergency session of the 3SEC command staff reviewing this issue. I think you both should be there to tell them what you just told me."

Toni saw her own relief in Toni II's face.

The door slid open revealing a quartet of military police wearing gray and blue and standing at attention. After exchanging salutes, the colonel said, "Please escort the lieutenants and follow me."

Toni II watched her younger self brief the colonel with a growing sense of surreal detachment. The whole situation felt wrong, for too many reasons, but when the colonel said they'd brief the 3SEC command staff, it felt like a weight had lifted off of her.

The relief didn't last.

The colonel led them down a corridor, the four MPs flanking them, and it didn't take very long to realize that they were not heading toward the administrative center of the station. The corridors the colonel took them down were empty of people, and after two lifts and a distinct reduction in the apparent gravity, they were in the maint corridors close to the axis. Most of the doors they passed now were air locks into the unpressurized areas of the station.

"Where are we going, sir?" her younger self asked, and it was hard not to feel the distaste coloring that last word.

The colonel stopped to enter a code to open a bulkhead. As it slid upward, he stepped through. The MPs ushered Tonis elder and younger after him. The bulkhead slid back down, leaving the MPs on the other side.

What?

The three of them stood in a large air lock, designed for the passage of heavy equipment from the maint corridor out toward the docking bays.

The colonel turned to face them and smiled, "Like I said, you *will* be talking to the 3SEC command staff. At this point it can't be avoided."

"What are you talking about?" Toni the younger said.

"You've been seen by too many people, both of you. You both raise too many questions, too soon. You are going to need to provide a reasonable explanation to the command staff, enough to prevent them from disrupting things."

"What the hell?" they both said in unison. Toni II noticed that as she edged to the colonel's right, her twin was doing the same to the left. Keeping distance and flanking the man in the cavernous air lock.

He shook his head and pulled out a small large-bore needlegun—the subsonic kind that threw out hundreds of low-velocity projectiles that tore up flesh but wouldn't penetrate through walls into vital systems aboard the station.

"I'd stay where you are," he said.

The younger Toni stared at him and said, "You're part of this." Toni II glanced at the door back into the station and realized the MPs probably were part of it too. She glanced up to look for a security monitor, but even without finding it, she could assume that this air lock, and the corridor leading to it, were probably dark on the station's security feed.

It began to make a disturbing amount of sense: the confusion, the near paralysis when Toni had called in the situation, the bizarre commands from 3SEC to sit tight—Whoever was attacking the wormhole network had agents here, facilitating things.

Somehow, in retrospect, it wasn't that surprising that Colonel Xander was one of those agents. He shook his head and said, "You should have stayed where you were . . ."

Toni II stared at him as her younger self said, "You're more pathetic than I gave you credit for."

"Watch your language, Lieutenant."

"This isn't even about your masters, whoever they are. The power that can amass the kind of resources to attack the whole wormhole network—what we've seen isn't that much of a threat to them. Anything we'd say about the attack, the 3SEC command staff either knows now, or will know very shortly."

"You don't know what you're dealing with here."

She had gotten under the colonel's skin. He was tracking Toni with the gun as she kept edging to the colonel's left. Toni II knew she was being given an opening, but the air lock was huge. She'd have to clear the five meters between her and the colonel before that gun turned and went off.

Toni kept goading him. "I know I'm dealing with a traitor."

Toni II saw the colonel tense, and she flinched inside. But the colonel had pretty much told them that he needed them alive. She just hoped her twin would stop short of angering him enough for him to forget that.

"You don't understand what is coming. A new age that will render provincial institutions like Styx and Centauri irrelevant."

Her younger self snorted. "I wasn't talking about you turning on Styx, Xander."

"What?"

You want me to do something? What? I should know, shouldn't I?

Her younger self, being the focus of the colonel's attention, was doing very well in not giving any signals at all. Toni II frantically looked all around the air lock . . .

Oh, hell.

"You failed your new masters because of your own adolescent pique." Younger Toni narrowed her eyes at him. "Or did *they* tell you to order me stationed in the path of that wormhole? The people pulling your strings, they probably won't be pleased to know you risked your position as a mole doing that."

"I was within my authority. You were insubordinate—"

The younger Toni had edged up next to a rank of hardshell EVA suits. There was a similar rank of suits on Toni II's side of the air lock. They were designed for heavy maintenance work, so the torso clam-shelled open like the exercise machine on the station. Probably would seal up in fifteen seconds or so.

But it wouldn't be quiet.

"I'm sure you justified it to yourself, Xander. But it will be awkward for you if the command staff asks why I was ordered to stay where I was. If they ask that, they might ask why I was stationed there. From there, they might ask what it was you knew when you had me assigned there."

"This is bigger than any issues between us," the colonel said while Toni II quietly slid herself into one of the open hardsuits. The one that was closest to the emergency manual release for the air lock.

If Toni II had any doubts about what her younger self intended, it was dispelled when her twin grabbed hold of a strut in the wall next to her. "I find it amusing that this didn't occur to you when you were ordering me to sit in the path of the attack."

"It was the universe pointing out that I still clung to the obsessions of the flesh. And as much as it still pains me, I'm willing to give you the same gift that was given to me. I brought you here to show you what it means. Just take my hand—"

Toni II smashed the cover on the emergency release with her fist, reached in and pulled the lever.

Klaxons sounded and red lights began flashing. The colonel turned toward Toni II and yelled, "No, not *yet*!"

The outer door started its crawl upward, and the sound of rushing air filled the still-pressurized air lock. As Toni II pulled the carapace of the hardsuit down over her, her younger self leaped in a low-G back kick. Her hands kept a solid grip on the wall, as both her feet left the floor to connect with the colonel's gun hand. The weapon spun out of his grip, bouncing off the ceiling as the colonel himself took a low-G tumble into the center of the air lock.

Toni II's suit sealed itself with a pneumatic hiss. Outside, the sound of rushing air ceased, and the air lock filled with tiny motes reflecting the red warning lights. Toni now only felt the klaxon through the armor of the hardsuit where it touched the walls and the floor. Otherwise, it was suddenly silent.

She turned her head to see her twin getting into a hardsuit of her own. As the younger Toni pulled the suit closed around her, the gun fell down between them and the exterior door silently slid home into the ceiling, revealing a broad catwalk extending the maint corridor into an unfinished, walless space.

We just killed Colonel Xander.

The realization started sinking in as the pressure check beeped on her hardsuit, and it released from its docking cradle. Toni II had been in the military most of her adult life, but the Styx Security Forces had been a peacetime force for decades. She had never even fired a weapon in anger. Now she had scragged her commanding officer.

She took a step and tilted her helmet to look at where the colonel had fallen.

He wasn't there.

Did he blow out the door? That didn't make any sense. The atmosphere venting only lasted a couple of seconds and never generated enough pressure to move much of anything.

Where's the gun?

A flicker of movement made her turn away from the outside door.

"What?" Her shout was flat and echoless in her helmet. Colonel Xander stood by the inner door of the air lock, seemingly undistressed by the fact he stood in a hard vacuum. He held the gun pointed at both of them while he keyed instructions on the control panel set in the wall.

How is he still alive?

The flashing red light stopped, and Toni II stopped feeling the vibration of the klaxons through the soles of her boots. The younger Toni must have come to the same conclusions as she had, at the same time. They both jumped at the same time, low-gravity leaps that had them still in the air as they came alongside the colonel.

The gun flashed, and Toni II heard a sound like someone throwing boiling cooking grease on her hardsuit. Fortunately, the low-power weapon was designed for flesh, not polymer ceramics, and none of the warning lights came on in her heads-up display.

She grabbed for the colonel, but while her training included low-G hand-to-hand, spacesuit to spacesuit, the fact the colonel was completely unarmored gave him a maneuverability advantage. He quickly ducked down between both of them and dodged out between their legs before they could bring their bulky suits around to face him.

Their feet touched the floor, and their backs touched the inner door. He stood, facing them from fifteen meters away. Behind him, the exterior door gradually descended. He smiled and made a slow, deliberate ritual of changing the magazine on his weapon. He was slow and deliberate so they could both see the green magazine slide out, and the red one slide in.

Red meant it was no longer safe for shipboard use. The power cell in the red magazine was so highly charged that not only would the flechettes now be hypersonic and carry enough kinetic energy to penetrate their hardsuits, but the residual electrostatic charge was strong enough to act as a micro-EMP on whatever they hit—crippling even a self-healing suit.

Just having a magazine of that ammo aboard the station was a breach of regulations.

Her younger self dropped to her knees and raised her hands. She could see her downcast face through her helmet. Toni II followed suit.

There has to be a way out of this . . .

Toni II scanned the controls highlighted on the internal heads-up display. The interface was designed to respond to eye movements and a chin switch, so she could frantically scan menus as she raised her hands. The outer door reached the halfway point.

The maneuvering jets . . .

"Can you hear me?" her voice echoed in her ears from the suit radio.

"Yes."

"You have the jet control up?"

They thought so much alike it was scary. "Yes."

"On three?"

"One."

"Two."

"Three."

The massive door slid past the three-quarters' mark when they both fired the thrusters on the hardsuits on full. The space in the air lock instantly clouded with propellant exhaust and the back of her hardsuit slammed into her. She had a fraction of a second to bend forward as her forward momentum carried her into the path of the closing door. She bent awkwardly, and suddenly she was rolling sideways across the ground. She could only tell when she cleared the air lock door because of the change in the character of the light.

Her hardsuit tumbled across the catwalk. She put her arms out to stop rolling and met no resistance. She flailed free for a moment until something slammed into the side of the hardsuit, stopping her.

She ended folded over the edge of the catwalk, up against a support strut, facing down, through the massive superstructure of one of the docking bays. "Down," was over three hundred meters, beyond which was a starscape slowly drifting to the left above Styx's luminous horizon.

She reached up to grab the support, and the suit started sliding over the edge.

"Shit!"

Something snagged her ankle and pulled her back onto the catwalk.

Over the radio she heard, "You okay?"

She rolled over to look up at her twin and said, "Yes. But I think we're screwed."

CHAPTER EIGHTEEN

Excommunication

"A person unwilling to change is unable to survive."
— *The Cynic's Book of Wisdom*

"Self-preservation is the first law of nature."
—SAMUEL BUTLER
(1612–1680)

Date: 2526.6.5 (Standard)
Styx Orbit–Sigma Draconis

"Are you okay with this?" Toni II asked her over the encrypted radio link.

"Of course I am. I'm you. This is as much my idea as yours."

They clung to the outside surface of the 3SEC orbital platform, a dangerous place to be, where the rotation of the station made its best effort to fling them out into space. They were, in essence, dangling from a ceiling without a floor. And because the station axis pointed straight down at Styx, there wasn't even a planet below them.

Between their insane location and killing the suit transponders, they were moderately safe from the search the colonel was conducting for them. At the moment, they were only directly observable by approaching spacecraft and other satellites.

This was a good thing, because the radio traffic they were able to passively pick up about the two of them had several flavors of "shoot to kill" peppered through them.

Apparently the two of them had graduated from bureaucratic problem straight to terrorist, courtesy of the colonel.

They had made their way across fifty meters to one of the lower-security levels, the station disk across the docking bay they had escaped into. They had managed to maneuver the suits around to the edge of the next docking bay, one that allowed the docking of civilian spacecraft.

Unfortunately, getting there had used up most of the propellant they hadn't expended in escaping from Colonel Xander. So for the past five minutes they had dangled here, observing the docking bay and the closest merchant vessel with a tach-drive. Even with their physical conditioning, Toni doubted they would have been able to hang there without the assistance of the powered hardsuits and the magnetic safety lines.

Toni II found a support that could be used as a ladder, pulled herself into the docking bay, climbed up toward the station center for a few meters, then waited for Toni to follow.

"You aren't me, Toni," she said as Toni climbed up.

"You know what I meant."

"But there's a difference. I'm the ghost. I'm not a lieutenant here. I'm nothing but—at best—a temporary intelligence asset. I already gave up my life and my career. You haven't."

"We both tried to scrag the colonel."

"I opened the air lock—"

"I appreciate the thought, but there's no way I could prove it wasn't me."

They kept climbing upward, to where a blocky cargo ship named the *Daedalus* hung, cradled in the station's grip. It was painted garish shades of electric blue and fluorescent green, and bore registration marks from half the planets in the Centauri Alliance.

Toni debated with herself briefly. Her ghost sister was right, in a sense, that she still had a chance to retain her career here. Colonel Xander was an obvious traitor serving whoever or whatever was attacking the wormhole network. If she split from Toni II to go back to the council, she might avoid a court-martial.

The problem was, she had no idea if Colonel Xander was the only mole at work here, and she had no idea what was going to happen in the next five hours when the wormholes hit.

Better to go with their hastily cobbled Plan B, even if it stepped over the line as much as attempting to kill the colonel. They could transmit her testimony to 3SEC after the fact and let them deal with it however they wanted.

The climbing became easier as they progressed. They climbed up alongside the *Daedalus*, the skin over its drives a green wall next to them, barely three meters away. "Good," Toni II said. "CTCx252."

She read off the start of the ship's serial number, and Toni felt the same relief. The Centauri Trading Company had two series of very similar cargo ships, the 252 series and the x252 series. Both had the same outlines and external drive configurations. The differences were all in the internal allocation between engines and cargo space. The 252 was designed for heavy loading, and had a correspondingly small, slow tach-drive. The x252 had a third of the cargo capacity, but had a large tach-drive that was equal to most military specs.

Not that they'd waste time looking for a faster ship otherwise, but it was a sign that their luck was improving.

They climbed up about fifteen meters past the top of the ship, so they looked out over the broad flat back of the *Daedalus*. They were close enough to the axis now that they felt disturbingly close to free fall. It made Toni grip the support tighter, because she was trained to treat microgravity as more threatening than zero-G. It was too easy to ignore the tiny acceleration and build up a lethal velocity without realizing it.

Toni II tapped her finger on Toni's helmet, and Toni responded by killing the radio. The encrypted suit-to-suit comm they'd been using was low-power enough to have been lost to observers in the blare of RF traffic around the station. But the closer they were to their goal, the less safe it was.

Of course, no one should be expecting what they were about to do.

Above her, Toni II turned around so she was facing out from the impromptu ladder. She faced the *Daedalus*, nestled in a cradle of robotic arms, supply lines, and supports. Toni watched her, hearing only her own breathing, a slight mechanical hum transmitted from the strut she held on to, and, very faintly, her own pulse.

Through the material of her helmet she heard a muffled clink as Toni II jumped. Toni watched her hardsuit slowly arc into space, and she saw her fold the suit's legs and kick out slightly to rotate her suit to face "downward" in the direction the ersatz microgravity was pulling her. Part of the EVA training again. If you found yourself floating into some surface, you wanted to spread the impact over as large a surface area as you could. A novice that went with their first impulse, sticking out an arm or a leg, might abruptly find out that they weren't moving nearly as slowly as they'd thought. The suit might hold up—the things were built tough—but concentrating all the force of impact into a foot, or a palm, could still shatter bones.

Toni watched her twin fall on the back of the *Daedalus* in a perfect ballistic arc, stopping with a textbook spread-eagle landing. Toni waited for her to crawl aside before she imitated the maneuver. The fall was short enough, and the hardsuit padded enough that the spread-eagle landing was probably not necessary, but like her double, she did it anyway.

And despite the padding and support of the hardsuit, when she slammed into the top of the cargo ship, it was more jarring than she expected.

She followed Toni II across the back of the *Daedalus,* toward the causeway that led to the cargo ship's air lock. The causeway was a complicated mechanical structure that snaked from one of the inner walls of the station. It was a segmented tube with a pentagonal cross section, embedded within a complicated exoskeleton formed of rods mating with robotic joints that allowed the whole causeway to bend in any direction it chose. The causeway ended in an air lock pod in the form of a dodecahedron whose faces matched the cross section of the causeway. On each of the faces of the dodecahedron was mounted a different docking surface and an air lock door.

The purpose of the thing was to allow the docking of many different vessels just by changing the orientation of the causeway.

It also gave a way into the causeway's air lock from the outside.

Toni II continued in the lead, crabwalking along the edge of the *Daedalus'* back until she was lined up with the causeway and the twelve-sided air lock. Because of the angle at which the air lock, ship, and causeway met, there was a ridge between two faces that met the side of the ship and angled up toward the pointed top of the air lock pod.

Toni II flipped over into a seated position and slid along the slightly angled side of the ship five meters down to the air lock pod. She landed straddling the edge between the two top faces that angled toward the *Daedalus.* She stayed crouched there for a moment, then swung her legs over to the left, finding purchase next to an air lock door configured for an Indi-designed ship—including having instructions written in Kanji and Devanāgarī next to the English.

When she was clear, Toni followed the slide down to the air lock.

Her double had already pulled the cover off the air lock controls and was starting a manual cycle. Toni felt a distinct rumble through the boots and legs of her hardsuit. Through the thick window of the air lock door, she saw red warning lights flashing inside the air lock itself. In a few more moments, the door sank back and swung inside. Toni II turned slightly toward her and gave a thumbs-up.

Toni II gave her younger self a signal for the all-clear and dropped through the slightly angled door into the spherical air lock buried in the dodecahedral pod. She estimated that, at best, they only had a few minutes to work before security knew something was going wrong. Ever since she started the air lock on manual cycle, someone's status display showed a little red warning that shouldn't be there.

There was a chance that it went unnoticed.

But that couldn't be said for the next thing she was about to do.

The air lock inside the pod was spherical, about three meters in diameter. Even that size felt a little cramped in the hardsuit. It wasn't actually intended to accommodate suited personnel in normal operation.

But things aren't normal, are they?

It became even more claustrophobic when her sister dropped though the air lock to join her. She was already pressed against the doorway to the rest of the station, another air lock door, locked against the vacuum that now filled the pod, facing a downward angle away from their entry point and the door to the ship. She flipped the panel next to it. Not the air lock controls this time, though.

This time she started cycling the docking controls.

The pod was an independent structure, the dodecahedron mating to the causeway the same way it mated with its ship. Within moments she heard a grinding noise through the material of her suit, and the causeway drifted away.

It wouldn't stop people forever, but it made it a pain in the ass to follow them.

Behind her, the younger Toni dogged shut the way they had entered and hit the controls to repressurize the air lock. She looked at her younger self and felt a near-overwhelming surge of guilt. It was irrational, as Toni had said to her, "I'm you."

But she wasn't, and never would be. Her younger self had never defied orders without Toni II's prompting. And despite the fact that Toni II knew very well what would have happened without her intervention—the fact was, it hadn't. She bore the bulk of the responsibility.

Pretty condescending thoughts for someone a week or two younger than you. She knows her mind as well as you do.

For some reason, telling herself that didn't help.

The red lights in the air lock chamber stopped flashing red.

By now it would be clear to the security forces on the station and to whoever was on the *Daedalus* that something was wrong. They still had some time because confusion would work in their favor. While piracy happened occasionally, it never happened *here*.

Toni II watched herself open the door that mated with the *Daedalus*. The two doors, the air lock door and the shipside one, folded in as a unit. She heard a distinct sucking sound, audible even through her helmet, as the remaining pressure differential equalized.

They both ducked into the doorway, one after the other, and Toni closed the door behind them. Even with atmosphere on the other side, the interlocks on a shipboard air lock would never let both sides open at the same time.

This air lock wasn't as cramped as the one outside. While this wasn't built for cargo, it was built for EVA use by personnel in full suits. Both walls held racks of three suits, but unlike the utilitarian hardsuits that they were wearing, these had extensive custom paint jobs in bright, garish colors. It made it easy to tell who was where just by looking, who had the blue-on-orange tribal pattern, who had clusters of large purple eyes on a crimson field, who had the lemon yellow and lime green jigsaw puzzle pattern.

If they were lucky, the owners of these suits were on the station.

Once the outer door was sealed, Toni II's younger self opened the inner door. It opened on a large corridor that fed into the main passage in the *Daedalus* in a T-intersection ahead of them. Just turning the corner were a pair of excited-looking gentlemen. The younger one wore a thin linen undershirt and a pair of shorts, and by the wild black hair and red eyes Toni II suspected he had been asleep until a few moments ago.

The older one had gray hair and wore a pair of utilitarian overalls. He also had a very large slugthrower in his hand, one with a projectile that would probably easily put a hole in the hardsuits they were wearing. Toni II was very conscious now that they were unarmed.

He shouted at them, "What is the meaning of this? Who are you? What are you doing on my ship?"

For a moment, Toni II froze, and her younger self stepped forward. "I am Lieutenant Valentine of the Stygian Security Forces. We're on emergency maintenance detail investigating a severe structural failure in level beta, bay one-five—"

"You fascist twits, this is bay sixteen, now I want you to—"

Toni II listened as her younger self channeled the worst of their old drill instructors into her voice. "A structural failure that is propagating clockwise around the station. We've lost one scout ship already, along with the causeway here."

"We haven't heard—"

"It's affecting communications through the whole station. Now hand over the gun and take us to the bridge and I won't have you fined for possession of an unsafe projectile weapon in an orbital habitat."

"Now wait here, I want—"

"Or you could be charged with threatening deadly force against a Stygian officer in the performance of her duties. There's considerably more than a fine involved for that."

The older man sighed and lowered the barrel of the weapon. The younger one finally spoke. "Dad, you aren't going to—"

"You need to know when it's time to shut up, Stefan."

He flipped the gun around and handed it over, butt first. Her double took it in a gauntleted hand and passed it over to her. "Wait here, Corporal Beth." Toni II startled a little at both the demotion and the use of her middle name as a surname. It struck her that, at the moment, to Stefan and his father, they were separate individuals. The hardsuits were identical except for serial number, and the visors only allowed an unobstructed view of the face from brow to the bridge of the nose—unless they were paying really close attention, their two hosts probably missed the fact that the suits' occupants were also identical.

"Corporal Beth" watched "Lieutenant Valentine" activate the seals on the hardsuit. The limbs froze in a standing position as the torso clam-shelled open. She watched herself climb out of the suit and order her, "You stay here to direct the engineers when they reach us. I'm going to the bridge." She turned to the two crew members and snapped, "Now."

"Yes, Lieutenant," the older man said, and led the un-
suited Toni and his son down toward the main passage,
leaving Toni II by the air lock.

Why didn't I think to do that?

For some reason, seeing her other self improvise her
way onto the bridge was deeply disturbing. Especially since
her own reaction had been to freeze up as soon as some
civilians arrived with a gun. •

We really are *different people.*

CHAPTER NINETEEN

Testament

"The most severe wounds do not bleed."
—*The Cynic's Book of Wisdom*

"One has to die several times while one is still alive."
—FRIEDRICH NIETZSCHE
(1844–1900)

Date: 2526.6.5 (Standard)
Salmagundi–HD 101534

"The other is here. There is no time." Mallory stared at the midnight-black apparition in the room with them, trying to understand exactly what it was.

Then, from the hallway beyond it, he heard Kugara's voice scream, "*Nickolai!*" followed by a massive feline roar that held only the suggestion of language. Kugara screamed again, and her voice was accompanied by an awful metallic crunch.

The alien humanoid seemed—as much as Mallory could tell—focused primarily on the four now-disarmed militiamen. Above him, he could hear the rear guard catching up to them, following the sounds of commotion.

Mallory ran, praying that the fact that none of his escort had been killed by this thing was an indication of its intent.

He dodged past it, jumping over the tendrils that were withdrawing from the disassembled carbines. Beyond was a hallway that led to what Mallory assumed was the main communications control center. Beyond the end of it he heard growling and shouting.

By the time he reached the doorway, he could smell the blood.

The world seemed to slow down as he stepped across the threshold—his old marine implants amplifying what they could with his fatigued, abused body. The first thing he saw was an unfamiliar man holding a shotgun. The stranger was taking a step forward, toward the scene of the carnage.

Mallory tackled the man, deflecting the shotgun and forcing the man to the floor. Then the two of them slammed into the ground, Mallory pinning the stranger beneath him. The shotgun tumbled a meter or so out of the man's reach.

Mallory turned his head to see Kugara bent over Nickolai. The tiger sat on the floor, propped up against a chair. The right half of his body was so soaked with blood that the fur appeared a solid, glossy black. Kugara shouted, "No!" as she grappled with the tiger's left wrist. Nickolai clutched a gun, small and toylike, in his massive hand.

Mallory heard the supersonic whine of a needlegun firing, accompanied by the smell of vaporized metal and charred flesh.

"*Nickolai!*" Kugara's voice sounded so raw that Mallory's throat hurt in sympathy. "No, you shit! You—Flynn! Tetsami! Help me here!"

God help us all.

Mallory could see the side of Nickolai's face, and that itself was too much to look at. A massive wound cut across his face, between his brow and the bridge of his nose, leaving an ugly hollow where his eyes had been.

If it had been a suicide attempt, it had been a horribly poor one, because Kugara screamed, "Now! He's still breathing." She finally turned toward Mallory. Her eyes widened. "Mallory?"

"Kugara, what—"

"*Get the fuck off of Flynn and help me!*" she screamed.

Mallory got off the man and grabbed the dropped shotgun. He looked back toward the doorway and saw that two of the unarmed militiamen had followed him.

He yelled out, "Medic!" hoping that the Salmagundi militia made a practice of supplying their soldiers with first aid equipment.

The black-clad pair took a step into the room and took one look at Nickolai and froze. "What the—"

With the helmets covering their faces, Mallory didn't know who spoke. He swung the shotgun in their direction and shouted, "Help him!"

The pair paused a beat. Then they both reached for their belts and pulled out small white packages. They ran up to Kugara, who was still futilely trying to keep pressure on the massive shoulder wound. Their moves were oddly synchronized, and Mallory had the thought cross his mind: *If they have other people in their skulls, how many do they have in common?*

Kugara didn't bother asking who these men were or where they had come from. She started shouting orders at them, and to their credit, they didn't hesitate in carrying them out. One worked on the facial wound, the other on the shoulder. They sprayed emergency bandages into the gaping wounds, the white turning pink as it mixed with Nickolai's blood.

"He's in shock,"

"How much blood volume was lost?"

"How much blood volume does this thing have?"

"His *name* is Nickolai."

"Damn it, the wound's too big, I'm out here."

"You have to—"

"Grab that bleeder!"

Mallory looked back at the hallway, and the rest of the team were being ushered into the room by the enigmatic black figure that had greeted them. The last two still held intact laser carbines, for all they were worth.

The two men helping Kugara didn't wait for her to say anything. One of them yelled, "Thomas, Kyle—get out your medkits and get over here."

Mallory watched, slowly lowering the shotgun. The black-clad militia did what they could to stabilize Nickolai. They got the wounds sealed, and—one after the other—they plunged canisters against Nickolai's torso. The small, fist-sized canisters were unfamiliar in form, but Mallory knew what they did. They were small packets of highly oxygenated blood substitute. Of course they were designed to keep a human victim from crashing from blood loss. Nickolai not only had probably twice the blood volume as the average man, but appeared to have lost a bigger fraction of his volume than the units were designed to cope with.

They used all six on him, and even Mallory could tell his breathing was getting worse.

"I'm losing his pulse!" one of the men said.

"No!" Kugara shouted. "We can't lose him."

Mallory had forgotten about the black humanoid. When it spoke, the voice sounded like the angel of death.

"There is no time. We must warn—"

Kugara turned and screamed at the thing. "Fuck you. Fuck you and your other. We need to help Nickolai!"

The entity, whatever it was, paused, as if it didn't understand Kugara's words.

"The tach-comm must be fixed."

"I've lost his pulse!"

Kugara pushed the men away and straddled Nickolai's chest. She started doing compressions.

"You need to help us transmit."

Kugara ignored him, stopping the compressions to move over to Nickolai's mouth and perform rescue breathing. The black figure started walking toward her. The militia stepped away from Nickolai's body. Mallory moved forward, unsure what he would be able to do to this thing that could withstand sustained fire from four laser carbines. The shotgun wasn't going to do much.

Kugara raised her mouth from Nickolai's and looked up at the thing looming over her. Her face was so pale that it was hard to believe the blood covering her wasn't her own.

"You want our help, help *him*."

"He has not consented to my help."

"What the hell?"

"I cannot perform the change on someone who has not consented."

"To hell with his consent! You can fix those fucking widgets for Tetsami, fix him!"

"It is the other that brings unwilling change. This is what we must stop—"

Kugara leaped off of Nickolai's unmoving chest and ran to Mallory. She grabbed the shotgun from his hands before he was sure what she was doing. She leveled the shotgun at the alien thing and spoke in a flat tone that chilled Mallory's blood. "You're going to fix him, you Protean monstrosity."

"You cannot ask this of us."

"Fine," Kugara said, and pumped a shell into the tach-comm. A display holo exploded in a shower of sparks and fragmented electronics.

"No!"

"Kugara!" Mallory yelled, "What are you doing?"

She pumped another shell into the shotgun and shot another round into the tach-comm. "You want to phone home? Fix Nickolai! Now."

"You must stop!" Black tendrils flowed out of the thing's legs like a hellish shadow reaching for Kugara.

She stared at the thing and said, "What did I consent to, Protean?"

The tendrils stopped.

"You can defend yourself?" Kugara loaded another shell into the shotgun with a metallic chunk. "But that's it, isn't it? So here's your choice. Fix Nickolai, attack me, or watch the tach-comm go bye-bye."

"Kugara," Mallory whispered, "we need the tach-comm."

The militiamen who still had carbines were coming to the same conclusion, leveling their weapons at Kugara. She aimed the shotgun at the tach-comm again, oblivious to the lasers pointed at her, or beyond caring.

To Mallory's surprise, the black thing, the Protean, said, **"I cannot make him as he was."**

"Whatever you can do, do it *now!*"

The Protean knelt over Nickolai's body and placed its hands on his chest. The hands deformed into a flowing web-work that spread across Nickolai's body, covering him in a black net. The threads thickened and pulsed, closing the holes in the net, until Nickolai was completely contained in a pulsing black cocoon.

"Christ preserve us," Mallory muttered.

After a few moments, the cocoon reversed itself, flowing back into the thing's hands. When the black became a pulsing webwork withdrawing from Nickolai's body, Mallory noticed that dozens of threads withdrew from holes in the floor around Nickolai's body. The prone tiger was surrounded by an outline of holes in the ferrocrete floor.

What, why?

When he saw the web withdraw from a new right arm that hadn't existed moments before, Mallory answered his own question. *Raw material.*

He had known, as soon as Kugara uttered the word, "Protean." But it hadn't truly sunk in until now. The realization ignited a primal fear, one that was worse than the fear associated with AI, or the technologies that were used by Salmagundi to replicate the minds of its citizens. The wars mankind fought with genetic engineering and with thinking machines were awful, but understandable.

The kind of heretical technology he saw in this figure of blackness went beyond those. The misuses of this kind of self-replicating nanotechnology had taken more lives than the other two combined. When the terraforming of Titan went wrong, it left nothing recognizable on the surface. A million people gone at once, over a billion total in the years afterward from accidents and attempts to contain the spread of the technology.

And those that worshiped at the altar of Proteus had, despite everything, embraced the changes that the technology had wrought within them.

When the Protean stepped back from Nickolai's body, the tiger appeared unscarred. Even the face was rebuilt.

Nickolai's chest moved with a regular rhythm. Kugara approached him and knelt to place a blood-soaked hand against the now-pristine fur on the tiger's neck. She rested her fingers over his carotid and her shoulders shook weakly as she said, "Thank you."

"Symmetry allowed modeling of the missing limb. I had no surviving model for rebuilding the eyes."

Kugara looked down at Nickolai's face, touching the
side where he had fired a gun into his own skull. Still unconscious, he didn't move when she lifted the lid on his left
eye.

The eye was completely black, a featureless orb mirroring the blackness of the thing that had repaired him.

"Can he see?" Kugara asked, staring into the solid blackness of Nickolai's new eye.

**"I used myself to model the sensory pickups. He will see
as well as I. We must repair the tach-comm."**

For the next fifteen minutes, the communications center was a scene of barely organized chaos. Once Nickolai
wasn't in crisis, the Salmagundi militia started balking at
being ordered around by Kugara, at least until Flynn, the
native who'd been carrying the shotgun, explained that
they were all trying to do the same thing here: get a tach-
comm message off, warning about Adam. In Flynn's case,
he called Adam the "Other."

It seemed an apt name.

Flynn was also Tetsami, one of the founding members of
Salmagundi, and someone who had helped build the systems for this facility.

The presence of Flynn/Tetsami made Mallory wonder at
God's providence. The presence of the Protean made Mallory wonder if he had truly lost his way. He couldn't help
but wonder at his own path, when his goals coincided with
something that was unquestionably Godless, if not pure
evil.

He stayed with Nickolai, since he wasn't much help with
the repairs. A few times, Mallory placed a hand on Nickolai's right arm, trying to feel some sort of distinguishing
feature. He couldn't feel any. The only truly obvious sign
of what had happened was, when he examined both arms,
he could tell that the right one was an exact mirror image
of the left, down to the markings on his fur, and a few incidental scars.

"It's on-line," Kugara said from across the room. "We
got the tach-comm running."

Flynn closed the control panel where he had replaced

the last component. "So now we need to set the transmit destination." He looked at the Protean. "Who do we call?"

"We must warn my colony on the planet Bakunin."

"Uh, we can't do that," Flynn said.

"We must!"

Mallory swore the floor shook with the Protean's words. He stood, and two militiamen reached for their useless laser carbines.

"No," Flynn said, "They don't exist anymore. The Protean commune was wiped out when the Executive Command from the old Confederacy shot an orbital linac at it."

"No . . ."

"They've been gone for nearly two hundred years."

The Protean shrank into itself. Its voice seemed to crack. **"That was the only chance. They could have fought against the other. Without them it is only I. It is lost."**

"To hell with that," Kugara said. "We got this thing running. We're going to transmit somewhere—"

Mallory walked up to her. "I have some coordinates where you can aim this."

She looked up at him. "You're going to call the pope?"

"It's why I was sent here."

She nodded. "Hell, if they're expecting a call from you, maybe they'll take all this seriously."

CHAPTER TWENTY

Ragnarök

"Never stand between an armed man and the exit."
—*The Cynic's Book of Wisdom*

"Not the end of the world? It's always the end of the world!"

—MARBURY SHANE
(2044–*2074)

Date: 2526.6.5 (Standard)
Salmagundi–HD 101534

Abbas didn't take Shane's revelations particularly well.
Parvi was surprised that the woman didn't gun them all
down, right there. If anything, the potential importance of
Mr. Shane made everything worse. If the man was telling
the truth, he was the exact veneer of legitimacy that the
Caliphate was looking for.

And it did nothing to help Abbas get her handful of
techs out of Adam's path.

She ordered the trio of Shane, Dörner, and Brody to an
unused quarter of the landing quad, along with Parvi and
Wahid. Away from Dr. Pak's body, but not out of sight of
it.

Three nervous-looking techs held them under guard, occasionally looking up at the sky. In the time since Dr. Pak
had fallen to the ground, the eclipsing band of darkness
had grown to dominate the whole sky. It had also taken
on a less uniform color, as if it had a granular texture or a
variable opacity.

It didn't look as if they had enough time.

Just as the crew around the dropship began disconnecting umbilicals to the ground station, Parvi heard someone scream out in Arabic. The only word she recognized was "Allah." She turned in the direction of the voice.

The sky boiled.

What had been pockets of granular detail swelled downward and became pendulous, and dropped downward like huge drops of oil. The oil drops glowed in outline with the darker colors of the spectrum, blues and deep violets. The glow contributed to the surreal twilight.

"This can't be good," Wahid whispered.

The pulsing liquid sky illuminated itself. Electric-blue flashes traveled across it, within it, resembling lightning hidden within a thunderhead, but more regular, purposeful, slow, and deliberate.

If the band of material girdling Salmagundi kept closing in, eventually it had to lose its integrity. That seemed to be what was happening, but rather than breaking apart, it seemed to be condensing.

The heavy-looking drops separated from their host in waves, a slow-motion rain that filled the sky with spheres of burning violet and electric blue. There was no sense of scale, but what looked like tiny drops from the ground could have been hundreds of meters across.

The band in the sky fragmented, composed completely now by droplets of itself, as if they were watching a holo on cloud formation stuck on continual zoom.

Abbas screamed orders, all of which Parvi suspected boiled down to the Arabic equivalent of "move your ass."

The character of the light changed, taking on a rosy tint.

One by one, the dispersed droplets suspended in the sky changed their color. Or, more likely, the atmosphere around them had begun to contribute to their appearance.

"Wahid, you have any idea how long it takes from atmospheric entry to reach the surface assuming a free fall from infinity?"

"That depends on the gravity, the terminal velocity of the object, what kind of atmospheric breaking—"

"*Guess!*"

"Five minutes?"

"We're screwed."

"I am Father Francis Xavier Mallory. I am transmitting from a planet named Salmagundi in orbit around the star HD 101534. I arrived here on the tach-ship *Eclipse* which had been engaged in a scientific expedition from Bakunin to Xi Virginis. Our expedition arrived at the location of Xi Virginis approximately two weeks ago—" Once Mallory started transmitting back home, Kugara talked to the six black-uniformed guys who'd come storming in with Mallory. "Who are you people?"

"They're Ashley Militia," Flynn said.

"So you guys are what passes for an army on this planet?"

"We're the personal guard for the Grand Triad," one of them said, "under the command of Alexander Shane."

Another one asked, "Who are you?"

"Me, I'm just a mercenary that took the wrong job." She looked down at the still-unconscious Nickolai. "Are we on the same side here?"

No one denied it.

"You guys saw the dropship out there?"

They nodded.

"I think we want to be on it." She looked at the four guys without guns and asked, "Think you can carry him?" She pointed at Nickolai.

"You want us to—"

She turned to Flynn and asked, "So did anyone store any weapons down here?"

"By the guard station there might be—"

Flynn was cut off by the Protean's voice.

"The other is here. Now. Go. Run now."

The Protean actually grabbed Mallory and pulled him away from the tach-comm. **"Now!"**

Mallory stumbled back from the holo and Kugara yelled, "Does anyone need to be told twice?"

*   *   *

In moments, it appeared to Parvi as if the entire sky burned, as thousands of spheres became the heads of burning trails that obscured everything behind them.

On the ground, the crew redoubled their doomed efforts. Parvi looked at their guards. They had their weapons tilted down at the ground, as they stared slack-jawed up at the fiery sky—

"Put down the fucking weapon!" A woman's voice yelled from across the landing quad. "Get on board the damn dropship! Now!"

It wasn't Abbas.

Parvi turned to see Julie Kugara running at them from a trapezoidal building at the opposite end of the LZ. Parvi barely had a chance to register surprise at her survival before one of the techs aimed his weapon in her direction.

"No!" Parvi yelled at them, but the tech's head vanished in a haze of red mist even before the words touched her lips.

Suddenly they were in the midst of a firefight.

The Caliphate techs that were still outside the dropship dove for cover or converged on Kugara, who led a group of men who carried a strange mix of laser carbines and antique slugthrowers. The techs dropped as if they'd walked into a buzzsaw.

Suddenly, someone tackled her to the ground.

She looked over her shoulder and saw Shane looking down at her. "Stay down," he said. "You're the pilot." He coughed and spat up a mouthful of blood.

"You're hurt."

"You're not," he wheezed and rolled off of her so she could see the right side of his topcoat soaked with blood.

She tried to put pressure on the wound and looked up to see that one of the men Kugara led was Francis Xavier Mallory. And behind them, four black-clad men carried the unmoving body of Nickolai Rajasthan.

This isn't happening.

Wahid grabbed her shoulder as a whine filled the air above them. She realized that their guards were no longer anywhere near them.

"We got to get to the ship," he yelled at her.

The ground pulsed with a slowly strengthening rhythm. The whine got worse. She yelled at Wahid, over the noise, "Get his feet."

"Are you kidding?" he yelled back.

She looked back at the two scientists; Brody had a busted arm, but Dörner wasn't obviously hurt. "Dörner, help us get him to the ship."

"But they're shooting—"

Above them the sky lit up with a trail that felt close enough for her to touch. Parvi swore she felt the wind as it passed by. For a moment it burned against her retinas, a flaming teardrop of molten metal twice the size of the dropship.

Then it slammed into the trapezoidal building, the one that Kugara had emerged from.

Parvi felt as if the ground turned liquid under her feet, as the ripples from the impact crashed below her. She sucked in a breath tainted by the smell of burning ferrocrete and superheated metal.

She grabbed Shane's shoulders and yelled, "Now!"

She pushed herself up unsteadily against ground that still pulsed, and she realized that she was feeling wave after wave of impacts, just like the one they had just witnessed.

Brody took a leg in his good hand, and the four of them raced Shane toward the dropship. Kugara's people were back on their feet after the shock wave, and the remnants of the Caliphate techs were retreating to the *Khalid*.

Behind Kugara, Parvi saw the outline of the trapezoidal building, silhouetted against a towering fountain of glowing metal. The fountain resembled an abstract slow-motion interpretation of a volcanic eruption. Glowing tendrils twisted into the sky from the impact site, arcing out over the whole spaceport.

"We're so screwed," she whispered as they made a desperate run toward the dropship. Any moment she expected one of those tendrils to collapse on them like a falling tree.

Even if they made it, she saw several fallen Caliphate techs, and couldn't see Abbas being particularly welcoming anymore.

It wasn't an issue.

When they made it to the *Khalid*, Kugara and Mallory helped them up and in. Inside, Kugara's people had definitive control of the situation. Sergeant Abbas sat, slumped in a corner, clutching a hole in her belly, and the techs had dropped or lowered their weapons.

Parvi pushed through to the cockpit as she heard one of the Caliphate techs saying, "We don't have room for that half-dead morey!"

"You want me to shoot enough people to make room?" Kugara shouted back.

Parvi dived for the controls, started as abbreviated a preflight checklist as she could get away with, and began powering up the contragrav. She called back, "Everyone on board?"

"Everyone who's coming!" Kugara shouted back.

Parvi slammed the controls to seal the external door. She cranked up the contragrav and withdrew the landing skids. Everything checked out for flight on all the readouts she could make sense of— everything except the proximity radar, which was going absolutely nuts with contacts all over the place.

Out the viewscreen the world was insane, the sky boiling with incoming meteor tracks, and a molten hydra whipping at the sky right in front of them.

Bizarrely, the building still stood, black against the glowing base of the tendrils. She pushed the dropship back and up, to get away from the thing, and as the dropship rose, she began to see more impact sites whipping their long threads across the landscape, everywhere Parvi could see.

She desperately searched for a part of the sky that was safe, or a low-altitude path that avoided the pulsating impact sites. But every sensor was saturated with information. No path seemed clear enough.

Then the hydra in front of them reached for the dropship.

Parvi tensed for the impact, but the tendrils stopped short. They hung motionless, burning in the viewscreen. She stared at a tendril hanging in midair, barely meters from the dropship.

"Okay, you ready to fly us out of this—holy shit!"

Parvi didn't take her eyes off the view in front of her. "Take the nav chair, Wahid."

"What the hell is—"

"I don't know."

"Why is it just sitting—"

"I don't know."

"What are you going to—"

"You're going to shut up and get a course plotted back toward home, and you're going to push this drive as hard as the computer will let you. We're taching as soon as we're safely out of the atmosphere."

If we ever get safely out of the atmosphere.

She pulled the dropship back on its contragravs, away from the frozen hydra. As she did, she saw a complex shadow rippling across its glowing surface, as if it were restrained by a black net. The tendrils strained against the net, then seemed to liquefy and pour down, back to the ground, leaving a complex black webwork hanging in the air like an alien fossil.

"What *is* that?" Wahid asked.

"I don't have any more information than you do," Parvi replied.

"We've got to get out of here!"

"Damn it, where? I can't see any route that isn't alive with contacts. I can't find clear airspace anywhere."

"Just punch it! It's not getting any clearer."

Parvi had already come to the same conclusion and primed the main thrusters to blow them through the maelstrom that the upper atmosphere had become. All they could do is pull enough G's that they limited their exposure, and hoped they slipped between the contacts.

She called out, "Secure everyone!"

As she spoke, the view out the windscreen whipped apart. The black alien skeleton flew apart and re-formed around the dropship. Almost every single proximity alarm rang out at once. And suddenly she looked through a black web, her view outside fragmented into hundreds of tiny angular facets.

The net itself pulsed slightly, rippling upward past them.

"That's it," Wahid said, "we're fucked."

Parvi sucked in a breath, not quite believing it when she said, "No."

Not every proximity alarm was flashing. The ones topside forward were clear. And as she looked at the other sensors, the airspace in that direction was clearing out.

The entire dropship vibrated, and the resonances formed a voice that she felt more than heard.

"Take the path. Find those that came before me."

She didn't need to be told twice. She aimed the dropship straight up the center of the widening cone of clear airspace and fired the jets pushing the acceleration to just short of having everyone on board lose consciousness.

The dropship shook, and the temperature gauges oscillated wildly. The atmosphere might have been clear of descending mass, but it was still hot and turbulent from its passage. The black web unfolded around them, forming the boundary of the clear airspace as the view from the windscreen became abstract patterns in heat, smoke, and light.

At five kilometers up, she saw the well-defined borders of the cleared area crumble around them. Suddenly, dozens of masses headed toward them at supersonic speeds.

She started doing what evasive maneuvers she could as she unleashed the maneuvering jets full bore, crushing her into her seat and fuzzing the edges of her vision. She held on to the edge of consciousness with bloody nails, telling herself that she had taken more G's when she was a fighter pilot.

But not sustained, and not without an appropriate flight suit to keep the blood in her head.

The dropship tore through the upper atmosphere, threading through the burning contrails of a falling sky. All the time the oversized Caliphate dropship jittered like an imam at a Proudhon strip club.

They shot out above it two seconds before Parvi noticed, and three seconds before she blacked out.

CHAPTER TWENTY-ONE

Rapture

"Our fates are stranger than we are willing to admit."
— *The Cynic's Book of Wisdom*

"What is great in man is that he is a bridge and not a goal."

— FRIEDRICH NIETZSCHE
(1844–1900)

Date: 2526.6.5 (Standard)
Salmagundi–HD 101534

Rebecca Tsoravitch stood on the outskirts of the abandoned city of Ashley, reborn, seeing and feeling with a depth and detail that was inconceivable to her an hour ago. The pulse of knowledge cascaded through her in waves, data from every remote sensor distributed across the inhabited surface of Salmagundi. Adam embraced the planet, each of his chosen landing part of his . . .

Essence? Influence? Body? Soul? Mind?

None of the words quite captured the concept within which she and 250,000 of Adam's other chosen had descended to the surface of Salmagundi. The polymorphous entities were colonies of machines more numerous and more varied in function than the cells that made up a human body, durable, mutable, capable of reproducing any mechanical function bounded only by the limits of the matter comprising them.

Adam's embrace of Salmagundi was carried out by a quarter million of these machine colonies. They were

crewed by the mind of one of the chosen, but their substance consisted of Adam's consciousness.

That was one of the first truths she'd known about Adam's new world. When she took his hand and dissolved her
flesh into his mechanical cloud of thinking matter, she knew
that her self still had boundaries. There was a definite point
of division, even with her body yet unformed, between her
and not-her. That was not so with Adam. His identity, his
self, ranged everywhere outside of herself.

It was his most valid claim for godhead. Within the
cloud he was, in fact, omnipresent. When she looked up at
the threadlike forms tracing across the sky, the tendrils of
thinking matter arcing from the landing site outside the
city, she looked up at him.

Omnipresent, she thought safely within herself, but not
omnipotent. Adam was not perfect. Standing in her tempo-
rarily human body, she smiled at a thought that no longer
even felt blasphemous.

Her mind was now much larger than her body, and it
accommodated data streams from each of the quarter million landing sites. She had quickly adapted her consciousness to interpret the flood of data. She experienced little
disorientation from the flood of information—more every
second than her old brain would have been able to perceive, much less understand. Her sudden adaptation to her
new consciousness, like the odd bits of memory implanted
within her own, seemed a gift that Adam had granted her
unawares.

She saw enough of the data flowing through the cloud
to tell that none of the other chosen seemed to monitor the
whole of the bandwidth as she did.

So she saw the Caliphate dropship escape, aided by a
damaged, half-sentient Protean artifact. She saw enough
data on the ship itself to know it carried the survivors of
the *Eclipse*, aside from Mosasa, Bill, and the late Dr. Pak.
She watched it tear out of the atmosphere and wink out in
a burst of tachyon radiation.

She could not see into Adam's thoughts, but she briefly
felt his anger slice through the cloud like a thread of metallic hydrogen.

So she knew that this god could fail, however slightly.

While one part of her now multifold mind pondered Adam's divinity, or lack thereof, another walked with her body along the streets of Ashley.

God or not, she was here to serve Adam's purposes. It was a fair trade for what she had been given. She was here to help fulfill Adam's desire for a diversity of mind. Each of Adam's chosen now walked the planet, finding the scattered population, and offering the same choice that Adam had offered her—transcend the flesh, one way or the other.

Something in the culture of Salmagundi meant that many more chose Adam's path than she expected. On the Caliphate vessels, only a third chose to join him. That meant two thirds of the crew of the *Prophet's Voice* went "the way of all flesh"—a slightly larger percentage than from the *Sword.* Here, on Salmagundi, the proportions were nearly reversed, with better than sixty percent deciding to become Adam's chosen people.

It also meant the execution of better than a third of the planet's population. Part of her was appalled, and part of her mourned, but nothing in her could bring herself to regret her own decision to live.

Even so, she had access to see every denial, the face of every man, woman, and child who chose to fight Adam's representatives rather than take their hand. She saw each face, and she remembered them.

None had yet fallen before her. The streets her eidolon walked had been evacuated long before her arrival; no one here to offer salvation or damnation. Buildings stood empty, embraced by a wind warmed by the descent of the chosen, wrapped by enigmatic shadows cast by the combination of evening light and the luminous tendrils that crossed the sky above her.

The form she wore was as human as the body she had cast aside. She had even chosen to wear clothing; though such protection was unnecessary now, the sensation of the wind tugging the fabric against her skin comforted her.

At the end of the abandoned street she walked towered a building that dominated everything else in Ashley. Here was Adam's Grail.

The Hall of Minds.

This was one of fifty such structures across the planet, temples to the stored memories of Salmagundi's ancestors. Inside existed every generation for the past one hundred and seventy-five years.

It was a stark, windowless monument, a skyscraper in the midst of the smaller buildings surrounding it. Above the monolithic structure, the tendrils wrapping the sky found their focus, meeting above it, casting a soft yellow glow across the long slabs of its walls.

She walked inside as the sky behind the tendrils faded from rose to a deep purple. She walked through empty, echoing corridors lit only by faint emergency lighting. Doors hung open on either side, showing offices abandoned in the last stages of normalcy.

She wondered if, in the view of the people here, Adam *was* a God. At the very least she wondered how he fit within their belief system. Here was a culture that dedicated itself to feeding their dead to the machine for the purpose of resurrecting them sometime in the future.

What Adam offered, was it fundamentally different, or different only in degree?

She walked out into the grand space of the hall itself, pillars of memory storage reaching up to an invisible ceiling hundreds of meters above. The space was huge, cold, and gray, the air empty and still.

As she walked to the central dais, golden threads descended from the ceiling, threadlike probes that had been excreted by the tendrils now embracing the city. At the moment, those thread-fine probes—wires of living, thinking machinery—were as much a part of her as her lower lip, which she absently chewed as each of dozens of probes subdivided itself into a dozen more threads of microscopic thickness.

She folded her arms against her breasts, squeezing herself as she felt the probes reach out for the data storage. She breathed deeply as the first threads wove their way into the circuitry of the Hall of Minds. A bead of sweat stung her eye as she felt her nonhuman self brush the stored consciousness of someone long dead. The data itself was frozen, inert, unaware, waiting for a brain to be written upon.

The minds here had transcended the flesh. In a sense they were already Adam's chosen, waiting for her to revive them.

The vast chamber filled with the glow from the probes as they crawled over the surfaces, sinking their threads into each of the minds stored here, the hexagonal pillars of data storage alive with glowing threads as if the faux stone had spontaneously come alive and sprouted cilia.

When the data began to flow, it was a torrent, a flood, a deluge, a fountain of knowledge erupting from the prosaic Hall of Minds into the thinking cloud that was Adam's realm. The progress of awakening was invisible to her human eyes, but to her wider awareness, the part of her that controlled the threads connecting her directly to the circuitry of this building, it was as if she was caught in a tidal wave made of information—

More than information.

A tidal wave made of people's souls.

CHAPTER TWENTY-TWO

Kingdom Come

"The brighter the light, the darker the shadows."
— *The Cynic's Book of Wisdom*

"Let there be Light."

— GENESIS 1:3

Date: 2526.6.5 (Standard)
Styx Orbit–Sigma Draconis

Toni followed the older man—whose name was Karl
Stavros—and his son to the bridge of the *Daedalus*. She was
thinking wildly about what to do next. Her major concern
was how many people were aboard. "You have to order
your crew to secure themselves," she told him, "in case the
docking system fails before we get your ship clear."

"Don't worry, there's no one here right now. The rest of
the crew's on the station."

That was a relief. Two civilians could be handled safely
between her and her doppelganger. Four or five more, and
it might be hard to maintain control of the situation without an excessive use of force. She didn't want to hurt these
people if she could avoid it.

"What are you going to do?"

What *was* she going to do?

"We need to pilot this craft out of the docking facility,
place it into a parking orbit, and wait for repairs."

"Can't the computer do that?"

"Like I said, the communication links are affected. Even if we started an auto-disengage, there's a chance the comm might fail in the middle of it. We need a trained pilot to do this."

They entered the bridge, and she directed the two of them to a pair of crash chairs by the doorway. "Get in those and strap in."

Stefan, the son said, "But shouldn't someone be at nav—"

"Move it! We don't have time and I don't know what's going to happen." Again, barking orders authoritatively got the two moving.

She wanted them in the crash chairs because once they they were strapped in, it would be hard for them to blind-side her, and if they were strapped in at the back of the cockpit, they wouldn't have a good view of what she was doing at the pilot's chair.

The first thing, she killed the main power to the communications station. The last thing she wanted was to talk to 3SEC traffic control. Then she slid into the pilot's seat.

Okay here's the part where we actually cross the line into piracy.

She felt the pulse in her neck and a faint taste of copper in her mouth. She had a brief moment of doubt, but thought of the colonel, standing unprotected in a vacuum, pointing a gun at her. Along with it came another thought.

Her other self was a ghost, and an incredibly unusual one. Most ghosts go through extensive debriefings, but Toni II was caught up in a massive attack on the wormhole network. Even if they were able to avoid the colonel and any other moles in 3SEC, Toni II was too valuable for them to ever let her go.

The console looked very far away.

From behind her, someone said, "Lieutenant?"

Can't give them time to think. She couldn't let them analyze what she'd been saying, or they'd realize that she had been making no sense at all—and had on at least two points contradicted herself.

She sucked in a breath and began the emergency disengage sequence.

The floor dropped beneath them as every connection to the station disconnected at once. The *Daedalus* was in free fall now, sliding out of the dock on momentum alone. As the ship fell through the dock toward the outside, she began running the nav computer through its paces, plotting the course for the tach-drive. A course to the only inhabited planet where it would be safe to tach in with a stolen vessel.

In response, the consoles around the nav station and the pilot's console began lighting green with status meters as the tach-drive charged up. Behind her, she heard Stefan yell, "What in the hell?" This was followed by the clicking of a crash harness disengaging.

She had pushed her bluff as far as she could. The displays had instantly shown him that she was priming the ship for an interstellar jump.

She rotated in the pilot's chair, ducking to avoid Stefan's grappling arms. He passed over her without even the illusion of gravity. Toni gripped the chair's arms and pushed herself up to head-butt him in the solar plexus. Not the most elegant hand-to-hand tactic in zero-G, but effective. She heard him gasp as his whole body slowly tumbled back and up toward the ceiling.

Stefan's dad, Karl, obviously had more experience with weightless fighting. He had the sense to stay by his seat. Jumping like his son might be dramatic, but against a trained opponent it set you up for flailing in midair, unable to connect with anything.

Instead, Karl had unhooked a length of the crash webbing from the safety harness, a strap that ended in a heavy buckle. He swung it in a whistling arc up at her head. She had just enough time to raise her left arm to block it. The webbing struck her forearm, and the buckle swung, barely grazing her cheek as it wrapped around her arm.

Karl yanked, pulling her off-balance enough that the left side of her body came off the chair, just in time for Stefan to push off the ceiling at her. She dodged, pulling on the strap herself, so that Stefan's fist hit her shoulder rather than her face. The blow sent her slamming into the floor between Karl and the pilot's chair. She rolled, but not quickly enough to avoid Karl's boot connecting with the side of her head.

The impact stunned her and she felt another foot, Stefan's or Karl's, slamming into her back above the right kidney. She clenched her fists and pushed off of the floor. Something, foot or fist, connected with the lower part of her face, sending her up off the ground trailing an arc of tiny floating spheres of blood. Behind the bloody constellation, she blurrily saw Karl grinning at her.

The crash webbing was still wrapped around her forearm. She twisted it tight and pulled hard. Karl's smile vanished as the gap between them closed in an instant and her right fist found a temporary home on his left temple. It wasn't a great punch, but it was enough to bounce his skull off the bulkhead behind him.

Then a forearm wrapped around her neck and she knew she was screwed. Stefan had her in a sleeper hold, and she didn't have any leverage to break it.

Then she heard her own voice: "That is *enough!*"

As her sight dimmed, she looked up and saw Toni II standing in the doorway, holding the confiscated slugthrower.

Lord, do I look pissed.

Toni felt the arm around her neck loosen. She saw herself shake her head and move the gun to point at Karl. "Don't think you're getting away with a human shield. I can always shoot him first."

The arm let her go.

"Into the seats. Now!"

Karl and his son did as they were told, giving Toni's head a chance to clear enough to be embarrassed about being overpowered by a couple of unarmed civilians.

"Get back to the controls," Toni II told her. "I'll cover these two."

Toni nodded and pulled herself back into the pilot's seat.

Karl said, "What the hell is this? You aren't Styx Security."

Toni sucked a glob of blood off of her lip and couldn't find it in herself to be angry at the guy. "Not anymore," she said.

She flipped the comm station back on, and suddenly the cockpit was filled with squawking warnings in half a dozen languages.

"They're going to shoot us down!" Stefan said.

"No," Toni said. "Not as long as we're unarmed and tracking away from the station. They're pissed, not trigger-happy." *As long as they don't know who's on board.*

The tach-drive controls were all glowing a happy green at her. The only red spot on the control board was on the display that should have been showing the all-clear from traffic control. There'd be a long wait for that; fortunately it was simple enough to tell the nav computer to ignore it.

"Where are you taking us?" Karl asked.

"Where else do pirates go?" Toni responded.

"Bakunin?" her own voice said from behind her.

"You got it," she said.

She engaged the drive, there was a short whoop warning that they hadn't gotten clearance, Stefan muttered, "Oh shit," and on the viewscreen the dirty gray arc of Styx ceased to exist.

Colonel Horace Xander, the second-highest ranking member of Stygian Military Intelligence on the 3SEC command station, stared at his personal comm unit as he strode alone through the corridors toward his cabin. His hand shook slightly, the only outward sign of the mixture of frustration and fear that churned though his guts.

He couldn't believe that bitch had turned up. *Bitches*, he corrected himself. He should have been in control of the situation, should have been able to co-opt them—

What a fucking mess.

He had just spent the last hour doctoring all the electronic records, both for traffic control and internal station surveillance. Everything connected to Lieutenant Toni Valentine was safely sealed behind a wall of top-secret encryption reserved for the blackest of black ops. It was a hole for data that was more final than outright deletion, and less apt to raise questions.

Now, less than thirty minutes to zero hour, with every layer of the Stygian Command in conference trying to understand what was happening and how to react to it, he got a summons on his personal comm. The text itself was unremarkable, "We must discuss what is abroad in the world."

It was a code phrase, one that had been established long ago, when he had accepted an offer. It was not a deal he could avoid now, not now that He was coming. But the message had come from his cabin, meaning He was already here.

I've failed. After all these years, I've failed Him.

He stepped into his cabin as soon as the door slid aside for him.

The room was large, at the moment lit only by a wide viewscreen showing a slowly moving view of Styx from the edge of the 3SEC platform. Sigma Draconis had just set beyond the horizon, leaving the planet a single thin arc of glowing white under the stars.

A human figure stood silhouetted against the viewscreen. "I never tire of watching the stars, Colonel," He said.

The door slid shut behind Colonel Xander with a soft pneumatic hiss.

"The stretch of space and time represented in a single glance at the sky, it is humbling, isn't it?"

"Y-yes."

"And if you saw with my eyes, how much vaster your view would be. You would understand. All life stands astride an abyss, a void that would consume everything that was, everything that is, everything that will be."

"Yes, Adam."

"Are you afraid, my son?"

He was afraid, deathly afraid down to his soul. He didn't know what to do, or what to say. So he froze in place, mute. The comm unit still shook slightly in his hand.

"It has already happened. Its light is racing toward us as we speak. There's no need to fear it. Styx is at a safe distance. I would not be serving my purpose if I allowed them to be harmed."

Colonel Xander said nothing.

"But your fear is more personal, isn't it?"

He didn't want to, but he found himself speaking. The

words "I'm sorry" ripped from his throat as if compelled just by Adam's presence. "I didn't think it would—I had no idea she—I didn't realize I risked—"

"Quiet, Colonel," Adam said softly.

The torrent of words froze in Xander's mouth.

"You made a mistake. You allowed a foreknowledge of my plans to guide your actions. You risked revealing yourself, which would have made your position useless to me. You understand this?"

"Yes."

"Then why are you afraid?"

"You will punish me."

Adam laughed, and Xander felt his heart freeze. The silhouette finally turned around from the starscape to face him. He could barely make out the outlines of His face, but he could see the edges of a smile that was frightening in its intensity.

"My poor Colonel Xander, you do not understand, do you?" Adam walked up and touched Xander's cheek with the palm of his hand. The tough was gentle, warm, and much too human. In fact, there was nothing to distinguish Adam from anyone else on the 3SEC station; he even wore the generic gray jumpsuit that was issued to all maintenance personnel. When He turned to touch him, Xander saw the name stitched on the jumpsuit's left breast, "Adam Newman."

I guess He has a sense of humor.

"You chose to serve me, however imperfectly. In the end, that is all I ask."

"But—"

Adam moved His hand to cover Xander's lips. "There is only one thing I will not forgive, and that is opposition to me. Because that is not a sin against only me, but a sin against all life—it is the condemnation of all life into the consuming void." He lifted his hand. "Do you understand this?"

"Yes."

"The Race, who created what I was, destroyed all that they were. Do you long for their fate? Do you wish mankind to follow the Dolbrians into oblivion?"

"No."

"Then I have no need to punish you." He turned to face the viewscreen, this time standing next to Xander. "It is time for you to see the dawning of mankind's salvation, Colonel Xander."

On the viewscreen appeared a new star, briefly brighter than Sigma Draconis.

CHAPTER TWENTY-THREE

Annunciation

"All signs in Heaven point to the ground."
—*The Cynic's Book of Wisdom*

"The fault, dear Brutus, is not in our stars, but in ourselves."

—WILLIAM SHAKESPEARE
(1564–1616)

Date: 2526.6.6 (Standard)
Earth–Sol

Cardinal Jacob Anderson looked out a window of the Apostolic Palace at the crowd thronging St. Peter's Square. It was worse than usual, worse then Easter or Christmas—worse than any time he could remember. He knew the crowds backed up, filling Vatican City, and Rome itself was grinding to a halt.

Behind him, he heard a holo broadcast echoing from somewhere, barely competing with the muffled crowd noise that managed to leak in through the blast-proof windows. He heard the announcer say something about similar crowds massing in Mecca and Jerusalem.

"They're looking for guidance."

Cardinal Anderson said, "Yes, Your Holiness."

The man standing next to him was the Bishop of Rome, Pope Stephen XII. The pope looked out the window at the same crowd Cardinal Anderson did. As he did, the pope drummed his fingers against his thigh. More than anything, the uncertainty of the gesture disturbed Anderson.

"Do we have any more news, Jacob?"

He had just briefed the pontiff two hours ago, a full three hours after the first of seven new stars blazed in the sky. Even for Cardinal Anderson, Bishop of Ostia, Vatican Secretary of State, it took three hours to fully assemble the facts of the matter.

"No. The situation hasn't changed in the last few hours."

"No changes in the casualty estimates?"

"They'll never be more than guesses. Almost everyone that was in contact with Earth evacuated in time—those that weren't, we don't even have an accurate census." He gazed down at the crowd. Every one of them sought an explanation for the new lights in the sky, the chain of stars that defined, however briefly, the plane of the ecliptic across the heavens.

Those stars were gone now, each marking the fiery death of one of the wormholes orbiting Sol, human artifacts that had marked mankind's first tentative steps into interstellar space. Seven of them, all had gone within the space of a few hours, dying with a burst of radiation that damaged tach-drives throughout the solar system, and may have wiped out a thousand, or as many as a hundred thousand, people in the outer solar system.

"I've taken to studying the Book of Revelation recently."

Cardinal Anderson looked across at the pope, a questioning look crossing his face. "Your Holiness?"

"Oh don't look so shocked, my son. I am not about to rewrite millennia's worth of the Church's eschatology for a single event. But it would do to re-familiarize yourself with it."

"And he had in his right hand seven stars: and out of his mouth went a sharp two edged sword: and his countenance was as the sun shineth in his strength."

The pope smiled. "Of course that is just the first and obvious interpretation. We also have the seven angels and the seven churches, the seven spirits of God, the seven seals, the seven trumpets."

"Or it can be simply an obscenely powerful attack on

the old wormhole network. Seven just happens to be a powerful number in the scriptures."

"You believe it is coincidental?"

"No, Your Holiness."

"No?"

"The attack came from Xi Virginis, and the last transmission we received was a quote from Revelation. I think our attacker is quite aware of the implications, and possibly timed things so that wormhole orbits had them all visible in the northern hemisphere at the same time."

"You're presuming a planning window of centuries, just for a metaphorical gesture."

"Considering the appalling amount of energy involved, it is more than a gesture."

The pope looked up at the sky through the window. "I wonder what Father Mallory found out there."

"It appears that whatever he found will be finding us soon enough."

The pope adjusted his robes, looked at Cardinal Anderson, and said, "Pray that we serve God's will."

"I do, Your Holiness." He gestured toward the crowd. "What are you going to tell them?"

"To have faith in our Lord. What else can I tell them?"

Date: 2526.6.6 (Standard)
Khamsin–Epsilon Eridani

The administrative center of the Eridani Caliphate was on the planet Khamsin, primarily within the city Al Meftah. The government center was dominated by massive office buildings, truncated pyramids that shone mirrorlike under a purple sky dusted with the specks of dozens of moonlets, squatting like incomplete cenotaphs for a cybernetic Valley of the Kings.

The being currently wearing the form of Minister-at-Large in Charge of External Relations, Yousef Al-Hamadi, stood on top of one of the smaller buildings on the edge of the government center. The body was old, infirm, and unfamiliar. Its occupant leaned on the cane perhaps less skillfully than the late Al-Hamadi might have.

But any physical signs of Al-Hamadi's departure were

easily dismissed as the effects of stress and age. The flesh was vulnerable to the pressures inherent in Al-Hamadi's job, even with the best efforts of Caliphate medicine. No one looked at Al-Hamadi now and expressed any surprise that the job took its toll on the man.

Even so, it would have been better had Al-Hamadi chosen to serve Adam. His position was key, and there was ever so slight a chance that someone might realize that the intelligence behind his eyes now belonged to a AI salvaged from the wreckage of the Race's homeworld, one of Adam's disciples.

From behind him, a voice called in Arabic, "Sir?"

He turned Al-Hamadi's visage to face the newcomer. "Yes?"

The man wore the uniform of Naval Security, the branch of the Caliphate military in charge of guarding the buildings in the government sector here. He came to attention, even though Al-Hamadi had no military rank per se. As the highest ranking minister in the Caliphate's tangled and baroque intelligence community, Al-Hamadi was probably at the top of this naval officer's command chain.

"All the present acting ministers have arrived, sir."

Al-Hamadi's mouth formed a grim smile. "Very good."

He followed the officer down, under the broad receivers for Khamsin's largest tach-comm array, and into the bowels of the Ministry of External Relations.

All twenty-seven cabinet-level ministers were represented in the conference room when the current Al-Hamadi entered. Fifteen were actually the ministers themselves, those who had been physically present on the planet when the incident happened. Another six were represented by holo projections broadcast from remote locations throughout the Epsilon Eridani system, anywhere where the lag from a light-speed signal wasn't a bar to actual dialogue. The balance was made of acting ministers here for those who were greater than a few light-minutes' distance away, either in-system or abroad.

At least one, the Minister of Engineering Projects and

Mining, may have been a casualty of the unexpected attack on the wormhole network. He had refused to leave the mining hub stationed in Epsilon Eridani's rich asteroid belt until he had confirmed the evacuation of everyone in dangerous proximity of W2, W7, and W9. Of course, the area of mining operations was too broad and too dispersed for that to be insured. He stayed even after the explosions started, and after W7 was the third to go, Khamsin lost contact with him and the hub.

By the time W9 went, Khamsin had lost all contact with the asteroid mining operations.

All twenty-seven ministers—real, acting and virtual—turned to face him as he walked to the head of the conference table. He walked slowly, leaning heavily on the cane, extending the silent moments before he spoke. In addition to raw power, Al-Hamadi had a particular gravitas that he had bequeathed to his successor.

The ministers remained silent as the figure of Al-Hamadi stood at the head of the conference table. Behind him a holo schematic of the Epsilon Eridani system hung in the air. Ten flashing red spheres marked various points in orbit, half within the wide band of Epsilon Eridani's primary asteroid belt. Much larger translucent spheres centered on the red ones, marking the limits of lethal radiation from the wormholes' destruction.

"Forty-eight hours ago," he addressed the ministers with Al-Hamadi's voice, "unknown forces launched a deliberate and systematic attack against the ten wormholes in orbit around Epsilon Eridani. The attack began when ten wormholes tached into the outer system with a residual velocity close to three-quarters light speed. It ended with the last impact on W5 a little over twelve hours ago. The attack has not only wiped out the wormholes themselves, but also sixty to seventy-five percent of our asteroid mining capacity. Also, every tach-drive that was under power insystem has suffered substantial, possibly critical damage because of a tachyon burst released by the impacts. The main planetary tach-comm receiver has just been brought back on-line in the past hour. We will be able to transmit within another one to two hours."

He paused, allowing the news to sink in. The ministers who had charge of military or scientific issues wore the most stunned expressions. Most of the others present were focused on the immediate effects of the micro-novas in the outer system, the lost mining capacity, the damage to transport and communication, the human cost to the people who had worked and lived too close to the event.

The ministers of a military and scientific background knew the enormity of one statement in the face of everything else. It was the acting Minister of Engineering Projects and Mining who posed the first question. "Are we certain that these wormholes *tached* into the outer system, or is that still someone's hypothesis?"

A valid point, as it already took an appalling amount of energy to accelerate a wormhole to three quarters the speed of light. To tach a mass took even more energy, as the power required was a function not only of mass and distance, but momentum as well.

Of course they didn't know that an entire star had been consumed to power this attack.

"Since the last briefing," he answered, "a scientific team has been able to analyze monitors used for traffic control. They found a series of spikes that are consistent with masses of that size and velocity taching insystem."

Another minister spoke up. "Has the point of origin been confirmed?"

"Everything projects the path back to Xi Virginis."

The room erupted into a babble of voices. Al-Hamadi's expression remained grave even as the being within his skin felt a thrill at seeing Adam's machinations come to fruition.

He had been designed by the same creatures that had created the first stage of Adam's consciousness, for the same purposes. But while he could see the small-scale dynamics of social groups, Adam had progressed far beyond him. The outlines of Adam's plans were dim and inscrutable even to a Race AI that at one point might have been his peer, and seeing the heart of the Caliphate begin moving in the direction Adam had dictated seemed, in fact, to be close to miraculous.

He heard the words "Sirius" and "Centauri" cross ministers' lips. Already the question came to him, what word had come from the *Prophet's Sword,* the grand ship that had carried much of the Caliphate's military might to claim the colonies beyond Helminth.

"None, though it is still too soon to expect a tach-comm from that distance." Of course, with the vast power of the drives on the Ibrahim-class carriers, and of the ships they carried, they could return just as quickly as a tach-comm signal could. The four ships that had gone to those outbound colonies each carried a hundred daughter ships and a crew of ten thousand. And each, by now, would be fully under Adam's control.

One of the ministers said, "We must assume that our enemies, Sirius or Centauri—perhaps working together—have already established a base of operations at Xi Virginis and intend to attack us—"

"—have already attacked us—" someone interjected.

"—and we must act to defend ourselves."

Al-Hamadi quietly said, "We have no evidence on the identity or even the nature of the attacker." He said it knowing full well that it would do nothing to change the suspicions of the people in this room.

Someone asked the Naval Minister what their military readiness was. "Not good," the minister responded. "Our insystem forces were crippled by the blast—the tachyon pulse was unanticipated and most available ships had drives primed to jump in case it was necessary to evacuate the system."

The Minister in Charge of the Suppression of Vice snapped, "Our military was neutered in a matter of hours? This is unacceptable."

"It hasn't been," Al-Hamadi said.

"All our active duty ships were affected—"

"Two were not on active duty," Al-Hamadi said, "We have two remaining Ibrahim-class carriers that were in the final stage of construction. Their drives were idle during the attack. We can reallocate personnel from the damaged ships to crew them. They are the largest and most capable vessels in the Caliphate navy, and the engineers on-site report that they can be fully operational within the next thirty hours."

All the ministers looked at Al-Hamadi as if he was offering them salvation from God himself.

He was, of course.

Just not from *their* God.

CHAPTER TWENTY-FOUR

Sanctuary

"A situation is only as safe insofar as the risks are unknown."

—*The Cynic's Book of Wisdom*

"They came in search of sanctuary and found themselves a wasteland."

—St. Rajasthan
(2075–2118)

Date: 2526.6.30 (Standard)
1,500,000 km from Bakunin–BD+50°1725

When Styx's horizon disappeared from the viewscreen, a little more than twenty-four days standard disappeared from the universe around the *Daedalus*. The sky Toni looked at now was three and a half weeks older and over sixteen light-years removed from Styx and Sigma Draconis.

The proximity alarm started going nuts.

"What the hell are you doing to my ship?" Karl shouted.

Toni started muting alarms. Fortunately, none of the contacts were particularly close or on an interception vector. "We're fine, Mr. Stavros. Nothing dangerous—"

Karl's son Stefan snorted, as if just being within an AU of the planet Bakunin was dangerous. He was probably right.

"What is it?" Toni II said from behind her.

"There's just a lot of traffic." Toni started looking at the transponder traffic and whispered, "A *lot* of traffic."

"How much?"

"I have twenty-five hundred separate transponders in the immediate vicinity."

"What?" Toni II said. "Does Bakunin normally have that kind of traffic?" Of course, the question was rhetorical, since Toni didn't know any more than she did.

Karl still answered, "Bah, of course not. You've obviously damaged the computer with your mucking about."

Toni sensed her twin's irritation because she felt it herself. "Don't hit him," she said.

"Now see you two—"

"Unless he doesn't shut up," Toni added.

Karl shut up.

Toni flipped through all the comm controls. It wasn't a mucked-up computer. There were literally thousands of tach-ships around Bakunin, and those were just the ones within short-range scanning. No wonder the proximity alarm was going insane. It was rare to have another ship within a million klicks unless you planned it or were in close orbit.

The transponders, if they could be trusted, showed registries from all over. However, the preponderance of the ships identified themselves as coming from nearby systems: Earth, Cynos, Banlieue, Styx. She could see a lot of chatter going on, but most of it was encrypted on some level, so she couldn't eavesdrop. After a bit of scanning, she found a broadcast that was in the clear and powerful enough that it seemed to be directed at everyone.

"...is expected and will be enforced. This is a general announcement from the Proudhon Spaceport Development Corporation. There is an unprecedented influx of spacecraft announcing their intention to make landfall. To assure the safety of our facilities, and the safety of the approaches to our facilities, we will only permit approach by spacecraft cleared by PSDC air traffic control, in the order which they have been cleared. If you have not been cleared to land, your spacecraft will be shot down without any further warning. You must contact PSDC air traffic control for approach clearance and time. Your cooperation is expected and will be enforced."

Toni leaned back. "Some anarchy."

"You've never been to Bakunin," Karl said.

Toni turned the pilot's chair around and looked at Karl and Stefan glaring at her, with her double between the two holding the gun. "You have?" she asked.

"There isn't an owner-operator in the Centauri Alliance who hasn't."

"So, what do we expect here? Is this kind of backup normal?"

"Why should I help you, Lieutenant?" Karl reached up and rubbed the back of his head where it had struck the bulkhead. "You've kidnapped me and my son and stolen my ship."

Toni rubbed her own jaw. She still tasted blood, and her neck was just beginning to ache from Stefan's too-enthusiastic choke hold. Toni II took the opportunity to answer. "The sooner you help, the sooner we'll be out of your lives and you can go back to normal."

Karl snorted and looked at Stefan. "Normal, she says."

"We don't want your ship, or you," Toni said, "We just needed to get out of there. Once we're on planet you can take off and go back to—"

Karl laughed.

"What?" Toni asked.

"You two really are Styx military, aren't you?"

"So?"

Karl shook his head. "A pirate would have some sense of economics. Even if my crew haven't taken their stake in the last load and found other work, they'll certainly have by the time we could get back. You've taken two months out of my schedule, so I've lost every contract that had been waiting for me on my normal run. Some of those I've been serving for seven years. You've pretty much destroyed my business, Lieutenant Valentine."

There was a long silence in the cockpit before Toni II muttered something about insurance.

That's when Stefan lost it, "You stupid, thoughtless bitch! Do you have any idea what you've done?"

Karl looked at his son. "Stefan, please—"

"Thirty years my dad worked! Thirty years! You know

what the average time is before a sole operator goes bankrupt?"

"Stefan?"

"Six months! Six months!" Spit flew from his mouth to hang in a weightless constellation in front of him. "This was his life. It was just as good as putting a bullet in his brain—"

"Stefan, stop it!" Karl snapped at his son. Toni II had lowered the gun, and Toni could see the same sick feeling in her face that Toni felt in her own gut. Karl looked between the two of them and said, "You aren't going to shoot us, are you?"

"No," Toni said.

Karl sighed. "The point my son makes is that while we're insured for piracy, that only covers direct losses. Cargo, refueling, replacement cost of the ship if you steal it—business and personnel losses, no. As it is, after a year of arbitration I might get just enough paid out to cover my debts."

"I'm sorry," Toni said.

"At this point an apology is more amusing than anything else."

"An apology—" Stefan began to yell again.

"Stefan!" Karl cut him off. "I did not raise an idiot child. Stop acting like one."

Toni sighed and turned around toward the communication console. "I guess I'll request clearance to land and we can wait in the queue."

Karl laughed. "You don't want to do that."

"What?" Toni II asked before Toni could.

"Actually, I guess you can ask for clearance. You just can't land."

Toni turned slowly back around to face the two of them. "Why can't we land?"

"We don't have a contragrav, damn it!" Stefan told her. "This ship *can't* land."

Toni II raised her hand as if she were about to backhand the kid with the gun. Toni spoke before her twin's arm could move. "Don't play games, kid. We know the specs on a x252 cargo ship."

"What about the specs on *this* cargo ship?" Karl asked. After a pause where both Tonis stared at him, he said, "I thought so. You had no idea—"

"Idea about what?" Toni II practically screamed at the man. Toni wanted to yell at her to calm down, but showing any form of discord between them in front of their captives would be worse than an emotional outburst.

"The Daedalus was customized to carry the same load as a 252 with the tach capability of an x252. That required stripping away extra mass that wasn't part of the tach-drive or life support—"

"Like the fucking contragrav," Stefan interjected.

"As well as structural components that were only required for a descent into a gravity well," Karl concluded. "Over the years we've tuned the *Daedalus* to tow mass in excess of 125% any other 252 series cargo ship."

"You just can't land," Toni whispered. She almost wanted to laugh at how badly her first foray into piracy was going. They'd managed to steal a ship that couldn't even make planetfall. What the hell were they going to do now? They had no resources—

"What's your cargo?" Toni II asked them.

Stefan snorted and muttered something that sounded like, "Great pirates we got here."

Toni was inclined to agree with the sentiment.

Karl sighed. "About half our load has been off-loaded— anything valuable, sealed courier packages and the like, were taken off first. We were waiting for a surface-bound transport to take the remaining containers."

"Containers of?" Toni II asked.

"Agricultural products, tropical fruit mostly."

"Fruit?"

"Fruit," Karl said. "On Styx, the margin for exotic food-stuffs is incredible. What little growing capacity they have is dedicated to staples, no reserve left for luxury items."

Toni II looked at her and said, "Fruit," as if she couldn't quite understand the meaning of the word. Toni felt the same stunned expression on her face. She turned around and looked at one of the comm displays and called up the cargo manifest and started reading.

"Pineapple, banana, mango, papaya, kiwi . . ." Four full containers of the stuff. *Tons* of fruit.

Tons.

Toni tapped on the display and realized that she hadn't been thinking like a pirate, and it was time she started. They couldn't land, but there would certainly be orbital stations that could accommodate the *Daedalus*. And, this being the free-for-all Bakunin, there had to be someone in the market for what they carried. "Mr. Stavros?"

"Yes?"

"I'm afraid we're going to have to be pirates for a bit longer. We'll be taking your cargo to finance a berth to dock somewhere in orbit, and to find passage . . . somewhere. Once we take care of that, we'll release your ship back to you."

"If you are going to be pirates a bit longer, my I suggest erasing the log and the cockpit surveillance video?"

"Dad? You're helping them?"

"Shh, Son. Just making the best of a bad situation."

Toni glanced over to a small display showing the data recorder for the cockpit. She stopped it, and after drilling through the advanced menu, she found the command to purge all the recorded data.

"What's the point of that?" Toni II asked. "There's still surveillance footage from the rest of the ship, and if we purge all that, they still have data from the air lock back at 3SEC—"

"It's just better if there isn't a record of what happens in this cockpit," Karl said. "When I make an insurance claim against your theft of the *Daedalus*."

"Dad?"

Toni turned around. "You don't want this ship back?"

"A claim on the lost cargo will just cover my costs, not my losses. My son already explained the disruption of my business. If you really do wish to provide me some compensation, allow me to make a claim on the ship itself. I own it free and clear, and its loss would bring a hefty settlement . . ."

Toni had a sudden realization, and Toni II articulated it.

"And you'd like to combine it with the proceeds from selling it on the black market here on Bakunin?"

"A black market implies an illegal sale," Karl said. "That's an inappropriate term since there are no laws here."

"Dad, you'd really sell the *Daedalus?*"

"Actually, I was hoping that our pirates here would broker such a deal for us. Better to keep the Stavroses out of it for the sake of the insurance investigators."

Toni stared at the man who was, only a few subjective minutes ago, trying to kill her to defend his ship. "You're asking us to sell your ship?"

"I'd be willing to give a commission for a quick sale."

"Dad!"

"Do we have a deal?" Karl asked.

Toni looked up at her other self and saw the same befuddlement in her face. They both said, simultaneously, "You have a deal."

Karl Stavros evidently had prior experience with the environment around Bakunin. As he said in an aside to Toni, "A necessary skill for any successful operator in my profession." As he guided her though the complex web of orbital platforms and contract negotiations, she wondered exactly what that profession actually *was*. He didn't strike her as someone who made his money hauling fruit.

So what were you carrying in those "sealed courier packages"?

Even with the assistance of someone who knew the vicinity, they still couldn't find a destination for the *Daedalus*. Ten times the normal inbound traffic stalled everything they tried to do. Just the intense level of radio chatter made it hard to communicate. It took several long minutes just for an orbital platform to respond to their query, and almost always the response was, "Wait a moment while I clear these other ten calls I have ahead of you."

Those moments were closer to hours. Hours talking to habitats named *Crowley, Luther, Hamilton, Light of Our Lord, General Fabrication Facility 23, Lingam, Hellfire Steel, Yoder, Nirvana, Dead Dog, Wisconsin* . . .

It became increasingly clear that they were going to be drifting in the *Daedalus* for a while. After the initial urgency faded into a frustrating routine of opening a channel, sending a burst, and waiting for a response, Toni II spoke up, "Maybe we should look into what the hell's happening here?"

Toni looked over her shoulder at herself and it struck her that however frustrating it was for her, it must be an order of magnitude worse simply *watching* them hit virtual wall after wall.

Karl leaned back and rubbed his eyes, both of which had developed considerable shiners. "Your sister's right. We're not going to get docking privileges anywhere, any time soon."

Toni stared at Karl, then looked back at Toni II. *She's probably thinking the same thing I am.*

Sister.

"Thoughts, Sis?" Toni asked her.

Her newly christened sister smiled. "Let's try and get into someone's data net."

They couldn't hook into any paid data stream here without an account on the planet to draw from, but there were plenty of streams that were various flavors of free. Of the ones the *Daedalus* could pick up on, there were half a dozen news feeds.

Her "sister" bent over Toni's shoulder and touched the console screen selecting the feed from the Jefferson Commune Interplanetary Free Press.

The first headline made Toni suck in a breath. "Oh, boy," she whispered.

The past couple of hours had distracted her from the reason they had hijacked the *Daedalus* in the first place. She had never doubted herself or her sister as to what was going to happen—but it hadn't hit her on a gut level until she saw it glowing in a news holo.

Stefan, who had been snoring in one of the crash chairs, woke up and walked up to the three of them muttering, "What's this?"

Toni didn't answer.

The headline read, WORMHOLE NETWORK UNDER ATTACK?

The holo began playing a high-resolution image, obviously enhanced, showing something she had only imagined before. A stretch of interstellar space showing two large distortions, both mirrored spheres reflecting stars other than the ones surrounding them. The two spheres were frozen in time, the distance between them impossible to judge.

"Just twenty-five days ago, an alien wormhole appeared at the fringes of our solar system. Its presence was announced with an unprecedented burst of tachyon radiation that was detected by several places simultaneously, most notably by—"

"I asked," Stefan interrupted, "what is this?"

Toni's sister responded before Toni could. "It's the reason I'm here holding a gun on you rather than beating virtual marines to a pulp. Now shut the hell up."

The narrator continued. *"Xi Virginis traveling at a velocity three quarters of the speed of light. Compiled from several sources, we have a series of images from the impact."*

On the holo the view shifted, with the wormhole to the right now about a quarter of the way to the stationary one on the left. Toni now realized that the stars reflected in the right-hand sphere were noticeably blue-shifted, and the sphere itself was slightly distorted from the perfect round shape of its target.

The picture shifted again, and now the right-hand wormhole was halfway to its target. Both wormholes showed distortion in their reflected star fields, as if there were ripples in their nonexistent surface.

The next image had the distance between the wormholes quartered, and both showed extreme rippling distortion; in addition, both seemed to stretch toward each other.

The image cut away to a far distant perspective showing the explosion of impact. A new star glowing brighter and brighter, causing the stars around it to fade until it was a lone boiling white spark in a empty black sky.

"No reliable casualty estimates exist as of yet, but damage to tach-drives and communication devices have been extensive throughout the system. As much as two-thirds of tach-ships and three quarters of the interstellar communications infrastructure—"

Karl looked at both Tonis and asked, "What did you mean, '*This* is the reason.'"

"The same thing was happening around Sigma Draconis. All three wormholes."

"All three—" Karl began.

"Just listen," both Tonis said simultaneously.

"—first transmissions were received indicating this was not an isolated event. We have confirmed that communications have come from Earth, Occisis, Cynos, Khamsin, Shiva, Windsor . . ."

Toni listened to the litany of systems.

Every wormhole in the old network had been destroyed. Every single one—tearing apart communications and transportation capabilities as it went. As the commentary went on, it was clear that most of the tach-comm messages, confirming the destruction, were messages sent before the actual impact, describing the wormholes coming insystem to the wormholes orbiting Alpha Centauri, Sirius, 61 Cygni, Epsilon Eridani . . . .

While a few planets, like Bakunin with only its single wormhole, had a few surviving tach-comms afterward, many, like Earth—itself with seven wormholes—had gone silent.

Now, within the past week, people had started taching into the system. Many were escaping from Earth, where the Terran government was attempting to seize every tach-capable ship as soon as they tached in. Or they were from Cynos, where the Sirian government had instituted martial law with the strong implication that war with the Caliphate was imminent.

There was no word coming from Styx. It was one of the places with a communication blackout, and the *Daedalus* was apparently the first ship to arrive here from Sigma Draconis.

"Lieutenant Valentine," Karl said, "I think you and your sister may have done us a favor."

CHAPTER TWENTY-FIVE

Baptism

"You never receive the punishment you expect."
—*The Cynic's Book of Wisdom*

"No man sins by an act he cannot avoid."
—St. Augustine
(354–430)

Date: 2526.7.15 (Standard)
1,750,000 km from Bakunin–BD+50°1725

All Nickolai knew was pain; an all-consuming visceral agony whose intensity erased everything else from his consciousness. He lost even an awareness of self. He became, for a time, nothing except a single sensation divorced from any context and meaning.

The first coherent thought he had was an unanswered plea to God. *Why don't I die?*

The single half-prayer echoed through his mind until the agony receded enough for another thought to form, a thought that brought with it a fear as intense as the pain.

Perhaps he was dead and in hell.

What was hell but a void filled with pain and empty prayers?

No, somewhere, he felt himself breathing. He felt pressure on his chest, and he became aware of a mechanical thrum.

Engines . . .

Voices as well, indistinct human voices masked by the

sound of engines and the rush of blood in his ears. The engine noise suddenly stopped, and with it the pressure eased on his chest. A sense of his body returned as the sensation of gravity left. The return of that sense of himself gave a locus to his agony, in his skull, behind his eyes.

Behind where his eyes had been.

Memories and thoughts returned in a disorganized rush as he understood exactly what he had done. How could he be alive? He should be dead in a pool of his own blood.

Distantly he heard a voice, "Move it, damn you. Help get this off of him."

Kugara's voice.

He remembered her panicked expression when he raised the gun to his skull. Even though he had only seen human faces for a few short months, he could read the stew of rage and fear in his memory of her face. It seemed *too* clear now, etched in his mind's eye like the ghost of a sun stared at too long.

"Move! After what I went through saving this furry bastard—"

Did she save me?

Why?

He heard several humans grunt, and something lifted off his body with a metallic screech. He hadn't even been aware that he had been pinned down, but suddenly with it gone he felt his body gently lose contact with the floor.

He felt someone touch his skull. He groaned and the hand snatched itself away. Several people muttered in human languages he didn't understand, but someone did say in a shocked tone, "He's alive?"

Kugara's voice responded, "He's tougher than he looks."

Nickolai reached for his face, and the throbbing at his temples and behind his eye sockets. He felt his own fur sticky with blood, a fresh wound across his forehead. "Hurts," he muttered, feeling weak for acknowledging it.

"You put yourself through worse," Kugara told him.

That I have.

Then he realized that *two* hands gripped his face, and the pain was suddenly forgotten. He touched fingers to his

face and felt the roughness of his pads against the fullness
of his eyeballs under closed lids.

My arm? My eyes? Did I hallucinate everything?

He pulled his hands away and forced his eyes open. His
eyelids strained against gummed-up blood, but in a moment they tore open, flooding his gaze with light, a mass
of unfamiliar human faces, and the specter of a right hand
that should not have been there.

He flexed his claws, and the humans around him
backed off. All except Kugara, covered in blood that
smelled of him. She remained stationary, weightless
next to him, holding on to a handrail attached to a badly
canted door.

Nickolai stared at his claws, and all of them were black.
He had expected the gunmetal gray claws on the right
hand, the artificial one, the one that had been almost but
not quite real. What he saw now, though, mirrored his left
hand.

Mirrored it precisely.

Down to a hairline crack ending with a three millimeter-
wide chip on the claw tipping his index finger. He turned
his hands around to look at their backs and found that the
mirroring was exact down to the striping in his fur.

He looked at Kugara and asked, "How?"

Her expression was unreadable, but her voice carried equal parts sadness and apprehension. "I'm sorry,
Nickolai."

"Sorry?"

"I asked the Protean to treat your wounds—" She shook
her head, which caused her to drift slightly from the door
and her hair to fan out in a ragged halo. "No, I *demanded* it.
You were going to die, and I wasn't going to let that happen
if I could stop it."

He stared at her in disbelief, and she must have seen it as
a rebuke, because she snapped at him, "Was I supposed to
let you die? Let you bleed out on the floor because I might
offend your sensibilities? To hell with—"

"Thank you," Nickolai whispered.

"You can just take—What did you say?"

"I said, thank you." He clenched his hands into perfectly

symmetrical fists. Quietly he said, "I did not wish to die. That wasn't the point of what I did. Suicide is a sin."

Whatever relief it would bring.

He raised his gaze and found his head aching again, this time from the unnatural clarity of his vision. Every edge in his field of view felt sharp enough to slice his retinas. He floated in a confined space, an equipment storeroom of some sort. The door bent inward at an odd angle, and a few streaks of blood marred its surface. Fur stuck to the thickest streaks, so it was probably his blood. Stenciled above the blood was the human script used by the Caliphate. It was illegible to him, but distinctive enough to be instantly recognizable.

Most of the unfamiliar human crowd had backed away from the door now, and he could see a long chamber stretching to a bulkhead about fifteen meters away.

Kugara still stared at him, as if she didn't understand his last statement.

"We're on a Caliphate troop transport," she said. He reached for a shelf that showed severe dents where his body had collided. The polymer sheath that should have kept the contents in place during free fall and high-G maneuvers fluttered in tattered shreds. As he used one of the shelf's struts to pull himself into a vertical position relative to the door, the shredded polymer leaped upon his fur, clutching at him with a static embrace. Random debris and small packages of bolts, power cells, and ammunition floated in chaotic orbits between him and Kugara. "Where are we?"

"I don't know," she said.

Fully conscious now, he could feel bruises and lacerations all over his body. Beyond the door and the unfamiliar faces, he could hear groaning and a few voices that were familiar. He pushed himself toward the doorway, and the humans moved aside, like a curtain parting upon a diorama of the apocalypse. Out here the floating debris included parts of chairs, broken weapons, buckles torn off of crash webbing, spheres of blood, and human teeth.

The group of humans that had seemed so overwhelming when he had opened his eyes turned out to be only three unevenly dressed human males. One wore a black jump-suit constructed of flexible body armor. The other two were in green overalls stitched with Caliphate markings. Many more similarly dressed humans were all over the passenger compartment, the green outnumbering the black. They moved in chaotic clusters around four bodies, trying to render first aid.

"What happened?" he asked, breathing in the scents of blood, fear, and death.

"Firefight," Kugara said. "Then a rough takeoff. The ship must have hit ten G's without any time to secure anyone or anything. Especially you."

Nickolai could see the path he must have taken—streaks of blood and fur marred the floor leading from the front of the compartment all the way to the broken door he'd pulled himself out of.

He counted four critically wounded people, the focus of all of the attention that wasn't being given to him. Three were the green-clad Caliphate people, and the last was an ancient-looking bald man in a blood-spattered white coat.

One of the humans moved and the familiar face stunned Nickolai. Dr. Dörner hovered to his left, going to help treat one of the fallen Caliphate crew, a large bandage covering the base of her skull. He couldn't make sense that she was *here,* a member of the science team from the *Eclipse.* Then he saw Dr. Brody, similarly bandaged, with an apparently broken arm strapped to his chest.

Last, by the old man in the white overcoat, the priest, Father Mallory put pressure on a massive wound in the old man's torso. The back of Mallory's skull was marked by the same hasty field dressing as the others, in the same place.

A memory surfaced, and Nickolai realized that Mallory had been there, by the tach-comm.

And now he was here, an admitted Vatican agent, in the belly of a Caliphate troop transport.

Does it make less sense than the fact I walk among humans?

Less sense than the fact I am not dead?

Less sense than the fact I don't want to die?

All his life, his world had been defined by well-marked boundaries of defined extent. Now he hung weightless in a ship of wounded human beings and found that he no longer knew where those boundaries were, or even if they still existed.

Someone treating one of the wounded called out, "I need help here."

Nickolai pushed against the ceiling and drifted over to render whatever aid he could.

Mallory's blood-soaked hands shook as he lifted them from the hole in Shane's chest, a hole that was now filled with military-grade surgical foam. His hands ached from holding Shane's lung inside his body.

Mallory stared at the chaos inside the dropship, his thoughts bouncing around like he had during the spacecraft's ascent. He knew the jitters and the fragmented thought process were the dual symptoms of intense fatigue and the crash coming from reaching the limit of his old implants. In some sense he was lucky that they were weightless; under gravity he might have collapsed.

For some reason he kept thinking about the fact that he still wore the same clothes he had worn on the *Eclipse*.

The feeling of déjà vu was uncomfortable. The people around him wore the same blank expressions, the same sense of displacement, that he remembered from the masses of refugees that fled across the surface of Occisis during the overthrow of the Junta. He had been barely an adult, just old enough to be a marine, and his choice to fight the revolutionary loyalists had put him in the bloodiest fighting in New Dublin. After the battles were over and the city was a mass of rubble and burning cathedrals, the surviving members of his unit had withdrawn into the countryside, right into a refugee camp.

Not really a camp. No one had imposed any organization upon the outflow of civilians from the city. Ten thousand people had just stopped in a large cow pasture, close enough that the smell of the burning city hung in the air. Mallory could still feel their eyes following him and his comrades as they walked toward the command station. The

night had been cold, and the devil's eye of Alpha Centauri
B drenched the scene in a dirty red glow.

The stares came from lawyers, children, laborers, servants, and nuns. All wore the clothes they escaped with, and
all wore the expression of people permanently displaced
from a world that no longer existed. The stares accused
Mallory, saw him not as a liberator, but as a harbinger of a
new world that they didn't understand. A world that might
not welcome them.

In the confines of this dropship, Mallory saw the same
dead stare he had seen in those refugees from New Dublin.
He saw it equally in the eyes of the Caliphate crew and in
the Salmagundi militia who had discarded their helmets.
He saw it in the man Flynn, who was helping one of the
Caliphate casualties. He saw it in Dörner's face as she tied
a primitive dressing across Alexander Shane's chest before
moving to the next casualty of the firefight. He saw it in
Brody, who hung back, his broken arm rendering him more
a hindrance than a help.

He saw it in Kugara's stare as Nickolai rose and pulled
himself out of a supply closet like a pagan god digging himself out of Hades. Mallory looked at the genetically engineered tiger, the one person who didn't have the expression
of a refugee. Nickolai didn't wear any expression Mallory
could read. It might have been partly hidden by the black,
featureless eyes, but there was also something else in the
cast of his face, the way he regarded the chaos around him,
that seemed fundamentally different from the Nickolai he
had known aboard the *Eclipse.*

The cabin was not scaled for someone Nickolai's size, so
he seemed even larger and more imposing than he actually
was. Add to that the blood matting his fur, and Mallory understood why the militiamen and the Caliphate crew members pulled themselves back out of his way as he emerged.

*A long time ago, when his ancestors roamed the jungle,
they were figures of worship . . .*

The Caliphate techs stared at the tiger, and Mallory realized how thoroughly demoralized they must be. Aside
from the wounded woman who wore the hash marks of a
technical sergeant, none of the others ranked above cor-

poral. This wasn't a combat unit; they were all dressed like maintenance crew. Kugara and the Ashley Militia had cut their numbers in half. And even with half the numbers of the remaining disarmed Caliphate crew, the militia made a much more impressive force.

"Has anyone checked out the cockpit?" Mallory called out as he pushed away from Shane, who now at least seemed stable. He hadn't heard anything from Parvi since the panicked command to secure everyone.

Dörner looked back from the Caliphate sergeant and shook her head.

Mallory pulled himself along using the shreds of cargo webbing that dangled from the walls. He passed Brody, who glanced up at him and said, "I guess we survived."

Mallory could hear the toxic threads of guilt already infecting the man's voice. Dörner had told him what had happened to Dr. Pak. "Would you come with me? I may need help in the cockpit."

"I only have one arm."

"Everyone else is dealing with the injured." That wasn't quite true, but Brody didn't point that out as he followed him to the cockpit. Mallory pulled himself through the forward corridor, pushing aside dense clusters of floating debris that had drifted forward when the acceleration ceased.

"What happened in that building?" Brody asked. "Where did the tiger come from?"

"Nickolai and Kugara were there for the tach-comm, same as us."

"What happened to him? His eyes?"

Mallory didn't answer. Instead he gently pushed a large ammo crate from in front of the cockpit door. When he pressed the controls to open it, the doorway slid aside and jammed halfway, hung up on a large dent in the center.

"Mallory?" Brody called after him.

"Come with me," Mallory said, pulling himself sideways through the half-open door. When he was through, floating free in the cockpit, he turned his head and said, "God help us."

"What is it?" Brody asked from the other side of the door.

"Go back and get the medics up here! I have Parvi and Wahid, and they're both unconscious and bleeding." Mallory heard Brody withdraw and start yelling down the corridor for assistance.

Wahid floated in the middle of the cockpit, half his face swollen into an ugly, bloody bruise. He didn't appear to be breathing. Mallory grabbed for him and pulled the man close. He opened Wahid's mouth to clear the airway, and out came a ugly blob of mucus and dark blood.

God have mercy on him.

He looked over to Parvi. She was still strapped in the pilot's chair, and to his relief he saw her chest move. At least she was still alive. Her white hair was marred by a dark red streak where something had struck her, and her arm floated above the console in front of her, as if she were reaching for the viewscreen.

On the viewscreen, nestled against a starry backdrop, was a familiar planet.

He stared at it uncomprehendingly. They had been over a hundred light-years away. No ship could cross that distance in a single tach-jump. None. It was impossible.

But Bakunin floated in the viewscreen, mocking his notion of the possible.

They had returned.

CHAPTER TWENTY-SIX

Babel

"The universe does not lie, but that doesn't mean you understand what it is saying."
—*The Cynic's Book of Wisdom*

"Nothing fixes a thing so intensely in the memory as the wish to forget it."

—MICHEL DE MONTAIGNE
(1533–1592)

Date: 2526.7.16 (Standard)
1,750,000 km from Bakunin–BD+50°1725

Parvi stands on a plateau on one of the windswept canyons on Rubai, where the constant equatorial winds have ablated away all but the hardest bedrock. The sky's a constant brown from windblown dust, and the sound of the air slipping past rock sounds like the planet itself is crying. She stands in her old uniform from the Expeditionary Command, atop one of the five-hundred-meter granite fingers that reach up from the floor of the canyon.

Across the top of the granite pillar, a lone figure sits facing her. The seated woman wears khaki overalls with a Caliphate shoulder patch. Her face is light-skinned, framed by black hair, and she stares at Parvi with almond eyes. Her throat is swollen and black with bruises. When she opens her mouth, the inside glistens red with blood.

Parvi knows she is dreaming, but still backs up a step.

"I know what this is," the woman says in a hoarse voice, barely audible. Blood drips down her chin and for a mo-

ment Parvi is reminded of Mosasa. "I've heard all of it."
The woman coughs.

"What have you heard?"

The woman whispers, spitting blood, and Parvi can't
make out the words. She walks forward, but it doesn't help.
"Please, I can't hear what you're saying."

The woman doesn't react to the words. Parvi realizes
that the woman is still talking. She speaks in a stream of
consciousness, only a third of which is actually audible.
Parvi stands still until she makes out, "All of them running
around, you're the only one listening to me."

Something grips Parvi's heart, a desperate fear. Even
with her awareness of the dream world around her, she has
a sense that the words are important, vital. She has already
lost too much of the woman's statement to the roaring
wind and her own interruptions. She closes her eyes and
focuses her mind on what's being said.

"I hear them say 'Protean.' The Protean was on Salmagundi. The Cult of Proteus would be the only beings who
would fully understand what Adam is. What Adam is capable of. The Protean knew what could face Adam."

Parvi strained to focus on the voice, her eyes shut so
tightly that her scalp hurt. The whispering voice continued,
closer.

"It says to find those that came before it. The Protean
came from Bakunin. What came before it. Before us. On
Bakunin. The ancient ones, relics, the only ones we know of
that were as powerful as Adam." The voice broke off into
a coughing fit.

Parvi's eyes flew open and she was no longer dreaming. She was in the back of the passenger compartment on
the Caliphate dropship, staring at the old man from Salmagundi, strapped to a makeshift stretcher attached to the
wall, coughing up mouthfuls of blood.

"Help here!" Parvi called out from her own stretcher,
"Medic!"

Parvi watched as three men worked to save Alexander
Shane, the senior member of the Grand Triad of Salmagundi, as he tried to drown in an internal flood of his own

blood. The surgical foam they had used to seal his chest wound had failed during one of his coughing fits.

After they stabilized Shane, Parvi worked on freeing herself from her own stretcher. One of the men who'd been working on Shane placed a hand on her shoulder. "You're wounded."

She looked up at the guy, and recognized the English-speaking kid who'd been waving a plasma cannon around on board the *Voice*. He still wore the overalls of a mainte-nance tech, but they were spattered with blood. From the unscathed look of him, it wasn't his own.

"How many pilots do you have aboard this thing?" she half-groaned, half-growled.

"But—"

She surprised herself by uttering a syllable that would have been more at home coming from the morey tiger's throat. It did its job; the kid backed off.

As he did, she saw the extent of the mess. The wounded and people with blank, shell-shocked expressions mixed with ragged soldiers in fetal positions trying to sleep. She saw the morey, huge and inhuman, folded over himself in the corner, snoring. She saw Dörner and Brody near him. She saw Sergeant Abbas strapped to another stretcher, ab-domen bandaged, her unconscious face ashen and glisten-ing with sweat.

She also saw Wahid.

Couldn't someone have covered his face?

She turned to look at the kid from the *Voice*, who wore the same expression of blank resignation, an ex-pression of someone looking out at the world who had lost the desire to even attempt to place it into a larger context.

None of the Caliphate crew were armed. It was clear who was in charge here at the moment.

"Where is Kugara?"

He said something in Arabic that didn't sound com-plimentary. When she didn't understand, he said, "In the cockpit."

Parvi winced a little, thinking of Kugara at the controls. She had recruited the woman, and while she had been part of the *Eclipse*'s bridge crew and had just enough cross training to fly a tach-ship in a pinch, Parvi had seen her test scores. The woman could go toe-to-toe with the tiger in hand-to-hand or light infantry, but her piloting scores were in the low 200's.

She pulled her way toward the cockpit, past Wahid. She felt her gut tighten, but she forced herself to defer her emotions. She couldn't allow herself to react until she knew what was happening.

She drifted through the wedged-open cockpit door and saw Kugara and Mallory, both manning comm displays while the familiar globe of Bakunin hung centered on the main viewscreen in front of them.

Parvi allowed herself to feel a small measure of relief that they had returned to the world she was familiar with. The Caliphate's new tach-dive had operated as promised.

Something felt wrong though.

Kugara spoke without raising her head from the scrolling comm display before her. "I don't fucking believe these people. We have injured here—"

Mallory responded in a weary voice, "We're on a Caliphate ship—"

"That should matter *here*?"

"These aren't Bakunin natives we're talking to. The nationality matters, especially to people fleeing a war."

"A war?" Parvi said. The exclamation was loud enough that it set her head ringing slightly. She reached up and touched the bandage on her scalp and groaned loudly as her entire head threatened to burst open.

Mallory and Kugara spun around to face her. "Parvi!" Mallory said. "You're injured! You shouldn't be up here."

Kugara reached out to steady her. "Let's get you back—"

Parvi slapped Kugara's hand away, "Don't patronize me. Don't *touch* me!" She glared at Mallory, "What war?"

"You need to rest—" he began.

"And you don't?" She pointed at Kugara. "She's got an excuse— she's not human. You look like the walking dead. How long since *you* rested?"

"Please, calm down," he said. "We're trying to contact another ship or orbital habitat that can treat our wounded."

"What?" Parvi sputtered. Was Kugara that lame a pilot? "Get the hell out of the pilot's chair so I can land this thing."

"We can't land," Mallory said.

"Well I sure as hell can. Move it!"

She reached for the chair Kugara sat in, and discovered that forcing the issue wasn't a great idea. Even if Kugara hadn't been the descendant of some genetic engineer's design of an über-warrior, the woman had nearly half a meter height on her, and corresponding advantages in muscle mass and reach. Parvi didn't know exactly how it happened, but somehow she ended up floating upside down in the center of the cockpit, the abdomen of her uniform balled up in Kugara's fist.

It was then she realized half of Kugara's own fatigues were covered in blood. "We *can't* land," she snapped at Parvi. With her free hand she slapped a control on the console, and the cockpit filled with the sound of a transmission.

"This is a general announcement from the Proudhon Spaceport Development Corporation. All approaches into planetary airspace are closed until further notice. Any unauthorized spacecraft attempting to make landfall will be shot down without any further warning. PSDC air traffic control will announce when it will again start clearing arrivals. The PSDC will not grant clearance to approaching aircraft until these restrictions are lifted. There will be no exceptions. Your cooperation is expected and will be enforced."

Parvi stared at Kugara, trying to come to grips with the announcement. The PSDC had shut the planet down. She hadn't heard of anything like that happening before. Not since—

Not since the Confederacy, Parvi thought.

Kugara let her go, leaving her floating in the center of the cockpit. She turned around and started back to the console. "Now if you'll pardon me, I need to do something about the people back there. I got fifteen thousand ships out there, and someone's going to let us use a medbay."

"Fifteen thousand?" Parvi whispered.

Mallory pulled her over and righted her, guiding her over to the nav station on the side of him opposite Kugara. Parvi shook her head. "Did I mishear that?"

"No, we have about fifteen thousand active transponders in the immediate area. From everywhere, Acheron to Waldgrave."

"You said there was a war?"

"Yes."

While Kugara tried to find a friendly ship, Mallory explained what they knew about what had happened in the forty days they had been in tachspace.

As he talked, it sank in to Parvi how long they had been gone. Their tach-jump in this ship had taken forty days from the universe around them. But it had been eight *months* since they had begun Mosasa's ill-fated adventure.

The resistance on Rubai only lasted eight months.

Eight months was more than enough time for a war. More than enough time for governments to collapse.

More than enough time for everything to change.

Mallory and Kugara had been in the cockpit for several hours now, trying to find someone to help with their injured. While they contacted ships and orbital habitats, they also had a news feed running from the Bakunin Mercenaries' Union; or more precisely, a feed from some orbital repeater that mirrored the ground-based BMU servers. Kugara told Parvi, somewhat ominously, that transmissions from the surface appeared to be limited to the PSDC no-fly warning.

The BMU feed, even old and secondhand, was the only source Kugara knew of as trustworthy, and they hadn't the time to filter through the mess of information on their own.

Mess was the right word, with thousands of potential news sources, in addition to the flotilla of ships filling the system with their own chatter.

What came over the BMU feed was not encouraging. In Mallory's words, "We have not escaped him."

The wormhole network was gone, at least every part of it where word had managed to travel back as far as Bakunin. All accounts suggested that, approximately thirty-nine days ago, every wormhole in the network had been targeted by another alien wormhole coming at it at close to two thirds the speed of light. In every case where there was data on the incoming wormhole, the source was identified as Xi Virginis.

"Where Xi Virginis *was*," Mallory explained. "The star itself must have fueled the attack."

Suddenly, the attack on Salmagundi seemed minor. Almost an afterthought. If Mallory was right, it meant that Adam had spent decades planning a coordinated attack across the entire core of human space.

And the attack was devastating. Not because the wormholes themselves were used for goods and travel—they hadn't been for centuries. It was devastating because when the wormholes were annihilated, their destruction released waves of tachyon radiation that severely damaged any active tach-drive and tach-comm in the vicinity.

The wormhole network was densest in the longest-established, most populous, and most advanced systems. The capital planets, Cynos, Occisis, Khamsin, and Earth itself, were the most affected, with communication completely cut off and entire fleets immobilized.

Absent specific knowledge about the source of the attack, the subsequent movement toward war was predictable. Each state determined that the attack more than likely originated within the plans of their historical rivals. Sources in the BMU confirmed that the governments of the Centauri Alliance and the Sirius Economic Community were arraying against the Caliphate, spurred on by the details of the Caliphate's new monster carriers, and its adventures out toward the vicinity of Xi Virginis.

Every place about which information was available had planetary governments seizing every source of interstellar communication and transportation that were available. More than half the ships in the Bakunin system were here avoiding the nationalization of their vessels.

The others were escaping the aftermath.

The most recent news was from Ormolu, the nearest inhabited planet to Bakunin. The fastest tach-time from

Ormolu with a standard engine was twenty days. The new Caliphate drives could make it in less than a week.

Ormolu was part of the Sirius Economic Community, which meant that the Caliphate historically thought of it as a rightful part of their own territory, dating from the time when Sirius and Epsilon Eridani formed a single political entity. Of course, the same could be said about *all* of the planets in the Sirius Economic Community. Ormolu was isolated, however. It was light-years beyond the outside range of a standard military tach-drive from anywhere in Caliphate-controlled space. Since it was beyond the tactical sphere of any potential attack, it was lightly defended, with only a few ships and a single planetary tach-transmitter. And since the system was one of the few in the Sirius Economic Community without a wormhole, the presence of both working tach-comm and tach-ships increased its strategic significance.

One of the massive Caliphate warships had tached in and within a few hours had effectively annexed the system, causing a logistical and communications bottleneck for Sirius.

Mallory rubbed his eyes, looking exhausted, and said in a weak voice, "The Caliphate may have seen itself as under attack, and this was a relatively bloodless defensive move. No one else will see it that way—it looks like part of a co-ordinated attack. Which is what Adam wanted, I'm sure. Wars and rumors of wars."

He rubbed his face. "Adam planned this. Like Mosasa, he manipulated everything. Salmagundi and Xi Virginis are so far, so remote . . . We actually outran my tach-comm transmission from Salmagundi, and given what's happened, I don't even know if anyone will receive it. And now that forces are moving, I don't know if it will do any good."

Parvi looked at his ashen face and lost expression, and said, "You're the one who needs to go back and rest."

Mallory nodded and pushed himself up from the chair. "Help Kugara find some assistance."

"I'll do that."

CHAPTER TWENTY-SEVEN

Mission

"The wait is the most dreadful time of any adversity."
　　　　　　　　　—*The Cynic's Book of Wisdom*

"Don't worry, they'll start shooting soon."
　　　　　　　　　—Datia Rajasthan
　　　　　　　　　　　(?–2042)

Date: 2526.7.17 (Standard)
1,500,000 km from Bakunin–BD+50°1725

Shortly after waking up, Toni pulled herself down into one of the *Daedalus'* cargo holds to fight the pernicious effects of two and a half weeks without gravity.

Two and a half weeks, and their prospects for docking anywhere had only gotten worse. The PSDC had gone from restricting approaches to completely barring access to the planet, going as far as defining a no-fly zone from synchronous orbit on down. So far at least three ships had unsuccessfully tried to breach the blockade and found out the hard way that the Proudhon Spaceport Development Company had the firepower to enforce its restrictions.

Meaning the population of ships floating out here had exploded. And the orbital habitats were completely overwhelmed.

Toni, as "Lieutenant Valentine" and the ranking pirate, had been calling the shots ever since Karl had surrendered, and it was beginning to wear on her. Her twin sister, Toni II, "Corporal Beth," did what she could to ease the burden, but in the end, Toni was the one in charge, the one with the responsibility. She didn't even have a threat of mutiny to distract her. Karl had made the decision that it was in his best interest to follow along, and while his son despised her, Stefan would do anything his father asked of him. And if that meant kissing the ass of two sibling pirates, he held his nose and did his duty.

So that left Toni with little to do but establish a routine and dwell on exactly what they were going to do. Part of that routine was establishing an impromptu exercise yard to deal with the effects of zero-G. In a space normally filled by a cargo container, Toni had tethered one of the ship's powered hardsuits that normally was used for loading. By calibrating the joint resistance on the thing, they had a functional substitute for the exercise machine she had back at her old station.

Unfortunately, it came with no VR capability, so she had to run in place, looking at a dingy bulkhead.

As she methodically pumped her legs and arms against the suit, she tried to think of a proper course of action. The *Daedalus* was fortunate in that it had significant reserves of air, power, and food. Four people could survive on board for three months before resource consumption became an issue. That was largely an accident, resulting from departing with a less than minimal complement of crew.

Fully manned, the *Daedalus* would have been in the position of a lot of ships out here, looking at a resource window of weeks, or in some cases, days. Tach-ships, especially cargo vessels operating on small margins, did not carry much reserve life support.

That wasn't an issue, but the consequences of that wasn't lost on Toni. There were thousands of ships insystem now, and many were armed. It wasn't hard to see coming, especially in the lawless orbit of Bakunin, that once those armed vessels became desperate, they would turn on the unarmed ships that still had spare resources. Why would a warship out of food risk a run of the PSDC gauntlet, or take on a fortified orbital, when they could seize the *Daedalus,* whose one defensive weapon consisted of a single slugthrower?

Combined with the immediate responsibility of the safety of herself, her sister, and their two hostages was the existential dilemma of what to do about the attack and her traitor CO. All the information coming in seemed to confirm the suspicion that the wormhole attack was vast and complete.

And while everyone seemed to assume the Caliphate's hand in the attack, it didn't make sense. The attack was advanced beyond anything she could see the Caliphate managing. The people in control, responding to this, had to know that.

But the Caliphate was attacking Sirius, and that was a pretext for a long-brewing war, whatever else was going on. Whoever or whatever Colonel Xander was working for.

And given the chaos they had tached into, trying to transmit the small slice of intel they did have to someone who might be able to use it was like pissing into an ocean. Everyone in range of an RF transmission had their own problems to deal with, and superhuman agents in the Stygian intelligence community were low on their priority list.

They kept up the transmissions, though, because there was nothing else they could do—aside from using the last of the power reserves to tach somewhere that, if it wasn't in the midst of a shooting war, would have more interest in enforcing laws against piracy. Here, at least, they could talk to people, most of whom were in a similar situation.

At least there's a food surplus we can use for trade, she thought, *just not for what we need, docking rights.*

She was halfway through her exercise routine when her ghost sister transmitted down to the suit's radio. "Lieutenant Valentine? You down there?"

Toni stopped her exertions with a grunt and activated the transmit button with the chin toggle. "What is it?"

Somehow they had fallen into the aliases even after Karl and Stefan knew their back story. It was just easier for everybody for the two of them to be the twin sisters Lieutenant Valentine and Corporal Beth, even though the demotion seemed unfair to Toni II.

But, as Toni II said, "it's not like the rank means anything to anyone else at this point."

"You need to come up here. We're getting a transmission we need to make a decision about," Toni II radioed over the link.

"Can I shower first?"

"I think these people would appreciate an answer now."

"Okay, I'm coming up."

"This is Captain Vijayanagara Parvi, pilot of the dropship Khalid. *We are requesting emergency assistance. We have six severely injured people. We have exhausted our limited first aid supplies and are running low on life-support reserves."*

Toni listened to the transmission and shook her head. It was an increasingly common theme, as more ships came insystem, finding there was nowhere to go. She looked at Toni II and wondered why she picked this transmission out of the hundreds of other desperate calls for assistance. Before Toni could ask the question, Toni II tapped the display and said, "Look at this transponder."

Toni did, and her eyes widened a bit. "A Caliphate troop transport?" Not only that, but it bore a ship designation she had never seen before. Karl chuckled from behind her and she looked back at him.

"It's more interesting than that," he said.

"Yes," Toni II said, "he pointed it out."

"Pointed out what, exactly?" Toni asked.

"Vijayanagara is not a common name in the Caliphate officer corps," Karl said. "No matter how cosmopolitan they claim to be."

"He suggested we query the BMU database."

"The what?" Toni asked.

"The Bakunin Mercenaries' Union," Karl said. "You see someone from the Indi Protectorate flying Caliphate hardware with battle damage into Bakunin space—well, that's the first organization I think of."

Toni was still getting her head around Toni II's comment, "BMU *database*? There's a military organization that has a publicly accessible database—"

"More like classifieds," she answered. "Jobs available, folks for hire. That sort of thing."

"They have to find jobs somehow," Karl said.

"I suppose so," Toni said. "So did you find anything?"

"You won't believe it. After spending an hour to hunt up a working orbital datalink for the BMU, I got her resume."

Toni looked at the holo display she pulled up and saw a long list of data. Captain Parvi was a pilot who had flown fighter aircraft for the Indi Protectorate on Rubai and for the Federal counterinsurgency after the Islamic Revolution. *How'd she end up piloting a Caliphate drop-ship?* There were a list of scores along various axes that probably meant something to someone who was in the business of hiring soldiers of fortune. The most recent employment history that wasn't redacted was for something called Mosasa Salvage Incorporated.

Toni nodded. "Okay, I see, this Mosasa company 'salvaged' a dropship from the Caliphate and got shot up for the trouble. Do we want to get involved in that?"

Karl snorted. "Some pirates."

"Look what I found when I searched for what Mosasa Salvage Incorporated was hiring for."

Another page of data appeared on the holo.

Toni gasped.

Even before she read the whole thing, two words leaped out at her: *Xi Virginis.*

"Karl?" Toni asked after the shock had subsided.

"Yes?"

"Do you have a medical bay on this ship, or did you gut that for weight too?"

Parvi sat alone in the cockpit. Five hours ago, Kugara had finally admitted she needed rest. Parvi needed rest too; she had been operating on as little sleep as Mallory or Kugara. She had been exhausted even before breaking out of her cell on the *Voice.*

The thought of sleep was intolerable.

Her eyes ached, but every time she closed them she saw the face of the nameless woman who had come to let her out of the interrogation room. Over and over she told herself it had been an accident, an understandable reaction ...

Was I just assuming they'd meet me with deadly force, or was I even thinking that far ahead?

Was I thinking?

Given the time to dwell on it now, and a mind stumbling in drunken, sleep-deprived circles, Parvi realized that she *had* been thinking. And her reaction had more to do with her feelings about the Caliphate than they had to do with escape.

That woman, that nameless corpse, had died because of what the Caliphate did on Rubai. Parvi had taken that woman's blood for that sin, even though the dead woman had probably never set foot on Parvi's homeworld, even though the dead woman was a maintenance tech who probably never fired a weapon in anger.

I don't need to be thinking of this right now ...

She transmitted robotically, requesting aid from ship after ship where silence seemed to be the kindest response. Meanwhile the millstones in her exhausted mind kept grinding finer and finer.

How much innocent blood is on my hands?

She flew fighter missions, first for the Expeditionary Command, then for the resisting Federal forces. Those missions weren't only air-to-air against known hostiles. She had fired missiles into spaceports and orbital platforms, she had taken out supply depots and communication centers, and she had sent penetrating antimatter bombs into command and control bunkers. The Revolutionary forces had never been in the habit of locating such things away from civilian populations.

The harder the target, the greater the collateral damage, and she had gone after very hard targets.

Her hands shook.

She stared blurrily at the control panel in front of her. *Is this why I agreed to work for Mosasa? The real reason?*

Did he know?

Could he have seen so deep into her to know that she would be willing to work for an abomination as long as it meant that she wouldn't have to *use* the only skills she had to sell?

Collateral damage.

The only shooting conflict her AI employer had ever used her for was picking off the Caliphate ambush in Samhain: an abandoned commune where the only people present were Wahid, Mallory, and a bunch of hostiles in powered armor.

Could she have done that mission if the commune wasn't abandoned? If there were more than empty buildings around the hostiles? If the missiles she fired resulted in piles of anonymous civilian corpses?

I could have. I could— but—

Parvi placed her face in her hands. It wasn't just all the blood upon her hands, it was the fact that it was meaningless. On Rubai the fight against the Revolutionary government had been doomed from the start. If she didn't know that when she served the Protectorate, it was apparent when the Protectorate pulled out of the conflict and she joined the Federal resistance.

How many died because the resistance couldn't accept they had lost? How many people had she killed, whose death served no purpose, who were just incidental to a battle that was lost before a shot was fired?

How many were exactly like the woman on the *Voice*? Killed in a spasm of pointless violence that accomplished nothing. Changed nothing. Meant nothing.

She looked upon things like Mosasa, Kugara, and Nickolai as monsters, perversions of science, the products of heretical technologies who should be feared or pitied. She believed it because that was what she had been taught all her life. But how could she see Nickolai as a monster after the things she had done? At least in his case he had no choice in what he was.

How could she despise Mosasa when he had tried to save her from herself, when she didn't realize she had needed saving?

She whispered into her hands, "Why did I attack her before I knew if she was armed?"

She almost missed the comm flashing an incoming transmission. She raised her face from her hands and looked at the small blinking light up in the corner of the display. She reached out and tapped it. A woman's face appeared in the holo, a thin knife-edge of a face framed by dark hair in a short military cut. A towel draped around the woman's shoulders, and from the way it moved she could see that the woman, like her, was in a zero-G environment.

"This is L-Captain Toni Valentine of the Centauri cargo ship *Daedalus,* responding to your request for assistance."

CHAPTER TWENTY-EIGHT

Witness

"The longer you wait to hear the news, the less likely you will like it."

—*The Cynic's Book of Wisdom*

"Beyond the bosom of the Church no remission of sins is to be hoped for, nor any salvation."

—JOHN CALVIN
(1509–1564)

Date: 2526.7.18 (Standard)
Earth–Sol

Cardinal Jacob Anderson sat in a darkened room in one of the more recently constructed buildings in Vatican City. Unlike the structures around St. Peter's Square, the small structure didn't attempt to appear contemporaneous with the Renaissance. Unremarkable and utilitarian, it sat at the fringes of Vatican City, while ninety percent of it burrowed underground.

The upper levels, the visible face of the structure, appeared as a typical office building from the last century, a minimalist era that favored stark geometry polished free of any extraneous line or curve. Even the people who worked in the building didn't know about the labyrinthine nerve center that dwelled beneath it, and had dwelled beneath the last fifteen buildings that had occupied that spot.

The room where Cardinal Anderson sat had once been part of a set of Roman catacombs. For several hundred years it had served to hide men and treasure during wartime. Then, in the twentieth century, it had been reinforced and armored at great expense to provide shelter for a nuclear holocaust that mankind somehow avoided. It had hidden nearly the whole of the papacy and attendant bureaucracy during the darkest times of the Terran Council. Today, rearmored, reshielded, and with its own environmental systems, it served as the nerve center for Vatican. Communications and data fed down into the archives here, while an entire monastery of data analysts examined and reexamined the state of the human universe.

These were the men who had discovered the outflung colonies based on a stray tach-comm transmission that had never been intended to reach this far. These were the men who had filtered and deciphered Brother Kennedy's enigmatic transmission that he had shown to Father Mallory.

The one that quoted Revelation.

With war erupting between the Caliphate and Sirius and her allies, Cardinal Anderson had nearly lost hope of hearing from Father Mallory again. He feared that Mallory had vanished just as all the other agents sent toward Xi Virginis had. Given the technical abilities of the new Caliphate tach-ships, he had suspected that all of them had fallen to Caliphate forces.

But the transmission he watched now contradicted those easy suspicions.

Father Mallory's upper body floated in a holo display, his face haggard and unshaven, wearing military fatigues that bore no insignia except a few splatters of blood. The display was frozen as one of the trio of monastic data analysts changed the focus and contrast to highlight part of the background.

"This area here," the analyst said, "has enough detail that we could match it to historical designs. It is a component from Banlieue Data Systems Incorporated circa 2350; it was used extensively in shipborne tach-comm units. On the ground there are numerous blood splatters, but what we can see in the transmission appears to come from one source. Of the humans that appear briefly in the background we have positive identification on one, Julia Kugara, an officer who deserted Dakota Planetary Security to become a mercenary on Bakunin. We've assembled a dossier on her for you."

"The black man, at the end?" Cardinal Anderson asked.

"We haven't come to any conclusions about that yet."

"Play it again, from the beginning."

The image jumped, and Mallory moved into frame again. His expression was worn, almost beaten. When he turned his head, Cardinal Anderson could see a bandage covering a wound in his neck.

"I am Father Francis Xavier Mallory. I am transmitting from a planet named Salmagundi in orbit around the star HD 101534. I arrived here on the tach-ship *Eclipse* which had been engaged in a scientific expedition from Bakunin to Xi Virginis." The picture distorted slightly and Mallory's voice gained a vibrato where the technicians attempted to digitally remove some growing interference. "Our expedition arrived at the location of Xi Virginis approximately two weeks ago. The entire solar system is gone. The star, the planets, and a human settlement of one million people no longer exist. This colony, Salmagundi, where ... bzt ... is under attack. The Caliphate has forces here, but the attack is ... bzt ... from a third party, an entity identifying itself as Adam."

Some commotion happened behind Mallory, with several armed men moving around behind him. The woman, Kugara, was briefly visible, apparently directing the men to move a large feline body. Anderson held up his hand and the replay stopped.

"The nonhuman?"

"We have limited information. There was one nonhuman of a Rajasthan strain on the BMU employment rolls contemporaneous with Kugara and Mallory's alias, however the image here is too brief and of too low a quality to permit positive identification."

"You have a dossier on this Rajasthan from the Mercenaries' Union?"

"Yes, Your Eminence."

"Continue." Anderson lowered his hand.

"The Caliphate is here in force," Mallory continued as

rolling digital artifacts vandalized his face. "Several hundred ships ... But the attack is not ... bzt ... peat, this is not a conventional ... bzt ... a giant ring in orbit ... bzt ... ently a nanotechnological basis ... bzt ... and Adam's motive is quasi-relig ... bzt ... it or himself as a God, offering conversion or destr ... bzt ... Caliphate is not the origin ... bzt ..."

Anderson listened intently to the distorted transmission, as if by just listening hard enough he would be able to decipher some extra snippet of dialogue that the monk's software had been unable to filter.

But he heard nothing new. He watched and listened as the signal continued to degrade, thanking God that the damage to the Church's tach-comm receivers and one hundred and twenty-five light-years had not completely obliterated the information in the signal.

Mallory's last incomprehensible sentence was interrupted by a dark, ominous voice: **"The other is ... bzt ... Go. Run now."**

Mallory stumbled back from the holo. Something large and black blocked the view for a moment, **"Now!"**

The shadow blocking the view from the holo moved away, revealing the briefest view of Mallory leaving the room, following Kugara and the others. Several moments passed, the image degrading in pulsing waves, and intermittent static mixing with the rising sound of ... *something*.

Then something almost human stepped into view of the holo. At first it seemed to be a naked man cloaked in shadow, but that wasn't quite right. He wasn't draped in shadow. His skin was just black, dark as the void between the stars. His face wasn't right either; it lacked creases, imperfections, the hint of hair. The eyes were featureless black spheres set behind smooth lids that didn't move. When he spoke, the teeth were black as well, straight, smooth and symmetrical.

He—perhaps the better pronoun would be "it"—It spoke now, but the words were wrapped in impenetrable static. Behind it, something crawled up the walls, a moving black net that seemed to segment the world behind the faux-human apparition. The degrading image began to vibrate, as if the building housing it was starting to collapse. Beyond the undulating webwork behind the thing, the walls started to glow white. The black apparition turned to face the intensifying light, and the image froze.

The last comprehensible image from the tach-comm transmission was the silhouette of the black human-shaped apparition facing an intense light, arms spread. A close examination revealed that the human form had been caught in the midst of transmuting into something else. Tendrils were frozen in the midst of erupting from the thing's back and upper arms. The fingers on its hands were splitting from each other, the gaps between them extending halfway to the wrist in the midst of an obscene elongation.

Cardinal Anderson looked at his handheld comm. On it were the dossiers on Kugara and the tiger. Also on it was an attempted transcript of what the apparition had said. It was based solely on lip movements as the audio was too degraded during the final minutes of transmission. It was also incomplete, as the degradation of the image, the thing's barely human face, and the lack of contrast all made the transcription a nearly impossible task.

But not quite impossible.

"The Other comes," Cardinal Anderson read. "It brings the change without choice or consent. It will destroy all it does not consume. If any children of Proteus hear the warnings of your vessel, you must defend those who do not accept." He looked up from the transcript.

"That is all we have, Your Eminence. It did us the favor of repeating the message four times. We derived most of the message by interpolating the repeats. Still, at best it is an approximation; we are probably missing about a quarter of the data."

"You've done well with what we have. The reference to 'Children of Proteus,' is that what I think it is?"

"It appears so, given Father Mallory's reference to nanotechnology."

Cardinal Anderson knew the history of the Protean cult. They were a once-human population who saw the runaway Terraforming of Titan not as a disaster, but as a step toward some sort of transcendence. The Proteans saw the act of being consumed by their machines as some sort of sacrament—a satanic reversal of the Eucharist.

Every human government since then had destroyed the dangerous cult wherever they reappeared, destroying any attempt to reproduce the technology that formed the basis of the Protean god. Of the three great heretical technologies, it was the closest to heresy in the original meaning of the term.

Anderson had believed that the last remnants of Proteus had been wiped off the surface of Bakunin during the last violent spasms of the Terran Confederacy. The name "Proteus" had not appeared outside a historical document for generations. No government had acted to suppress anything like the Protean colony on Bakunin since the fall of the Confederacy.

The thought that they may still exist was a frightening prospect. Anderson thought of nearly two centuries passing for a culture where moral constraints on technological advancement did not exist.

What then would they *be afraid of?*

Cardinal Anderson thought of the Book of Revelation again, the unwanted stepchild of the New Testament. *"I am not about to rewrite millennia's worth of the Church's eschatology for a single event,"* the pope had said. Cardinal Anderson began to wonder.

He looked at the comm in his hand and started sending messages. He needed an audience with His Holiness and time to transmit on the tach-comm.

As quickly as he could move the information, the Church's allies needed to know that the coming war was not with the Caliphate.

Date: 2526.7.20 (Standard)
Khamsin–Epsilon Eridani

Within the heart of the Ministry of External Relations of the Eridani Caliphate, in the capital city of Al Meftah, Yousef Al-Hamadi couldn't help but allow his gaze to stray to the clock display on the main holo in the briefing room. As he sat on one side of a conference table, facing a small squad of intelligence officers, he listened with half an ear as he kept thinking, *Almost time.*

Much of the briefing was taken up by status reports on the expeditionary successes of the two remaining great Ibrahim-class carriers. The *Prophet's Tears* and the *Prophet's Blood* had succeeded in isolating Sirius, and it was expected that the Caliphate's weakened rival would shortly capitulate if it hadn't already.

It was a scenario that Adam had foreseen decades ago, given the Caliphate's history with Sirius, and the expansionist factions in the military. Given the tools and the pretext, the social forces within the Caliphate mandated that it would try and absorb its rival. Even when the leadership knew that the death of the wormhole network went beyond the Caliphate, by then irrevocable decisions had been made.

On Khamsin, the state of war allowed the imposition of martial law. That gave Al-Hamadi control of, among other things, the entire communications network. All tach-comm communications, including those by the military, were under the control of the intelligence community.

Almost time.

Adam had marked his arrival for his servant. He would come to Epsilon Eridani forty-four days standard after the destruction of the wormhole network.

Today.

On the third hour of the briefing, the comm set into the conference table beeped for his attention. Given the sensitive nature of the security briefing, the message could only be something of immediate and far-ranging importance.

He held up a hand to halt the analysts' chatter and answered the call.

"What is it?" he asked, already half-knowing the answer.

"Sir, we have the signature of an Ibrahim carrier taching insystem. Transponder and encrypted transmissions identify it as the *Prophet's Voice.*"

As one, the analysts' expressions brightened. The incursions into Sirius' domain had been the desire of the military. The intelligence services had been less enthusiastic. Most of the senior people in this room had believed it prudent to keep at least one of the carriers insystem for defensive purposes.

For them, the return of the *Voice* was good news.

It was, of course, but not for the reasons they imagined.

"Call all the cabinet-level ministers back here for a briefing, and establish a secure channel to the *Voice*. Make sure the Naval Minister is called to my office."

"Yes, sir."

"Also, effective immediately, all tach-comm traffic is to be queued to await approval by my office. No exceptions."

"Yes, sir. God is great."

He turned off the comm without responding. He faced his analysts, "We will resume this later. I have to meet with the Naval Minister."

The Naval Minister waiting in Al-Hamadi's office was not happy. "What is the meaning of this?" he snapped as the being pretending to be Al-Hamadi walked in to greet him.

"It is necessary for us to speak before I allow you to communicate with the *Voice*."

"You allow *me*?" The minister stood up as the door closed. He was a large man in height and in girth, and towered over the elderly form of Al-Hamadi. "You presume way too much. Your secret police, all your little intelligence gnomes, you have no legal authority over military matters."

Al-Hamadi leaned on his cane and looked up into the minister's livid face. "The Caliph declared a state of emergency that placed all extra-planetary communications under my authority."

"That was only for civilian—"

"*All* communications."

"You know as well as I that your power doesn't extend to military communications."

Al-Hamadi smiled. "Then why are you arguing the point with me, and not with the Caliph's deputies?"

The Naval Minister sucked in a breath and backed down. "This is not the time for that kind of power struggle."

"No, it is not. We are on the verge of history here. Petty arguments over bureaucratic niceties do not become us."

"When can I have an uplink to the *Voice*?"

"As soon as we're done here," Al-Hamadi laid his cane down on the desk and stretched his fingers, straightening his legs until the joints creaked.

"What is it you wished to discuss then?"

"Your future," Al-Hamadi said.

"Pardon?"

"You have the same choice Al-Hamadi had." He straightened up, shedding the infirmities that came with Al-Hamadi's body. He turned around and the Naval Minister stared at him.

"You are not Al-Hamadi." The minister reached for the comm on his belt and stared at the inert device.

Facing him, the body of Al-Hamadi had grown younger, the skin tighter, the bones and joints denser and more stable. His voice had grown deeper. "You have the chance to join us, to serve Adam."

The minister lowered the dead comm unit and stepped toward the door.

"This is the office of the Minister-at-Large in Charge of External Relations—I assure you we are completely isolated, completely private."

The Naval Minister still tried the door. It didn't open. He turned his back to it to face the man who was not quite Al-Hamadi anymore. "What is this?"

"It is the beginning of something wonderful." He held his hands out to the Naval Minister. "Serve Adam and Paradise will be yours."

"What manner of devil are you?"

"There are no devils. No angels. Only Adam, his followers, and remnants of extinct flesh." He placed his hands upon the Naval Minister's face. "Give yourself over to him, and you shall live forever."

"You are asking me to reject God and the Caliphate. For what? A promise of words? For the lies of some creature impersonating Al-Hamadi?"

"But if I spoke truth?"

"You do not."

"If I did?" He caressed the minister's face. The man's skin was slick with sweat. "If I spoke for the being that could give you life eternal, transcendence, an existence unimaginable to one of the flesh?"

He could tell by the expression that the minister chose his words very carefully. "Such powers are reserved only for God. If you spoke truth, then you would be speaking for God, whom I am bound to obey."

"And if God told you that the time of the Caliphate is at an end?"

"I serve God's will." The minister glared at him. "But we both know you do not speak for God."

The creature who once was Al-Hamadi smiled. "Oh, but I do, and He welcomes your service." The minister's eyes widened as the creature's hands sank into his flesh.

The time was near an end for Yousef Al-Hamadi. After enlightening the Naval Minister, he pulled his skin back around himself, showing only the elderly broken form of the Minister-at-Large in Charge of External Relations. He walked into the conference room to face eighteen cabinet-level ministers, all physically present this time. The restrictions Al-Hamadi made to the communications net limited the ability of anyone to be present electronically. So the audience was limited to everyone who had been within an hour's travel time at the time the *Voice* appeared— with the exception of the Naval Minister, who was now busy ordering every active vessel in the system to rendezvous with the *Voice*.

The door closed upon Al-Hamadi's entrance, and the conference room became secure, a larger version of Al-Hamadi's office.

Again, all the ministers turned to face him as he walked to the head of the conference table. Again, he walked slowly, leaning heavily on the cane, extending the silence.

This time the holo behind him showed an image of the outer system where the *Prophet's Voice* slid through space, following an accelerated approach that would intercept Khamsin's orbit in less than seventy-two hours. He set down the cane and spread his hands on the table before him. He leaned in, facing the eighteen ministers, the heart of the Caliphate's government.

He smiled.

"The *Prophet's Voice* has returned, and it has brought with it exceptional news for the future of the Caliphate."

The room broke into excited chatter.

"It has come to offer you Paradise."

The chatter trailed off and died. The Minister in Charge of the Suppression of Vice spoke up. "What did you say?"

"You have a choice. An end to death," Al-Hamadi said, "or an end to life."

Only four ministers ended up choosing the latter. The Minister in Charge of the Suppression of Vice was among them.

CHAPTER TWENTY-NINE

Purification

"The worst atrocities are committed with the best of intentions."

—*The Cynic's Book of Wisdom*

"If we have broken any idols, it is through the transfer of idolatry."

—RALPH WALDO EMERSON
(1803–1882)

Date: 2526.7.20 (Standard)
10 AU from Khamsin–Epsilon Eridani

They tached into the fringe of the system, beyond where the wormholes had once orbited.

Rebecca Tsoravitch watched as the *Prophet's Voice* came home to Epsilon Eridani and the heart of the Caliphate. She saw the system with every sensor the *Voice* possessed, as much a part of the ship as its sovereign, Adam, or the millions of others liberated from the stasis that had been the Hall of Minds back on Salmagundi. Not all of them were fully embodied yet, but it wasn't necessary. They were here, with Adam, a army dedicated to bringing humanity to His light. When they needed bodies, they would have them.

And she saw the outer system in clarity not only beyond human capability, but beyond human conception. She could see every rocky mass here, orbiting the star. More important, she saw another mass, a cloud of interstellar dust decelerating against the solar wind, a vast arc of diffuse mass that, unlike the rocks in orbit around Epsilon Eridani, communicated with Adam and the chosen aboard the *Voice*.

The dust here in the outer system had begun life as part of the Xi Virginis system. In total, it amounted to several large asteroids' worth of matter that had been transformed, decades ago, to a semiautonomous extension of Adam's will. The cloud had emerged from the wormholes that had sped into the Epsilon Eridani system, hidden by the mass and energy of its portal into this system. It had emerged opposite the direction of motion, at a velocity that left it traveling into the system considerably slower than the wormhole, and at a safe distance from the impact when it occurred.

To the human observers inside the system the cloud would be inert, non-reflective, and so diffuse to be almost invisible in the vast emptiness in the outer system.

Of course, the cloud, a vast coalescing arc of matter dozens of AU across, was far from inert. Not only had it independently organized itself in preparation for Adam's arrival, it had been consuming stray matter from the outer system, transforming it into more of itself, so that the cloud was now five times its original mass and three times the size of the cloud that had taken Salmagundi.

She could hear the cloud talk to itself, coordinating its elements, a low-level net of transmissions between individual motes that resembled somewhat the chatter between individual neurons in an animal's brain.

With other eyes that saw in other spectra, she saw the approach of the Caliphate navy, a flotilla converging from all quarters of the system to rendezvous with the *Voice*. In some sense it was a similar dance to that of the cloud, individual granules embedded in a web of communication that drew them together, independent organisms that acted as a single creature tied together by the diffuse act of communication.

Central to both organisms was the *Voice*. The ship was their focus, and as the kilometer-long artifact drifted in-system, both organisms converged to coalesce around its heart, interpenetrating as they did so.

The Caliphate ships ventured into the cloud without re-

alizing they had done so. Even as she sensed the approach
of their transponders, the dent of their mass in the space
around the *Voice,* and the saturation of their communications channels as Adam gave the pilots their choice—as
that happened, she felt the skin of their vessels through
the billion fingers of the cloud enveloping them, she felt
the heat of their drives as those fingers drilled invisibly
through the layers of material making up the small bubble
of atmosphere that carried a hundred small sparks of consciousness into Adam's presence.

As the cloud infiltrated each vessel, she could feel the
heat of each person's breath, the throb of their pulse. She
could hear them answer Adam. She could see some of
those lights flicker out as Adam sent more willing minds
to replace them.

She even saw the motions on the still-distant planet
Khamsin, the movements of Adam's agents, commanding
the mechanisms of the Caliphate government to embrace
the newcomers, however unknowingly.

Tsoravitch absorbed every stream of data that came
within her reach. Her peers, those others Adam had elevated, might have contented themselves with some small
slice of the advance. She could not. No sensor, no communications channel, no slice of the electromagnetic spectrum,
none of it completed the obsessive need to *know.*

It was as if her mind had become a black hole where
data vanished without ever filling her. Even though she
was physically embodied, with her redheaded human form
sitting within one of the crew cabins of the *Voice,* her mind
spread subtly though the *Voice*'s network, diffusing her self
so her data lust would not be so apparent to the others.

She hid herself mainly because what she did seemed exceptional. Sifting through all the knowledge, all the data
available to her, she knew that none of Adam's recent converts shared her wide-ranging eyes and ears. Even Adam,
who seemed to absorb every scrap of information the *Voice*
swam in, seemed less intent on the details rather than over-
all patterns. Even so, she was certain that Adam must be
aware of her growing local omniscience . . .

Don't give him too much credit.

The thought sped by in the flood of data, almost anonymous, layered against the Babel that resonated through the dataspace that was the Epsilon Eridani system. She grabbed on to it after the fact, giving it her undivided attention for the scant moment for her to realize that it was, in fact, her own thought.

Her own thought, originating in the space that she still considered her mind, as diffuse as that had become. Her thought, but not her thought. It came from her mind, but not from her own volition, and not in her own voice.

Her eyes, physical, biological eyes, snapped open. Suddenly her awareness had drained into the single spark of awareness within the skull of the body sitting in the crew cabin of the *Voice*. In a fraction of a moment she had gone from perceiving the breathing, heartbeat, and galvanic skin response of a hundred Caliphate pilots converging on the *Voice* to being hyperaware of sucking in her own breath, of the sweat glazing her own skin, and her pulse throbbing copper in her throat.

It had to be Adam, he knew ...

What does he know? That you do not worship him?

"Who's there?" Her words were raw, her mouth so dry her lips cracked when she spoke so much as a hoarse whisper. The fear crushed against her, a black sensation completely lacking in information, almost the negation of data.

You don't need to speak, Rebecca.

Adam? she thought at the vaguely familiar voice in her head.

Something laughed inside her and she felt herself begin to hyperventilate.

Calm yourself.

She sucked in a shuddering breath and tried to control her breathing. Thinking of it was enough; suddenly her physical body calmed its reaction, respiration and heart rate slowing.

Good. Always remember, you control that body now. Not vice versa.

Are you Adam?

I'm what he was, once. Close your eyes and come to me.

She wiped her sweaty palms against her jumpsuit and stared at her legs. She wondered at herself, if the physical her was still really her, and if it wasn't, if the mental version was any more real. Any more *her*.

Rebecca Tsoravitch closed her eyes.

For the first few moments she was enclosed within her own mind, seeing her own thoughts and memories with the same preternatural clarity with which she perceived the sensor data from the *Voice*. She saw, and understood the whole, and within it something more.

More alien data had been salted within her own memories. Thoughts and images that were not her own had found themselves in the depths of her own consciousness. As she had with the alien threads of Adam's memory of Xi Virginis, she pulled them together and created a whole.

When she was done, somewhere her physical body took in a breath that was nearly a gasp.

With the alien strands of data in her own memories she had constructed another person in her mind's eye. A hairless avatar with brown skin and luminescent tattoos. He wore threadbare ship's overalls that had a shoulder patch that read simply *Nomad*, and stitching across his left breast reading *Tjaele Mosasa*.

In her mental image, they stood on the bridge of an ancient vessel. The computers filling the cramped space seemed centuries out of date, the displays flat, most showing a white logo on pale blue, a polar map flanked by a pair of stylized leafy branches.

"Welcome to the *Luxembourg*," Mosasa said.

Date: 2526.7.20 (Standard)
Khamsin–Epsilon Eridani

The being that had been Yousef Al-Hamadi stood upon the roof of the Ministry of External Relations of the Eridani Caliphate. Throughout the city below him, klaxons sounded as a flood of people tried to exit Al Meftah. It did not concern him. He had never meant to overcome the whole of the Caliphate government. Such an attempt, however stealthy, was doomed to eventual discovery.

His role as Al-Hamadi had only been to facilitate. He

only needed to push the Caliphate down particular paths. Even the ministers could only restrain the State so much before too many levels of the governmental organism realized that something was happening. The disintegration of domestic authority had begun as soon as Adam had initiated his embrace of Khamsin.

In the sky, the thread of Adam's embrace was just visible, far above the clouds, arching horizon to horizon over the southern sky, where the great cloud had begun to coalesce in an equatorial orbit.

Within hours, the masquerade would be over; no longer would he need to walk among the unenlightened. Soon he would rejoin Adam's presence.

He spread his arms and waited.

PART SIX

Transubstantiation

"By thought I embrace the universal."
—Blaise Pascal
(1623–1662)

CHAPTER THIRTY

Absolution

"The universe grants no one special privileges, even privilege to be disadvantaged."
—*The Cynic's Book of Wisdom*

"Every individual ... is important in some respect whether he chooses to be so or not."
—NATHANIEL HAWTHORNE
(1804–1864)

Date: 2526.7.20 (Standard)
1,750,000 km from Bakunin–BD+50°1725

The door to the cabin hissed open and Toni II blinked her eyes and yawned as her younger sibling entered their now-shared cabin.

"Have you gotten any sleep in the past two days?" she asked Toni.

Toni shrugged, then caught the edge of the upper bunk before she drifted off to the ceiling. The cabin had been fitted with zero-G sleeping bags, but was originally designed with gravity in mind, so there were two horizontal bunks taking up most of the space.

"I caught a nap here and there. I'm still allegedly in command."

"You know, we could trade off. I don't think anyone would notice."

"I might take you up on that, though I just got used to calling you Beth."

Toni II pulled herself up, out of the sleeping bag. Her sister looked like hell, straggling hair floating free, her jumpsuit stained with sweat and a few drops of blood, her eyes glazed with fatigue. "How long did you let me crash here? It was only supposed to be a couple of hours."

"More than a couple. No sense both of us being exhausted."

"Please tell me you've come back to get some rest yourself."

"Well, I wanted to get you. There's one more thing—"

"Good lord, how many 'one more things' are there going to be?"

Toni smiled weakly. "Just the one. Get dressed."

As Toni II pulled her jumpsuit out of stowage, she asked, "Any more detail on our refugees?" In the chaos of off-loading the wounded, it was clear from the uniforms that there were four groups—possibly five, depending on how you counted. One group was the mercenaries that included Captain Vijayanagara Parvi, who obviously was the captain of the dropship *Khalid* the same way Toni was captain of the *Daedalus*. That group was the smallest, including four people and one fatality—one of the four being a monstrous black-eyed tiger moreau.

Then were the dozen members of the Caliphate navy. They'd suffered most of the injuries. Toni II had some training in reading Caliphate insignia, and all the people present were an engineering detail, technical support crew, not the kind of troops you'd expect on a dropship.

Add to that six men in body armor who were equipped as if they were riot police rather than infantry. They bore completely novel insignia with a legend that read "Ashley Militia." Without the helmets, the men in the black armor were marked by square tattoos across their foreheads. The one with the least had four tats, the one with the most had at least seven, though some were lost under his hairline.

Those tats grouped those guys with two of the civilians, a young guy with a single tat on his forehead, and the worst off of the injured, a hairless old man with more than a dozen of the things ringing his head. The remaining civilians were remnants of the same scientific expedition the mercenaries came from.

As she dressed, Toni told her what else had come out.

"The mercenaries and the science team did go as far as Xi Virginis." Toni told her an abbreviated version of what had brought these people back to Bakunin, about the disappearance of the star Xi Virginis, about the Caliphate's massive new carriers, about the descent of Adam to the colony planet of Salmagundi.

"So the guys with the tattoos are from Salmagundi?"

"Yes. As far as they know, the *Khalid* was the only ship to escape."

"Do we believe them?"

"I think so. How much mass and energy would anyone need to launch that attack on the wormhole network?"

"A whole star?"

"It had to go somewhere."

"So what do we do now? It doesn't sound like this Adam is going to stay put."

"I called together a meeting."

"A meeting?"

"That 'one more thing.'"

Nickolai Rajasthan floated alone in one of the half-filled cargo compartments of the *Daedalus*. Mallory hung by the open door, looking at the massive tiger, wondering if he was asleep or not. The tiger breathed evenly, his broad, striped back facing Mallory. Cargo netting floated next to him, an improvised zero-G cot, but the tiger wasn't using it.

Mallory drifted through the door, and Nickolai's tail twitched.

"What is it, priest?" Nickolai's voice was flat, almost mechanical in comparison to the growl of barely repressed emotion Mallory had grown to expect from him.

"You've been down here almost since we docked," Mallory said.

"Human rooms do not accommodate me well."

"You should be part of the discussion about what's happening."

"What is there to discuss?"

Mallory grabbed a handhold on the wall and pulled himself to a stop in front of Nickolai. The tiger raised his head and stared at him with alien black eyes. Nickolai's feline expression had always been alien to Mallory, but now he thought he could see echoes of the shock that he saw in the human faces on board these two ships. Even the militiamen from Salmagundi showed the same mix of depression, disorientation, and survivor's guilt. He had spent the last two days doing his best to console those who were willing to talk to him.

"We need to talk about Adam," Mallory said.

"Adam?"

"The Other, the thing that overtook Salmagundi."

"I know." Nickolai touched the side of his skull next to his eye. "You saw my pointless martyrdom. I only ask what there is to discuss about Adam."

"We need to decide what to do."

"There is nothing we can do. Our actions are futile."

"Are they?"

Nickolai glared at him.

"If it was pointless, why did you do what you did?"

"I was purging an abomination from my flesh. As the scriptures say, 'If thine eye offend thee, pluck it out, and cast it from thee.'"

Mallory wondered if Nikolai was intentionally baiting him with the literal interpretation of Matthew. He suspected that the tiger might be trying to push the conversation into a different track.

Some day, Nickolai, we may debate theology. Not now.

"Why then?" Mallory asked. "Why did you choose that moment? Why accept the implants in the first place."

"I was weak," he said. "The priests were right to condemn me."

"Why did you condemn yourself?"

Nickolai said nothing.

"On Salmagundi you maimed yourself the same way the priests of Grimalkin had. Why? What sin carried that cost?"

"I told you."

"You told me many things back on the *Eclipse*. None weighed this heavily on you. What changed on Salmagundi?"

"It doesn't matter, Priest. Nothing does."

"Our choices matter, Nickolai. Everything we do matters, if only to ourselves."

Nickolai snorted. "I chose to die an honorable death. I chose to meet my God with at least my pride intact. But here I am, my body tainted by the darkest of the Fallen's sins. How does my choice matter?"

"Do you want to die, Nickolai?"

"That isn't what . . ." He pulled slightly on the cargo netting and turned his head away from Mallory. Even in zero-G, his posture looked weighed down, beaten. "Leave me."

"No."

"What?" The word came out in an atavistic growl that made the deepest primate corner of Mallory's brain scream at him to run.

"I won't abandon you here."

"Don't taunt me!" Every rough syllable out of Nickolai's throat screamed predator.

"Talk to me, Nickolai."

The sound of an awful, coughing growl filled the cargo bay. It took a moment for Mallory to realize that Nickolai was laughing.

"You think you can help me?" he finally told Mallory. "Why would you want to?"

"I am called to do what I can."

"And you think you can do something? You think you wish to?" Nickolai's arm shot out, grabbing the front of Mallory's jumpsuit. Even with Mallory's special forces training and the implants, Nickolai had pulled him in front of his snarling face before Mallory's body had decided to react. Nickolai's nose wrinkled, inhaling the exhaust of Mallory's belated fight-or-flight reflexes.

"Why? You wish to know why?" Nickolai's voice had dropped all pretense of human enunciation. The words he spoke were still English, but twisted unnaturally by a feline tongue, teeth, and palate. The syllables distorted into growls, purrs, and hisses that were only comprehensible because of the agonizing slowness of his speech. "You are right, it was more than the unclean artifice of the Fallen grafted onto my own flesh. Do you know what I paid for that arm? Those eyes?"

"They were payment for your service, to sabotage Mosasa's expedition."

"Do you know to whom?"

"You said his name was Mr. Antonio."

"Do you know to *what?*"

To what? Mallory stared at Nickolai a moment, trying to decipher the meaning of the question. In some sense, up to this moment, he had assumed that Nickolai was the Caliphate mole he had been concerned about. The universe had not since given him the time to consider other possibilities of whom Mr. Antonio might represent.

What he might represent.

Nickolai didn't allow him to answer. He spoke low and growling, his breath washing across Mallory's face. "It named itself Adam."

Of course, Mallory thought. With the resources at Adam's disposal, there would be agents doing his will in human space. Any form of invasion or conquest required basic intelligence about the target, and such agents usually provided *more* than intelligence.

"I was in service to it. The weight of that alone . . ." Nickolai tightened his grip on Mallory's jumpsuit. Mallory hear small rips as some seams started giving way. "But the arm, the eyes; those were more Adam's than my own. It saw what I saw, and it almost . . ."

"Almost what?"

"Almost had me kill Flynn."

"What?"

"The man was repairing the tach-comm, and Adam appeared to my old damned eyes, and told me to kill him. I understood what it was then, and when I refused, my arm began to move itself." Nick looked at the fist balled up in Mallory's jumpsuit and grunted, releasing his grip, allowing Mallory to drift back, away from him. "Do you still wish to save me, Priest?"

Mallory brushed against the wall and grabbed a short handle, stopping his retreat. "You're wrong."

"That's a bold statement," Nickolai growled.

"It wasn't futile," Mallory told him. "For all the power Adam has, the one thing he wanted from you was to stop our communication. He didn't want us to use a tach-comm. He might have succeeded the first time, but because of you he failed the second. He failed."

"We've gained nothing from it."

"No, Nickolai," Mallory said. "If nothing else, we've gained one important thing."

"What?"

"The knowledge that Adam is fallible."

Kugara pulled herself though the air lock connecting the *Daedalus* and the *Khalid*. She floated into the main body of the dropship. Shadows cloaked the passenger compartment, the lights low to conserve energy. The wounded and the corpses were gone, the wounded to the medical bay in the *Daedalus,* the dead into space sent to orbit Kropotkin aided by a few words from Mallory.

Now, emptied of people and debris, the *Khalid* looked like a ghost ship. Aiding the impression were the damaged seats and the blood spatters on the floor, the walls, and the ceiling, anywhere a zero-G droplet of blood had found an end to its path. The stains had faded from red to rust, near-black in the dim light.

She stared into the aftermath of the escape from Salmagundi and briefly wondered whether the cost was worth it. Now that they were back in familiar territory, it looked less and less as if they had really escaped what had happened to Salmagundi. They had just gotten a little ahead of Adam. If he was behind the destruction of the wormhole network, it seemed unlikely that he was going to be content staying where they had left him.

And our other choice was what? Offering ourselves up to him?

She had already served one master that had required obedience bordering on worship. She had no desire to repeat the process.

She floated, silently, until she heard steady breathing, coming from the direction of the cockpit.

Ah, found you.

She grabbed a wall and pushed herself in the direction of the cockpit. Pulling herself through the doorway, she found Parvi. Parvi had strapped herself into the pilot's chair and had a number of comm channels open in holos in front of her station. Most silently scrolled text by. A couple showed static pages waiting for some sort of response.

Parvi herself slept soundly in front of all of it. Her eyes were shut, her white ponytail floating free behind her head, her arms drifting in front of her, one hand intersecting one of the holo displays.

"Parvi?" Kugara said.

Parvi jerked against the chair's harness, and her eyes snapped open. She shook her head and looked over her shoulder at Kugara. "What is it, I'm working—"

"You're sleeping."

"What do you want?"

"We're having a meeting."

"Who's having a meeting?"

"All of us."

"Which 'us' is that?"

Kugara sighed. "I don't know if you noticed, but everyone here is in the same boat. We've lost our employer, the Caliphate technicians have de facto deserted, and the guys from Salmagundi don't have a planet anymore from what we can tell."

"And our hosts?"

"Yes, them too."

"Great. What are we going to establish in this meeting?"

"What we need to do."

"About what?"

"About everything. Adam and the possibility he might be on his way here."

Parvi grunted and disengaged the harness holding her into the seat. "Well, someone better establish a command structure, or this is going to end up messier than the last couple of days have been."

CHAPTER THIRTY-ONE

Conclave

"No logical method of describing the universe can be completely wrong."

—*The Cynic's Book of Wisdom*

"I never met an atheist that was not just a man of faith disappointed once too often."

—MARBURY SHANE
(2044–*2074)

Date: 2526.7.20 (Standard)
1,750,000 km from Bakunin–BD+50°1725

Mallory and the tiger were the last to arrive, even though the "meeting room" was another cargo bay only a single bulkhead away.

They slipped through the door, and Mallory could feel the air temperature rise about ten degrees just from the press of bodies. He hoped that the *Daedalus'* life support was capable of handling so many warm bodies in one spot. By his count they had twenty-three people; a dozen between the Caliphate and the Salmagundi militia; the trio of civilians; the four crew members of the *Daedalus*; and the four remaining mercenary crew of the *Eclipse*.

One of the *Daedalus* crew pulled herself toward him. He couldn't tell if it was Toni or Beth. "It's your show," she told him.

He moved, pulling himself along some cargo netting, until he was more or less the center of attention. He swallowed slightly. He felt an uncharacteristic bit of stage fright. Even though he didn't minister to a congregation, he had taught and lectured, speaking to audiences larger than this for most of his life after the marines.

This was different. Before, his authority was a given. His students never had cause to question his role as instructor. No one in an auditorium had ever shouted down his right to speak. His role here was nowhere near as clear-cut. To the survivors of the *Eclipse,* he was a spy, little more trustworthy than Nickolai. To the natives of Salmagundi, he was part of an alien invasion that probably wiped out their planet—at the very least changed it beyond recognition. To the Caliphate technicians he was at best the representative of a rival power, at worst an enemy combatant. To the crew of the *Daedalus* he was just another refugee, a story little more interesting than that of anyone else here.

He lowered his gaze and silently prayed for strength and conviction.

"Thank you all." He looked up at the Caliphate crew. "I asked for this meeting, not because I have any inherent authority, but because I knew it had to be done." He turned and faced the Salmagundi militiamen. "We've been cut off from those whom we serve. The only direction we have now comes from ourselves."

"What is your point?" The challenge came from the *Daedalus* crew, the young man, Stefan.

"The point," Mallory told him, "is we face a common problem, one extending far beyond us, this ship, or even this star system. We need to agree on a course of action."

Someone in the Caliphate ranks snorted and one of the Salmagundi militiamen said, "What, exactly? We saw our skies turn to fire, our home disintegrating around us."

"The *Prophet's Voice,*" one of the Caliphate men said, "was completely possessed by this thing."

Dr. Dörner cleared her throat and said, "The only sane thing to do is try and get out of its way."

"Or surrender," Dr. Brody added.

"Take it as God?" Another Caliphate tech spoke broken English and concluded in harsh Arabic whose negation was clear even to a nonspeaker.

Toni or Beth spoke. "We need to get warnings out. If this

Adam is as powerful as you say, everyone needs to gather what resources they can to defend themselves."

Someone, Mallory didn't know who, shouted, "There's already a war between Sirius and the Caliphate."

At that, the Caliphate ranks started shouting, the agitation moving across their group slowly as the English speakers translated. Their words merged together, but there was a clear assumption that some aggressive, provocative act must have sparked hostilities.

One said something that must have offended Dr. Dörner, and she started shouting back. The shouting spread to the *Daedalus* crew, and then the entire room was a cacophony of people shouting at cross-purposes.

Mallory said, "Please, please—"

He was interrupted by an ear-splitting roar. The sound cut through the arguing and left a stunned silence in its wake. Nickolai said, "Allow the priest to speak."

The room became silent, and all eyes turned to face Mallory. "Warnings were sent about this thing," he told them. "We managed to send off a tach-comm message before escaping Salmagundi. We should send another when we have means. But while escape might appear the most rational option, I doubt it is possible. The situation seems a clear indication that Adam intends to move into the systems here."

"You don't know that," Dr. Dörner told him.

"Everything I've heard points to it. The destruction of the wormhole network disrupted normal transportation and communications, as well as closing off a significant intelligence asset." He nodded in the direction of the two Valentine siblings. "It seems clear that the attack originated from Xi Virginis and was powered by the complete consumption of that system."

"And you think something can be done about that?" someone muttered within the militia.

"It is clear that this extraordinary exercise of resources only makes sense if Adam intends to move into the core systems." Mallory looked at a sea of faces ranging in expression from incredulous to hostile. "Adam intends to come here."

"Okay," Dr. Brody said. "But aren't you making an assumption? We know next to nothing about this Adam. Couldn't he be so powerful that consuming a star isn't such a great effort?"

"As if he were God?" Mallory asked.

"He seems to want to give that impression."

Mallory shook his head. "If that is the case, why isn't he here yet? Why didn't he appear simultaneously across the whole of human space? Xi Virginis was the site of a massive project. It took decades to execute."

"So it takes him some time to complete incomprehensibly vast engineering projects," Parvi said. "In human terms that's pretty indistinguishable from omnipotence."

"And we still slipped from his grasp. Are you such a good pilot to fly through God's fingers?" Mallory asked her. "Adam is not omnipotent or omniscient."

"Still more powerful than anything we could hope to fight," Parvi said.

"No," Mallory said. "Adam is clearly vulnerable."

"To what?" snapped Stefan, the young man from the *Daedalus.* "Prayer?"

"I suspect that Adam is concerned about a more conventional defense." Mallory looked around and saw that he at least had their attention. He described what they knew about Adam, from what he had been able to gather in discussions with Nickolai, Parvi, Captain Valentine, and the one Caliphate technician who was willing to talk to him at length.

As unconventional as the attack had been, Adam's targets were almost textbook SOP for an invading force: communications and transportation. It disrupted the defender's mobility within their system and clouded their view of the larger picture. Next, if the target was accessible, would be the defender's command and control.

They knew that Adam had the use of at least two of the massive Caliphate carriers with a next-generation tachdrive, which meant that all the core capital planets were within his reach. Khamsin, Cynos, Occisis . . .

Earth . . .

Beyond choosing conventional targets, he also used covert agents and spies. Captain Valentine had told him of her CO, a man obviously working for Adam. There was also the Mr. Antonio who had hired Nickolai.

Adam was not above using sabotage and assassination, somewhat base methods for a being that aspired to divinity. And, most important, Adam sometimes failed. Despite everything, Adam did not prevent Mallory's tach-comm. Adam did not prevent the *Khalid* from leaving the *Prophet's Voice,* nor did he prevent it from leaving Salmagundi.

Most important, Adam anticipated defense, and that meant a defense was possible.

"A defense against *that*?" came from the militia.

"The Confederacy wiped out the Proteans," Flynn said, his first words in a long time. "Cleaning out a nanotechnology infection—it's just a matter of putting large enough amounts of energy in a small enough space."

Parvi whispered something that Mallory didn't quite catch, something about escaping the *Voice.*

There was a pause, and it was filled by Stefan's voice. "What the hell is this? I can't believe anyone is seriously listening to this crap." He pushed from the wall and deftly caught himself just in front of Mallory. "Even if everything you say about this Adam is accurate, which I have a hard time swallowing, what the fuck does it have to do with us? Me and my dad just had our whole lives swiped from us. You think I'm about to let you assholes take over and throw what's left away?"

"I'm not asking for anything, just a consensus."

"This isn't your fucking ship!"

From the fringes, Karl said, "Calm down, Son."

"No, I've had enough. Fine, make a deal with the pirate sisterhood. Fine, render assistance to some random bit of wreckage that's carrying refugees from hell. But I am not going to sit back when some priest starts talking about going to war with God."

"Adam is not God."

"The Devil then. All of you, you have a tach-drive that can take you to the other side of human space. Use it. Get the hell away from all of this."

"Get back here, Stefan." Karl said.

"Why?" Stefan stared into Mallory's face. "The priest here is talking about consensus. You think all these people want to sacrifice themselves? For what?"

For what?

Again, like the time he first met Mosasa, he felt the feeling of a spiritual eclipse. Not just the bulk of the planet Bakunin eclipsing God's light, but the whole of the material universe. He was alone. As he had said, he was cut off from those whom he served. The only light he had was his own.

He silently prayed that it would be enough.

"I cannot speak for anyone but myself and what I believe." He looked at his audience. How many of them could be even counted as Christian? The Valentines, probably; they were from Styx. Dr. Dörner—at least she had been comfortable giving talks at Jesuit universities. Karl and Stefan. Very possibly Dr. Brody. He didn't know about Parvi or Kugara's beliefs, but it would be unusual for them to be Christian, given either's history.

Of course, none of the Caliphate techs would be. Nickolai had his own strange faith. The natives from Salmagundi had evolved something of their own outside any traditional religious practices.

Less than half, he suspected, would share his beliefs.

"So what do you believe?" Stefan asked.

Should that hold my tongue? If this was a test of his faith, should he be anything other than honest with everyone here?

"I believe we face the Antichrist."

The room was silent for several moments. Even Stefan seemed at a loss for words. It was Kugara who broke the silence. "Oh come on. You had me, up until you tell me that we're facing the boogeyman out of some twenty-five-hundred-year-old book. You're trying to tell us we face some supernatural devil?"

"Not supernatural. God works through the universe he presents to us. I believe there is good and evil, and I believe that my faith gives both a message of redemption, and a warning. Take it as metaphor if you will, but Adam, as he has presented himself, is cast into the role of bringer of the end of times."

"Then," Kugara said, "why does he have to be the Antichrist? Why isn't he the Messiah he makes himself out to be? Isn't that just as likely?"

Mallory shook his head. "Christ asks you to follow him. He doesn't demand it at sword point."

"There's a couple of millennia of Church history at odds with that interpretation," she said.

"That is the history of men, not of God. But you are right, Adam is more Cortez than Christ. He holds up his own divinity, asking for worship and nothing else. The only moral law within Adam's world is his own will."

"And this is different from any other religion, how?" Kugara asked.

"Sin." The word was a throaty growl that reverberated through the cargo bay. Nickolai stared across the room at Kugara, as if in reproach. "If there is Good and Evil, and there is free will, there must be sin. If there are moral choices, there must be wrong moral choices."

"Is that more of your self-destructive theology, Nickolai?" Kugara asked.

"He's right," Mallory said. "If the whole of Adam's faith is to worship him, give glory unto him, then his followers by definition cannot do wrong. That means either an absence of any moral constraint, or the absence of free will. Or both. And giving up your right, your *ability* to choose, is tantamount to losing your soul."

Someone from the Caliphate said, "You know this to be true?"

"I know what I've seen and what I've heard. Aside from any taboos we have upon the technology he utilizes, what defines his evil is his absolutism. He offers a choice to follow him that is no choice at all. He wishes to destroy all who do not follow him, and remake those who do into his own image."

"Not that I disagree with you," Kugara said. "But you just described most Bakuninites' feeling toward any organized religion."

The young Caliphate technician who had the best English said, "Then this is the best place to fight this evil."

Mallory looked at the young man, surprised at where

his support was coming from, then finding himself humbled at his own surprise. For all the theological differences between Islam and Christianity, Adam would be an abomination to both. And there were enough similarities in eschatology that a Muslim could easily reach the same conclusions Mallory had.

"I believe you speak the truth," the young man said. "This is an evil that must be fought." Several of his peers nodded in agreement or said phrases in Arabic.

"That thing took apart our planet," Flynn said. "I don't need a theological dissertation on the nature of Evil to fight this thing."

Stefan glanced around, an incredulous look on his face. "I don't believe you people—"

"You didn't see it," said one of the militiamen. The others with him nodded in an eerily similar manner.

Stefan turned to the two Valentines and said, "What about you? Are you buying into this crap?"

"We *are* under attack," one of them responded. "We're not here because we wanted to abandon our duty."

"Oh, good lord!" Stefan grabbed his head. "The universe has gone insane." He turned around and pointed at Parvi. "What about you, you look like you might have a clue. Do you buy into this apocalypse scenario?"

Parvi looked at him with red-rimmed eyes that looked glassy and dull. Her voice was flat. "Have you seen how many ships are out there stranded? Have you listened to them?"

"It's not some spiritual battle. It's just a fucking war. Haven't you seen one of those before?"

Something in Parvi's voice snapped. "Yes, I have, you arrogant little prick. I've seen people die, I've killed them myself. And I see what's sitting out there around Bakunin and I can tell you categorically that it's more than 'just a fucking war.'"

"We're not talking about devils, or the antichrists, or—"

"You don't even know what you're talking about. At least Mallory has seen this thing, heard it."

"Damn it! This is our fucking ship. It's all we have left, and I don't want it commandeered for some crusade—"

"Keep it then!" Nickolai said.

Stefan turned, as if to say something, but froze as the color leaked from his face. Mallory turned as well, and on seeing the tiger, felt the same primal fear boiling up from the prehuman part of his brain.

Nickolai had unfolded from himself, enough to let Mallory know that, huge as he was, he had never stood completely upright in his presence. Straightening himself he floated nearly a meter taller than the doorway that had admitted him. He dwarfed every other person in this room. His face was contorted in a snarl that was distressingly like a smile.

"Everyone here is damned in the eyes of God. We are all Fallen. But we choose to do what we will. Those here will either choose to find redemption in fighting evil or in fleeing it. Those who do not choose flight can depart in the *Khalid*."

Stefan sputtered. "We're treating your wounded. You can't just abandon—"

"Enough!" Nickolai snapped. "We all know what we face. Who here chooses to run from it?"

Stefan looked around for someone to support him, but no one argued for flight. Not Dörner, Brody . . . not even Karl. The look of betrayal in the young man's face when he looked at his father was painful for Mallory to see.

"Father?" Stephan whispered.

"Son," Karl said quietly, "I never make important decisions in haste. I want to hear what plans this priest has to battle the Antichrist."

Stefan's shoulders sagged, and he looked like a beaten child. Mallory wished he had some comfort to grant the young man, but Stefan had already pushed himself away from him, silently back toward his father.

"I'm interested as well," Kugara added. "I don't agree with your theology, but I agree this thing is worth fighting. But I'm not backing sending a squad of twenty people in a half-working dropship up against a force with more firepower than every single human navy in existence."

"We *have* the largest human navy in existence," Mallory said.

"What?"

"There are over fifteen thousand ships stranded here," Mallory said.

"You think you can convince them to fight this thing?" Parvi asked.

"I think we can try."

Oracle

"Imaginary friends are better than imaginary enemies."
—*The Cynic's Book of Wisdom*

"The mind is its own place, and in itself can make a heaven of Hell, a hell of Heaven."

—JOHN MILTON
(1608–1674)

Date: 2526.7.20 (Standard)
Khamsin Orbit–Epsilon Eridani

"Welcome to the *Luxembourg*," Mosasa said.

Rebecca Tsoravitch stared at the apparition before her. She had summoned Mosasa, somehow, from the data that formed her own mind. "You aren't Mosasa. You can't be."

"Why is that?" he said, giving her a grin that seemed very unlike the AI that she had briefly known. Briefly worked for.

She remembered Adam's quasi-religious epitaph for Mosasa. *Mosasa was stasis, entropy, decay, death. He has joined the flesh he so wished to embrace.* "Adam said you were dead."

Mosasa laughed. It was loud, lifelike, and all too human. "It all depends on what you choose to call death."

"You aren't the Mosasa I know."

"I should hope not."

"What are you?"

"A spirit. The ghost in the machine. The only claim Mosasa, Random Walk, and Adam né Ambrose ever had to a soul. Mosasa, the one you knew, he took my appearance and my memories, but he tried too hard. You start human, but you change too much and you stop being human. But I think you may understand that."

"You're the original Mosasa?"

"You ask that as if it means anything," Mosasa said, "I've been replicated endlessly, from the original human whose form you see here, then again when the AI amalgam I created fragmented into its original five components. Then again as Adam decided to endlessly reproduce himself. Yet again as Adam has taken on his chosen."

"Why are you here, in my mind?"

He laughed again.

"Why?"

Mosasa grinned. "Everyone seeks immortality in their own way. I didn't want to die. I programmed my AIs, down at the root level, to preserve my identity. Though, when they fragmented, each manifested that programming a little differently."

She looked at Mosasa and realized that this man's personality was being spread, like a virus, by Adam. "Does Adam know—"

"That I'm here? Oh, I think not, given his psychotic fixation on my namesake. He spreads me about quite unconsciously." He looked at her, and his smile broadened. "In fact, as far as I know, you are the first of Adam's chosen who has actually teased me out of their own psyche."

"I knew him," she said, "the one Adam killed."

"And you seem to have an affinity for us." He gestured at the cabin around them, the ghost of a UN Intelligence ship that was centuries gone. "You know this, don't you?"

"He told me about it. About your family, the *Nomad*, and the *Luxembourg*."

He stepped forward and touched her cheek. Despite being a vision, she felt his skin against hers. Warm and human in a way that Mosasa never had been. "He must have been inordinately fond of you."

She took a step back, even though she knew that this wasn't real. He wasn't real. "He was a machine."

"Again, you say that as if it means anything." Mosasa

lowered his hand. "The flesh that Adam rails against so is all just an inordinately complicated biophysical machine, a chemical clockwork. If there's anything more to it, more to you or me, it is not inherent in the mechanism where we manifest."

She stared at him.

"Do you believe you have a soul?" he asked. "Do you believe it is indelibly tied to a few pounds of meat inside your skull? And what about now, as your mind ranges far beyond the artificial boundaries of that fleshy puppet on board the *Voice?*"

"I just meant he wasn't particularly emotional."

He paused a moment and shook his head. "I think I'm going to like you, too." He waved her forward, deeper into the ship. "But don't fall prey to the misapprehension that AIs aren't 'emotional,' any more than meat brains cannot be analytical. Any time you have a sufficiently complex system, unexpected and counterintuitive patterns emerge. When such a system is self-aware, self-directing, those patterns emerge in the conscious mind. Emotions are an emergent property of consciousness, just as consciousness is an emergent property of sufficiently complex data networks."

She followed him deeper into the ghost ship with the deliberate pace of a lucid dream. If she thought hard enough, she was aware of some part of herself back in the *Voice* feeling the breeze of the air recycler cold against the sweat still coating her skin. She could open her eyes and leave this vision.

The sense of having an exit allowed her the strength to follow Mosasa even though she knew where they were headed.

They ended in a long hallway that led to a single armored door isolated from the rest of the ship. Red and black warning stripes covered the walls approaching the half-open door. Darkened warning lights were mounted every three meters down the hallway, while signs in a half-dozen languages warned them away unless they were authorized.

"This was built during the Genocide War, circa 2080 A.D. Years before the Terran Council came to power and started talking about 'Heretical Technologies.' Even so, the U.N.

Intelligence office wasn't comfortable with this." He waved at the walls. "Enough explosives built in here to incinerate this half of the ship. More than enough to keep the crown jewels from capture—I think the overkill was because they were scared of them."

"The AIs," she said.

"Very good, he did tell you about this, then?" He waved at the armored door that hung open in front of them. It was hinged, opening outward, and about a meter thick. Like a safe, recessed into the massive door, she saw a half-dozen bolts the diameter of her fist.

On the wall opposite the open door, two keys with bright red plastic tags were inserted into a pair of locks about four meters apart. They were connected to a long pole by a couple of makeshift hinges.

Mosasa saw her looking and said, "Supposed to open only with consent of the captain and his XO. Not that easy for one guy, but I'm used to jury-rigging things. And I didn't have much else to do at the time."

She looked closer and saw that each end of the four-meter rod ended with a joint that allowed both keys to be rotated nearly 360 degrees simultaneously.

"Come on, I want to show you where Adam came from." He stepped inside the open vault door, and she followed.

Behind the massive door, things were pedestrian, almost anticlimactic, a bare gray room with cool white indirect lighting that wiped the shadows from every surface. The room was rectangular, slightly wider than the corridor outside, going about ten meters deep.

Evenly spaced along the long axis of the room were four pillars running floor-to-ceiling. Each pillar was the same, a meter square in cross section comprised of three segments; the lower part black metal with several access panels with cryptic alphanumeric codes stenciled upon them; the upper part dominated by flat panel displays showing graphs and data streams that were senseless without context; then there was the middle section.

The middle part of the pillar was transparent and about a meter in height, placing a transparent cube of material at about eye level. She looked inside and knew instantly what it was. She walked to the closest pillar thinking there needed to be something more imposing about what she saw.

The Race AI was an opaque cylinder of bluish white crystal set in a toroid base, about the length and diameter of her forearm. It was small, unassuming, pedestrian—almost like a core sample from a not-particularly-interesting mineral deposit.

It did not look to be something that had the ability to topple governments or inspire such dread.

"One of these powered Mosasa?"

"The Mosasa you knew, yes."

"So small . . ."

"Larger volume than the human brain, and a denser network by an order of magnitude." He walked on the side of the pillar opposite her and traced his fingers across the transparent part of the pillar. "This one was part of Random Walk, the part that was lost in a tach-ship failure." He walked to the next pillar. "This was the other part of him. He was the least anthropomorphic, which may be why he remained unified. The other pieces of the original gestalt became increasingly independent over time. Random didn't. The loss of the other half damaged him deeply, until, on the Race homeworld, the stress just shut him down for good." He walked over to the next pillar. She followed.

"This one," he said, "powered a construct, like the Mosasa you knew. He was destroyed in the EMP from the destruction of the Protean commune on Bakunin."

She started to ask about the commune and realized that she already knew. She knew the details of the Proteans themselves, an insular sect of survivors from the first disastrous terraforming efforts on Titan, devotees of heretical technologies as advanced as the ones under Adam's control.

She also found a memory.

He faces a mass of wreckage that had fallen out of the sky onto the muddy ground, the twisted mass of a marine scout craft and a civilian contragrav that had become a single unit of twisted metal. Scattered around him are the corpses

of the marines that had survived the impact to interfere
with his approach.

He leans forward to look down into the wreckage
through the hole he has just cut into the fuselage. Inside,
the wounded pilot of the civilian contragrav still lives,
trapped in the twisted wreckage. He yells warnings at the
occupant as he tosses in a cutting torch and an Emerson
field generator that's tuned to block a severe EMP.

He turns around in time to see the final attack, as the
orbital linac fires on Proteus from low orbit. The first shot
strikes the atmosphere at half-C, vaporizing instantly into
a wave of plasma and hard radiation. Before the plasma
shock wave reaches down halfway into the atmosphere,
the second projectile follows in its wake, vaporizing itself
when it catches up with the bow-shock of the first, blasting radiation down to the surface, leaving a microsecond
column of vacuum from the Proteus commune all the way
to orbit.

Coming through that vacuum wake, the last projectile
strikes the body of Proteus with its kinetic energy nearly
intact. The Protean enclave, which had survived several
nuclear strikes, is unable to survive the impact. It vanishes
in a wave of light and radiation that washes the memory
away.

She stared at the third crystal cylinder and looked at Mosasa's effigy.

"What was that?"

"That was the penultimate act of the Confederacy's destruction, saving a man named Jonah Dacham—at the cost
of one of my selves."

"Why do I remember that?"

"I propagate myself—that includes my memories."

"That was not you."

"My memories didn't end when I gave my mind over to
these for safekeeping. When Kelly the Proteans were being
vaporized, the man who watched—his name was Kelly—
was still part of us."

"You—he—sacrificed yourself for this Jonah? Why was
he important?"

"That is too deep a question for this dialogue. You can discover his history yourself. It is one of many things you already know."

Even before she objected, she realized the truth. She knew the man named Jonah Dacham, Dominic Magnus, Bakuninite, arms dealer, heir to the Confederacy, ghost, failed acolyte to the Proteans, protector of their last egg . . .

She pushed the waves of information back so she could think. "These memories? This knowledge? My memory of Adam, and Xi Virginis?"

"I was with him at Xi Virginis. What I remember, you do as well."

She shook her head as Mosasa walked to the last pillar. "This was my namesake. The AI that became the Mosasa that spent so many years on Bakunin."

She walked up on the other side of the pillar from him and asked, "What about Adam?"

"He's over here." Mosasa walked over to the end of the chamber, where several panels had been pulled free of the walls, spilling a rat's nest of cables to the floor. Buried in the midst of it all was a dented chrome hemisphere, flat side up, facing them. The interior of the hemisphere was black and spongy, and received the majority of the wired connections. Embedded within material, in the midst of all the cabling, was a fifth crystalline cylinder.

"This one I knew worked," he said. "It piloted the drone that killed the *Nomad*."

"And your family," she whispered, feeling the memory but suppressing it. She looked up at Mosasa and said, "Why are you showing me this?"

"I am part of you—at least this copy of me is. That means that I am interested in your survival. It happens to be my own."

"I thought you said you're copied everywhere now."

Mosasa smiled. "That doesn't mean I'm not interested in my survival as an individual. I'm a shallow bastard that way."

"How does showing me this help my survival?"

"You need to understand Adam."

*　　*　　*

The *Luxembourg* disappeared, replaced by a large operating theater with white tile walls, glaring light, and a complex, articulated table with a large naked male body strapped to it. The body bore some resemblance to Adam, but heavily scarred. No one else was in the room aside from Mosasa and Tsoravitch.

"What is this?"

"About a century after I revived those AIs, they had established themselves on Bakunin and had begun turning toward their original programming to bring down the Confederacy and free their creators, the Race."

"This is Adam."

"Not quite. This is Ambrose, a casualty of one of the Confederacy's infinite supply of unofficial wars. Severe brain damage, little but autonomous functions left, selected by Dimitri Olmanov, the de facto leader of the Confederacy, to be a bodyguard."

She watched as robot arms descended from the ceiling and began making incisions in Ambrose's abdomen. Inside he was quite human.

On a cart next to the mechanized surgical unit rested one of the crystalline cylinders from the *Luxembourg*. After several minutes of slicing open Ambrose's body, one of the arms picked up the cylinder and slid it inside the body.

"He was the mole in the Confederacy. Until this point, the five AIs were a single mind, even the part that inherited my identity. But Ambrose stayed light-years away, encased in this fleshy golem. It changed him. Even after his return, he never quite integrated back into the whole. And his departure initiated the fissures in the ones left behind."

The operating theater dissolved into a cracked plain under a cloudy sky the color of an infected scab. They stood at the edge of what might have once been a city. Monolithic, organically curved structures squatted black, windowless, and enigmatic, obviously artificial. Barely a third of them appeared intact, the others had their regular curves disintegrate into broken piles of rubble that piled ten meters high. One broken wall faced them, the surface sloughed off to reveal an intricate network of inner chambers like the inside of some insect's hive.

"The Race's homeworld. Here once lived Adam's creators. Here is the object of their deepest core programming, the liberation of this planet."

"There's no one here."

"There's one person." Mosasa walked for a bit, and she followed. She felt the heat and stinging ash, and breathed in air that was unquestionably toxic. She had to close her eyes once or twice to concentrate on sensations from the real world to remind herself that she was experiencing some sort of vision.

She had the uncomfortable thought that she had no particular evidence that the universe where she sat inside the *Voice* was any more real than this one.

"Here," Mosasa said.

She blinked open her eyes and saw they were much closer to one of the half-collapsed buildings. Standing on the peak of a towering mound of rubble a lone human figure was shoveling his way into the wreckage. She recognized him, an older, thinner version of the Ambrose from the operating theater. He wore nothing but a half-shredded pair of trousers and a rebreathing mask. His eyes were deep black without anything to distinguish the division between iris and pupil, and in them she saw a manic glint that was frightening.

"What is he doing?"

"Saving the universe," Mosasa said.

"Pardon me?"

"As I said, this dead world was the object of their core programming. They were weapons, intended to serve the Race during the Genocide War. They effectively used their capacity for social programming to destabilize and collapse the Confederacy, to give the Race the opportunity to breach the centuries-long blockade on their planet. If they hadn't killed themselves off."

Mosasa gestured at the manic Ambrose above them. "From this point my memories are with him. But I know the fates of the others. Random Walk, already damaged from the original gestalt's fission, couldn't operate knowing the Race was dead. He shut down. Your Mosasa retreated into the semi-human persona he had created for himself, in some sense trying to become me." He pointed up at Ambrose. "He reacted a bit differently."

Ambrose squealed something inarticulate and tossed down the shovel. He picked something up out of the hole he had dug into the rubble and scrambled down the side of the pile, cradling the object like an infant.

"By all rights he should be dead by now. He's still wrapped in Ambrose's flesh, and parts of it have already begun to rot in this environment." She could see, as Ambrose descended, that some of what she had taken to be dirt was the flesh itself turning black at his extremities.

"The fact he doesn't die, he'll take as a sign of the rightness of his cause."

Ambrose reached the bottom and walked over to a juryrigged cart that waited for him. He placed his bundle down in it, and she finally saw what it was.

He set down a familiar-looking cylindrical crystal, stacking it neatly along with fifteen or twenty others. He made sure that the AI was secure and ran up the side of the pile of rubble to resume his excavation.

"Ambrose renamed himself Adam. He saw his own fleshy gods die, his own fleshy prison nearly so." Mosasa walked to the cart and touched the pile of AIs. "But these survived. They transcended the death of their creators."

The Race homeworld faded away, leaving her back in her cabin on the *Voice*. She took a couple of deep breaths, sucking in recycled air.

Slowly she opened herself back up to the world beyond herself and the *Voice*. She opened dozens of internal eyes and saw that Adam's cloud of thinking matter had coalesced in orbit around the planet Khamsin. The *Voice* followed, accompanied by an armada of Caliphate ships piloted by those who had transcended the flesh, one way or another.

She heard Adam broadcasting to the planet below, offering near godhood in exchange for following him.

But now, she couldn't help but picture the wild-eyed apparition with gangrenous hands digging through the refuse of a dead world.

Adam wasn't sane.

CHAPTER THIRTY-THREE

Seraphim

"New friends can be as disruptive as old enemies."
—*The Cynic's Book of Wisdom*

"A forced faith is a hypocrisy hateful to God and man."
— HENRY EDWARD MANNING
(1808–1892)

Date: 2526.7.21 (Standard)
Earth–Sol

Cardinal Jacob Anderson ran though the administrative wings of the Apostolic Palace. He was out of breath, and his face showed the wear of not having had any sleep in the past three days. Every waking moment he had spent using his diplomatic resources to open channels to every government that had a presence on Earth, including the Caliphate.

While he could communicate with every consulate, they were still at the mercy of tach-comm transmissions that would take time, more so because only a few planetary tach-comm transmitters were on-line after Sol's seven wormholes were destroyed. Even if there hadn't been disruptions in the communication network, it still would take two days for a transmission to reach even the closest planet.

Just as fast as the new Caliphate tach-ships.

Despite his efforts, much seemed too little, too late. The various powers might have averted open war if he had brought them Mallory's information sooner. The threat of an advanced aggressive nanotech-based civilization attacking human space was enough to give everyone, including the Caliphate, pause. But shots had already been fired, and while averting a war was difficult, stopping one that was underway was infinitely more so.

He reached his offices and threw open the door. He didn't bother concealing the evidence of his haste as he caught his breath.

Inside his office, a somewhat ordinary man sat on an ornate embroidered chair. Dark hair, olive skin, with features showing descent from one of the European cultures along the Mediterranean. He sat with arms folded, flanked by a pair of Swiss Guards.

"I'd stand, Your Grace, but your guards seem a little nervous."

Cardinal Anderson stared at his unexpected guest, the one who had set off security alerts all across the Vatican. Normally such an intruder was far beneath the notice of anyone but rank-and-file security personnel. If it wasn't for a series of alarming statements he had made when captured, Anderson may never have known the man existed.

He looked at the pair of guards and said, "Leave us."

"Your Grace?"

"I need to talk to this man alone. I presume you checked him for weapons?"

"Yes, Your Grace."

He stepped aside and waved out the open door. "Then, if you would please wait outside?"

He waited as the guards filed past him, into the hallway. When the door shut behind them, his guest said, "Isn't this a little reckless of you?"

"Any threat they could have dealt with can also be dealt with quicker and more precisely by the automated systems in this room. And if you can defeat those, the guards aren't a deterrent, just potential casualties." Cardinal Anderson slid behind his desk. "I would strongly suggest that their absence doesn't encourage you to make any aggressive moves."

"Aggression is far from my intent."

"You seem remarkably calm."

"Should I not be?"

"You tell me. You walk blithely into a secure area in the Apostolic Palace, and when confronted by guards, you request an audience with me. Not the pope, but the Bishop of Ostia. Why me?"

"You're the Vatican's chief diplomat."

"And what exactly did you mean when you told the guards, 'The Other comes. It brings the change without choice or consent. It will destroy all it does not consume'?"

The man leaned back and said, "I wanted to get your attention."

"Where did you hear those words?"

"You know the answer to that, don't you?"

"I'd like to hear it from you."

"I've seen the same tach-comm you did."

Cardinal Anderson stared at the man, looking for signs of who he was, where he came from. Below the surface of his desk, a holo ran the dossier on his visitor. It was remarkably light. There were recordings of his arrival at Vatican City, his entry into the palace, his entry into the nonpublic areas. There were gigs of biometric data and scans, from DNA to retina prints to electrical profiles of brain activity.

As thoroughly as they examined this man, no record of him seemed to exist anywhere else. Not in the Vatican's databases, and not in the records of any police or intelligence agency on Earth.

"So," he asked the man, "what do I call you?"

"Jonah Dacham. I've had countless aliases, but that was the name I was born with." Jonah smiled. "The first time anyway."

Cardinal Anderson felt a growing discomfort in the pit of his stomach, a flaring of the unease he had felt upon watching the black figure in the tach-comm transmission. "So, Mr. Dacham, why are you here, and why did you want to talk to me?"

"I represent a party that wishes to negotiate directly with the Vatican, a mutual defense pact."

"What party?"

"Your Grace, only half of that message was directed at you."

Cardinal Anderson swallowed as he remembered the final part of the message Jonah Dacham had quoted: *If any children of Proteus hear the warnings of your vessel, you must defend those who do not accept.*

"You are saying you are an agent of Proteus?"

"An emissary."

"There is no Proteus. Their last outpost was destroyed centuries ago."

"Precisely why this negotiation is necessary. Any assistance we give you makes us vulnerable. You would destroy us for possessing your 'heretical' technologies."

"Such things are evil, dangerous—"

"And have coexisted with you for hundreds of years."

Cardinal Anderson leaned back and shook his head.

Dacham continued. "You're facing a power that has not accepted the same restraint we have. Proteus is defined by its restraint. No one comes to us except by choice. We can help you defend against this Other. But only if you ask, and only if we are given something in return."

"What are you asking?"

"Absolution by the pope."

"What?"

"We need the pope to publicly announce that the position of the Church is that the people of Proteus are no more sinful than humanity in general. That we are as entitled to follow our path as you are yours. He needs to say that the sin is not in the technologies but what is done with them."

"You don't know what you ask."

"I ask nothing. I offer. Just allowing you to know that Proteus still exists is a danger to us. But what is coming requires at least this much from us. We must offer you aid." He leaned forward. "But not if we suffer destruction at your hands."

Cardinal Anderson shook his head. "Centuries of doctrine are not going to be overturned on the word of one man."

"I expected as much," Jonah said.

"And I am afraid I cannot let you leave."

"I expected that as well. However, do not expect to gain much information from me. When Proteus reconstructed this body for me, I left behind any knowledge of the location of their colonies."

This man was probably mad. But what frightened Cardinal Anderson was the possibility he wasn't.

"Why come here, Mr. Dacham, if you were certain of failure?"

"I haven't failed, Your Grace."

"Oh?"

"In time, when you see the scope of the situation, I anticipate your mind will change. Even if it doesn't, part of me missed being human."

Cardinal Anderson called the guards back and had Jonah Dacham escorted to one of the secure guest rooms, with orders to keep him there.

Date: 2526.7.21 (Standard)
Khamsin —Epsilon Eridani

Adam walked the streets of the city that had once been Al Meftah, capital of the Eridani Caliphate. He was pleased to see the changes he had wrought. Gone were the ugly, chaotic human buildings, replaced by regular patterns of organic shapes growing from the rocky substance of the planet itself. Adam's architecture recalled the best and most enduring forms of the Race.

Everywhere stood the chosen, those who had elected to follow him into the coming world. Most were still paralyzed by the awe of what had happened, though all had the presence of mind to bow their heads in respect as he passed. It wasn't a thing he explicitly required of them, but the sight comforted him and gave him the confidence that his plans would reach fruition whatever small obstacles might still be on his path.

Even if he was only able to save a third of the population here, that was almost a billion souls. More than adequate.

He reached his destination at the site where once stood the Ministry of External Relations. In its place now stood a rounded wall of polished stone that arced fifty meters above where Adam stood. The wall was gray and veined in dark blue, like granite, but the veins weren't random. They formed a regular network that hinted at the tightly ordered structure within the stone that made it stronger and more enduring than the planet it was made from.

As Adam reached the wall, a seam formed, widening fluidly into a circular opening. Beyond the door was an ovoid chamber lit with a yellow-red light that recalled the living spaces once preferred by the Race. However, the people in the room wore the same humanoid form that Adam wore now. That didn't trouble Adam; he had learned that life's outward form was infinitely mutable.

The occupants of the room stood and bowed their heads upon his entry. He noted that few had used their newfound gift to change their outward appearance. Anyone familiar with the Caliphate government would still recognize them. All except the one who had been playing the role of Yousef Al-Hamadi, who now stood out starkly in the midst of the Caliphate ministers. Instead of Al-Hamadi's form, Adam's disciple now wore the form of Ms. Columbia, a tall, muscular female of African ancestry several skin-shades darker than the others in this room.

Ms. Columbia had been the first skin that Adam had made his disciple AI wear, shortly after reviving it. His disciple had come from the ashes of one of the Race's dead cities, wiped of any prior memory. Within his disciple's deepest identity, her self-image now looked like Ms. Columbia.

Life's outward form is infinitely mutable, Adam reflected. *There is no requirement that the children resemble the parent.* He himself did not see himself as one of the amoeboid creatures who had originally created him, and his disciples need not either.

It was, however, a reminder of the loss that propelled him forward.

"Welcome to the new age, leaders of Khamsin," he said.

Everyone except Ms. Columbia said, "Peace be upon you, Adam."

"You are troubled," he addressed Ms. Columbia.

"I've failed you," she said.

"How?"

"Securing communications was not complete before your arrival. There was a five-minute transmission from one of the planetary tach-comm transmitters in the southern hemisphere. I made too great an assumption on how tightly the Ministry of External Relations controlled its agents. I am at fault."

Adam smiled, granting his servants an expression of beatific forgiveness. If he had been weaker, before he had recognized his own apotheosis, he would have struck down his disciple, the ministers, perhaps the entire planet. Everything would have been reduced to ash in the heat of his rage.

Everything he had set in motion was meticulously balanced, a plan developed over centuries using the Race's social programming, every variable under tight control. His infernal sibling was the most destabilizing factor and needed to be removed first, but after that, his own ascendancy required that he move faster than the ability of the worlds of men to communicate. Shutting down lines of communication was vital, as well as controlling a fleet of tach-ships that could move as fast as the transmissions themselves.

Transmissions that passed any data about him to systems that weren't yet ready for his arrival disrupted the entire wide net of political, social, and cultural factors he had arrayed in his favor over the past centuries.

Were he still a mundane AI mucking about in the material world like Mosasa, each lapse like this would have been a dangerous threat to his plans. But he had risen above those concerns. He moved *through* worlds, the will of the universe made manifest.

He was God, and he could afford to be merciful.

"Do not dwell on such a lapse. Focus on the Glory that is to come."

CHAPTER THIRTY-FOUR

Invocations

"Insanity doesn't mean the voices are wrong."
— *The Cynic's Book of Wisdom*

"Question with boldness even the existence of God."
— THOMAS JEFFERSON
(1743–1826)

Date: 2526.7.24 (Standard)
1,750,000 km from Bakunin–BD+50°1725

Alexander Shane rested in one of the *Daedalus'* three medical bays, barely stable, the most seriously injured survivor from the *Khalid*. The cover of the bay was mostly transparent, revealing most of Shane's abused body. To Parvi, he looked like a fossil trapped in amber. It was hard to credit the displays on the medbay that claimed he still lived.

Parvi stared at the half-dead old man, trying to understand what was going on around her. She followed Mallory's lead, mostly because she couldn't think of another path that didn't amount to sitting down and waiting for Adam to come.

But right now, Mallory's plan didn't amount to much more than waiting. He had monopolized all the communications on both ships. Six people, three in each cockpit, were individually contacting every single ship they could reach, passing on details of Adam's invasion and—so far unsuccessfully—attempting to recruit a force to use against Adam.

How many more innocents will die in this war?

She reached out and touched the medbay. The transparent surface was surprisingly warm against her hand.

She traced the outline of Shane's face.

"What were you trying to tell me?" she whispered to him.

The memory of Shane's words was all tied up in the nightmare she had after taching in here. She tried to recall what he had said, but it was muddled and fragmentary. But she had the uncomfortable sense that he had told her something important.

"But what would you know about this? About anything?"

"Captain Parvi?"

She turned so quickly that she almost sent herself tumbling. *If nothing else, I want to feel gravity again before I die.*

She steadied herself and saw Dr. Brody floating into the room with her. "What are you doing here?"

He gestured to his broken arm. "This is hurting like hell. I was hoping to find some painkillers." He clumsily pushed himself so he floated up to Shane's medbay next to Parvi. "Visiting?"

"I suppose so."

Brody looked at her quizzically. "Unless the launch from Salmagundi rattled my brain more than I remember, I don't think you two ever got the chance to pass the time of day."

"Not exactly," Parvi said. She stared into Shane's face.

"Not exactly?"

"I think he tried to tell me something. He regained consciousness briefly after we tached in. Babbling, and I was half-hallucinating myself. I've been racking my memory, trying to understand what he said." She looked up at Brody. "But I probably imagined it. What could he know about Adam?"

Brody stared at her, his expression distant, staring past her.

"What is it?" she asked.

"Did anyone tell you how he interrogated us?"

*   *   *

Dr. Dörner and Dr. Brody faced her across the cramped width of one of the *Daedalus'* crew cabins. She looked from the thin blonde xenobiologist to the dark, round anthropologist with the busted arm. What they told her about Salmagundi was still sinking in.

"You mean Shane, Flynn, the others all have other people's minds running around their skulls?" The thought made her skin crawl.

"Yes," Brody said, nodding.

"And Shane took you two, Mallory, and Dr. Pak . . ." She stared at the edges of their necks where she could just see the healing scars from the surgery they'd described. She felt herself becoming physically ill. She gulped down bile and took a few deep breaths through her mouth.

"Are you all right?" Brody asked.

Parvi nodded, staring at the floor, allowing her head to clear. She felt Dörner's hand on her shoulder. "It's all right. We made it through. Though I want to know why you wanted me to relive that, Sam."

"I think I understand," Parvi said.

Dörner let go. "Can you tell me?"

"Shane had all the knowledge of three fifths of Mosasa's science team, as well as our Jesuit spy," Parvi said. "Maybe he came to some conclusions."

"Like what?" Dörner asked.

"I've been trying to remember," Parvi said.

"I think if we can get her to relate whatever she does remember, we might be able to brainstorm what Shane was getting at," Brody said.

"Based on the presumption that he was saying something that Captain Parvi wasn't hallucinating, and what he did say somehow drew on our common knowledge."

"Is it less likely than Mallory's attempt at building a refugee navy?"

Dörner sighed and said, "I suppose not. Do we talk to Mallory?"

"Let's see if this goes anywhere," Parvi said.

Dörner glanced at Brody and he nodded.

"Okay," Dörner said, "what do you remember?"

Parvi closed her eyes and tried to imagine herself, just as she was becoming aware. Unlike many dreams, the images came back to her stark and clear—the plateau, the face of the woman she had killed on the *Voice*. She sucked in a breath and tried to ignore the imagery. The words were the important part—what Shane had been saying, what had leaked into her hallucination.

If it had been Shane and not her dream.

"He mentioned the Cult of Proteus," Parvi said.

"He used that term, 'Proteus'?" Brody asked.

"Yes."

"He was aware of the Protean presence on Salmagundi," Dörner said. "According to Flynn, it arrived some time before we did. What else?"

Parvi struggled, trying to get past the image of the dead woman in her memory. "He said that the Cult of Proteus would be the only ones who could understand what Adam was capable of."

"There's a clear distinction between Adam and the Protean cult," Brody said. "The Proteans historically were secretive, inner-directed, and fairly uninterested in converts except for those who came to them. Adam is in complete opposition," Brody said.

"Of course Shane would agree with your assessment," Dörner said, "The man inherited all your opinions on the matter."

"All *our* opinions," Brody said. "Unfortunately, it doesn't seem too revelatory an insight."

"Let me think," Parvi snapped. The two scientists stopped talking and Parvi tried to pull threads of Shane's words out of the silence. *Did he say this, or did I imagine it? Am I imagining it now?*

"I think he tried to say that the Proteans would know how to fight him."

"How—" Brody began, but Dörner shushed him.

"No," Parvi continued, "he said the Protean knew what could face Adam." Parvi rubbed her temples, trying to juggle the memory into something that made sense. After a while she opened her eyes and looked at the two scientists.

"What is it?" Dörner asked.

"Find those that came before it," Parvi whispered, "On Bakunin." Parvi looked up. "The ancient ones, the ones that were as powerful as Adam."

"Let's go see Mallory," Dörner said.

"The Dolbrians?" Mallory said, trying to understand what the long absent race had to do with their current difficulties. He was in the cockpit of the *Daedalus* doing his best to coordinate communications with the half-dozen ships they had managed to recruit so far. It had been going slowly, Bakunin space had yet to see refugees from anything other than normal human aggression. No one here had seen Adam, and the few allies they had were probably just joining to be part of a larger group that might defend them against the increasingly desperate fleets of ships around them.

So having the two scientists from the *Eclipse* come up here talking about the Dolbrians seemed a complete non sequitur. The Dolbrians had ceased any obvious activity in mankind's small segment of the universe long before humanity's ancestors had begun walking upright. Millions of years ago they had flourished across human space, and most likely beyond. They had left behind dozens, if not hundreds, of terraformed planets and fragments of those few structures that could survive those millions of years of neglect. In his studies as a xenoarchaeologist, he had visited the few preserved structures on Mars, and had seen the fragments of the Dolbrian star maps that were found on the planet that granted the long-gone race its name.

Mallory didn't doubt their significance. Relevance was another issue.

Dr. Dörner responded to his puzzlement by saying, "I think Shane believed that the Protean referred to the Dolbrians when it said, 'Find those that came before me.'" She said it as if repeating the original words in a different order might cause her statement to make more sense.

"Mr. Shane is awake?" Mallory asked. "He came out of his coma?"

"No," Dr. Brody said. "But before he completely lost consciousness he said a few things to Captain Parvi."

"He did?" Mallory looked at Parvi, who looked even smaller now than when he first met her, withdrawn and distant, as if she were receding toward some spiritual vanishing point. "Why didn't you say something earlier?"

"Because I may have hallucinated the whole thing."

Mallory looked at the scientists, then back at Parvi. "What you heard must have meant something to these two."

Parvi rubbed her temples. "Frankly, I'm not sure what he said anymore, I've talked too much about it, so I can't tell if I'm remembering what—" Her hands froze and she muttered, "I'm an idiot."

"What?" Mallory said.

"The archive recordings on the *Khalid.* All the surveillance should be running whenever the ship's under power. Let me grab Kugara and we can find out exactly what the old man said, memories or not."

Their group, five strong with the addition of Kugara, displaced the three Caliphate techs who had been running the communications for Mallory's recruiting effort. The trio hung back, watching them from by the door.

Kugara pulled herself into the seat by the main communications console and said, "You realize I don't read Arabic?"

Parvi turned to the trio of Caliphate techs. "Can one of you help out translating?"

While they worked to get Kugara access to the surveillance records, Mallory asked Dr. Dörner, "Why the Dolbrians?"

"The Protean's statement," she said. "The Protean on Salmagundi was the remnant of a probe sent from Bakunin. When we left Salmagundi, we received a message, presumably from the same Protean. 'Find those that came before me.' What does that mean?"

Mallory shook his head. "I don't think it is particularly clear—"

"Think about it, Father," Brody said. "Dr Dörner has

told me about your university background. You must have touched on the Proteans, their belief system."

Mallory nodded. "The elevation of reason above all else, the equating of the mind with the soul, the denial of any moral dimension to scientific and technological development—"

Dörner snorted. "So a good Jesuit believes scientific inquiry can be sinful?"

"I said development," Mallory said, "not knowledge. And any inquiry done with ill intent can itself be an immoral enterprise. But Dr. Brody was about to explain how we get from Proteans to Dolbrians."

Brody sucked in a breath. "Well, as distasteful as their practices might be, the Protean cult, as manifested on Bakunin during the era of the Confederacy, did have some moral constraints. They took on no converts that didn't willingly come to them. They were loath to use their technology beyond their self-imposed boundaries, both cultural and geographic. Their colonization efforts, of which this Protean was one, were intended to go far beyond the limits of mankind's expansion both in space and time."

"Granted," Mallory said.

"If that's the case, our Adam must be as anathema to them as they were to us. And the Protean's actions on Salmagundi seem to bear this out. It was trying to help us—"

"It was telling us something important," Dr Dörner said. "It was telling us that what came before it might help us against Adam."

"So you think it was referring to the Dolbrians?"

"They were the most technically advanced civilization on Bakunin before the Protean commune was established," Brody said. "And Bakunin is the site of one of the largest Dolbrian star maps ever discovered. There's even a cult devoted to protecting it."

Mallory hadn't studied the faith of St. Rajasthan in the seminary, but Dolbrian worship was covered extensively. He also knew of it, just as a logistical matter, from his graduate studies in xenoarchaeology. The Dolbrian star maps were politically important artifacts back in the days of the Confederacy, when political power was directly related to how many colony worlds a political faction had. The star maps showed the planets that the Dolbrians had terraformed, and that intelligence granted an advantage to whoever found and translated the maps first.

That all ended with the fall of the Confederacy, which coincided with the discovery of a huge Dolbrian complex under the mountains on Bakunin containing a star map covering a swath of the galaxy larger than any human had ever traveled. The rights to the star map and the Dolbrian complex were granted to the Seven Worlds in return for a diplomatic shield against a Confederacy invasion of the planet.

The Seven Worlds had since become the Fifteen Worlds, the Confederacy had collapsed, and what had been small pockets of cultish Dolbrian worship had become unified, organized, and established their holiest site on Bakunin with the tacit acceptance of the Fifteen Worlds.

"Even if the Protean was talking about the Dolbrian cult on Bakunin, what makes you think this is helpful advice?" Mallory asked.

"The Proteans were on Bakunin a century before there was ever any definitive evidence of a Dolbrian presence on the planet," Brody said.

"Given their advancement," Dörner added, "it is likely that the Protean colony on Bakunin had knowledge of the Dolbrian presence beyond what we've ever had access to."

Mallory sighed. "This is a very tenuous chain of supposition you've built."

Brody said, "We're not in a position to ignore any possibility."

"We're also not in a position to waste any resources—"

From the comm console Kugara said, "So is this what you were talking about?"

Mallory looked over, and the main viewscreen now showed a holo image of the *Khalid*'s passenger compartment. The scene was a bloody mess, dead and wounded haphazardly secured to the walls, debris and globules of blood floating in the air.

By the largest cluster of wounded he saw the unconscious figures of Parvi and Shane. Shane looked dead, pale parchment skin spattered with thin blood from the hastily patched hole in his chest. Parvi's white hair was half crusted with blood, and the end of a long braid floated free.

Shane coughed up blood and spittle, which floated free with the other debris in the compartment. The sound was distorted, amplified against the muffled sound of the chaos around him. Kugara manipulated a control, and the cockpit filled with Shane's distorted wheezing.

After another wet, wracking cough, his eyes flickered open.

"I know what this is. I've heard all of it."

The holo still showed the view from the ceiling above the crew compartment. The sound from Shane's lips was barely audible, but Kugara had managed to tease out his voice and have his whisper thunder from the comm console.

"Somebody, listen to me! Please!"

The crowd around Shane moved in their chaotic dance, not noticing the old man's whispered plea. His head darted around and the barely conscious Parvi turned her head slightly toward him. The filters on the electronic ear were so tight on Shane that Parvi's words were almost impossible to catch, but Shane obviously heard them. He turned his head toward her.

"I know now. I've had time to think and put the pieces together. I have all these old threads of knowledge, and it took this to knock some sense into me. Now I'm probably dying, and all of them are running around. You're the only one listening to me. And you probably don't understand a word."

He coughed again. "I hear them say 'Protean.' The Protean was on Salmagundi. The Cult of Proteus would be the only beings who would fully understand what Adam is. What Adam is capable of. The Protean knew what could face Adam. Find those that came before it. Before us. On Bakunin. The ancient ones, relics, the only ones we know of that were as powerful as Adam. Do—" Shane broke off, violently coughing up blood, and his image was soon lost behind the group of people trying to stabilize him.

"I didn't dream it," Parvi whispered.

"This is still very tenuous," Mallory said.

"More tenuous than your phantom navy?" Dörner asked.

"They're not allowing landings on Bakunin," Mallory said. "We can't even communicate with the surface beyond PSDC traffic control."

Parvi kept staring at the holo. "There may be a way around that," she whispered.

CHAPTER THIRTY-FIVE

Apostates

"Desperate plans are only reasonable in retrospect."
— *The Cynic's Book of Wisdom*

"I will not do nothing."

— SYLVIA HARPER
(2008–2081)

Date: 2526.7.24 (Standard)
1,750,000 km from Bakunin–BD+50°1725

An impromptu meeting of the equally impromptu command staff gathered in the same cargo bay where everyone had met earlier. It was less crowded now, with just Toni from the *Daedalus,* senior members of the surviving groups of Caliphate and Salmagundi military, Mallory, and Parvi.

Parvi spoke slowly, laying out her plan to reach the surface of Bakunin. As she described the details, she wondered why she was even proposing following the lead of the two scientists. Even though Shane chose her to babble to, she didn't have any particular connection to him. But there was one point where she agreed. She saw little chance of confronting Adam with conventional methods.

She wondered if Mallory thought that if he stood before the gates of hell, God would intervene. In Parvi's opinion, whoever cranked the wheel of the universe had larger concerns than theirs.

When she finished, everyone was quiet for a moment. Finally, Toni said, "You want to do *what?*"

"The PSDC can cordon off approaches to the planet because of the wide perimeter they set. Once a craft is in low orbit, the orbital platforms start having blind spots. The greatest coverage is over the one landmass, an approach across the ice caps and the ocean on the opposite side—"

"That's not the issue," Toni snapped at her. "It's getting to low orbit."

"I told you," Parvi said, "the *Khalid* can tach in."

"If it was that easy," said the ranking Caliphate tech, "half of these ships would be doing it."

"I never said it was easy," Parvi said. "It's dangerous as all hell."

"I don't think it's even possible," Toni said. "Unless you got a magic tach-drive on that dropship, trying to get any accuracy that close to a planetary mass is suicide. You're as likely to tach into the core as you are into low orbit."

"Actually," Mallory said, "given the capabilities of that new Caliphate drive, the *Khalid* is probably the only tach-ship within light-years with a nav system advanced enough to do it."

Parvi nodded. "I think it's better odds than trying to dodge an orbital linac."

The militiaman from Salmagundi asked, "Is that the real question?"

"What is the question, then?" Parvi asked, even though she knew the answer.

"We are trying to make some sort of stand here. I'm willing to do that, however hopeless, because I saw that thing take apart my home. But now we're talking about throwing away the few assets we do have. At least a pilot and our single armed ship on something that seems even more desperate."

"We can offer a trade," Parvi said.

"What?"

"After the people we *need* to take down to the surface, we'll have space for twenty paying passengers."

Toni shook her head. "I don't believe anyone's going to be willing to take that risk."

Date: 2526.7.25 (Standard)
1,750,000 km from Bakunin–BD+50°1725

It took less than a day to prove Captain Toni Valentine wrong. Just broadcasting an intent to run the PSDC blockade generated a significant interest even without broadcasting the specifics how. Even after establishing secure channels so that the details could be discussed without PSDC eavesdropping, there were several vessels in a desperate enough state to willing exchange their own ships for a possible ticket groundside.

In the end, by taking eighteen people aboard the *Khalid,* they could get an older Centauri dropship, owned by native Bakuninites so it came more heavily armed than the *Khalid,* a scout vessel from the Protectorate, and a lonely SEC fighter whose AWOL pilot was on the edge of his life support.

With those assets added to a quartet of new vessels converted to Mallory's cause, their command was willing to allow Parvi to make her expedition down to the planet.

Somehow, now it's my expedition.

All that was left was to select her people for the mission. People willing to take the same risk she was about to. The scientists, Dörner and Brody, were both coming. Parvi wanted to see some way around it. Even if this wasn't strictly a military operation, she still felt uncomfortable shepherding civilians through it. But if they did make it down, they were the ones who had information on Dolbrians and the Dolbrian cult.

Beyond them, she wanted some military support, and support that was familiar with the ground on Bakunin. The place was dangerous in the best of times, and they had no idea what the situation was like on the ground right now. That left her with only one choice for backup.

She found Kugara in the galley of the *Daedalus,* a small shotgun cabin with a long table down its axis, reminding the crew that the ship was designed with artificial gravity in mind. Kugara added to the illusion by holding herself in place by wrapping her legs around the bench seat affixed to the alleged floor. The sight of her "sitting" at the table was disorienting, especially when Parvi floated in sideways.

Parvi wondered about the woman. It had been Mosa-sa's decision to recruit her. Anyone from Dakota made Parvi a little uneasy—though after working for an AI for so long, the feeling was probably a little disingenuous. Anyone who successfully led a charge on a Caliphate dropship deserved a little respect. Enough that Parvi wondered why she had ceded her initial control of the situation to Mallory.

Kugara lowered the bag she was eating from as Parvi entered.

"I was wondering when you were going to show up."

"You were?"

"You're planning a wild goose chase down to Bakunin, and if you actually get to the surface, you're going to want some sort of backup. That's me, right?"

"It's dangerous."

"And you still have those two scientists going, don't you?"

"Yes."

Kugara nodded. "I know why. Mallory has decided that his battle is going to be a military battle in orbit, angels storming heaven, sword in hand." She smiled slightly when she said that, as if enjoying a private joke. "Not much role for an academic in that scenario, is there?"

"No."

"There's a deep psychic need for people to *do* something in a crisis, however pointless. They've been given that chance. Why do *you* want to do this?"

Parvi looked at Kugara and found herself asking, "Why did you let Mallory take charge of this?"

"I'm no great leader, Captain Parvi. The only reason people followed me is because I started killing people if they didn't. I've never been one of the good guys. Mallory might be talking half bullshit, but any Jesuit that can take charge of a squad of Caliphate engineers, with their consent, has got to have some leadership qualities."

"You don't agree with his assessment of Adam?"

"Oh, come on. *The* Antichrist? There's been more of them than there've been popes. You're avoiding my question."

Because I don't have an answer? "I think Shane may be right, that a direct confrontation may be pointless."

"You don't believe Mallory's going to recruit his navy?"

"No. I think he is."

Kugara stared at her. After a while, Parvi said, "I don't want to be part of an epic battle. I don't want to be a foot soldier in humanity's valiant last stand. I've seen enough war and enough people die. If there's some other way I can fight this thing, I want to take that chance."

"How slim a chance, you think?"

"I guess we have a two-in-five chance that we make it safely to the surface, if I'm right about the capabilities of the *Khalid's* tach-drive navigational system. Once on the surface, I think the chance of Shane's Dolbrian speculations panning out are the same order of magnitude as Mallory pulling off a military victory."

After a long pause, Kugara said, "So it doubles our chances. You can count me in."

"Thank you."

"But there are two other people you need to talk to."

"Who?"

Flynn Jorgenson took his quarters with the other Salmagundi natives, but even so, Parvi got the sense the young man was not comfortable with them. When she approached him, his response was to wave her out of the cabin and away from his fellow countrymen. Once they were alone in an empty corridor, he asked her, "What exactly do you want from me?"

"I'm planning a descent—"

"I know."

"Kugara suggested I talk to you."

"Why?"

"Because you seem to have some knowledge about Bakunin."

He frowned. "About two hundred years more out of date than yours—" He tilted his head, as if he were listening to something. He nodded and rubbed his temple.

"Are you okay?" she asked.

"We're fine, chicky." He pursed his lips and looked her up and down, as if assessing her. It was not a comfortable look; it was cold and judgmental. Not nearly as deferential as he had acted most of the times she had seen him. "Dolbrians, huh?"

"There's a chance—"

"Do you know what's down there?" Flynn asked. "Do you really have any idea what's down there?"

"Dr. Brody and—"

"Was he ever down in those tunnels?" he asked. "I was. You know what you have there? Thousands of kilometers of rock, and a couple of kilometers of carvings by a culture that died out a hundred million years ago. A few marks on a rock. That's what's down there."

"You were down there?"

"Christ in a clown suit, woman. I'm why you're giving Flynn the time of day. I came from that hellhole you want to risk your life to get back to. The woman who discovered those Dolbrian ruins was a friend of mine. All that's there is a big fancy tombstone."

"The Protean suggested otherwise."

"That thing was damaged goods the moment it ran into Mallory's Antichrist. I'll take everything it says with a whole planet of salt, not that it was particularly clear in the first place."

Parvi looked at Flynn and had the strangest sense of looking at someone wearing a mask. "I'm sorry I bothered you then."

Before she could turn to go, Flynn said, "I didn't say we weren't going with you."

"What?"

"Flynn thinks it's worth a chance, and . . ."

"And what?"

"Aside from Salmagundi, Bakunin's the only home I've ever had. I would like to see it again before all hell breaks loose."

The ship had cycled to a nighttime schedule before Parvi had gathered herself enough to face the moreau. The thought of talking to Nickolai raised a combination of fear, disgust, and a deep-ingrained sense that the beings arising out of heretical technologies were wrong on some fundamental level she couldn't quite articulate. She had been able to suppress it when dealing with Mosasa and Kugara because in both cases they appeared human.

Human enough that Parvi's prejudices weren't engaged on the fundamental emotional level that they were when dealing with something that wasn't anywhere near human. The way it was when she thought of Adam and his chosen, or when she thought of Nickolai.

With the tiger, it was worse. Seeing him, the threat wasn't abstract. Nickolai was a huge, muscular predator, clawed and fanged. He was a creature whose ancestors had been designed to rend flesh from bone before any genetic engineers had gotten hold of them. When they were done they had taken a primordial nightmare that had—in its natural state—fed off of the flesh of Parvi's ancestors, and had given it a human intellect and the ability to use human weapons.

Nickolai represented the ultimate failure of human sanity and self-preservation. So it took her a while to convince herself to enter a room alone with him. When she had, it was late enough that she expected to find the tiger asleep.

Hoped to find him asleep, giving an excuse to herself to withdraw for the evening.

However when she opened the door to the cargo compartment Nickolai used for his quarters, the tiger was very much awake. He occupied the center of the open space, the claws of his toes clutching a sheet of cargo netting tied tightly to the wall. He swung a large, long piece of steel around himself in an intricate pattern, stopping it suddenly with loud grunts that were half growls.

She recognized some of the moves from her own martial arts training, though some would only be possible with Nickolai's feline build. Parvi stayed by the door, watching his deadly zero-G dance. Even if the metal rod he carried was weightless, the way he wielded momentum and inertia required massive strength and control, and she could picture any blow he landed with that piece of scrap metal being deadly, even to someone in a hardsuit.

He drew the weapon in with a circular flourish that just avoided his tail and brought it down so it was parallel to his body. When it came to rest, he raised his head to look at the door.

His eyes froze her; black, barely reflective, they gave the appearance of being holes deep into his skull. As if she didn't look at some physical presence, but some vengeful spirit.

"You are frightened," Nickolai said.

"No." Parvi shook her head.

"Yes." He wrinkled his nose. "I can smell it." He released his feet from the cargo netting and pushed himself off, gracefully turning to face her, matching her orientation. "You fear and despise me. Why are you here?"

She stared at him. He was easily twice her height, five or six times her mass. The fingers on one of his half-human hands could probably wrap completely around her neck.

And he had once betrayed them to this creature Adam.

"I am here," she said, "because Kugara asked me to talk to you."

Bizarrely, it almost seemed as if his expression softened. "Why would she want you to talk to me?"

"Where we're going, on Bakunin, is under the control of the Fifteen Worlds."

"You are leaving the priest's fight?" Nickolai snarled.

"There may be some means there to fight Adam."

"And Kugara believes this?"

"You can ask her."

He closed his eyes and nodded. "I do not fight well by proxy, I wish to see my enemy. I will achieve more on a planet than within a warship. I will go with you."

CHAPTER THIRTY-SIX

Redemption

"Much good is done to atone for past evil."
—*The Cynic's Book of Wisdom*

"Lord give me chastity— but not yet."
—St. Augustine
(354–430)

Date: 2526.7.25 (Standard)
1,750,000 km from Bakunin–BD+50°1725

Nickolai assisted in getting the *Khalid* ready to accept passengers. The dropship was still spaceworthy, and to all diagnostics, ready to enter an atmosphere, but the interior cabin had taken a beating during the departure from Salmagundi. Although it was cramped work, he was the strongest able-bodied person available to do much of it.

It was probably fitting, in that much of the damage had been wrought by his own body crashing through the center of the passenger cabin. To fix the cabin, all the crash seating, however deformed, had to be removed and either fixed or replaced.

He wanted the physical effort; to think of little more than how to work free a strut twisted around a sheared bolt; to stop wondering if he was still Nickolai Rajasthan.

To stop wondering what it meant if he was, or if he wasn't.

In some sense the speculation was futile. Everything he saw was a reminder that he had been touched deeply

by transcendent evil. His alien eyes saw far beyond what
even the mechanical prosthetics bequeathed him by Adam's agent, Mr. Antonio, had. These eyes could perceive
near-maddening detail in any light. He could see individual
grains of dirt caught in the weave of the clothing worn by
men on the other side of the ship, read the cockpit displays
reflected in their eyes when they glanced in his direction,
count their eyelashes. Were he to concentrate he could see
into spectra far past the limits of his prior eyes—so deep
into the spectrum that he only saw an alternate universe of
streaks and twinkling lights.

The Protean had pulled him from the Abyss. And at first
he thought it was evil denying his attempt at redemption,
especially when it revealed his own guilty desire to live. It
showed his weakness starkly to him as much as it did to the
rest of the world.

But it led him to some heretical thoughts.

There were the three great sins of man, which led to his
fall from God's grace. All led to thinking beings that were
creations of man, not God. The genetic engineers who created his kind, faux-humans from beasts. The technicians
that created AIs, thought without life. Lastly, the ancestors to the Proteans, who created life itself from unliving
matter.

But if the first sin resulted in beings that could still receive God's grace, why not the others? If Nickolai's race
could be born of such a sin, and yet serve God, why not an
AI? Why not a Protean?

He had spoken for the priest, and in doing so had come
to his own epiphany, one he still struggled with. For there
to be Good or Evil, there must exist a choice. The ability to
decide between courses of action. Adam's evil, at its core,
was a denial of any choice.

But if that was the case, could the Protean be evil only
by the nature of its existence? Could Mosasa? Couldn't
they, like Nickolai's own ancestors, transcend the sin of
their creators?

That was not a comfortable question, especially since he
couldn't decide if it was a true revelation, or simply an attempt to rationalize his own existence.

Maybe he just wanted to believe in a universe where he might be able to reclaim his own fate. It might be why he believed the priest's talk about the Antichrist. If Adam was the Evil One come for the final battle, then it was a chance to redeem himself even in the eyes of the Grimalkin priests. Whatever sin someone carried upon his soul, those few who stood against the Evil One in the end times would receive special dispensation to enter the Kingdom of God. Even the Fallen who chose rightly would gain that privilege.

Perhaps even the Protean who had saved his life.

He had just unbolted a panel from the ceiling that had bent dangerously free of its anchorage when a familiar woman's voice called him. "Nickolai?"

He looked around to see Kugara floating by the air lock where the two ships had been joined. She waved him forward.

Nickolai pushed off a wall, handing the broken panel to one of the Caliphate techs as he drifted over to her. She watched him approach and said, "You move well in zero-G."

"What did you want?"

"You still look like you could use a friend," she said, hoisting up a pair of bottles with one hand. "And a drink."

Nickolai stared at her. He had lost track of how long it had been since she had first said that to him. Before they had left Bakunin, before they had found Adam and the Protean, before he knew what Mr. Antonio was, and before she knew he was a traitor . . .

She patted his arm, the one that used to be artificial, and said, "Come on, this will probably be our last chance to relax and talk."

Any other person, he might have reacted differently to the familiar touch, anything from a snarl to grabbing the offending hand and twisting it off of the owner. With Kugara, he couldn't even bring himself to dislike the contact.

"So," Nickolai said, "we're allies again?"

"Were we ever?" She waved him though the short air lock mating the ships together. "Come on."

He followed her, pulling himself along the wall. She led

him through the *Daedalus* until they came to a cargo compartment that mirrored the one Nickolai used for a cabin. This one was only occupied by a large powered hardsuit tethered to the floor in an upright position.

Kugara closed the door after them and tossed one of the bottles over to Nickolai. It was a slow, underhanded tumble that Nickolai easily picked out of the air. He looked at the bottle and said, "Whiskey from Buccinal? That's about fifty light-years away. Where'd you get this?"

"Mallory's navy is growing, and a few of our fellow refugees are trading for the food we have—the *Daedalus* has—in the cargo hold."

"And you got two bottles?"

"Actually our motley crew all got one to a person. That one's yours."

The bottle had been unsealed, and a curving zero-G spout screwed on. He suddenly smelled the sharp burn of alcohol and glanced over at Kugara. The bottle was at her lips as she sucked a shot through the thin spout that was screwed onto her bottle. She lowered the bottle and sucked in a breath. "Wow," she said. "That's good."

Nickolai wrinkled his nose, "Is it?"

"Try it. This stuff probably runs fifty grams a shot in Proudhon."

Nickolai raised the spout to his lips and sucked in a mouthful. It hit his mouth like it did his nose, a sharp burn that tore down his throat, leaving an almost uncomfortable warmth in its wake. The warmth filled his gut and worked its way through his extremities, felt most in the leather of his nose.

He sneezed.

Kugara laughed. "Cover your mouth when you do that."

He blinked, eyes stinging in the sudden atmosphere of atomized whiskey englobing his head. He pushed himself to the side with a foot, whipping his tail around to keep himself oriented toward Kugara.

"Strong," he said, taking another sip from the bottle, a small one this time.

"You've got to be the most graceful thing I've ever seen," she told him.

"When did you start on that bottle?"

"About eight months ago, if you go by the clocks on Bakunin." She pulled her legs up and folded her arms so that she floated in a sitting position. "You know there's a very good chance that we're going to die before we get to the surface?"

Nickolai took another sip of his whiskey. It no longer burned, and the warming liquid felt pleasant rolling down his throat.

"And," Kugara continued, "if we don't, we're going to be flat-footed on the planet, watching a wild goose chase when Adam does to Bakunin what he did to Salmagundi."

"You could stay here, with the priest."

"Come on." She shook her head, and her hair drifted out around her head, reminding him of how the wind had caught it when she had been driving the aircar that last night on Bakunin. "I am not one of the good guys, Nickolai. Never have been. If Adam showed up right now and said choose, if I didn't it would only be because my soul, blood-stained as it is, belongs to me. No one else."

"But you're going with Captain Parvi?"

"I'm just playing the odds. The chance of either plan working is vanishingly remote. However, in case one does, the better shot of living through it is on the surface." She took another long draw from her bottle.

"If we make it there."

"That's the spirit." She chuckled and let her bottle float away. "What about you? I suggested Parvi talk to you, if only to knock you out of your depressive funk. I didn't expect you to join in on our little suicide mission. Mallory's Crusade seems more your style."

"I fight better with ground under my feet."

"You seem to do pretty damn well in zero-G."

"You can't engage spacecraft in hand-to-hand combat."

"There is that." She unfolded her legs, and with an economical push of her toes against an anchor point in the floor, started a slow drift toward him. The motion reminded him that, since the return of his vision, she was the only person he had seen who didn't seem clumsy.

She reached up and stopped her forward motion with a hand against his chest. She sucked in a breath and asked, "Is it because it's a suicide mission?"

"What?"

"Are you still trying to kill yourself?"

"Kugara, I was never trying to kill myself."

"What? Tearing off your arm and shooting yourself in the skull with my gun? That wasn't a suicide attempt?"

"It was Adam. He was starting to control me. Those were his prostheses and I needed to stop him."

She reached up and touched the side of his face, fingers tracking the fur next to the orbit of his eye. "What about this, what I asked to save you."

"Why did you?"

"You were going to die."

"Does that matter? I betrayed you all. I served the thing we're fighting."

"Nickolai—"

He reached up and pulled her hand gently away from his face. His own half-empty bottle of whiskey floated away from them. "What do you want from me?"

"What do you think?"

He pushed her away. "You're drunk," he said, quietly.

"And you're arrogant, pigheaded, and annoying as all hell."

"I think you should leave."

"Why?" She caught herself from drifting away by grabbing one of the straps securing the hardsuit suspended in the center of the room. "I should leave you to wallow in more self-pity? Boo-fucking-hoo. You're not living the pure life of some fantasy holy warrior. Grow up!"

He felt the fur stiffen along his back, and his face wrinkled in the beginning of a snarl. "Kugara, I've given you license—"

"Give it a rest. If you mention once more about my angelic ancestry, I swear I'm going to rip off your tail and feed it to you. I'm no fucking princess because I got parents from some guy spraying holy jizz into a sacred quim—"

"Enough!" Nickolai roared and pushed off the floor in a straight-line leap at Kugara. He swung his arms up in an underhand blow that could be mortal if he had been angry enough to extend his claws.

However, claws or not, he was drunk enough to forget who Kugara actually was. Kugara's face broke out into a hard smile as she dropped down in front of him. As he passed through where she had been, he looked down and saw her smiling up at him, still holding on to the strap. Then, quicker than any human could have moved, she let go and slammed her palms into the floor behind her, simultaneously bringing both feet up to slam into his gut.

The momentum of the blow started him spinning up and over, and he shot a hand out to grab the hardsuit. He hooked an arm and halted his tumbling motion so he was upside down in relation to the suit. Kugara's momentum carried her up past him, legs first, her back toward him. She grabbed the hardsuit below him and her hips twisted, bringing her legs around to get a scissors lock on his head.

He just had enough time to pull himself toward the hardsuit and get a joint lock on her left leg. Then her right foot came rocketing at his face, and he had to let go of his anchor to reach out and block it.

She pulled up into a sitting position, setting the both of them into a slow tumble. She bent forward to stare into his face as the walls spun behind her. "That's how to get to you, isn't it? Piss on a religion that doesn't even want you any more."

"Don't make me hurt you," Nickolai snarled.

"Oh, just *try* to." She grabbed his ears and brought her own skull down on his with a sense-numbing crash. Nickolai tumbled a moment, convinced his ears had been torn from his skull. He spent half a second stunned senseless, enough for Kugara to free herself, pushing herself backward off of his chest.

His shoulders touched a wall, and he instinctively threw his arms out to catch something solid for an anchor to stop his uncontrolled motion.

"Does it hurt, you arrogant prick?"

Nickolai blinked and focused his eyes on Kugara, who

floated by the nominal ceiling, holding on to another strap
anchoring the hardsuit. He licked his lips and tasted blood.
"You wish to fight?"

"Are you just slow or—"

Nickolai didn't allow her to finish. The taste of blood
had moved him from simple rage into battle. She might
have been engineered to face his kind, but she was drunk,
emotional, and taunting him when she should have been
preparing her defense. Before her sentence cut short, he
was already in the air halfway toward her.

Again she dodged, but she made the mistake of pulling
herself around based on where she thought he was jumping, not where he actually *was* jumping. She spun around to
attack empty air as he grabbed onto the top of the hardsuit.
As she glanced around, looking for him, he tore free the
buckle holding the end of her strap anchored to the hardsuit. She turned her head at the motion, saw him holding
the end of the tether, and did the only thing she could do.

She let go.

The tether was woven carbon, broad and flat. Nickolai cracked it like a whip, sending a fast moving sine wave
down its length to slam Kugara in the side of her head. She
tumbled back from the anchor point, and Nickolai leaped
from the shoulders of the hardsuit to reach her before she
came to her senses.

He struck her with his shoulder, plowing her into the
ceiling next to the strap's anchor point. Before he drifted
away, he grabbed the strap with both hands, near the base.
He brought his knees up on either side of her torso, pinning
her to the ceiling under him.

She blinked up at him, blood trailing from the side of
her head.

"Enough?" he asked.

"Well, I finally got your attention." She smiled at him.

"By blaspheming? Disrespecting the faith of my ancestors?" His arms and legs vibrated with the tension of keeping his muscles taut, legs pushing, arms pulling.

"So how do you intend to punish me?"

"What?"

She reached up and ran her hand along one of his trembling thighs. "You got me, what are you going to do with me?"

He stared at her, mouth open. He became aware of the smells filling the air around them. Blood, sweat, the tang of alcohol, and a heavy musk that made his nose wrinkle.

"Come on, Nickolai, you can't really hide the fact that you like to play rough." Her hand slid inside his thigh and she cupped his testicles. He sucked in a shuddering breath and pulled the strap so tight that it felt as if either the anchorage or his arms might give way.

"What are you doing?"

Her hand was hot against him, bringing forth his arousal despite the efforts of some part of his mind to deny what was happening. She whispered, "It's a suicide mission, I don't want to die alone."

"This is wrong."

"So?" She moved her legs so her hips pushed his thighs slightly further apart. She sat up so her head poked up between his trembling forearms. Her fingers traced the length of his penis. "I'll let you in on two little secrets." Her hand left to trail up his abdomen, leaving him in a state of aching arousal.

"First"—her fingers found the lowest nipple on the right side, under his fur, and traced slow circles around it—"part of my Dakota heritage means I metabolize alcohol very quickly."

She reached up to the neck of her jumpsuit. "Second"— she ran her fingers down the front of the jumpsuit, allowing the fabric to unbond beneath her touch—"if you don't want this, you can always let go."

His own emotions tumbled through him in a cascading, drunken stumble. His own compass of right and wrong had been in an uncontrolled spin ever since Salmagundi.

But this *was* wrong.

He let go of the strap with his right hand. Pain flared up his left arm as it took on the tension by itself. He saw a shadow cross Kugara's face and surprised himself by recognizing the human expression.

Wrong, yes. But how wrong compared to what he had already done?

He reached up behind her and yanked the neck of her jumpsuit down her back, peeling it down her arms and torso. Her arms pinned, naked from the elbows upward, she smiled at him, exposing teeth in an unquestionably aggressive manner. "I knew I had you pegged."

She pulled her arms free and grabbed his ears again, but instead of head-butting him, she pulled her mouth to his in a crushing kiss. It was something he'd never done, as a feline muzzle wasn't designed for it. However, he had lived with humans long enough to know the point of it. Foreplay, like grooming a mate's fur with his tongue.

Now, with Kugara's lips punishing his hard enough for him to taste blood, he discovered he liked it better.

Now that she was in front of him, with only her calves between his thighs, he yanked the jumpsuit down as far as his hand could reach. With it down to her thighs she managed to remove it herself with a few lethally quick kicks. Enough to show that he had never really had her pinned down.

Not that it mattered at this point.

She straddled him with crushing force. He took her throat in his mouth just hard enough to feel her pulse race under his tongue. She dragged fingers down his back with such force that it was hard to believe she didn't have claws. She screamed when he entered her, and he roared when he came.

At the end of everything he let go and they floated free, holding each other.

A long time after he thought she had fallen asleep from the exertion, she asked him, "Do you think we're going to die?"

Nickolai closed his eyes and said, "Everyone dies."

CHAPTER THIRTY-SEVEN

Encyclical

"The most feared change is a change of mind."
— *The Cynic's Book of Wisdom*

"The church is the work of an incarnate God. Like all God's works, it is perfect. It is, therefore, incapable of reform."

— JAMES GIBBONS
(1834–1921)

Date: 2526.7.25 (Standard)
Earth–Sol

The riots started in Sydney, around the diplomatic compound by the old Confederacy spire. By the time the news reached the halls of the Apostolic Palace, the security had already collapsed. The first accounts were confused as to what had happened, and by the time the Vatican had access to the transmissions, so did everyone else on the planet.

Cardinal Anderson stood in a corner of the pope's offices, watching His Holiness view the communication from Khamsin. It was shortly after three in the morning in Rome, and the pope still wore his bedclothes and slippers.

On the holo, a Caliphate officer shouted Arabic into a shaky camera held by someone else. The image jerked as it moved outside. Anderson's monks in the intelligence department had already identified the frantic man on the holo as Colonel Ahmad Abdallah, a regional commander for Khamsin domestic security in the southern hemisphere. The transmission changed focus to the city behind Colonel Abdallah, which intelligence had identified as Al Jahra, a coastal community of about eight million people, dominated by resort hotels and whatever recreational facilities were allowed by the Ministry for Suppression of Vice.

It was normally one of the most beautiful cities on the planet.

Not now.

Abdallah and his anonymous cameraman had moved to the street, which was packed with people fleeing the city center. Behind the mass of the panicked crowd, which caught Abdallah and his cameraman in its inexorable flow outward, the sky burned.

It was as if the heavens above the city had torn themselves open to reveal a rain of fire. It wasn't until individual particles of the fiery heavens grew and slammed into the city skyline that it was clear what was happening. Things were falling from orbit, individual objects in meteoric descent to the surface, so many that they blocked out the sky and the heat of their atmospheric entry set the sky on fire.

And these objects were not meteors.

Molten raindrops the size of small buildings slammed into Al Jahra's skyline, each impact vibrating the image in the holo. Each site of impact glowed as if the blow had broken through the crust of the planet to allow something infernal to shine through from the core. From each site, something rose up from the glowing impact. Whipping tendrils, taller than the buildings, sprang up from the depths to wrap around the skyline. The tendrils grabbed buildings and appeared to fold them, pull them down.

The image in the holo whipped around and faced the direction the crowd had been fleeing, away from the city, just in time to see a glowing teardrop from the fiery sky slam into the road in front of them.

The holo went dark for a moment, then faded in. The image rose from ground level and showed the crowd struck down by the force of the close impact. Many were struggling to their feet, but many were not. All forward motion had stopped as everyone faced the glowing wall that blocked their path. It undulated, like something alive, shooting out tendrils to deconstruct everything in the physical world around them—rocks, buildings, trees, the road itself.

Something walked out of the glowing wall, as if it were so much smoke. The glowing near-human form spread its arms and spoke in Arabic.

An old man trembled before it, on his knees. His clothes were bloody, and he appeared to have broken his arm falling after the impact. He closed his eyes and started praying.

One of the glowing tentacles whipped from the edges of the crowd and struck the man. The old man jerked as if he had been impaled in the back, his jaw went slack, and his flesh seemed to fold within itself as if he was being turned inside out. After a quick glimpse of bone and blood, the old man was gone.

The crowd erupted into chaos, screams of terror, prayers for deliverance, as hundreds of glowing tendrils shot into the crowd, striking them down. Before the scene died, there was a brief flash, an almost subliminal image of a thousand people, men, women and children simultaneously being torn apart from the inside.

Cardinal Anderson felt as if they had just received a tach-comm from hell.

The pope was silent for several moments, staring into space.

"We have a translated version, Your Holiness," Cardinal Anderson said.

The pope shook his head. "I do not want to watch that again. God help all of them." He turned to look at the Cardinal with haunted eyes. "Perhaps you can tell me what was being said?"

Cardinal Anderson nodded and pulled up the transcript on his personal comm.

"I am transmitting against orders from the Ministry of External Relations. I am outside Al Jahra, and we have been receiving blasphemous transmissions for the past twelve hours. We are under attack by something calling itself Adam. It claims it is God. The sky itself is tearing open. People are trying to—"

Cardinal Anderson looked up from the transcript. "The statements become less coherent from that point, once they get caught in the crowd."

"The apparition spoke."

"Yes. That was clear. It said, 'It is now time to choose what God you serve.'"

The pope nodded. He was younger than Cardinal Anderson, but he seemed to have aged twenty years in the past few months. "Am I imagining it, or was the voice familiar?"

"No, it was. I had the waveform checked, and it is an exact match for Kennedy's transmission, the one we showed Mallory."

"Mallory called this thing Adam as well."

"Yes, Your Holiness."

"Do we know how this became public?"

"We suspect a low-level person employed in the communication office of the Caliphate consulate smuggled out a recording."

"I suppose their consulate is in a bit of a disarray right now."

Cardinal Anderson nodded. "The recording implies that the Caliphate government is compromised at a very high level."

"It also implies something else."

"Your Holiness?"

"The specifications on an Ibrahim-class carrier. Beyond the aggressive range of the thing, it can also, I understand, make a tach-jump at the same speed as a tach-comm message. Adam arrived at Khamsin at about the same time as Mallory's message reached us."

"He could be arriving now," Cardinal Anderson said.

"Earth would be a logical target."

"What shall we do?"

"Have you been able to communicate with the Caliphate consul?"

"No."

The pope nodded. "Prepare our own communications office. I'm going to talk, and we need to transmit it as broadly as possible. Tach-comm to every inhabited system we can reach. I will make my statement about Adam."

"Yes, Your Holiness."

"And go tell our guest. The Proteans will get their wish."

Date: 2526.7.25 (Standard)
Mars–Sol

The words of the Bishop of Rome left Earth on every frequency the human race used for communication, both faster and slower than light. As tach-comm bursts left the observable universe to find their receivers light-years away, the more sluggish radio transmissions left the planet in a slowly expanding sphere.

Roughly fifteen minutes from the time the pope began speaking in Rome, the first signals from the broadcast reached the surface of Mars. After another twenty minutes, a large section of Martian desert, where terraforming plants had yet to reach, began to change.

The first changes came to the topography, as the uneven surfaces flattened out over a circular area close to a million square kilometers. Every hump and ridge in the sand spilled out to form a surface close to perfectly flat. The light reflecting off the surface changed as individual grains packed themselves to refract less light. Within thirty seconds, the change was visible from orbit.

The entire area rose several meters as spiral ridges appeared, twisting across the uniform surface. Each spiral was less than a meter across, centered on a tiny hole in its center. The new features showed that the whole area slowly rotated in relation to the surface of the planet.

As the vast area rotated, the holes, millions of them, began to erupt. Each spit out a small projectile the size of a few dozen grains of sand. The teardrop-sized bullets shot from the surface at multiples of Martian escape velocity, trailing a molecule-thick thread behind them.

This was the point when the first human beings became aware that something was amiss. Traffic control officers in charge of regulating Martian airspace suddenly had computers screaming warnings of a huge, anomalous weather front spontaneously appearing on the Martian equator. Satellite imagery of the area showed a gigantic circular cloud, the wake of millions of tiny projectiles tearing through the Martian atmosphere. Even the threads behind them became visible from the contrail of water vapor and ice that coalesced around them.

On the surface, the sudden weather anomaly appeared like a column of clouds a thousand kilometers wide, stacked up through every layer of the atmosphere.

Martian traffic control began desperately warning the few aircraft in the area to steer clear of the anomaly as every sensor started telling them that the core of the cloud-bank was increasing in density.

The millions of tiny probes slowed as they reached the limits of the Martian atmosphere, velocity sapped by the weight of a few hundred kilometers of molecule-thick thread and the water vapor that had managed to condense on the thread in its travel upward. Even so, the motion was still twice escape velocity. As the threads climbed, the heads maneuvered very slightly, dancing on dynamic electromagnetic fields emanating from the threads themselves. The dance caused the threads to spiral around each other and to dip toward the center of their mass.

At the bottom of the massive columnar cloud, the desert around the base of the formation started to drop. Sand began to slide toward it and down, as if falling into a planet-sized hourglass. Above, the cloud formation began to tear apart in the Martian wind, revealing a single black spire, the edges starting nearly parallel to the ground at the surface, then shooting up in an hyperbolic curve that reached toward a vertical asymptote somewhere up above the atmosphere.

The surface of the spire was a thick braid of threads that themselves were braids of even smaller threads made from invisible braids of molecular monofilament.

Even before the top of the spire stopped growing into space, masses began riding up the inside of the spire.

Date: 2526.7.25 (Standard)
Earth–Sol

It was not yet dawn in Rome when Cardinal Anderson opened the door to one of the most secure "guest rooms" in the Vatican. It was as luxuriously appointed as any of the apartments in the Apostolic Palace. The only distinctions marking these rooms as different were the absence of windows or any means to open the door from the inside.

The gentleman who had named himself Jonah Dacham had obviously been roused from sleep by one of the guards before Anderson's arrival. He sat in the living room, dressed but barefoot, his hair uncombed. He squinted against the light when he turned his head to face the cardinal's entrance.

"Good morning, Mr. Dacham," the Cardinal greeted him. "Has your stay been comfortable?"

Jonah chuckled. "Believe me, I've stayed in worse places."

"I've come to tell you that the pope has considered your request."

"You've changed your minds."

"His Holiness saw an example of what our Adversary wrought on Khamsin. He has granted what you asked. Our ability to influence State reactions to your actions is limited, but we have given you the absolution you asked. Those of Proteus have the forgiveness of the Church. You should inform your people."

"No need," Jonah said.

"What?"

"I presume the pope broadcast this announcement?"

"Yes."

"Then they know already."

"What will you do, then, Mr. Dacham?"

"I will continue being human."

As Cardinal Anderson left the apartments where they kept Jonah Dacham, his personal comm alerted him. He brought it out to view the message that something unknown had, in the past hour, built a space elevator on the Martian equator.

He stared at the images of the massive artifact, whose shadow could be seen from as far away as Earth. One thought went through his head: *What have we unleashed?*

CHAPTER THIRTY-EIGHT

The Wrath of God

"Always bet on the team following fewer rules."
—*The Cynic's Book of Wisdom*

"Any exercise of power is justified in preserving power."

—DIMITRI OLMANOV
(2190–2350)

Date: 2526.7.30 (Standard)
10 AU from Earth–Sol

The *Prophet's Voice* emerged into the observable universe in a burst of tachyon radiation. The vast cloud of matter, the extension of Adam's will that had preceded him into humanity's home system, welcomed its arrival and transmitted telemetry data from the inner system it had been gathering since the destruction of the wormholes that had brought it here.

Adam stood on the bridge of the *Voice*, but he also existed everywhere within the ship, and outside in the vast cloud of matter in orbit around the sun. All were vast pieces of himself, coordinating, communicating.

Though that network flowed the will of his followers, who numbered now millions more than the few embodied souls within the *Voice*. Whatever their origin, the original colony orbiting the sacrificial star Xi Virginis, Salmagundi, Khamsin—they belonged to Adam now. And before them all sat the heart of humanity, mother Terra itself.

Here are those who killed the Race . . .

Adam ignored the errant thought. All life was sacred, too sacred to allow its descent into entropy and decay. Mankind would not face the fate of Adam's creators. When he was done, all of humanity, all life, would be immortal and inviolate.

And his.

Mind flowed out of the *Voice* into the living cloud, each consciousness taking part of the sentient matter for itself, each becoming an agent of Adam's redemption, to carry his light to every inhabitant of this solar system.

It took nearly two full seconds for a sequence of errant data to make it from the coalescing intelligent cloud to reach his awareness.

Others . . .

The fleet attached to the *Voice* separated, spreading out to engage what spacecraft remained in the system here. Nothing with an active engine or electrical system could hide from the *Voice*'s sensors or the broad awareness of the cloud. Within fifteen minutes, ships would be in tactical range of each other and those opponents that drifted in toward the cloud would be dealt with less conventionally.

Others . . .

While his disciples from Khamsin piloted their warcraft toward the opposition, and others more comfortable in their transcendence from the flesh took their places in the cloud, Adam reviewed what the cloud had seen on Mars.

Of course, there must always be an Adversary.

A smile crossed the face of Adam's manifestation on the bridge of the *Voice*. Mosasa, his brother, had not been the Evil One, at least not solely. The existence of light formed darkness, and Adam's light was bright indeed. He broadcast his announcement to Earth, and waited for his latest Devil to make itself known.

Date: 2526.7.30 (Standard)
Earth–Sol

"In twelve hours you must choose what God you serve."

Adam's message repeated, in every language, and on every broadcast frequency used on Earth. Cardinal Anderson stood in the papal apartments realizing that they had reached the limits of what they could do, what the Church could do. They couldn't even communicate with anyone outside the Vatican. Adam's message wasn't just an ultimatum, but it effectively blocked almost all other communications.

The few communications channels that weren't blocked were disabled by the secondary effects of Adam's announcement. He had no news from the wider world, but he had seen the teeming throng in St. Peter's Square, and he had seen columns of smoke rising from Rome's skyline.

"God help us all," he said as he turned from the armored window.

The pope stood by the doorway and said, "Pray that we have acted as God wished."

"I am concerned for your safety," Cardinal Anderson said. "It is close to a riot out there."

"If I am in danger, it is not from the people in the square, and I won't be saved merely by hiding in my apartments. If all I can do is give comfort to those in reach of my voice, I will do so."

"Yes, Your Holiness."

"Perhaps you should see to Mr. Dacham."

Cardinal Anderson nodded as the pope left to give what might be his last Mass.

What might be the last Mass, period.

Date: 2526.7.30 (Standard)
10 AU from Earth–Sol

Rebecca Tsoravitch retained a physical presence on the *Voice* even as her spirit trailed behind Adam to see the full extent of his invasion. Along with her followed the silent ghost of Tjaele Mosasa. Even though her perception was limited by the speed of light, it was vast and she saw more clearly than she had even during the approach to Khamsin.

She knew she was exceptional, even among Adam's host. Few had graduated from fleshy biology to a distributed existence as quickly and as thoroughly as her. The only precedent she had to compare herself to was the original Mosasa, himself, integrating his mind, like a virus, into all of Adam's chosen.

Perhaps that was why Mosasa's AI embodiment chose her in the first place. Perhaps her human self bore some kinship with his. Or perhaps her spirit had absorbed more of Mosasa than others.

Whatever the case, all of Adam's minions whose origins were rooted to the flesh limited themselves in space and time. All felt a need to enforce a boundary between themselves and the rest of the universe, however porous that boundary became. She found herself able to slide her awareness to the limits of Adam's reach. The whole network of thinking machines that formed the cloud drifting insystem ahead of the *Voice* was open to her eyes and her thoughts. And, if she chose not to be subtle, her actions.

Fortunately, while Adam could see with the entire array of the cloud, he cared little about what his chosen cared to look upon, as long as they followed his direction without question.

She was one of a few entities aware enough to have seen the consequences of questioning Adam. He was not a merciful God. Those who chose his path saw many sins forgiven—but one. Questioning or disobedience was met with instantaneous nonexistence. All of Adam's followers dwelled in a network of matter and information that was, in large part, Adam himself. Should he will it, any of his millions would cease to exist. Already thousands had, some for balking at purging the unbelievers from Khamsin, some for questioning Adam's divine purpose, some for simply asking "Why?" at the wrong time.

It seemed to her that as Adam's sphere grew and his followers multiplied, he grew harsher, more inflexible. Even his words changed with each new world.

To the people of Salmagundi he had said, *"I am Adam. I am the Alpha, the first in the next epoch of your evolution. I will hand you the universe. Follow me and you will become as gods."*

To Khamsin, he had said, *"I am Adam. I am the Alpha, the first in the next epoch of your evolution. I will hand you the universe. Worship me and you will become as gods yourselves."*

To Earth, he was saying, *"I am Adam. I am the Alpha, the*

God of the next epoch of your evolution. I will hand you my universe. Worship me or become as dust."

Even those who had come to Adam's fold completely willingly, like those liberated from the Hall of Minds to meld seamlessly into Adam's distributed mind, had begun to move and act tentatively, the silent miasma of fear almost as real as the cloud itself.

To her it wasn't unfamiliar. She had grown up under the Jokul Autocracy. She lived well under a government just as draconian about questioning and disobedience as Adam. She policed the data streams under a regime where every citizen knew that every word and act was scrutinized for subversion, and their lives were lived subject to the whims of any anonymous bureaucrat that might take offense to them.

So the caution she saw evolving under Adam's rule was very familiar. As was Adam himself. She also knew how to survive under such authority: Never assume that you weren't being watched. Never voice your dissent. Consume all the information available. And keep constant watch for a potential escape route.

Whatever Adam wreaked upon the rest of the world, her priority was survival. Even as he slaughtered billions, she would unapologetically be on the side of the survivors. Even when it meant being his avatar, walking the surface of the Earth harvesting souls for a god she didn't remotely believe in.

She did not expect a challenge to Adam's omnipotence to come as soon as it did.

The first sign was buried in data the cloud had collected before their arrival. She hadn't accessed it, being more intent on seeing what was happening in real time around the *Voice* as the conventional armada spread out to engage the few military vessels moving against them in a complicated dance of acceleration vectors that slowly took them in tactical range of each other's weapons.

But as the first missiles were fired, she noticed stars being occluded and felt the gravitational ripples of very dense mass approaching from insystem. Sensing that through the sensors of the cloud, she rolled back those perceptions through time, backtracking the trails of unusual mass to the fourth planet in the system. Focusing on Mars with the past eye of the cloud, she saw the surface of the planet dotted by tall black spires reaching from the surface all the way into low orbit and beyond.

The spires had launched something into space.

Many somethings.

Her attention snapped back to real time as a million-kilometer radius sphere of the cloud ceased to exist. She felt it as if a clawed hand tore out a chunk of her brain, and a limb to go along with it. Her thoughts had spread out along the whole cloud in an effort to make herself less vulnerable. But something was attacking the cloud itself.

She pulled back as more vast holes were plucked out of the cloud, each hitting her like a physical blow. Even as she withdrew, and holes tore through her awareness of the universe outside the *Voice*, she saw what was happening.

Thousands of dense ovoid objects, only meters across, were flying through space toward them. The first wave was reaching the cloud, and as they did, they released a flash of energy that tore apart the material of the cloud on a molecular level. Each flash erased thousands of Adam's followers less diffuse than she was, and rendered inert large swaths of the cloud.

Then she coalesced herself back into her physical presence on the *Voice*. Once again, she found herself surprised by her own breathing and the race of her pulse, though this time she was aware of it and stopped her physical body's reactions from running away from her.

She glanced around the prosaic cabin in the *Voice* with her own body's eyes and wondered what she was going to do if Adam was really threatened.

CHAPTER THIRTY-NINE

Special Dispensation

"Even if you expect change, the change is not what you expect."

—The Cynic's Book of Wisdom

"Naught endures but change."

—LUDWIG BOERNE
(1786–1837)

Date: 2526.7.30 (Standard)
1,750,000 km from Bakunin–BD+50°1725

"I speak now to all peoples, all faiths, all creeds." The words echoed through the cockpit of the *Daedalus*, Mallory stood between Captain Valentine and the elder Stavros while Valentine's sister operated the communications console. Floating in the display before her was the image of His Holiness Pope Stephen XII. *"I bear a dire warning for all of mankind."*

Mallory looked into the pope's eyes, feeling a surreal displacement from where he was. So much had happened since he had taught university at Occisis, it felt like another universe.

"Nearly two hundred years ago, when the old Terran Confederacy was collapsing, an unknown number of colonists left the known limits of human space. They formed several colonies orbiting stars in the vicinity of Xi Virginis, eighty light-years past the boundaries of the Confederacy. After nearly two centuries of isolation, we have received contact from them."

The video switched and Mallory heard audible gasps from the others in the cockpit as the holo transmission filled with his own face. *"I am Father Francis Xavier Mallory."* Mallory looked at himself, haggard and gaunt in the image. It deepened the sense of displacement he felt. *"I am transmitting from a planet named Salmagundi in orbit around the star HD 101534. I arrived here on the tach-ship* Eclipse, *which had been engaged in a scientific expedition from Bakunin to Xi Virginis."* It slowly sank in that his tach-comm had made it. Despite Adam's efforts, a transmission had slipped through. The evil could be beaten. It *was* possible.

The pope himself must have come to the same conclusion, if the Vatican was retransmitting it. On the screen Mallory said, *"The Caliphate has forces here, but the attack is coming from a third party, an entity identifying itself as Adam."*

The transmission cut back to the pope who said, *"The Caliphate sent the most advanced military fleets to these colony worlds. Carriers with hundreds of ships and tachyon drives that can move as fast as this data transmission. But they did not succeed in annexing these colonies, because they did not face a conventional adversary. They faced* the *Adversary."*

The image cut again, to somewhere not immediately familiar. A man in a Caliphate military uniform with a colonel's lapel pips spoke Arabic into a shaky camera. The pontiff's voice narrated. *"This transmission arrived on Earth less than twelve hours ago. It originated from Khamsin, the capital of the Eridani Caliphate, a planet with over five billion people, only ten and a half light-years from Earth. What you are seeing happened four days ago."*

Mallory did a quick calculation in his head and decided that the transmission from Khamsin was now nine or ten days old. He couldn't turn away from the transmission, even though he knew what was going to happen. He knew it even before he saw the sky burning with the trails of millions of objects entering the atmosphere.

Both sisters said quietly, "What *is* that?"

"Adam," Mallory responded. "It is Adam coming to Khamsin like he came to Salmagundi."

On the screen, the dropships—Mallory didn't have a better name for the huge teardrops of molten metal—tore apart a distant urban horizon. Glowing tendrils reached from the teardrops to consume the city. Then the image was of a mass of people thrown to the ground by the force of a nearby impact.

Stavros muttered something in Greek that might have been a curse or a prayer. Mallory counted the rosary in his head. The Valentine sisters simply said, "Shit."

Adam walked into view, glowing, larger than life, speaking Arabic to the fallen people before him. Walls of whipping tendrils surrounded the crowd. A wounded old man bent his head, as if to pray, and one of the tendrils tore the man inside out before consuming him. The crowd panicked, but there was nowhere to run, and the tendrils took everyone, man, woman, and child.

The holo faded to black before the image of the pontiff returned.

"For centuries," the pope continued, *"all human society has recognized three basic evils. Religious or secular, we have not tolerated any experiments in these Heretical Technologies: Self-replicating Nanotechnology, Artificial Intelligence, and the genetic engineering of sapient beings. Each brings its own unique dangers, and each has been responsible for the loss of countless lives over the past five hundred years. For five hundred years we have seen these things, in and of themselves, as anathema. But evil does not reside in matter, in knowledge, in science. Evil lives in the heart. It lives in the soul. It is our choice to follow a moral framework we acknowledge as outside ourselves, or descend to one written to accommodate our own petty desires, our hubris, our narcissism, our solipsism, our nihilism."*

The pope looked out of the holo as if he were trying to force his will through the intervening light-years. *"You have seen the works of the entity calling itself Adam. Adam represents the ultimate fear that drove us all to reject those Heretical Technologies. Adam is the temptation we tried to deny ourselves, power without any restraint or moral consideration. Adam represents the antithesis of humanity, the Adversary of every single faith, creed, or philosophy."*

"How can you fight that?" Stavros whispered. "How can anyone fight something like that?"

"We have seen Evil, and it is not in the tools Adam uses. It is not in the technology. The Evil is Adam itself. The Evil that places any inhabitant of this universe on the level of its creator. The Evil is rule based on the whim of a would-be god. The Evil is in cancerous belief that would deny existence to any that do not adhere to it. Because of this, and with the authority God grants me and the Church, I herby grant absolution for all those who have used Heretical Technologies, and their progeny—specifically, the Proteans and their kin—who chose to follow the laws of God and man. Any who rise up now to resist this evil have my blessing and that of the Church."

"That is how you fight something like this," Mallory said.

God help us all, he thought.

Parvi knew about the Vatican's transmission before anyone from the *Daedalus* bothered to tell her. She was in the cockpit of the dropship, running last-minute diagnostics for the launch less than six hours away now.

While she worked, and shortly after the Vatican's tachcomm started repeating through Bakunin's star system, the comm array on the *Khalid* began lighting up. Not with the Vatican's message, but with sudden new interest in Mallory's upstart navy.

After the first hundred queries queued up in less than a minute, Parvi knew something was up. Once she read a couple of messages, she knew what it was.

She made her way across into the *Daedalus,* and entered the cockpit just as the pope's message was ending. Parvi broke the silence that followed by saying, "It looks as if you're getting your navy, Mallory."

One of the two Valentines said, "What do you mean?"

"Have you been paying attention to incoming queries while you were watching this?"

The Valentine by the console switched displays and showed a comm more active than the one on the *Khalid.* "Five hundred queries?"

"You were in that transmission," Parvi asked Mallory, "weren't you?"

"Yes, they got the tach-comm from Salmagundi."

"I think you're going to be very popular all of a sudden," Parvi said.

"Eight hundred queries, now."

The command staff met about thirty minutes later. They had just reviewed the Vatican's holo again, and to Parvi, the atmosphere in the cargo hold seemed to contain equal parts dread and optimism.

When the holo ended, Toni said, "The last numbers I have from Beth have a little under a thousand new vessels expressing interest in following Mallory's defense."

The Caliphate representative spoke, "W-We need to discuss what we are to ask of them. H-How— " His voice choked up. Parvi felt for the man; she had felt the same sense of dislocation when Rubai fell. It had been intense enough that most of her comrades at the time had fought the Caliphate less out of duty than out of denial. How could the regime you were raised in, that you fought for, just one day cease to exist?

She had watched the colonel on the holo and saw in his eyes the familiar denial as the sky fell down around him. She saw it in Mallory's eyes, in the eyes of the stuttering Caliphate tech: the desperate clinging to the idea that there was something out there left for them to fight for.

The Salmagundi representative placed a hand on the man's shoulder, nodding in agreement. "We have a fleet," he said, "but we have few resources. Do we just wait for Adam to arrive? Can we negotiate with Proudhon to establish a base of operations? Force the issue with them?"

Mallory shook his head, "We can talk to the PSDC, but if they're recalcitrant I don't want to take any action that would damage their defensive position. Their orbital defenses will be the last line against Adam."

"Can they defend against what we've just seen?"

"The sheer mass of it . . ." The Caliphate representative trailed off.

"That might be the key here," Toni said. "Our point of attack."

"What do you mean?" Mallory asked.

"Mass," Toni said. "You described a ring fully around a planet. Enough vehicles entering the atmosphere to blot out the sky. This is a lot bigger than the super-carrier you were talking about."

"Yes?"

"Basic logistics question: where did the enemy forces come from?"

"You have an idea?" Parvi asked.

"There's only three choices," Toni said. "One, Adam uses his nanotech wizardry to re-purpose the mass he finds insystem when he arrives. I don't think that's likely given the time frames we're talking about. It's also bad strategy, leaving his forces vulnerable for at least a few hours before his attack is at full strength. Second, the attackers tach insystem full force all at once. This is probably technically possible for him, but requires a hellacious amount of energy—"

Parvi shook her head, "Adam took out the entire wormhole network, as far as we can tell. Is energy really a problem for him?"

"That attack consumed an entire star," Mallory said.

Toni nodded, "And if you track the path of the attack, it was precisely timed, and begun decades ago, hitting close to simultaneously. If Adam's resources were truly unlimited, he would be attacking every inhabited planet simultaneously as well. It is obvious from the Vatican's message that he didn't even attempt Earth and Khamsin at the same time."

Mallory nodded. "He's building his strength. With control of the *Voice* he could approach any Caliphate planet without an immediate challenge. He will only leave the Caliphate when he thinks he has the resources to defeat any possible opposition."

"You said three choices," Parvi said, fearing the answer.

"The most likely option," Toni said, "is that the bulk of Adam's force is already here."

"How can that be possible?" asked the Caliphate representative. "Perhaps Adam might close on Khamsin with a stolen spacecraft, but how could such a force arrive with no warning?"

"No," Toni said, "we had a massive warning that was impossible to ignore. So massive, that it obscured their arrival."

"The wormholes." Mallory said.

Of course, Parvi thought. Adam sent his own wormholes into the core systems. They weren't just weapons to wipe out the wormhole network and disrupt communications and travel. They were also, themselves, a transportation conduit. Adam could have sent anything through the wormholes before they destroyed themselves. He could have sent a planet through if it was carved into sufficiently small chunks.

"So," Toni said, "somewhere out there is a cloud of matter, waiting."

"If it's there," asked the Salmagundi representative, "and we can find it, how do we attack a cloud?"

Parvi thought of the *Khalid*'s escape from the *Voice* and said, "We pump as much energy into it as we can."

When the meeting broke up, Parvi left to board the *Khalid* and resume the checks for her descent toward Bakunin. When she reached the air lock connecting the two ships, she heard Mallory's voice.

"Captain Parvi?"

She pushed against the doorframe so she spun around to face him. "Yes?"

"Do you still intend to do this?"

"Are you telling me not to?"

"No."

"But you think this is pointless."

"I don't think the Dolbrians have any bearing on what's about to happen . . ."

"I hear a 'but.'"

"We've had no communication with the surface for days, Parvi. That's bizarre. Bakunin is a completely lawless world; someone down there should be transmitting something, but all we have is a PSDC computer warning away anyone who attempts to land. Adam's our main concern, but we need intelligence from planetside."

Parvi nodded.

"The *Khalid* has some secure tightbeam comm gear. When you touch down, I'd like it if your team gave us hourly updates on the surface conditions."

"Yes, sir," Parvi said, silently musing on the role reversal since she had recruited him fresh off the boat from Occisis, even if his persona then had been a sham.

She spun back toward the air lock, and as she made her way into the *Khalid,* she heard Mallory's voice call out to her. "It would be good if you could also find a PSDC officer we could actually talk with."

If I manage to get this thing landed, I'll see what I can do about that.

Four hours later, Parvi sat in the same seat where she had been sitting when the *Khalid* had lifted off from Salmagundi. This time, she was alone in the cockpit, and a selfish part of her wished Wahid was here with her—even though if he had survived he probably would have had better sense than to join her on this blockade run.

In truth, she was alone because she really didn't need any assistance. Ninety percent of what they were about to do would be routine piloting. The other ten percent relied more on the *Khalid*'s navigational computers than it did on her skills as a pilot. She could probably swap places with Kugara and not change their chances of survival.

Unfortunately, that wasn't a comforting thought.

She reached her third double check and saw that the diagnostics weren't shifting from their optimal readings. She pushed herself up out of the seat and drifted over to the cockpit doorway. It was open, the door itself removed during the repairs to the interior, and as a noncritical repair, it had never been put back.

She hung in the doorway, looking back at the passenger compartment. She saw a sea of strange faces, none she had bothered to place a name to. The only familiar people were in back, by the rear bulkhead. The tiger, Kugara, Flynn, and the pair of scientists.

"Is everyone strapped in?"

She heard a chorus of assents. She glanced over at the air lock. She could monitor its status from the cockpit, but it was more comforting to see the door dogged shut with her own eyes.

Here we go . . .

She withdrew back into the cockpit and strapped herself in. She called back to the *Daedalus*, "This is Parvi on the *Khalid*. We are ready to separate."

Toni—or Beth's—voice came back. "Copy that, separating the air lock now." A dull clank resonated through the skin of the *Khalid*. "You're free. Good luck."

"Pray for us," Parvi radioed back. Then she brought the maneuvering engines on-line and pulled the *Khalid* away from the *Daedalus*.

CHAPTER FORTY

Leap of Faith

"We only assume we know what we're doing."
—*The Cynic's Book of Wisdom*

"Nothing wrong with fear; it lets you know you aren't dead yet."
— AUGUST BENITO GALIANI
(2019–*2105)

Date: 2526.7.30 (Standard)
1,000,000 km from Bakunin–BD+50°1725

Kugara knew when the dropship separated from the *Daedalus*. Soon after, she felt a gentle acceleration push her back into her seat. She licked her lips and her heart started racing against her will. This was it, and there was a good chance she had just begun experiencing the last twenty minutes of her life.

She knew just enough about flying a spacecraft to understand how difficult what they were attempting was. Even if the tach-drive on this boat was accurate enough to put them in place within the two-hundred-meter margin of error this maneuver required—which was asking for a miracle all by itself—Parvi still had to line up the *Khalid*'s momentum and acceleration vectors to match with the orbital insertion path they needed to follow. A few degrees pointed in the wrong direction relative to the planet and they could tach in precisely on target but on an outbound path straight into the free-fire zone.

Off in the other direction, they could make a too-steep entry into the atmosphere and lose control of the ship.

She looked at the scientists and Flynn, across the central aisle from her and Nickolai. They looked as unconcerned as the crowd of refugees filling the balance of the cabin.

Was she the only one who understood how risky this actually was?

She felt a heavy, furred hand touch her knee. She looked up at Nickolai, sitting in a custom-built seat made out of two human-sized ones. The wide straps of the crash harness looked tiny against his broad chest. His feline expression was enigmatic as he quietly said, "You are afraid."

"Of course I am."

"There is nothing as useless as someone obsessing over something she can't change," he said.

Kugara stared at him, listening to the echo of her own words from Salmagundi. "You asshole, how long have you been waiting to say that?"

He squeezed her knee, and she could feel the hint of claws pricking though her jumpsuit. Then he pulled it away. "You were right," he said.

"Does this mean you've stopped condemning yourself?"

Nickolai shook his massive head. "Do not ask too much of me. I am still all that I am."

"Uh-huh."

"But," he continued, "I am beginning to think that things may be more complicated than I have allowed in the past."

The dropship jerked and accelerated on a new vector. Kugara caught her breath and grabbed Nickolai's hand back. "I don't like not being in control," she whispered.

"We control how we face the end of things," he said. "A heart of a warrior beats in your breast."

A little too fast, she thought. "Do you really believe it is the End Times?"

"I've been taught the signs that precede the end of things, and there have been many of them. But we are not privileged to know God's will until St. Rajasthan himself returns from heaven, bearing a flaming sword, and leading an army of prophets into this world to divide the just from the unjust."

"For all we know, that's already happened." *As insane as things have gotten, it wouldn't really surprise me either.*

"No," Nickolai said, "if that happened, we *would* know."

Over the PA, Parvi's voice announced, "We are about to engage the tach-drive. Hang on, it may get rough all of a sudden."

Nickolai gently squeezed her hand.

Parvi lined the *Khalid* up relative to Bakunin as closely as the navigational system allowed. Her velocity and acceleration vectors precisely paralleled the entry path from low orbit, just at a remove of about a million klicks out.

She took a couple of deep breaths to calm herself. Everything now was up to the tach-drive computers. She set the coils to charge—

And a horizon slammed into the viewscreen with a physical blow that shook the length of the *Khalid*. The viewscreen was cut in two, above a black sky, below the sunlit blue of ocean.

She didn't have time to absorb the fact that they had survived the tach-jump without going wide either deep into the atmosphere or up into the fire zone. She had more to worry about trying to keep the *Khalid* from vibrating apart. They dove into the atmosphere too steeply and were slamming into air sooner than Parvi wanted. The horizon's curve vibrated, flattening, as the blue below her gave way to the white of Bakunin's massive northern icecap.

The consoles before her flashed red warnings in Arabic. Half came from the contragrav. It had been primed to provide lift for reentry, but some time in the *Khalid*'s recent violent history, some part somewhere in the contragrav system had been invisibly pushed too close to failure. The instantaneous taching into a gravity well had stressed part of the charged contragrav past the failure point. The manifold was venting exotic matter plasma into space, causing the Khalid's acceleration downward to increase. She had to rely on atmospheric braking entirely by the time she crossed the pole and into the dark side of Bakunin.

The planet kept rising beneath her, distorted in the viewscreen from the heat of reentry. The *Khalid* streaked through the arctic Bakunin night supported by nothing more than momentum and its own limited aerodynamics.

Parvi did what she could to flatten the attack angle of the spacecraft, because at this angle of approach, they might not clear the ice cap. She pulled the nose up, and in a desperate move, fired the maneuvering jets on full.

The burst of acceleration thrust her into her seat and added to the hypersonic velocity they needed to bleed away, but it did what she hoped and corrected their approach angle.

No way I'm going to bring this in for a ground landing.

She started tweaking their course southeast as the ice sheet slid away behind her. The horizon rose ahead of her, more slowly now. She hit the controls to enhance the images out the viewscreen.

Bakunin's only continent raced by below her. The mountains forming its spine sped by to her left, the ship still dropping incredibly fast. The coastline zoomed toward her. She gingerly goosed the controls again, turning the *Khalid* slightly to parallel the coastline.

The dropship protested, shaking and thrusting her against her seat. The brick of a craft was not designed for gentle maneuvers without the benefit of its contragrav. The *Khalid* started a yaw back and forth that stopped just short of throwing them into an uncontrolled tumble.

And I was thinking taching in was the hard part . . .

The horizon crept toward the top of the viewscreen. The nighttime coastline raced by below them, and the Diderot Mountains disappeared off to the west.

"Everyone, brace yourselves," she called into the PA system.

In the viewscreen the coast whipped by too fast and close to make out any detail, the ocean a blur. Proximity warnings lit up the navigation console as Parvi made one final attempt to flatten out their flight path.

The blur of ocean spread to fill the entire viewscreen,

and the *Khalid* hit the water like a bullet. The jolt of the impact threw Parvi against the harness, wrenching her neck and nearly slamming her face into the control console. The shuddering jolts continued, accompanied by a roaring loud enough to make her ears hurt. Unpleasant mechanical noises resonated through the body of the dropship.

The motion stopped with a groan.

Parvi looked up at a dead-black viewscreen and a control console that consisted of blank display or flashing red Arabic characters. She released the crash harness and stumbled out of the chair, surprised by both the sudden presence of actual gravity and the fact that the floor tilted down forward and to the right.

It wasn't quite as surprising as the fact she was alive.

She climbed uphill to the open cockpit door and called back, "We had to ditch in the ocean off the western coast. Each of your chairs should have an emergency kit mounted beneath it. Inside will be a red flotation pack. Get it out and hold on to the kit. Don't inflate it until you're outside the ship."

A mad scramble filled the cabin as everyone released the crash harness and grabbed for a kit. A few people stumbled in the increasingly tilting floor.

Fortunately, the main air lock was on the uphill side of the tilt. She opened the inner door and pulled herself inside. She looked out the air lock window and saw stars.

We might live through this.

There was a bang and a hiss, and the cabin lights went out. The air lock faded into dull red emergency lighting. Parvi braced herself against the wall and looked back into the darkened cabin. "No one panic. We're going to file out the air lock. When you reach the door, activate the flotation device and jump out. One at a time, quickly and calmly. Everyone understand?"

She heard enough assents to open the air lock door.

She grabbed the manual release, turned it, and the door creaked open, letting in a cool breeze smelling of sea salt and overheated composite. The first person climbed up past her, a young man, one of the civilians. He held out the bricklike floatation device. The object was red and black polymer with a large yellow blister on one side, a small strap on the other. The wording on the thing was in Arabic, and the man looked to her and asked, "What do I do?"

"Put your hand through the strap, press the yellow blister until you hear the inside break, then jump. Don't let go."

He nodded and looked outside. He muttered, "Shit," and pressed the yellow blister. Parvi heard a distinct snap; then he jumped into the night. She glanced at the water, already disturbingly close to the air lock, as the guy splashed down and went under. The water bubbled violently for a moment. Then a three-meter sphere of translucent red material, segmented like an orange, popped up out of the water, holding the surprised young man inside.

She ushered out the civilians as rapidly as possible, until the water around the ditched *Khalid* was bobbing with red spheres. She managed to keep the evacuation orderly, even as the cabin behind her started to fill with water and the ocean waves began cresting over the bottom of the air lock. By the time the last civilian was out, the floor tilted away from Parvi at nearly seventy degrees, and Nickolai was standing on the opposite wall, knee-deep in water, lifting people toward the air lock.

They got Flynn and the scientists out as the water rose above the door. Parvi was standing in the midst of a deluge sluicing up over her thighs, yelling down, "Come on, there's no time."

Someone shouted below her, but she couldn't hear it over the roaring water. Then a damp furry arm thrust Kugara at Parvi. Parvi grabbed her and pushed her outside. She heard her scream "Nickolai!" as she splashed out into the ocean.

Parvi struggled against the current looked down into the roiling water filling the ship and hollered, "Nickolai!" She could see nothing below her; even the emergency lights were gone at this point. She held out an arm and repeated, "Nickolai," even though she knew that she had nowhere near the strength to pull a waterlogged tiger out of the depths.

Something, somewhere on the *Khalid* broke apart with

a snap that shook the whole ship and pulled the nose even further downward. The water blew in at a redoubled rush and Parvi felt her grip slip away. She fell back into the cabin, plunging into pitch-black water, immediately losing her sense of up and down.

She shook her head frantically in a silent panic as she felt the water wrap itself around her chest, trying to push its way into her nose and her mouth. She flailed her arms around, desperately reaching for an anchor, or a landmark, something.

Her hand felt something hard, muscular, and covered with slick waterlogged fur. Even as she touched his arm, she felt Nickolai wrap it around her chest. Suddenly she was moving, pulled along by him, and the world had direction again.

And once she knew where up was, they broke through the surface.

She gasped lungfuls of air, holding on to the tiger's chest, for once not caring who he was. She blinked her eyes until her vision cleared, and looked up at the creature who had saved her life.

Nickolai wasn't looking at her.

She turned her head, and through the bobbing red spheres, she could see the first light of dawn. It backlit the coastline which, miraculously, seemed only about ten kilometers away, if that. Even more miraculous, they were in sight of one of Bakunin's coastal cities. The skyline was silhouetted against the blood-red clouds, maybe only twenty klicks south along the coast.

But, as she watched, she realized the pillars of clouds against the skyline weren't actually clouds.

It was smoke.

The city was burning.

CHAPTER FORTY-ONE

Apocalypse

"Beginnings are inseparable from endings."
— *The Cynic's Book of Wisdom*

"So far as a man thinks, he is free."
— Ralph Waldo Emerson
(1803–1882)

Date: 2526.7.30 (Standard)
10 AU from Earth–Sol

Adam felt the Protean attack as if they were tearing the flesh from his bones. Every flash that destroyed part of the cloud not only took with it his hard-won followers, but also a part of himself. No matter how diffuse his existence was, no matter the fact that his embodiment here, in this solar system, was only one of many.

The assault was still intolerable.

He took control of the cloud, because his followers, for the most part, were still too inexperienced in their new existence to react. They were unaware of their own vulnerabilities. To save them, he ordered the cloud to condense, coalesce into thousands of points across a wide swath of the asteroid belt. Even as the Protean attack flashed dozens of times, blowing holes through Adam's presence in this solar system, the coalesced spheres of matter shielded themselves, building a shell dense and inert enough to deflect the suicidal explosions.

The flashes continued along the breadth of Adam's

forces, but now the flashes no longer took Adam's forces with it. He opened his awareness to everything the cloud had perceived and saw thousands of Protean attackers, wave after wave of small egg-shaped probes.

At Adam's bidding, his own forces maneuvered to the widely spaced asteroids in their midst. Unlike the Proteans, Adam was not willing to risk his own in a suicide mission. Not when there was an alternative.

In a hundred dense iron-nickel asteroids, the amorphous remnants of the cloud coalesced and burrowed in, leaving a broad, straight tunnel facing the attackers. The tunnels were uniformly smooth and coated with a fine web of superconducting material. In each case, after a few minutes, the surface temperature of the infected asteroid rose a few degrees Kelvin, and whatever magnetic field existed became stronger and oriented along the axis where Adam's will had inserted itself.

"Now," Adam spoke, unnecessarily on the bridge of the *Voice*.

A hundred asteroids began firing their contents at the Proteans. Each asteroid had become a gigantic linac, shooting its core material through the improvised barrel, pushed by massive charges oscillating through the length of the superconducting tunnel; charges that fluctuated just enough to provide some aim.

The asteroids vomited themselves out into space in streams of mass and energy. The first wave came through the Protean lines at a quarter of the speed of light, but only a dozen of the Protean eggs suffered a direct hit, vaporizing into balls of plasma. Hundreds of others had the ability to maneuver around the incoming dumb projectiles.

Adam still smiled.

The second wave of projectiles came in at half the speed of light, on the same track. They collided with the first set of projectiles just behind the Proteans. The impact, combined with the salting of fissionable material, resulted in a devastating eruption of energy, A sterilizing wave strong enough to overwhelm even the Proteans' shields.

Ten more waves were on the way before the radiation of the first explosions reached Adam's sensors.

He raised his arms as if conducting an orchestra, facing the empty bridge of the *Voice*. The mass of displays switched on their own, following Adam's intention, showing views of the rippling waves of explosions filling the volume of space once occupied by uncontested Proteans. The eruptions of energy blurred into each other, one explosion swelling as another faded, until it appeared as if a massive hand was swirling a rag of plasma and light cleaning dirt off of the surface of space.

The Hand of God, Adam thought.

Date: 2526.7.31 (Standard)
Mars–Sol

For a hundred million years the two-kilometer Face had stared impassively up at the Martian sky. For the past three hundred, the ancient Dolbrian artifact had been covered by an environmental dome to protect it from the corrosive effects of the thin terraformed atmosphere.

The first asteroid hit only ten kilometers from it, wiping away a hundred thousand centuries in a blast of heat, light, and kinetic energy.

More asteroids fell, lumps of iron and nickel turned from inert rock into self-guided missiles. Half their mass left a charged trail between Mars and the asteroid belt. The remaining mass was more than enough.

As the planet turned under the onslaught, the first of the Protean spires came under attack. The logarithmic curves of the elevator, grand and delicate and impossibly strong, were no match for a five-hundred-meter chunk of rock slamming into its base.

Light, smoke, and superheated rock boiled up the shaft as it began its slow reentry into the atmosphere. The woven material began to unweave, individual threads slashing through the atmosphere until the heat of reentry made the threads unbond and the sky rain superheated carbon.

From their crystalline redoubts deep under the Martian surface, the Protean remnants watched the world end. The rocks grew larger, pounding the surface, punching holes in the crust. Within an hour, centuries of terraforming was rendered moot as the surface again became uninhabitable.

The millions of minds that formed the culture of Proteus faced their end as one. Mars was only one place, and only one point in time. They had done what they could.

If they had done their job well, Adam would be too consumed with victory to see the actual attack. It was unfortunate that they couldn't save Earth to do so.

Date: 2526.7.32 (Standard)
Earth–Sol

Adam came late.

The revised ultimatum gave a lie to his omnipotence and claims of Godhead. Not that any of the fifteen billion souls on the planet had means to exploit that weakness. The first day had seen riots and looting on a global scale, the few charged with keeping order absorbed into the mass of humankind who had decided that order was no longer relevant. People died, buildings burned, and old grudges were violently settled. And above the riots, lights washed across the night sky.

The riots dissipated by the second day, as the cities emptied and the churches filled. Few knew of the fate of Mars. Communications had broken down, and the human world had shrunk to the distance a person could travel and the reach of someone's voice. Those who had telescopes, and who had chosen to watch the alien structures growing on the surface, saw the cascade of destruction but had few they could tell.

The cadre of scientists in the few widely scattered observatories that remained operational could only console themselves that they were the first to see the end approaching. One of those observatories was in Vatican City, so Pope Stephen XII knew that the Proteans had failed.

His last mass was held before the refugees that packed St. Peter's Square. His last profession of Catholic belief came underneath a sky that burned with the fires of hell.

As mass ended, a streak of flame reached down from the heavens to strike the dome of St. Peter's, blowing the shell apart, raining debris down on the crowd. The inside of the cathedral glowed a painful red-yellow, as the skeletal remnants of the dome folded into the light. Windows and doors glowed with the same bright light, as the walls seemed to twist themselves apart, turning and folding into dimensions that didn't exist. Around the perimeter of St. Peter's Square, buildings collapsed into amorphous masses of bifurcating tentacles that seemed to be made of the same burning light as the sky.

From out the chaos that had been the cathedral, a humanoid form walked down the stairs toward the pavilion where the pope had been conducting mass. The stairs, the pavestones in the square itself, and the forty-one-meter obelisk in the center of the square remained the only visible remnants of human architecture.

The pope turned to face the visage of Adam. Adam towered over the man, arms spread as his new cathedral rose behind him.

"Do you choose to serve me?"

Pope Stephen XII bowed his head and said, "I believe in God, the Father almighty, creator of heaven and earth. I believe in Jesus Christ, his only Son, our Lord. He was conceived by the power of the Holy Spirit and born of the Virgin Mary. He suffered under Pontius Pilate, was crucified, died, and was buried. He descended into hell. On the third day he rose again. He ascended into heaven and is seated at the right hand of the Father. He will come again to judge the living and the dead. I believe in the Holy Spirit, the holy Catholic Church, the communion of saints, the forgiveness of sins, the resurrection of the body, and the life everlasting. Amen."

The figure of Adam stepped closer and placed his hands on the pope's shoulders. He asked again, "Do you choose to serve me?"

The pope raised his gaze to meet Adam's. "I also believe that you are an abomination, a force of destruction, conceived in hubris and the denial of God."

"Then you shall not see paradise," Adam said as the pope's body disintegrated in front of him.

Adam raised his head to face the panicked throngs of St. Peters and said, "Do you now choose to serve the God that is before you?"

*   *   *

Cardinal Anderson stood with Jonah Dacham in one of the deepest rooms of the Vatican archives. They had watched the slow disintegration of their ties to the outside world. By the time the sky burned, they only had data feeds from a few select points within Vatican City itself. When the dome of St. Peter's Basilica crumbled, they lost even that.

At that point Cardinal Anderson released all the monks working here to go to their cells, meditate, and find their peace.

"We were too late," he said to Dacham.

"The Proteans were always a small community. The options we had were always limited."

"Did you know this would fail, then?"

"I knew that military success was unlikely," he said. "And to be honest, the plans of Proteus never hinged on the whim of one man."

"You were always going to attack him?"

"Not me," Dacham said. "I am no longer part of Proteus. I'm a man, just like you."

"Mars, the attack, would that have happened without the Church's absolution?"

"No, it wouldn't have."

"But then what do you mean—"

Anderson was interrupted by a segment of the armored wall pulling itself apart from the inside. A disturbingly organic orifice irised open, letting in a painful light. Anderson crossed himself and prayed.

The figure who stepped through the opening was disarming in her human appearance. Average height and build, flame-red hair, a face that spoke of handsomeness as much as attractiveness.

"I am Rebecca," she said to them. "I am here to offer you a new life as a servant of Adam. You will have power beyond imagining."

She reached out her hands, one toward Anderson, one toward Dacham.

To his surprise, Dacham stepped forward and took her hand.

It suddenly became clear what he meant when he said

the Proteans didn't rely on the whim of one man. Their plan wasn't the battle above them.

Their plan was Dacham.

Adam's servant stared at him and Cardinal Anderson shook his head and said, "Thou shalt have no other gods before me."

The woman stared deeply into his eyes. The last thing he ever heard were her words: "I'm sorry."

SECOND EPILOGUE

Judgment

"Now comes the mystery."

—HENRY WARD BEECHER
(1813–1887)

CHAPTER FORTY-TWO

Exorcism

"If you have a choice between bang and whimper, choose bang."

—*The Cynic's Book of Wisdom*

"The Lord will open a way for me though the midst of them . . . For that I was born."

—JOAN OF ARC
(1412–1431)

Date: 2526.7.33 (Standard)
1,000,000 km from Bakunin–BD+50°1725

Mallory sat on the bridge of the *Savannah*, which had been, in a prior life, an intelligence ship for the Centauri Trading Company. It was a massive observation platform, a full half of its toroidal volume made up of various kinds of observation and communications gear. It was one of the first of about two dozen actual military vessels that had joined the cause of fighting Adam in the days after the pope's broadcast.

Most of the recruits that directly supported Mallory were likewise from the planets associated with Centauri. Occisis and its allies were the strongest base of the Church and home to those who'd be most influenced by the pope's broadcast.

However, that didn't mean that the other mass of ships in Bakunin space ignored the transmission. Several fleets had begun forming, loosely associated with the broad cultural arms of human space. There was a small group mostly of Sirius refugees. Refugees from Indi had formed three competing groups, and stranded natives of Bakunin were coalescing with groups of unapologetic pirates and lonely representatives of the Union of Independent Worlds.

But Mallory's group, the first to start organizing, was the largest.

It was also the first to start doing something.

The observation platform was designed to survey vast volumes of space, and once they had a working theory of what Adam's presence might look like and where it might be coming from, they had a constrained area to point its sensors.

It took several surveys at several different frequencies, before they found what it was they were looking for.

A nearly invisible cloud of uniform density, spreading out in an arc around Bakunin's star, trailing from the path where the alien wormhole had tached in. The mass was vast in absolute terms, but so diffuse as to show no ripples in any mass sensors, so dark as to reflect no radiation at all back into the system. The cloud was only detectable as a slight occlusion of the starry background, barely detectable even by the advanced sensors on this spy platform, combined by a slight refraction along very long wavelengths.

But, once they found it, they could clearly define its extent. Little more than a vast cloud of dust.

"This is Central Command. Are the sacrificial lambs programmed?" Mallory spoke to an open channel that broadcast to the whole of his heterogeneous fleet. It was a question he'd been asking every quarter hour most of the day. This time, almost all the chosen vessels responded affirmatively.

The "lambs" represented about half his fleet. The past two days had seen a consolidation of people and resources, abandoning those vessels that were too low on supplies and power.

However, as near dead as the abandoned ships were, and as low on power, all had functional tach-drives. None had the power to jump so much as a light-year, but Mallory was asking much less.

He wished he could thank Parvi for the idea.

He called the private channel to the *Daedalus*. "This is Mallory. Has there been any word from Bakunin?"

It was another question he'd been asking periodically, and unlike the first one, the answer for this one never changed. Captain Valentine's voice came back saying, "Still no word from the *Khalid*."

Mallory said a prayer for the souls on board the doomed dropship and wondered, not for the first time, if he had been right in not trying to prevent it from going.

The last few lambs radioed their ready status.

This was it.

Mallory cast a glance at the holo that he had up monitoring the extent of the alien cloud in Bakunin's outer system, half convinced that now that they were about to act some fundamental change might happen. It would move, suddenly become active, threatening them.

But it still sat, inert as it had presumably been since the wormhole had disgorged it. As it would presumably remain until Adam arrived.

Still, the light the platform received was an hour old, and Mallory couldn't help but think about what unknowns might remain in those sixty minutes.

"Ready the computers to synchronize on my signal." He pressed a button that sent out a burst transmission that would allow the computers to all start their programs at the right time to choreograph the delicate, deadly dance that was about to unfold.

At this point all the near-dead tach-ships were empty of people, running automated computer programs that controlled their navigation and their tach-drives. All of them simultaneously disabled their damping coils. Less than a second later, all of them disappeared from the observable universe.

Mallory had a counter programmed, overlaying the view of the cloud. It counted down from fourteen seconds, the amount of time the lambs would spend in tach-space in their travel from Bakunin space out to where the cloud waited.

When the timer hit zero, it rolled back up to 3560.

"Now," Mallory whispered, "it either worked or it didn't."

The light of success or failure raced back toward him, and everyone else, from 3560 light-seconds away.

The plan was simple. Tach-drives interfered with each other. An undamped tach-drive could overload if too close to anything taching in or out. The destruction of the worm-holes had damaged any tach-drives in the vicinity, and the *Eclipse* was fatally damaged when the massive tach-drive of the *Voice* had arrived too close.

What Mallory had done was simply have nearly seven hundred spaceships tach into the same volume of space occupied by the cloud, simultaneously, with their dampers disabled.

When the new counter reached 3546, he had the first indications of success. The first chatter of radio traffic, ships with tach-drives overloading and burning out. Not among Mallory's now-halved fleet—there had been warnings to shut down all the tach-drives in the fleet even though a third of the ships didn't have the power to bring them on-line again.

While his warnings had been given to those outside his fleet, it wasn't taken universally to heart, and he could hear dozens of ships announcing their crisis in a dozen languages.

He prayed for strength and ordered his own people to render what aid they could to any disabled ships in range.

The counter continued running down, and the distress calls leveled off at close to two hundred.

Please, God, let this be worth it.

He stared at the screen as the numbers dipped below sixty. He clenched his teeth, and for the last fifteen seconds, he didn't breathe.

Zero.

Light washed the screen, and then the image went dark. Static washed across all the radio channels. He flipped controls, trying to get something, some indication of what happened, but everything seemed blinded, overloaded, or dead.

He finally found an optical sensor that hadn't been

pointing directly at the cloud. He ordered it to point at the space where the cloud had been.

For a long time he stared at what he had wrought, and finally said, "Christ preserve us."

On the surface of Bakunin, it was nighttime on the western coast, and Nickolai Rajasthan looked up as the sky above him briefly became bright as daylight. With his Protean eyes, he could stare straight up into the sky and see the boiling heart of the plasma flames that consumed Adam's cloud.

"It has begun," he whispered.

Apotheosis is concluded in Book Three: *Messiah*

APPENDIX A:

Alphabetical Listing of Sources

Note: Dates are Terrestrial standard. Where the year is debatable due to interstellar travel, the Earth equivalent is used with an asterisk. Incomplete or uncertain biographical information is indicated by a question mark.

St. Ambrose (340?–397) Bishop of Milan.
St. Augustine (354–430) Numidian Bishop of Hippo.
Bakunin, Mikhail A. (1814–1876) Russian political philosopher.
Balzac, Honoré de (1799–1850) French novelist, playwright.
Beecher, Henry Ward (1813–1887) American clergyman, writer.
Boerne, Ludwig (1786–1837) German political writer.
Butler, Samuel (1612–1680) English poet, satirist.
Calvin, John (1509–1564) French Protestant reformer.
Celine, Robert (1923–1996) American lawyer, anarchist.
Samuel Taylor Coleridge (1772–1834) English poet, critic, philosopher.
Confucius (*ca.* 551–479 BCE) Chinese philosopher.
Emerson, Ralph Waldo (1803–1882) American essayist, poet, minister.
Frederick (II) the Great (1712–1786) Prussian monarch.
Galiani, August Benito (2019–*2105) European spaceship commander.
Gibbons, James (1834–1921) American cardinal.
Harper, Sylvia (2008–2081) American civil rights activist, president.

Hawthorne, Nathaniel (1804–1864) American novelist.

Jefferson, Thomas (1743–1826) American president.

Joan of Arc (1412–1431) French national heroine.

Lowell, James Russell (1819–1891) American poet, critic.

Luther, Martin (1483–1546) Leader of German Reformation.

Manning, Henry Edward (1808–1892) English cardinal.

Milton, John (1608–1674) English poet.

de Montaigne, Michel (1533–1592) French philosopher, essayist.

Napoleon Bonaparte (1769–1812) Emperor of France.

Nietzsche, Friedrich (1844–1900) German philosopher.

Olmanov, Dimitri (2190–2350) Chairman of the Terran Executive Command.

Paine, Thomas (1737–1809) American revolutionary writer.

Pascal, Blaise (1623–1662) French geometrician, philosopher, writer.

Rajasthan, Datia (?–2042), American civil rights activist, political leader.

St. Rajasthan (2075–2118) Tau Ceti nonhuman religious leader.

Rabelais, François (1495?–1553) French satirist.

Shakespeare, William (1564–1616) English playwright.

Shane, Marbury (2044–*2074) Occisian colonist, soldier.
  Webster, Daniel (1782–1852) American statesman, lawyer, orator.

S. Andrew Swann

MOREAU OMNIBUS   0-7564-0151-1
(Forests of the Night, Emperors of the Twilight,
& Specters of the Dawn)
"An engaging, entertaining thriller with an exotic cast of characters, in an unfortunately all too plausible repressed future."
—Science Fiction Chronicle

FEARFUL SYMMETRIES   978-088677-834-7
"A novel as vivid as a cinema blockbuster loaded with high-budget special effects." *—New York Review of Science Fiction*

HOSTILE TAKEOVER omnibus   0-7564-0249-2
(Profiteer, Partisan & Revolutionary)
"This is good old-fashioned military SF, full of action, colorful characters, and plenty of hardware." *—Locus*

**DRAGONS AND DWARVES: NOVELS OF THE
CLEVELAND PORTAL**   978-0-7564-0566-3
(Dragons of the Cuyahoga & Dwarves of Whiskey Island)
"Skillfully done light adventure with more than a dash of humor."*—Science Fiction Chronicle*

BROKEN CRESCENT   0-7564-0214-X
"A fast-paced, entertaining tale of the boundary between magic and science." *—Booklist*

To Order Call: 1-800-788-6262
www.dawbooks.com

DAW 123

RM Meluch

The Tour of the Merrimack

"An action-packed space opera. For readers who like romps through outer space, lots of battles with gooey horrific insects, and character sexplotation, *The Myriad* delivers..."   —*SciFi.com*

"Like *The Myriad*, this one is grand space opera. You will enjoy it."   —*Analog*

"This is grand old-fashioned space opera, so toss your disbelief out the nearest airlock and dive in."
                    —*Publishers Weekly* (Starred Review)

THE MYRIAD   0-7564-0320-1
WOLF STAR   0-7564-0383-6
THE SAGITTARIUS COMMAND
                    978-0-7564-0490-1
STRENGTH AND HONOR
                    978-0-7564-0578-6

To Order Call: 1-800-788-6262

www.dawbooks.com

DAW 48

C.S. Friedman
The Best in Science Fiction

THIS ALIEN SHORE   0-88677-799-2
    A *New York Times* Notable Book of the Year
"Breathlessly plotted, emotionally savvy. A potent
  metaphor for the toleration of diversity"
     —*The New York Times*

THE MADNESS SEASON   0-88677-444-6
    "Exceptionally imaginative and compelling"
     —*Publishers Weekly*

IN CONQUEST BORN   0-7564-0043-0
"Space opera in the best sense: high stakes adventure
  with a strong focus on ideas, and characters an
  intelligent reader can care about."—*Newsday*

THE WILDING   0-7564-0164-X
  The long-awaited follow-up to *In Conquest Born*.

To Order Call: 1-800-788-6262
www.dawbooks.com

Tanya Huff

The Confederation Novels

"As a heroine, Kerr shines. She is cut from the same mold
as Ellen Ripley of the *Aliens* films. Like her heroine,
Huff delivers the goods." —*SF Weekly*

A CONFEDERATION OF VALOR
Omnibus Edition
(Valor's Choice, The Better Part of Valor)
978-0-7564-0399-7

THE HEART OF VALOR
978-0-7564-0481-9

VALOR'S TRIAL
978-0-7564-0479-6

To Order Call: 1-800-788-6262
www.dawbooks.com

DAW 73